WARNING

THIS TEXT CONTAINS GRAPHIC DESCRIPTIONS OF VIOLENCE AND ACTS OF UNRESTRICTED WARFARE

X-DAY: Japan
Copyright 2015, Shawn D. Mahaney
Published by Stone Lake Historical,
an imprint of Stone Lake Press,
Seneca, South Carolina, USA
ISBN 978-0-9963101-0-9 (paperback)
ISBN 978-0-9963101-1-6 (e-book)
Cover art and design by Catherine Gurri
This printing October, 2015, with errata corrected.

Visit xdayjapan.com for downloadable maps, more references, and a freely distributable sample of the book.

A companion volume is available – X-Day: Gaming Olympic is a full color book which illustrates the battle day-by-day in maps and photos with running commentary. Visit xdayjapan.com/gaming-olympic for more information.

To the 54

The most honest agents of history

http://www.54warcorrespondents-kia-30-ww2.com/

Table of Contents:

Guide for the Modern Reader..4

Editor's preface, Kyushu Diary, 2nd Edition 6

July 16, 1945 : San Diego, California 9
Map – Pacific 1942 16

Map – Japan and Ryukus.......................................17

July 21, 1945 : Oahu island, Hawaii 21

July 26, 1945 : Saipan, Marianas 28

August 3, 1945 : Pacific Ocean 42

August 6, 1945 : Okinawa, Ryukus..............................45

September 10, 1945 : Okinawa, Ryukus 56

October 20, 1945 : Okinawa, Ryukus 75

November 11, 1945 : X-4....................................87
Map – Southern Kyushu and Nearby Islands 94

Map – Southern Kyushu and Invasion Outline............95

November 15, 1945 : X-Day – Kyushu, Japan............97
Map – Western Kyushu.......................................115

Map – Details from Army Maps 116

November 20, 1945 : X+5 – Tanega-shima 124

November 21, 1945 : X+6 – Ariake Bay.....................128

November 26. 1945 : X+11 – east of Kanoya, Kyushu 158
Map – South-central Kyushu..................................167

December 2, 1945 : X+17 – west of Hoyoshi-dake 181

December 8, 1945 : X+23 – Miyazaki, Kyushu..........................197
Map – Eastern Kyushu 207

December 14, 1945 : X+29 – northeast of Miyakonojo, Kyushu 212

December 16, 1945 : X+31 – west of Miyazaki, Kyushu 221

December 21, 1945 : X+36 – Sea of Hyūga.................230

December 23, 1945 : X+38 – Kanoya, Kyushu 236

December 31, 1945 : X+46 – Kushikino, Kyushu 250

January 8, 1946 : X+54 – north of Kagoshima Bay....................262

January 14, 1946 : X+60 – north of Miyakonojo 270
    Map – Central Kyushu..274

Press Release, January 17, 1946...285

Postscript 286

Thank You 289

Glossary – Military Structure and other 1940s Terminology.......290

Additional Reading and Resources 294

Brief Historical Context 297

More Tuttle Columns 303

Scuttlebutt..308

A freely distributable sample of this entire book (not just he first portion) is available from the project web site, <u>xdayjapan.com</u>.

Guide for the Modern Reader

The book Kyushu Diary was originally published in 1946, in which Walter F. Tuttle combined his own columns and other notes into an edited compilation. The second edition of 1952 was also by Tuttle's own hand, with added footnotes, a map, some previously censored sections, and a post-script from the author. We are not calling this new book a 3rd edition. We have left Tuttle's own 2nd edition of his compilation intact. X-Day: Japan starts with the second edition of Kyushu Diary and expands on it with extra features for a 21st century presentation.

The target audience of Walter F. Tuttle's original Kyushu Diary is a newspaper reader of 1945. That person speaks a slightly different language from someone in the 21st century. That reader was persistently exposed to an argot of military affairs during six years of global war. Some of the words and concepts novel to that reader are mundane to us now, and many common phrases or jargon of that fast-changing time quickly became anachronistic or forgotten.

Tuttle wrote that "logistics" was a new word to many people then, as fielding a large army into undeveloped territory across a vast ocean was an unprecedented concept. In our modern post-jet-age economy, "logistics" is found in perky ad slogans of major companies.

Our modern world has been shaped by things we call "low intensity conflicts", "limited war", and "counter-terrorism operations". These are all terms that would have been completely unknowable to a reader of the pre-nuclear 1940s. To help the modern reader bridge those gaps of time and language, we have included a section of brief historical context, and a small glossary.

Histories are generally either top-down views, summarizing the whole situation, or narratives from an individual perspective. Tuttle's Kyushu Diary is at its heart a personal narrative. But Tuttle went to some trouble to paint a complete picture of the scene in the Pacific, from the home front all the way across to the battlefields in Japan, for the benefit of American readers who had

4

been shown mostly news from Europe in the preceding years. Toward that effort we add this guide, additional maps, a list of further reading, and a judicious few additions to the text footnotes. The format of any notes added in 2015 will be as below[*] on this page.

Tuttle believed in the spontaneous uncertainly of momentous events, which could turn out vastly different from changes in decision making or from natural flukes, and he was keen to communicate this to readers. In that spirit we also include a list of books of alternate histories or historical fiction novels, fantastic explorations of entirely possible what-ifs in this part of history. Popular topics in this genre are 'What if we forced Japanese surrender by dropping atomic bombs on cities instead of military targets?' and 'What if we dropped atomic bombs on cities and they kept on fighting anyway?'

The book is not a parade of military hardware or a treatise on combined arms tactics. It does not get into any high level politics or command decisions. As before the war, Tuttle wrote about people and how they over came their own local problems. As a reporter he provided regular updates about the progress of each battle and the larger situation, but his real interest was in setting the stage for human stories to play out.

The text of Kyushu Diary varies considerably from the columns that were published under Tuttle's byline during the war. The columns were worked over by many editors, and parsed out to fill some number of column-inches three days a week. Tuttle did not actually write to a format or deadline; he submitted when he could. The book was written directly from Tuttle's own notes and original submissions. Many boring days are skipped, and some busy days have a dozen pages of dense material. That's war for you.

---

[*] [Editor's note, 2015: This is how foot notes added for a 21st century reader will appear. – sdm]

Editor's preface, Kyushu Diary, 2nd Edition

The greatest historians remain those who tell the story as it happens, with fidelity but without theories to advance and without trying to build a story by selection and speculation. We believe that Walt Tuttle's "Kyushu Diary" is just that sort of direct honest work – history from the own eyes of the historian, which will be cited without caveat or argument for generations.

In this time of uneasy peace and 'containment' policies, we are pleased to present the second edition of Kyushu Diary. Great armies are again poised across imaginary lines from each other, as tangled webs of ancient rivalries, incompatible cultures, territorial ambition, and new existential threats challenge the lasting peace and trust many hoped they had fought for in the preceding generation. What we have learned, mostly the hard way, about the new epoch of nuclear warfare may temper impulses to action, or drive them with desperate immediacy. Only time will tell.

History may be a never ending game of unfinished business. Only the last person left in history will have a clear view to say. For his part, Walt Tuttle has limited his post-war edits of this book to a few footnotes which highlight the unknowns of battle, some choice historical quotes to caption each chapter – to remind the readers, politicians, generals, and citizens alike that very little changes in human history – and a reflective postscript. Walt refused to put any preface before the journal entries, which might color perspective of the reader.

The Defense Department has let us re-submit the material through the military censors. A number of details are no longer redacted. Some paragraphs flow better, stories are more complete, and details such as the planned positions of maneuvering units are now in print.

We didn't get everything through though. The military is wary of letting loose information on tactics that may still be current. No one will say if Japanese imperialists, Chinese communists, Russian communists, or some other group will present the next military challenge, but for once the U.S. military is ready to admit in a post-war time that there will be a next challenge.

As a book, Kyushu Diary is substantially different from a simple collation of newspaper columns. Walt Tuttle went back to the original source material, his own notes and unedited submissions, and constructed the book under one structure. A close eye will catch a few themes and clever call-backs.

One of the original editors cautioned Walt that the 200 pages of conventional combat stories were, "repetitive. The writing is interesting, but what it describes over and over is somehow both brutal and boring."

Walt Tuttle replied succinctly, "If that's how it reads, then good. Because that's exactly how it was."

> Francis Dixon, Stone Lake Press
> February, 1952
> Saratoga, New York

Kyushu Diary

Walter F. Tuttle

July 16, 1945 : San Diego, California

They made me a corporal today. It's completely ceremonial, of course. Civilian war correspondents do not have a rank. While normally billeted[†] with the officers, and wearing the same uniform, the uniform has no insignia and we are outranked in the field by the lowest one stripe private. Still, they for some reason thought I had done enough to merit some sort of recognition[‡], so there was a slightly farcical "ceremony" in the corner of the HQ office courtyard.

Commander Samuel "Sammy" Adelanto, XO of the sprawling and ever growing naval base, pinned an oversize medal on my chest that one of the mess cooks had fashioned from a large can lid . A few words were said half in jest about getting me out of their hair. A couple veterans from remote islands in the central Pacific earnestly wished me luck – they said I hadn't seen the worst of anything yet. Two young recruits about to deploy chatted me up, probably hoping to get their names in the paper (Marine Corps 2nd Lieutenant Victor Saldano of east Queens, New York, and Marine Private Smithy Batson, of Knoxville, Tennessee).

I was writing dispatches from the field in Europe for three years more or less non-stop. Two weeks here in the ever-expanding Navy base is the longest I've been in one spot since 1942. Here the world has sped by me instead. There are so many bodies and ships moving through San Diego it's dizzying trying to keep up.

My first job here was to pick up a fresh military ID card and get my "orders". Each correspondent is always assigned to a particular unit and commanding officer. They gave me a temporary

---

[†] A billet in formal usage is a description of the details of a military posting, down to what special (e.g. cold weather) equipment will be issued, rules of the local base, and how many pair of socks a soldier is expected to keep in his locker. It is often used to mean just the room one is assigned to sleep in.

[‡] [Editor's note: Walt Tuttle's reporting under fire through the European campaign is already a growing legend, as readers of our previous compilation of his work can see through his stubbornly modest accounts.]

assignment attaching me to the naval base when I got here. I can go anywhere I like, but technically have to check in with the senior officer of the command to go outside its area of responsibility. That wasn't a concern here in a U.S. city.

I expect to head across the Pacific soon. My time off in the States has been refreshing, if surprisingly hectic with planned and impromptu public appearances, but now I will head west. I plan to tell you about what I see out there, on those dots in the middle of the great ocean, and how different they are from dots on the maps of Europe. Men and machines are being prepared on those islands for the next big action. I plan to be with them when it comes.

Today I signed an updated copy of the standard agreement for war correspondents. It's documented right in the unusually compact code of regulations the War Department issued just for us journalists. The rules basically say that we are to be given as free reign as possible, subject to local exigencies, and all we have to do in return is not try to cheat the censors. There are plenty of censors[§], both to keep an eye on us and ensure quick turnaround of material headed back to home town newspapers and syndicates. The military also pledges all the radio and teletype time they can spare, after military traffic is sent, and air shipment of news photo film, if there is free space on military transports. Ain't they swell?

Now that I have my final agreement signed, I really don't know where I'll want to go. Most junior officers I've met so far have been agreeable to take me in on-the-fly, so I asked them to make it as general as possible. Oh boy did they! For the next year I am attached to "CINCPACFLT" – Commander-in-Chief, United States Pacific Fleet. Somehow I don't think I'll ever actually check in with Admiral Chester Nimitz.

AGREEMENT

[§] This paragraph was not deleted or trimmed in any way by the censors in the original printing of this collection. Many others were, too many to call them all out individually, but I will point out a few later on, to illustrate the difficulty of their task and just how much they really did try to let us tell the unvarnished story.

In connection with authority granted by the War Department to me, the undersigned, to accompany <u>CINCPACFLT</u> for the purpose of securing news or story material, still or motion pictures, or to engage, in radio broadcasting, I subscribe to the following conditions :

1. That, as a civilian accredited to the Army or Navy of the United States within or without the territorial limits of the United States, I am subject to the Articles of War and all regulations for the Government of the Armed Forces Issued pursuant to law.

2. That, I will govern my movements and actions in accordance with the instructions of the War Department and the commanding officer of the unit to which I am accredited. I further agree that I will submit for purposes of censorship all such material even though written after my return, if the interviews, written material, or statements are based on my observations made during the period or pertain to the places visited under this authority. This includes all lectures, public talks, "off the record" speeches, and all photography intended for publication or release, either while with the armed forces or after my return, if they are based upon my observations during this period or pertain to the places visited.

3. That, I waive all claims against the United States for losses, damages,

or injuries which may be suffered as a result of this authority.

4. That, this authority is for the period *7/16/45* to *7/15/46*, and subject to revocation at any time.

Signed: *Walter F. Tuttle*

Representing: *Stone Lake Syndicate*

I spent the afternoon idly shopping in town near the beach. The place is thick with servicemen, enough that the military has MPs out on patrol in addition to the local authorities. The retailers closest to the bases and barracks have adapted to cater to them, carrying supplies, trinkets, and services directly in the interest of a freshly paid solider or sailor. Prices that aren't regulated are higher than they would be in a place not stuffed full of young men with new money burning holes in their pockets and little time to spend it.

I have my own agenda, which includes finding a new pair of field glasses, as mine got lent to a desperate young officer in France, who I expect kept them in use through a substantial portion of western Germany. I also want to add to my collection of local newspapers. It's been a great way to make new friends, running a small lending library of home front newspapers.

It doesn't matter where the it is from, or what size town, guys far away like to catch up on the little things that don't make it into the news sheets that the military takes care to send forward. A race for county drain commissioner means more to a soldier than world geo-politics. A man in a dirt hole just wants to know that life back home is carrying on as always and waiting for his return.

My trip out is probably coming up soon, so I took a last stroll down the boardwalk, stopping in a souvenir stand to get my picture taken with my fake "medal." After dinner in a crowded soda shop I picked up the photo print, headed back, and dumped the medal in a scrap bin at base – they say we need every bit of loose steel we can get.

12

Two of the afternoon papers I picked up have an identical short article off the wire about an explosion at an old weapons dump in New Mexico. It was south of Albuquerque, near a small town called Alamogordo. There were some chemical shells, and people are advised to stay away and possibly be ready to evacuate should the winds blow toxic fumes toward town. It's disturbing to think about what might happen if unconventional weapons get unleashed in what remains of this conflict. They have been treated to undoubted technological development since the so-called "Great War." I wonder to myself just what horrible weapons might still be unleashed in the fighting to come. [**]

July 17, 1945 : San Diego, California

In preparation for my adventure in the Pacific, I took to reading up on the Japanese and what it is they read. In Japan they look at ancient Chinese texts the way we read ancient Greek plays, history, and philosophy. One of the oldest texts on the topic at hand is a short treatise called The Art of War, by a fellow they call Sun Tzu. At the time of writing, Chinese lords had been fighting back and forth for territory and prestige for over a thousand years. They'd made a regular business out of it, and Sun Tzu had plenty of examples to work from.

One section caught my eye, about fighting far away from home and how enormously expensive it is. Sun Tzu even listed tables of expenses and his commentators gave logarithmic ratios of how it's a hundred times more expensive to fight ten times farther away. When there are chariots carrying nothing but spare parts for other chariots, and food for the chariot drivers, and food for the troops guarding the chariots, only a fraction of the supplies that

---

[**] [Editor's note, 2015 : It is now well known that on July 16, 1945, at the "Trinity" test site outside Alamogordo, the first atomic bomb was detonated. The weapons dump story was circulated to satisfy anyone who had seen the flash, with the chemical shells angle in case an excuse was needed to evacuate nearby towns. – sdm]

leave home will actually get to the army in the field. Fighting far away from home is terribly expensive.

In this war we literally could not be fighting any farther from home, unless the Japs have a base on Mars and we decide to attack that too.

I took a walk around the commercial end of the harbor today. At least they call it the commercial end. There's not a single match stick being moved through here for civilian commercial ends. It may have been a colorful scene a few years ago when a wild flotilla of different ships jockeyed for loading berths, all of them hastily pressed into service for the military. But now it's an unbroken line of nearly identical gray Liberty ships and Victory ships, purpose-built for the war effort.

Across the bay the marinas for private boats, mostly pleasure craft, are practically deserted. Fuel rationing has dried up the tanks of any motor boat. The few sail boats left in the water I expect must belong to Navy officers, stationed here inside the heavy security blanket draped over everything in the vicinity of the military complex.

The scene would be dull and repetitive, actually it definitely is, but I looked at it for more than an hour, watching a couple ships leave and another come in. The harbor pilots bring each ship in and out through a channel so well 'worn' it seems remarkable the water doesn't show permanent marks on its surface. Each ship takes position at a pier with cranes and longshoremen and a scheduled line of trucks ready to stuff it full.

Each hoist of a crane starts a bundle of material on its way halfway around the world. In each bundle is one item, say a can of beans or pair of socks, which someone in an office somewhere assigned to that bundle on that boat expecting it to meet up with a member of a particular company of a particular battalion on a particular island fifty-odd days from now.

One has to feel for the soldier so far from home. It doesn't matter so much to him how far it is, for out of sight is out of sight, but all that stuff headed his way is headed his way based on someone's months old guess by the time it gets there. No matter

14

how much we produce at home, know that he goes without some times.

Still, they've been at this for a while now, and have the numbers down pretty tight. Including food, ammunition, and everything needed by the facilities directly supporting him, the fighting man is allotted 45 pounds of stuff per day. Giant ship-sized bundles of all that stuff is fired toward the far away front by this cargo cannon at regular intervals. Of course the supply chain itself needs supplies, and there's a compounding effect of doing the fighting so very far away from home ports.

It takes about 110 days for these cargo ships to make the round trip all the way to the Philippines[††] so more and more ships are sitting in the pipeline, and more tankers are hauling fuel just for the cargo ships themselves. They say we moved over five and a half million tons of stuff from the west coast last year, and this year the west coast can't even keep up. Ships are sailing around to New Orleans and Charleston and anywhere with an open loading dock to pick up cargoes headed directly to the Pacific.

A network of spies in all the major harbors could probably do a creditable job divining our strategic plans just from counting the number and types of ships heading west. Of course that still leaves the matter of doing anything about it, when there is such a massive flow of men and materiel steaming toward enemy held lands.

Logistics is a new word in the public lexicon. I have to think when this is all over, it won't go away but will open up a new global economy. We've gotten too good at this.[‡‡]

[††] In the Philippines we finally held the only port worth holding so far, at Manila which also had good warehouse space. It greatly sped up the unloading of ships and allowed all that 'stuff' to be stored.

[‡‡] The reader will notice close runs and then gaps in the date lines of these reports. At the time my column was running twice weekly, but I was writing almost every day, sometimes saving up material for later publication. The dates are the actual days of writing. Some entries were never in a printed column or were heavily edited.

PACIFIC OCEAN and key islands
Map is approximately 8500 miles wide at latitude of Hawaii

━━━━━ ━━━━━ ━━━━━ ━━━━━ JAPANESE LINE OF CONTROL, MID-1942

Map – Japan and Ryukus

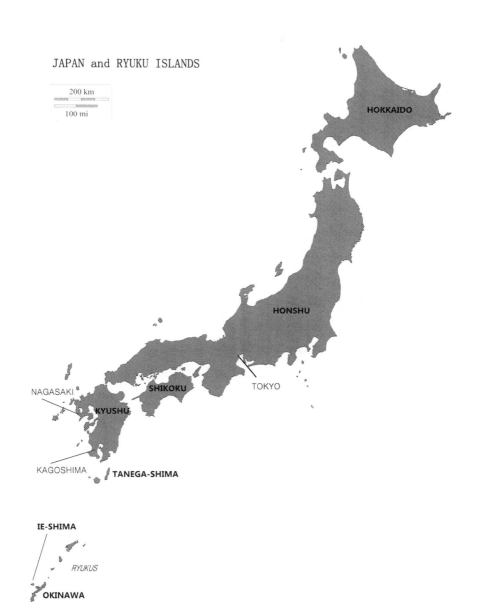

JAPAN and RYUKU ISLANDS

200 km

100 mi

HOKKAIDO

HONSHU

NAGASAKI   SHIKOKU   TOKYO

KYUSHU

KAGOSHIMA   TANEGA-SHIMA

IE-SHIMA

RYUKUS

OKINAWA

July 19, 1945 : San Diego, California

Something mighty peculiar went on today, and I'm not sure how much I'll be able to tell you about it. So, I'm writing it down with all the details intact, and will hash it out with the censors later.[§§]

Early in the afternoon all traffic at the naval air field was halted to make way for a VIP C-54[***], coming in on low fuel. While on the ground a sizable party from the aircraft sought out the communications office of the base. In less than three hours they were gone again, heading east.

Dinner time found me in the company of an officer from the intelligence section, because I asked him. Commander Cecil Lambert, of Lucedale, Mississippi, is a conscientious intelligence officer. I expected he would tell me all he could about the curiosity at the air field without being indiscrete and risking trouble for either of us.

"No, you can't buy me a drink," was his initial reply to my invitation. "First of all, because I've got more beer ration chits than I could use if the war went on ten more years," He did drink, but only on occasion, and 1945 had been occasion-free. Even the V-E Day celebrations didn't mean much here on the west coast. "Secondly, you simply can't. It's against the rules." He did let me pay for the cab as we got a bit away from the base to a restaurant that wasn't overrun with young representatives of our armed forces, trying to impress a local girl or a WAC that finally gave into his pestering for a date.

"We weren't expecting that plane," he told me over dinner, "not until it made radio contact from a few hours out. They came

---

[§§] This is one of those sections that got eaten up by the censors, but not directly. The young lieutenant who first read my report at the base sent it up to his superiors for review. They in turn asked for higher review. And so on until it was too late for normal publication, so my column for that day was about yet-another-war-plant-tour. Now [1952 edition] I get to print it in full detail.

[***] The C-54 is the military passenger and cargo version of what we now call the DC-4 airliner.

18

in all the way from Johnston Atoll, skipping Hawaii entirely. They were in a really big hurry, flying all night at maximum range. I can tell you everything that anybody who was there on the ramp saw for themselves. And honestly I don't know much else."

"The second guy off the plane was Lieutenant General Richard Sutherland, General MacArthur's own chief of staff. The first guy off I think was General Charles Willoughby, head of intelligence for MacArthur, which is why I know of him. The plane was the Bataan, MacArthur's own plane, so his guys aren't here on leave."

"They went to the radio room to try to get a private phone line to Washington [D.C.], and to put a stack of coded dispatches into the operator's hand. They left after more than an hour on the phone and took off again east bound with a full fuel load."

"From there I can only speculate." I naturally encouraged his speculation. "MacArthur wants something, and is going to the highest levels to get it. Truman is away, still on a boat heading to Europe[†††]." Commander Lambert poked the air with his fork to emphasize the next point, "It would be just like MacArthur to make an end-around play and put his guys in front of the real decision makers while the President is away."

I asked rhetorically if they would be in such a hurry if it was a scheme planned in advance. The Potsdam conference was scheduled months before. It looked to me more like something had come up suddenly, and they wanted a quick decision, before some other impending thing happened.

Commander Lambert considered it a moment and agreed. "It's one of those things we'll probably never know about. Things will just happen one way, and we'll never even think about how it could have been done differently, with who knows how different a

---

[†††] President Truman was traveling for the Potsdam Conference for most of late July and early August, 1945. His ship the USS Augusta was outfitted with the latest communications equipment and could receive dispatches at sea anywhere in range of radio relays.

result. People have a funny way of thinking about history as a string of inevitable outcomes."

On that we also agreed, as we split the bill and looked for a ride back to base. My own flight out is due to leave tomorrow. After one last check of my luggage I will turn in and get ready for the long passage west to the other end of the world.

July 21, 1945 : Oahu island, Hawaii

I woke up a little before dawn, and forced myself back to sleep for a while, still tired from a long trip that went from dull to busy and back again. The Navy has me in a wing of rooms for transient officers just east of Pearl Harbor. The building would be at home in a brochure for a modestly priced tropical getaway. Everything here looks that way, in this island paradise, no matter how many buildings the Seabees put up for military use. The low sloping roofs, long overhangs, and ubiquitous palm trees conspire to slow everything down to a pulse in sync with the gentle waves hitting Waikiki.

The only breaks in the idyllic scenery and architecture are the vast rows of corrugated steel Quonset huts they've set up in a few clear-cut areas. There are also the well burdened lines of new utility poles bringing electric power and telephone lines to all the busy new compounds. Still, my quarters are off the main drag in a quiet corner, and I rested long and well after the lengthy flight and hurried tour of the area facilities.

I don't regret taking the trip here in a patrol plane, but a PBY Catalina makes less than 200 miles per hour when it's pushed hard, and for a routine ferry mission in a brand new airframe it's not normal to push it hard. My companions for the long haul were just the pilot and co-pilot, Navy Lieutenant Robert Abell and Flight Officer James Wirz, from coastal North Carolina and central Ohio, respectively. Both officers claim to have been inspired to flying by the famous 'first' of the Wright brothers, which both States claim jealously[‡‡‡]. I graciously declined to take a position on the matter.

Our twin-engine seafaring mount was one of the very last of her type. In fact they closed the San Diego line weeks ago. This plane and a few others were held back to correct faults found at delivery (I didn't care to ask just what the faults were). The

---

[‡‡‡] The Wrights made the first controlled powered flight on the coastal dunes at Kitty Hawk, North Carolina, but had their home and workshops in Dayton, Ohio.

21

Catalina was introduced in 1936, which is ancient history when looked at from this stage of the technological explosion that has accompanied the global struggle. Still, the type hasn't been completely neglected. Lieutenant Abell took a short detour en route, to a location where Mr. Wirz could show me how good the latest radar equipment fitted to these birds is.

The Catalina did well hunting at night, with a previous generation radar set. I can't say exactly where we were or how finely we could see what my hosts put on the scope, but I would not be surprised if the new radar was actually effective for snipe hunting. A Japanese ship of any size hoping to evade these planes is surely full of praying seamen – there isn't much else the sailors can do. They also have more machine guns and bomb racks than the first models.

Today I wanted to see some of the island myself before I saw more of the military side. I looked for a ride over to the famous Waikiki beach a bit to the east of downtown Honolulu and Pearl Harbor. A poster of bus routes reminds riders that priority should be given to military personnel and civilian war workers going about their needful business. Some people tell me that my work is important to the war effort, but I still looked around for busier looking riders before getting on a bus.

One errand they ran me through yesterday was to change out some of my currency for "Hawaiian" money. Wary of Japanese invasion, which seemed inevitable just three years ago, the government called in all the paper money from people in Hawaii so that it couldn't fall into enemy hands. But with a half million inhabitants and likely millions of servicemen and support people about to be moving in, there was a need for replacement cash, pronto.

The expedient-if-inelegant solution was to stamp "HAWAII" on the front and back of millions of existing bank notes. I suppose a lot of the marked notes will become souvenirs someday. Right now mine is marked for lunch money and bus fare.

22

July 22, 1945 : Oahu island, Hawaii

Pearl Harbor is a deep branching fissure in the middle of the southern coast of Oahu, itself a roughly trapezoidal shape, 25 to 30 miles along each side. Honolulu city is just east of the Navy and Army bases on the harbor. East of that is the famous resort strip. Yesterday afternoon a local bus took me out of the sprawling military compound-of-compounds, past downtown Honolulu, and through the tourist district along Waikiki beach. There are three multi-story hotels and a line of smaller hotels and beach houses all along the sand, which ends at the base of Diamond Head mountain.

The locals might be glad that the hotels are perfectly free of pesky tourists these days. The tourism bureau says that their count of annual visitors jumped from 22,000 in 1940 to over 31,000 in 1941, as leisure air travel just began to make itself felt[§§§]. But they are instead busy catering to mobs of freshly paid servicemen on liberty after duty elsewhere. Of course the merchants and performers have adapted – they had little choice once the cruise liners and airplanes quit coming.

I spent some time walking along the oceanfront. Everyone here is smiling and playful, soaking up all they can of this 'happy place in an ocean of peace', as one pre-war tourism flyer called it, while they can. The only tell that there is a war going on is that most of the tourists look the same – all roughly twenty year old American men. They outnumber the *wahine* by a tremendous margin, a source of irritation to both genders.

Another tell might be the row of barbed wire fencing in from the beach, and regular patrols of uniformed MPs. But it gets to where one doesn't notice these things, like not seeing power lines until after taking a photograph of a stunning landscape from just the right vantage point.

[§§§] [Editor's note, 2015 – The reader is reminded that pre-jet-age travel excluded jaunts to exotic tropical islands for all but the few people with lots of both time and money to spare. Current visitor counts for Hawaii run over 8 million a year! Most of them are accommodated in unbroken blocks of high-rise hotels that line Waikiki several blocks deep. – sdm]

A soldier, sailor, or Marine can find something to do or see on any budget of time or money. Small shows run all afternoon and well into the evening, as late as the recently relaxed curfew and blackout rules will allow. Surfboards and small boats can be rented. Young men are always looking for a contest. It is now regular sport for crews from different units to race the fast traditional outrigger row boats as soon as they learn how to handle them with even minimal proficiency. You can bet some wagers are taken on those races.

Speaking of vice, prostitution was still legal here until late last year. The tax office is not happy about the regulated trade going away. The Army and Navy medical staffs are worried about a jump in venereal disease rates. What hasn't changed is that there are thousands of young men here with time and money on their hands.

I didn't bother to tour the fortifications at Diamond Head. I certainly couldn't tell you about them in any detail even if I did. But we know that there are tunnels and caves and gun portals and very big guns ready to fire out of those portals.

Diamond Head is an old volcanic crater, about 700 feet high at the rim and a half mile in diameter. The bowl of the crater is high and flat and could hold a substantial and well supplied garrison. Nature handed this island an almost perfect natural fort. Looking back along Waikiki from the west I notice that the basic setup is a mirror image of what the Marines faced landing on Iwo Jima this spring.

On Iwo they had to land on a long straight beach with Mount Suribachi to the left looking straight down the water line. Gunners in the mountain waited for the maximum concentration of troops and equipment to pile up on the beach, as the third wave came in, before opening fire. The Marines had no choice but to keep landing, turn toward the mountain, and fight straight up it to silence the well-protected Japanese guns.

It's interesting to think about what might have happened if the tables were turned and the Japanese had tried to land on Oahu. We might get to read about fanciful accounts of it in some of the

24

inevitable historical fiction that is bound to be published years after all this settles out.

Back on the west end of Waikiki, I am writing my notes outside the largest hotel on the island, the Royal Hawaiian, still probably the finest large hotel in the Pacific. The Royal doesn't currently have to worry about tourists, or any other sort of rent-paying visitor, as there are none. The entire place was booked by the military for-the-duration after hostilities broke out. It is reserved for convalescing servicemen in from the front. They get first-class treatment, whether going back home or returning to their units.

Tonight a USO variety show is running several performances outside the Royal Hawaiian. I'm due to have dinner between shows with a big group of USO people, including a band of entertainers who are heading the same way as me through the Marianas and maybe Okinawa. The headliners tonight are Eddie Bracken and Peggy Ryan[****].

July 23, 1945 : off Maui island, Hawaii

The Hawaiian islands may sound like a magical place to be stationed, if one is in the military. Indeed it is, for many of the officers and men assigned to fixed posts in the coastal towns, each of them a vacation spot for well-heeled travelers before the war. Be sure that these people work long and diligently, but when off-hours come, they can be almost instantly a world away from a busy shipyard with its hot blowtorches and flailing yardarms, or a frantic warehouse where sweaty men move stenciled crates all day. But these islands are big enough to hold a few of paradise's version of 'bad neighborhoods.' This is where the military saw fit to put the bivouacs of some large units in training for combat.

[****] [Editor's note, 2015 – You may remember Peggy Ryan as the secretary Jenny on the original Hawaii Five-O and Eddie Bracken as the founder of Walley World in National Lampoon's Vacation. – sdm]

The 4th and 5th Marine Corps divisions have been in camp on the islands of Maui and the big island Hawaii, respectively. The 5th in particular drew a very un-Hawaii-like place. Camp Tarawa is on a high arid plain in the middle of Hawaii, well away from any town or amusement, and even out of sight of the ocean. It might as well be on the moon.

What the camp does have is plenty of open space to exercise the troops, and lots of nearby rocky hills to practice assaulting. For small scale amphibious rehearsal units are trucked down to the coast of Hawaii. For larger amphibious exercises a battalion or more will embark and sail over to Maui and invade it, repeatedly. Maui may go down in history as the most invaded island anywhere.

I heard all this from a Navy liaison officer, Lieutenant Victor Logan Jr., of Albuquerque, New Mexico, who is assigned to coordinate these things with the 5th Marine Division. I arranged to tag along on a dry run Maui assault. There were no Marines this time, just a lot of fresh Navy ensigns and warrant officers who needed to learn their jobs. The Navy likes to rehearse these things before doing it in front of company.

We were observing from a brand new destroyer escort, DE-510, the USS Heyliger. DEs are slower and smaller than regular destroyers (DDs), but good for their intended job of escorting lumbering convoys of transports and cargo ships. These are about the smallest named warships in the Navy, but they pack an oversize punch.

Today our DE was playing the part of shore bombardment destroyer. We would cut across the path of the assault boats before they headed in, firing a few practice rounds for effect. Lieutenant Logan told me to watch for a twist as the boats got close to land.

We found three of the large amphibious transport/assault ships waiting for us under a clear sky with two miles of calm sea between them and the shore. Two of the ships had great doors in the front which open to launch amphibious tractors and landing craft. The third ship only had boats that are lowered over the side.

The last boats were still being lowered when our ship started her passes on the beach.

The Heyliger ran parallel to the beach, from left to right, in front of where the assault boats were lining up at the hands of their green crews. We came about and made another pass in the opposite direction, as the three or four dozen boats finalized their formations (with much yelling and flag waving and not a few expletive-laden constructive criticisms).

Then the boats were off. We made a lazy turn out to sea to let them pass, then hurried in to move across behind them. At this point they were still about a mile from shore. Our five inch mounts roared out more shells, shooting over the heads of the men in the tiny bobbing craft, as many more and larger ships would do in a real assault.

Lieutenant Logan assures me that all the sailors have piloted these boats many times in practice. But this is their first live-fire test, and it shows. The natural instinct under fire is to duck – but it's hard to drive a boat that way. Some boats drifted out of their lanes, then jerked back into formation. Some kept drifting, and I saw a couple near misses.

We got past the lines of assault craft, where I thought we would stop and watch. But we kept up speed and turned inland, quickly overtaking the first wave. Just when I was sure we would run aground the ship made another hard turn back out to sea, and we started making smoke.

The breeze was up and down today, but right then it was up. The smoke screen walked briskly down the shallows of the beach. Visibility couldn't have been more than twenty feet. We couldn't observe the boats any more, of course, but by this time observers on land were moving in to greet the boats, grading each young 'captain' on where he put his boat, compared to where it was supposed to be. It hardly seems fair, but unfairness is what some say is practically the definition of war.

July 26, 1945 : Saipan, Marianas

The Navy runs a fine airline. I am just settling in from a series of flights, island to island, on NATS, the Naval Air Transport Service. It must be right to call NATS an airline, because it has its own in-flight magazine, updated monthly. The magazine has everything one would find in a commercial airliner publication: travel tips, information about destinations served, news about partner airlines, and features about the different aircraft flown and general airline operations. Except, in this case the details are decidedly special interest: safe handling of explosive souvenirs, care of the injured in Guam, the Navy taking over planes and routes from Pan Am, and forced-air warming of planes which stop in northern Alaska.

The humor section of the current magazine includes a bit about one hard-fighting Marine who swears he is done fighting forever, even with his mother-in-law. Letters to the editor and assorted amusements fill out the magazine inside its two-color cover. I left the Jean Parker pin-up photo for the next fellow.

The Navy has brought me to the Mariana Islands, specifically to a base they call Marpi on the northern coast of Saipan. Saipan is the northern most of the three major islands we hold here. It is part of what the Japanese took to be the main line of defense of their enlarged empire. It took several flights to get here from Hawaii.

Seats on NATS flights are normally hole-in-one carnival prizes for anyone who doesn't have explicit orders to move across the ocean at aircraft speeds. On short notice I squeezed on to an already overloaded R5D (Navy name for the C-54, which is the Army name for the DC-4) cargo plane which was going straight through to Manila, stopping only for gas. The hold was jammed full, mostly with a 'confidential' cargo[*]. The crew was happy not to have the usual load of VIP passengers to fuss over. With

---

[*] An unnamed Army general insisted that all the office furniture for him and his key staff be brought over from San Francisco. Somehow a Navy plane got the job.

their plane full of cargo they had just one passenger seat to offer, and they practically recruited me to fill it instead of someone actually important.

My "air hosts," including the actual air host, showed me one special feature of our plane. It has refrigerated storage, just for bringing whole blood across to combat areas, several hundred crated pints at a time. There were a few dozen units loaded on my trip, and you may wonder why, as there is little active combat and the blood only lasts a few weeks if well cared for. Not all injuries come from combat. In fact, only a narrow majority of casualties in most campaigns are a direct result of being bombed or shot at. We have well over a million men out here moving around, building things, or practicing destroying things. Injuries happen, and all of them are a long way away from anything you would recognize as a hospital.

The hosts I mentioned for the flight were Lieutenant Frank Spalek and Lieutenant Carl Kube on the flight deck, and Flight Orderly Raymond Holman, coincidentally all from different parts of Nebraska. A flight orderly is to the passenger just a steward or flight attendant, but they also do half the work of the ground crew and all the work of the galley crew on a civilian flight. If a box of cargo comes loose or a life jacket is misplaced or a passenger gets a cold cup of coffee, it's on the record of the flight orderly.

We were an overnight flight, and technically it took us almost three calendar days to get here. We crossed the international date line somewhere between Johnston and Kwajalein atolls at nearly midnight. The date went practically instantly from July 23rd to July 25th. With a break to rest the crew, it was the morning of the 26th when we landed at Marpi with the sun behind us. I hadn't thought at all about the date line until I was reminded that I was on a Navy plane and that it is long standing naval tradition to do a line-crossing ceremony at the equator and other key limits of passage.

You may have heard about the equatorial ceremonies, where "pollywogs" are put through torments by the veteran "shellbacks," before the Court of King Neptune. Even President F. D. Roosevelt was taken under by such sundry festivities a few years ago, though likely watered down from the sometimes notorious details of proceedings with regular Navy crews. I had no thoughts of such stories as we droned through the featureless night over an imaginary line in the sea.

Lieutenant Kube came back to offer me a toast for the occasion, bypassing FO Holman, which should have been my first clue. I was offered a bottle of beer, which was opened in front of me, to toast my first date line crossing. I accepted with a smile and took a hearty swig, which was immediately spewed all over a bulkhead in front of the small seating area.

"Sorry, old fellow, but that's the way all the new guys get it!" the grinning young lieutenant explained. "We have that bottle topped off with avgas and re-capped every time back in Honolulu. It's nothing like how they'd work you over on a surface ship, but we don't have a certificate for you either." They did have a few cans of real beer for a chaser though, so it was all good sport. Of my own will, and to show proper servitude to the good King Neptune, just in case I did have to ditch in the ocean at some point, I washed the bulkhead for them.

July 27, 1945 : Saipan, Marianas

It was another late start for me today after the string of flights to get here. The sun was well up when I got moving, and I missed the first session at the galley. Satisfied with a generous dose of coffee, I walked around the base for a bit until I could get in for lunch. I still didn't even know who I was bunked with, in the transient officers' quarters here on Marpi Naval Base.

I doubt sleep would have been possible for all the noise, was I not only tired but also now well accustomed to the sounds of hard working aircraft engines. The Navy airfield is a busy place, and there is a large bluff along the south side that echoes sound right back over the base. It's not a large base, by the standard we set for the Marianas, but that is a very high standard. This airfield would look at home serving the needs of some larger cities.

30

As a Navy facility, its main job is service of carrier planes. New models ferry through for assignment to the actual carrier they will fight from. Other planes come back for heavy maintenance or battle damage repair. Not all of them are saved. Many beat up planes are strewn in rough order in the nearby fields. Quite a few obsolete models have simply been pushed off the bluff into the ocean to make room. To Navy fliers Marpi Point is essentially another very large but very slow moving aircraft carrier.

Over lunch I talked to some of the technicians based here. They work in different units, each of which has a job to do that changes as each base evolves. The Navy has got base building itself down to an art form, after lots of practice. Building an airfield, operating an airfield, operating planes out of the airfield, and doing heavy maintenance are jobs of different units. They each move into a new area in that order, just as some of the people and gear from the previous units are moving on to the next raw island.

Warrant Officer Lloyd Daniel, of Livingston, Montana, ran a team of earthmovers as the Seabees[*] were expanding the small air strip the Japanese had here before. That airstrip is now almost twice as long as it was, and it has new brothers. His bulldozers are somewhere in the Philippines now, and most of his team is right behind them. He expects to fly out after finishing paperwork here.

Herman Davis, from Bowling Green, Florida, is an electrician's mate with the unit that actually runs the base. They take over from the Seabees, and "make it civilized," as he says. Sitting next to him is aviation ordnanceman Tom Close, of Pensacola, Florida. Tom works on guns and bomb racks, and often runs parts for the heavy maintenance guys.

I found these guys from different units sitting together not because of their common professional interests, but because of baseball. They are the core of the infield for the base team, and they're worried about what to do for a shortstop once Mr. Daniel leaves. I'm sure they'll do fine, but they're from a relatively small base. The other bases each have a top notch squad, as does each

---

[*] "Construction Battalion", or CB, the Navy units that build things, in a hurry, often under fire, anywhere they're asked.

combat division in the Marianas. They have a competitive league going, and big games coming up.

I asked the guys about other topics of interest, like the British election and the big conference at Potsdam, Germany. I couldn't get a stated opinion on any of it, though they get regular world news here. They are much less concerned about how Prime Minister Clement Attlee will get along with President Truman than the number of combat aircraft they can help get in the air over Japan. They will debate the Potsdam proceedings only after the Japanese throw their own guns into the sea and give up.

After lunch I found a pilot who has to run a Marine Corps plane to Guam tomorrow and he agreed to take his time at it, giving me an aerial tour of the Marianas.

The Marianas were taken at considerable cost. They formed part of a key defensive line for the Japanese. Each of the larger islands carried a heavy garrison, with tens of thousands of troops plus thousands of conscripted civilians to build fortifications for them. U.S. Army, Navy, and Marine Corps forces concentrated on each in turn.

The Imperial Japanese Navy turned out to repel the invasion, and formed up a large attack on the fleet supporting the troops. With U.S. aircraft carrier strength ten times what it was at the start of war, and with better equipment all around, the Japanese fighters and attack planes were swatted out of the sky en masse. Several days later the Americans found the Jap fleet and attacked in force, sinking many capital ships. The Japanese Navy task force limped home shattered while the American ground forces picked their way across the islands hill by hill and hole by hole. (This will all be old news to some readers, but many of you had your attention focused on the action in France going on at the same time.)

Not that the Japanese were satisfied with simply giving up the Marianas. While we still only held some of them, very long range air raids were organized, which continued to the end of last year. A dozen or two planes from Japan would refuel at Iwo Jima, make the long trek to attack the American bomber bases, and

32

theoretically land on one of the small islands they still held. It was a one-way trip for all of them. Still, the Japanese traded a number of older fighters and attack planes for damage to our new, large, expensive, B-29s.

The shoe is on the other foot, now that we hold Iwo Jima[†]. Fighters from there can escort bombers from here, and the bombers can even stop for gas on Iwo if needed. In fact, that is happening tomorrow. A flight of B-29s will make a night run to a city far in the north of Japan. I'm not giving away any secrets there – we're going to tell the Japanese ahead of time that the bombers are coming. I'm not sure yet what the bomber crews think of all that, but I can guess.

July 28, 1945 : airborne over the Marianas

Each of the 3 main islands in the Marianas is about five or six miles wide and 15 to 25 miles long, north to south. Captain Thomas Campion, from Boston, flew us from Saipan, the northernmost, over Tinian just to the south, and finally to Guam another hundred miles south. I arranged to have the bulk of my gear sent to Guam after me and met the Captain near his plane, a two seat Curtiss dive bomber, a long-serving SB2C "Helldiver", headed to the navy base on Guam for an overhaul.

Captain Campion, call him Tom he says, has been flying with Marine Corps close air support groups for as long as such things have been around in this war. Navy pilots flew ground support early in the war, but the Marines formed their own squadrons dedicated to the job, and now the Army calls in Marine Corps planes whenever they can. Yesterday Tom was telling me about flying over, and into, the fights on Peleliu and in the Philippines. At times on those islands pilots would fly from captured fields a mile from the front, not even raising landing gear

---

[†] There was also a large new-design radar installation set up on Guam to detect any further raids, but I couldn't mention it at the time.

the whole trip. They made many attack runs every day, over and over, each one a complete stressful mental adventure.

After some forced R&R at Hawaii, Captain Campion has been doing training and ferry duty, waiting patiently for the next combat assignment. "I didn't want the time off, but they insisted," he explained. "I have to say now, they were right. I'm a much better pilot now than I would be if I'd kept grinding it out. Truth is, I'd probably be dead. I'm still ready to fight, but not itching for it like I was."

The fight will wait at least another day, or so this tourist hopes. I wait for pre-flight checks to be done, get my own flying outfit checked by the ground crew and we are off. We take off to the southwest, against the prevailing wind, but the unladed carrier plane doesn't need a quarter of the runway to get her wheels up.

Our plane ascends into an expansive blue field of distant white puffs, scattered high clouds well above our sight-seer's flight plan. We start west bound, with a warm mid-morning sun behind us. As we gain altitude Tom makes a long lazy turn to the north. We level off and he points out some of the minor islands north of Saipan. After the big fighting was over we secured a few of them. Others are simply cut off. Whatever Japanese garrisons are left there will be tending vegetable gardens until the end of the war.

Turning back to the south, we pass Saipan on our right. Some areas where the fighting was hard are still pock marked and denuded. Other substantial areas are clear-cut and developed, including multiple airfields larger than the one we left. The 2nd Marine Division is camped somewhere between the clusters of runways and rows of Quonset huts. The rapidity of development since just last fall is awesome.

Tinian comes up quickly, and if our bases on Saipan are impressive, Tinian is simply gob-smacking. The whole island looks like it lost a fight with a giant cat. Parallel lines of broad white scratches cut across it at irregular intervals, with raw blisters of new buildings and other facilities ringing each big paw swipe. The largest 'wound' is called simply North Field, which has four parallel 8,000 foot runways and scattered parking for a secret but triple-digit number of heavy bombers.

Tom intends to cut across the middle of Tinian, to get me a better look, and communicates that to the appropriate party by radio. He is reminded to steer clear of the north end of the island, but otherwise cleared. We cut altitude and airspeed and move toward the center of the island, which from a low approach still looks tranquil and lush with green fur. Clearing the first line of trees, and conspicuous gun emplacements, the scene changes quickly.

I can barely see the ground for all the variety of patrol planes, long range fighters, inky black night fighters, and broad acres of shiny metal bombers. Most are parked out in the open, on pads off of curving paths that slink off of the runways and service ramps. The pads are scattered and staggered so an attacker can't wreck a bunch of parked aircraft at once, but I think I could drop a rock from this plane at random and have even odds on dinging two of them in one go.

A southerly turn and another twenty some minutes flying brings us to Guam. I am still writing notes about Tinian as the facilities on Guam make themselves clear. Guam is the new home-away-from-home for a large part of the United States Marine Corps. The scene from Tinian is repeated, a dense clutter of war material making up most of the landscape. But the shiny bombers are here replaced by long rows and expansive clusters of tents, Quonset huts, and a growing variety of more permanent structures.

Guam today hosts two divisions of the United States Marine Corps. Before the war there wasn't even such a thing as a Marine Corps division. Now there are six.

The rows of tents sit along bright white gravel roads with cluttered signposts at every intersection. The square shape and sharp creases of each tautly staked tent add to the sense of industrial order that has overtaken much of this tropical isle. Each of those tents houses a small unit of Marines. One might argue a squad of Marines is the equal in combat power to one of the giant bombers and her aircrew. It would be entertaining to see the debate between them.

July 29, 1945 : Guam, Marianas

As we approached our landing yesterday, we came across the great naval base established here, which is still being improved and expanded. Guam offers a large natural harbor, four miles deep and a mile and a half wide, with another sizable inner harbor leading inland from the outer anchorage. It was a priority target for the Japanese at the start of the war. Their attacks on it began barely a European lunch break after the strikes on Pearl Harbor.

Scores of warships of every size and type are anchored in the harbor. Others are tied up near the shore, where the land is bristling with protrusions like porcupine quills, each one a service pier or loading dock or crane reaching out into the air. This facility can do almost any repair job, even putting a battleship or aircraft carrier into dry dock. Giant floating dry docks were towed here all the way from California.

One can hardly say enough about the Seabees and what they've done out here. Graded land and hard surfaced roads are placed almost as if the Seabees have them in suitcases ready to fold out when they check in to each tropical hostelry they visit. I understand a great deal of dynamite was actually involved.

If you've ever complained about the quality and condition of roads in your home county, instead of writing letters to the local newspaper editor, I suggest you write to some ambitious foreign power asking to be invaded. With any luck, the Navy will have a hand in taking your town back, and will bring the Seabees with them.

I am housed in the bachelor officer's quarters of the Navy base. While technically Quonset huts of pre-fabricated design, these are two-story buildings with every detail thought of. Housing for all the military personnel here was built from scratch, and also for thousands of natives who were left with nothing after the back-

and-forth fighting. Beside the other obvious building types, we have constructed here warehouses, ammunition bunkers, hospitals, radio studios, tank farms, and maintenance shops for everything from typewriters to heavy trucks. I took advantage of the typewriter shop services myself.

Seabees are still at work here. The larger units, together with their Army cousins, have moved on to do the same jobs in the Philippines and Ryukus as they did here. Those that remain do every job imaginable, from running aviation fuel pipelines to filling in as longshoremen unloading ships.

Last evening a large flight of bombers assembled and headed off for a night raid over Japan, and I took notes as it happened.

The large Army air bases are fifteen miles from where I am near the giant naval station, but the bombers can be heard before they even get airborne. The insistent hum from thousands of cylinders in hundreds of radial engines shoves through the few gaps in the range of hills that cover Guam. The hum becomes an angry buzz as the engines rev and the 200 inch diameter propellers rip into the warm evening air, pulling the planes in close groups down parallel runways. The sound sharpens and takes focus as pairs of bombers come into view past the hills that had hidden them, slowly climbing over the water.

The evening sun warms each shiny silver bird with a fiery orange hue. I think it must look much the same when they circle back over a freshly fire-bombed city, widespread fires lighting up the sky as the injured city calls out her attackers in the sky.

The planes turn and continue climbing, moving to where they will meet bomber groups from the other islands. On each mission dozens or hundreds of planes from Guam meet a similar number from Tinian and/or Saipan. Together they pick up dozens or hundreds of fighter escorts near Iwo Jima.

The whole force moves toward Japan, where it will either split up or focus on just one large or important target. At night aiming points are found by radar. Coast line features, river junctions, and large landmarks show up well on even the most basic set. Thankfully Japanese defense radar and night fighters haven't been very effective so far. That was a big unknown when the Army Air Force first started night bombing runs last spring, and at that time they had no option of fighter cover.

I got the run down on all this from Navy Captain Lee Clary, a former river boat pilot from Memphis. Despite his experience handling big boats, the Navy put him in the intelligence section. His group didn't have much to do until the bombing mission got back in the morning and they developed the first photos of the fires. Follow-up recon flights would get daylight pictures of the area after the smoke cleared.

It's an Army job from here. Captain Clary expects to go to Okinawa soon to work Navy attack missions. He showed me some of the pictures from previous missions, and how they estimate and report total area destroyed in an area bombing mission.

"But here's the thing about fire bombing," he was anxious to explain. "We can burn down all the wooden buildings easy enough, but that's just the shells. Look here…" He produced a series of prints for damage assessment from a job on an aircraft manufacturing complex. "See all around here, all these shapes sticking up casting hard shadows?" The scene was an ocean of blackened earth and charred timbers, but I could see the shapes he meant, popping up out of the barren landscape like cacti in the desert. "That is practically a forest of drill presses and small lathes. That's why we bomb out large areas – production is distributed to small shops and even homes all around every factory. So there are machine tools in every back yard. I'd bet most of them could be cleaned up and put back into use. Hell, by now they probably are!"

Captain Clary is sure that we're doing much to frustrate the enemy with regular bombing, but he is not among those who think air power alone could ever end the war.

July 30, 1945 : Guam, Marianas

When I met Captain Clary in Navy intelligence yesterday, he shook my hand excitedly and gave me a personal welcome. "Of all the reporters who come through here, I'm glad it was you who happened in here today." He unlocked a drawer from which he pulled a thin file. He opened the file and I was surprised when he asked me to autograph the third piece of paper in the stack.

On the paper was a blue mimeograph version of my own column from about six weeks ago. Some notes in Japanese went down the right side. That column was generally about labor problems back home, and what the fighting men in dirty trenches thought about striking war workers (using what words I could put in print). I looked over a few other pages in the packet. Each had a piece out of or information derived from American newspapers, with annotation in Japanese. The material ranged from collation of military death notices in local papers to editorials criticizing the American generals over the Okinawa campaign.

Captain Clary gave me some context, "We found this at a small Japanese command post just over a week ago. It came in with a bunch of other captured material for us to look at. They send out summaries of our news with the regular intel reports." He marked over the "Restricted" stamp on the folder with another stamp, initialed a box just made by the second stamp, and put the souvenir folder in his own bag. "Remember, Mr. Tuttle, that your work is light reading back home. To the Japanese, it's all intelligence. They manage to get newspapers from all over, through foreign embassies if not by agents."

"What they read must be horribly confusing to them. There is so much open criticism in our papers and magazines, the Japs think we'll be in open revolt any day now! It's just so different from what any of them have seen their whole lives. The Japanese comments on those sheets are a riot some times. We think there are three guys who do the markups; they each have their own style. One of them we call 'Chicken Little', he's so sure the sky is going to fall, right on the capital dome."

After closing up the intelligence office, Captain Clary and I went to find a radio to listen to. The mission that night had a radio reporter on board with gear set up to do a live broadcast, all the way back to the States. It will have been a week or two ago by the time you read this. Ray Clark, from a station in Omaha, transmitted directly back to Guam, and the feed was relayed along through several hops from here. I'm pleased to say the broadcast worked, and all the planes made it back from that mission. I'm not too pleased to wonder what this means for us old-fashioned typewriter-wielding war correspondents.

Baseball is nuts here. Every base has a team, with natty custom uniforms and groomed fields to play on. Every field unit, down to battalion size or even smaller, has a competitive team with whatever equipment they can get a hold of. Somehow every ship with more than 9 sailors on it shows up with a team itching to play (I suppose they practice over the water with sharks and rays as bases). Leagues form up spontaneously any time two teams are within a day hike of each other. The Navy formally organizes a larger league for the whole Marianas. You've probably read about the top level leagues run by the military. If you don't follow, know that last year Navy beat Army for the "Pacific World Series" in Hawaii. Both are dead serious about putting up good teams for the rematch this year.

Today a top-flight match was played on a professionally laid field. Construction teams here did not neglect sport and recreation facilities, and Trimble Field is one of their best. Named after Jimmy Trimble, who passed on a pro contract to fight with the Marines and was killed at Iwo Jima, the field has a fine scoreboard and a few small grandstands. The top teams of the Third and Sixth Marine divisions faced off for a full nine inning game. It's an open secret that major leaguers in the military are kept out of risky combat roles, but the Marine divisions still have plenty of ringers.

I hitched a ride up to the field, which wasn't hard because practically everyone was heading there. Upon arrival I gave up hope of watching much of the action. The few grandstands were burdened with brass, and guys were standing ten or twenty deep along the foul lines, all the way out further than Ty Cobb's longest home run. People watching was going to be my sport for the afternoon.

It's another open secret that anywhere sports are happening, or anywhere American servicemen are together, there is wagering going on. This place had both sports and servicemen in spades. It didn't take long to find a cluster of fellows putting cash into the hands of an entrepreneurial soldier with a busy pencil and notebook. The huddle was off to one side, just a bit into right field. Each man was anxious to stuff a few bills into the hand of the man in the middle, except the known few who had credit and looked to see their names written into his notebook.

Army Corporal William Isley, off duty from airfield security, is here from Winston-Salem, North Carolina. I got to talk to him for a minute after the second inning, when he finally stopped taking proposition bets for a while. He filled me in on the line for the day's game, and some of the other action going in his book.

I wasn't interested in the lines, though it is curious what servicemen will bet on, for entertainment or enrichment or to tempt fate, who can say. The odds of Japan surrendering before the next action are followed closely, of course. Then there are propositions like the number of women in the next USO troupe or which aircraft carrier will show up in port next.

I was more interested about Mr. Isley, the gambler, for every bookie I've ever met is an inveterate gambler. Whatever margin a bookie makes in running lines for others, he almost certainly spends more than that betting with someone else. My questions were transparent enough that Corporal Isley cut me off with a laugh in the bottom of the third. "I know the story, pal. Don't you worry about little ol' Bill – I've got it all leveled out. I've sent home ten times more money than you've seen go by today." He tapped his notebook for emphasis. "My job here is just to play these other fellows against each other, settle their bets, and save what's left over. I'm doing just fine." I'm sure he believes it, too.

August 3, 1945 : Pacific Ocean

The last few days are still a blur to me. At the baseball
game (the 3rd Marine Division won, on a late triple from minor
leaguer Ray Champagne) I hooked up with the crew of a Liberty
ship in port refueling. They only had time to catch the game
because of some overdue repair work – their ship had been banged
up by typhoon Connie back in June[‡]. The ship was pulling out at
first light, straight for Okinawa.

Impulsively, I jumped at the chance to go with them. I was
pretty well settled in on Guam. Official, discrete, word to me was
that I had some time before I had to fly out[§]. But I had never been
with a cargo ship, and it's been made abundantly clear to me how
important they are in this trans-oceanic campaign. So I signed on
to the crew of the USS Red Oak Victory.

I am without many of my personal possessions on this trip.
They have to be packed up and shipped to meet me on Okinawa. I
called in a bunch of favors that nobody owed me to get everything
done as I ran to the pier. I missed a USO show I was looking
forward to, featuring some of my friends from Honolulu. But they
too are due to follow after me to Okinawa.

I called the Red Oak Victory a Liberty ship, but she is
actually a newer "Victory" ship, technically of the Boulder class.
The Victory ships carry a little bit more than the Liberty ships, and
go a lot faster. They take more than a week off a trans-Pacific
route, and then get back another week sooner ready to take another
load.

Mariners will have noticed that I called this ship a "USS"
and I am not mistaken in that. The Red Oak Victory is under U.S.

[‡] Typhoons had been a real nuisance, or worse, for the Navy. You
probably heard about typhoon Cobra of December 1944, which tore up Admiral
Halsey's fleet, sinking three destroyers and putting dozens of other ships into
port for repairs. Typhoon Connie was not as bad, but still killed sailors, threw
planes in the water, and took two large aircraft carriers out of action.

[§] At this time Operation Olympic, the invasion of southern Kyushu,
was set for November 1st.

Navy command and crewed entirely by officers and sailors. She is not a civilian Merchant Marine vessel. Her main job up to now has been hauling ammunition, and delivering it directly to other ships while the fleet was still at sea.

This ship is armed almost as well as the small destroyer I was on in Hawaii. Small and medium caliber guns ring the upper decks, making air attack dangerous (to the aircraft). The one big gun is on the back, all the better for making distance between us and a submarine running on the surface. These guns would be run by a Navy contingent on a Merchant Marine ship. Merchant Marine ships have seen plenty of action in this war, some scoring multiple aircraft kills in a single attack.As I write this Okinawa is already in sight. A ship like this can get from the Marianas to the Ryukus in four days, even when running a zig-zig course to frustrate a submarine captain trying to time a torpedo into the same place as our ship. The run is not done in convoys; the whole shipping lane is patrolled from the air. Navy sea planes get regular catches of big tin fish with bombs and depth charges, but the situation makes the Atlantic veterans in this crew nervous. A line of well armed destroyers would certainly make a more reassuring security blanket.

We made this run without incident, and are ready to unload. But we're on the familiar military schedule of 'hurry up and wait.' Okinawa still does not sprout enough piers and cranes for our ships to be unloaded fast enough. We will anchor in the far spread arms of what has been renamed Buckner Bay on the east side of the island, before getting directed to a pier, which could be at the nearby naval base or all the way around the island at Naha.

I am taking the opportunity to catch up on reading. The ship has a decent little library, and takes on new magazines and books when it can. Much of the recent news is from the big conference at Potsdam, Germany. President Truman should be just on his way back from that big to-do, where it is supposed that the whole post-war world was neatly drawn up.

Except of course that sketch depends on the Japanese playing their part according to the artists' vision. Toward that end they issued an ultimatum to the Japs, that people are already referring to simply as the 'Potsdam Declaration.' It is not a long document. It spells out concisely that we intend to completely re-make Japan, not just defeat her, and that we have the means to do both. I read the whole text, and took particular note of the end.

> "We call upon the government of Japan to proclaim now the unconditional surrender of all Japanese armed forces, and to provide proper and adequate assurances of their good faith in such action. *The alternative is deliberate and thorough destruction.*"

We are here to unload a full cargo of heavy bombs for the heavy bombers. I survey the vast mob of other ships anchored here waiting to unload assorted deadly cargoes, and I have no doubt about the thoroughness we intend to exhibit.

August 6, 1945 : Okinawa, Ryukus

Okinawa is the newest target for the Army engineers and Navy CBs to aim their shovels and hammers at, but they've had a whole four months to remake it now. They even got to work the entire last month without getting shot at! That's plenty of time for those ferociously determined engineers to remake an island this size. New wide gravel roads run all directions, between and through camps and bases of every size and variety. On my first day I came ashore on the north end of Buckner Bay and was driven ten miles down to the south end near a Navy air base called Yonabaru.

On the way I saw Navy functional and headquarters buildings to rival anything they have this side of Pearl Harbor. Land around the headquarters buildings is groomed and terraced, with young landscaping starting to grow in. The buildings are multi-story Quonset huts, but the people in charge of idioms need to snip off "hut." They dwarf my previous quarters on Guam, and are ringed with boardwalk porches behind white picket fencing that may have been commandeered from a neighborhood in Indiana.

I am quartered in a tent camp which overlooks Yonabaru airfield with the water of the bay behind it. My tent mates include another reporter and two officers from a patrol plane squadron, none of whom I have met yet. With little on my person to stow, I was only at the tent camp for a few minutes.

My escort, Army Captain Clarence Southard, is a public communications officer. That means he's a censor. But just to show that they're not all bad guys, he offered to drive me around the island. So by jeep we wandered over the newest American possession while Captain Southard narrated over the sound of our engine.

"Job one here was air fields. The Army went right for the two big ones when we landed here at the beginning of April. By mid month they were flying fighters out of there directly into the fight." We crested the center ridge line of the island just then and I could see the handy work of the engineers at Kadena and Yontan airfields. New long runways, composed largely of local coral, shone in the sun. Aircraft parking areas ran off in all directions, and more were being graded. "The 8th Air Force is still coming over from England, picking up B-29s along the way. Two other air forces are already here, running long range fighters and medium bombers."

I asked about some large tent camps that were briefly in sight at the northernmost leg of our journey. I could just make out barb wire topped fences around the camps. "Those are for the Okinawan civilians, and the Jap POWs. For now they're one and the same to us. Interrogators are sorting them out, which is gonna take a while. But it's not like there's anywhere for the actual civilians to go anyhow."

We turned to the south, along the west coast of the island, and the narrative turned to shipping. "Once the airfields were laid down, the top priority was getting the ports dolled up. Naha," he pointed just ahead and to the right, "has the only port to speak of here, but it's small. As you saw we set up dozens of new piers in the other bay to add capacity."

The race is on to get enough port capacity to support the big bombers once they get up to speed here. All that bomb tonnage has to go from shore-to-ship-to-shore before it is delivered by air to Japanese factories and harbors and airfields. I was deposited back on to the largely naval side of the island, where I could forage for basic essentials I would need until my luggage showed up from Guam.

A stunning bit of news came and stuck around today. Unofficial reports say the large cruiser USS Indianapolis was sunk with great loss of life over a week ago. I checked up and there is no official word or press report about it, but guys 'in the know' swear that radio traffic went around about a big search and rescue operation that should be still going on.

One of my new tent mates is particularly anxious for news. Warrant Officer Henry Weber served on the Indy with her float plane team until last October. He was an old salt compared to most recruits coming in. "We had just taken on a batch of new kids in the aviation group when I was transferred. I took a real shine to my one machinist's mate. I hope Mitchell got off, and good word gets to his momma. He used to write home just about every day."

August 9, 1945 : Okinawa, Ryukus

I've met my other tent mates for this stay. They are the aforementioned Warrant Officer Weber, his boss Chief Clayton Holt, and Major Peter Lawless (British Army, retired) who is reporting for London's Daily Telegraph. The bespectacled Mr. Lawless is the elder statesman of the camp, at 54. Since he picked up his military rank in the trenches of WWI, he says camp life here is not the slightest hardship. He is also an experienced rugger and is teaching me a lot about the game of rugby football.

Actually camp life truly isn't hard here. The tent cities are well graded and drained. We have elevated wood floors. The climate is mild. And we can get to a hot shower without too much effort. I've been in worse shape at a cheap hotel in South Dakota.

I'm getting the feel of the place, and it has a real living pulse. A routine flow has taken hold, now that the fighting is over and facilities are up enough to support operations. Not that we're by any means done building up Okinawan bases.

Every expansion is met with a ready need for more. A tank farm is barely filled for the first time before a line of trucks or ships or planes has formed ready to take on fuel. Each new mess hall only slightly shortens the lines at three others. Freshly paved road lanes are set upon promptly by hordes of loaded trucks, requiring constant maintenance.

This morning I walked with Major Lawless over the island to watch planes take off for a big raid that we were tipped off to. From the right vantage point one can see the airfields at Kadena and Yontan, which we took from the Japanese and promptly expanded, plus a new extra-long airstrip at Bolo point.

We were sending everything including the kitchen sink for a remodel of southern Japan that day. Long range fighters were going up almost side by side with Liberator bombers. Bunches of our new twin engine attack planes formed up over the East China Sea before droning off into the high overcast sky.

We watched for over an hour as the formations came together for their deadly migration. Thousands of men on the ground wrangled equipment, shifting from the hustle of fueling and arming planes to preparations for receiving them back, making repairs, and starting all over again.

There is still no official word about the loss of the heavy cruiser USS Indianapolis. She may have been taken by a torpedo. One story is that a swarm of long range fighters from some tiny island we skipped invading set upon her. Others say she was on a secret mission and not on any table of movement. Rumors are pretty consistent at this point that about 300 of her crew are accounted for. She left port with almost 1200.[**][††]

August 10, 1945 : Okinawa, Ryukus

The bombing raid yesterday went well, as far as these things go. The cold accounting that goes with such operations recorded three fighters and two bombers lost to enemy action, survivors doubtful. Another one of each was seen ditching into the sea with mechanical trouble. Float planes are unable to search for airmen from those planes because horrible weather moved in late in the day.

I hung around Kadena airfield for the rest of the day. Watching all the aircraft move through space got me wondering how they're kept from co-locating on a regular basis. Mid-air collisions seem inevitable with ten airfields on this roughly five-

---

[**] This paragraph was originally embargoed. Official announcement of the sinking was not made until August 13. Details became public when her Captain Charles McVay faced court martial long after, including testimony from the Japanese submarine captain who sank the Indy with two torpedoes.

[††] [Editor's note, 2015: Captain McVay was formally exonerated by act of Congress in 2001. He died in 1968. – sdm]

by-fifty mile island, most of them clustered together in a quarter of that space.

I talked my way into the air control room for Kadena. It was busy, as expected, and the atmosphere was tense. Bad weather was moving in earlier than predicted. They would need to recover planes under thick clouds bearing heavy rain. Radar screens and radio stations received the keen focus of the controllers' attention.

Added to the mix was a flight of new B-29 bombers coming in for deployment at Bolo point to the northwest. Those pilots would likely be unfamiliar with the airfields and landmarks around them. Most of the landing strips here are parallel to each other, running with the prevailing winds. Controllers don't need to give multiple headings and control crossing flight paths, if they can get each plane into the right corridor. They have a system for it, but sometimes it's not enough.

Late in the day, with minimal sunlight pushing through the low rain clouds, a B-29 came down in front of me, right on top of a smaller plane. The A-20 "Havoc" had just landed, gun belts and bomb racks emptied, coming to a slow roll only halfway down the generous runway. It was completely demolished. The pilot of the B-29 probably lined up on the wrong runway. We'll never get the chance to ask him or his co-pilot. The nose of their bomber broke off cleanly and bounded down the runway in a violent twisting tumble. It remained intact but their bodies were shattered.

I stood at the window watching ground crews scramble to put out fires and clear debris from the wet coral pavement. Calm but forceful voices behind me issued rapid instructions to dozens of inbound planes, diverting them to other fields. The rain kept coming into the night so I found a quiet corner of the base office block to camp in.

August 12, 1945 : Okinawa, Ryukus

Heavy rains continued into today. Combat units are still expected to work through maneuvers out in the field. We can see them come and go every morning and evening toward the oft-assaulted hills south of here. The lucky ones are buttoned up in tanks and truck cabs, until they get stuck in mud. Engineers are getting practice with their big tracked recovery vehicles, and if the rain keeps up they'll be practicing recovery of stuck recovery vehicles.

People who don't have to be outside are cooped up and getting restless. Poker games with well-worn decks are running continuously in the usual tents, campaign currency and paper IOUs moving around fluidly. No one has much stomach for setting up pranks in this depressing weather. Most write letters or sit and read in their off hours.

One well-worn bit of reading material is a copy of Yank magazine from back in June. The big cover story is a piece that directly asks the question, "How Long Will We Have to Fight the Jap War?" It's the standard question here, and it has a lot of standard answers. Answers run from confident predictions to uncertain humor like "Golden Gate in '48!" to more somber reflections that other soldiers don't want to hear.

The piece in Yank gives a summary of the situation, and plenty of stats, but nothing in the way of any predictions. It ends with an admonition from the war department that however tough it gets, we have to keep up the pace or it will only get tougher. "The War Department plan calls for redeploying men from the ETO[‡‡] and the States so fast that the Japs will not have time to build up defenses or assemble reinforcements at spots where the Japs may figure the next invasions will come. 'Speed is essential, for it is vitally important that we do not give the enemy time either to rest or reorganize his defenses.'"

Last I looked, there still weren't any units from Europe in the Pacific. I suspect the boys already here will carry on with what they have for at least the next big job.

The tattered magazine has the usual letters and funnies and requisite full page pin-up photo (Nancy Porter in a sharp looking

---

[‡‡] European Theater of Operations

50

two piece). But my attention is drawn to the last page, which is filled by an article on "The Soccer Situation" from Corporal Tom Shehan. There is a thought that young Americans being exposed to soccer in the various countries they visit will make them bring the sport home. U.S. based soccer officials look especially to troops who spent considerable time in England and Australia. I find this odd.

I would expect that our soldiers, Marines, and airmen, mixing with the virile men of other nations, from their combat units, would pick up sporting pursuits more suited to smart athletic young men. Soccer has always looked to me like a gaggle of flightless birds running around a stolen egg. It's proper rugby football that I expect our service men to bring back, and I'll be happy to see it.

August 16, 1945 : Okinawa, Ryukus

Heavy rains have let up, but overcast and drizzle continued intermittently through today. There is hope for predicted clear skies tomorrow. Tent residents are becoming moldy cave dwellers, in desperate need of dry air to move through their odor fouled canvas homes.

Moods were brighter today, and not just because of the expected sunshine. Last afternoon a delayed USO show put on three performances in the largest amphitheater. Columns of poncho wearing soldiers, sailors, Marines, Merchant Mariners and civilians working here paraded into the bowl in rotation. A light rain was not going to stop them from seeing the only live entertainment for a thousand miles.

The USO typically rotates troupes around the island, working them ten or twelve shows a week, twice daily at theaters near each major base. But most of them are outdoors, so shows have been limited all this week to small affairs with no PA in mess halls and airplane hangars. There is pent up demand for a full show.

I hiked over with my tent mates and the rest of our attached unit. Engineers have been busy keeping the roads passable, filling in muddy ruts with more of the seemly inexhaustible piles of coral they have blasted from the sea and crushed into gravel. It is still a damp adventure, as we are shooed to the puddle ridden road edge by passing trucks that have work to do as we pursue a scarce pleasure.

Among the list of #1 priorities for the engineers here, and all their jobs are #1 priorities when making up a whole functioning civilization from practically nothing, was theater areas. They have multiple uses, not just entertainment, but today this one was dedicated to fun.

Curving rows of stout benches, most with straight board backs, run in semicircles up a terraced curving hill side. They arc almost 180 degrees around a tall Quonset-hut-style building at the bottom of the strategically chosen hill. A stage platform extends twenty feet out from the building about four feet off the ground. Everyone has a good view when the performers come out.

My companions took over a block of bench space about twenty rows back from the front. The rain took a break just then and most men took off their ponchos before settling in. Down front the usual "bald headed row" of high ranking officers and VIPs showed themselves true to form, reflecting some of the bright gray sky in the middle of a sea of olive green. I kept my own hat on as I walked down to the stage.

Most of the performers tonight were the friends I made back in Honolulu, crossing paths again with them on Guam. I pulled rank to get back stage, showing my press ID, and got to catch up with them again before their second show of the day.

For my money, not that I was spending any, the centerpiece of the show was pianist Arthur Zepp. He supported every act in the show, and in the middle took center stage for a couple solo pieces. The troops heard comedy from Dell Chain and songs from Emma Lou Welch. Virginia Carroll also sang, but what got the troops to sit up and lean in was her acrobatic act. The headliner was the surprisingly funny Betty Hutton. She sang until they drug her off stage, and I had a side stage view of all of it.

August 30, 1945 : Okinawa, Ryukus

Whatever else a military encampment is built for, it is sure also to be a highly productive rumor mill. Word is passed around among men at every instance of idle time. The story can be rated "straight dope" or "scuttlebutt" depending on the teller's reputation and storytelling skill.

Some guys make a sport of it. One fellow will deliberately start something, seeding his story with just enough inconsequential detail and unverifiable sources to make it sellable. The game is to see how quick it comes back around, and how the story got twisted or exaggerated along the way. Like anything else, there are sometimes wagers that go along with these things.

For me it is strictly a spectator sport. I don't care to encourage such things. But that doesn't stop me from doing my own experiments, using strictly factual material, of course.

I didn't start my rumor from scratch. Buried in one of the American newspapers I had brought over was a regular table in the business section on awarded government contracts. I happened to be reading something else nearby when a fellow began pointing out one of the line items to his buddies.

"Look here! The Navy just bought another 125,000 purple heart medals[§§]. Forget what they said about Japan keeling over before we get there!" He had a point in that – whatever the Navy said, it would have to buy hardware to go with what it really thought.

Seeing my opportunity to add a marker to the story, a tag for me to watch it run around, I interjected something else I'd learned. On a tour of the Philadelphia mint just a few months

---

[§§] The purple heart is awarded to persons who are seriously injured or killed in combat.

before, they showed me how the medals were being made of molded plastic instead of more precious materials. It had as much to do with holding the thing together as conserving war materials, but I didn't include that part.

I hung out near the mess tent coffee urns for the rest of the day. Within hours the Navy order had jumped to a quarter million. The Army got in on the act for another 400,000[***]. No one really knew what a purple heart medal was made of in the first place, so quickly there were critical shortages of: brass, copper, silver, or even purple paint. The best story had a German spy try to blow up Fort Knox, causing a run on gold.

Satisfied that the rumor mill here was working at full efficiency, I took a walk through Naha in the warm setting sun. I wondered if when the sun came up again there wouldn't be a story about crates of medals being air dropped to us, 'just in case.'

September 2, 1945 : Okinawa, Ryukus

It has been said that this is "the Engineers' war." I wouldn't dispute that, and I can say that right now Okinawa is their biggest playground. They are and have been busy remaking the world, starting with its level. Causing flat land to exist seems to be their number one occupation.

On top of the largest flat spots go airfields. Others get everything from hospitals to workshops to giant latrines – there are a million people living here after all.

Every sort of vehicle imaginable is here to do the work, and many which have never before been imagined. Okinawa is the proving ground for some mechanized contraptions that range from clever to brutish to whimsical.

[***] In fact, both services were mostly catching up with demand, delivering medals late to previously injured servicemen. That would continue past the war's end, until the total number of purple heart medals produced topped 1.8 million.

Wheeled truck mounted cranes wander the hillsides, fetching and rearranging things where even tanks dare not go. Speaking of tanks, funny looking tanks also wander around with crane arms on them, but no gun turret. They are tank recovery vehicles, with massive counterweights and a winch strong enough to pick up a stuck tank. Since they are essentially just small cranes, they also get put to every other kind of utility that a lifter can provide.

It is also not unusual to see a bridge drive by. Not a truck carrying bridge sections, but an actual self-propelled self-deploying bridge. It can drive up to a river bank, fold itself out over the span, and be driven right over.

Oh, there are people here besides the engineers. The bombers and long range fighters make some racket as they sortie and return. Ships come and go, taking supplies and liberty, heading back out into the fight or to bring us even more stuff.

The ground combat units here, who mostly just stayed on after conquering the place, are the 1st Marine Division, the 7th Infantry Division, and the 27th Infantry Division. The Army and Marine Corps units are camped generally on their respective sides of the island. They are refitting and retraining, as you might expect, but the pace of it leaves some of them restless.

Pranks are to be expected. Inter-service pranks especially. Add in the presence of a hundred thousand technical specialists, and the jokes can get intricate.

Colored smoke grenades are a favorite booby trap device so far. A delay mechanism is set in some way, so a machine will get along a ways before green or red smoke billows out from the engine compartment – or fills the driver's cab. One group of on-looking Seabees thought it was hilarious to see an Army crane run straight over a jeep, the driver blinded by a well timed smoke bomb, until it turned out that it was the personal jeep of a Navy captain, who only got out a minute before.

Those Seabees kept the Navy officers' latrines spic and span for the duration of their stay.

September 10, 1945 : Okinawa, Ryukus

Late into the evening before last, word went around to check tent ropes and put anything under cover which we wanted to be sure stayed dry. A big storm was moving by. The center of it was sure to miss us but they said it was still big enough to bring serious wind and rain. They weren't kidding.

Me and my tent mates had set up our canvas home to serve well in any weather. We had a wood plank floor which kept us up off any wet ground, but Major Lawless and Chief Holt had worked on a drainage system that kept water from getting under the tent in the first place. Berms and ditches worked to divert water from the tent farm above around us and on down toward the airfield below. A small amount of fresh rainwater was collected from our roof, handy for shaving and some cleaning.

When word of the impending storm came the earthworks were improved a little, though we were sure it was good already. I looked over the tent rigging and redid some of the knots, getting better and more even tension on the ropes. I thought they must have been tied by army men, not sailors.

The storm came just a bit after dark. The wind peaked near 10 pm, the rain near midnight. It was over by two and only then could we finally sleep.

The noise of fast wind like that from inside a tent was something new for all of us. Inside a solid building one hears strong wind whip around the corners and whistle through certain fissures when it turns just right. In a tent one hears the wind blowing around the tent, the tent fabric shifting and billowing, and every sound from outside as well. We couldn't see the source of each noise, so every bump, crack, and rustle was a mystery.

One specter startled us like a noisy ghost. A rhythmic thump and rumble drew closer, quickly, from the direction of the bay. We all leaned that direction, straining to hear better. I for one jumped a foot off my cot when something suddenly pushed into the side of the tent, shoving the wall in a good foot.

I got volunteered, since I was up anyway, to go see what it was. I took one of the two lanterns we had lit and sloshed out into the rain, down off our wooden deck which had indeed stayed dry so far. Shortly I was standing over a rough wooden spindle, three feet long with 30 inch diameter rims. Someone had left an empty cable spool laying around and the wind took it. We had a new table.

Other tents were not so lucky. By daylight I took a quick survey and found many fellows wringing out their belongings, while their tent mates re-tied guy lines or added more heavy stakes. A few fellows walked by with borrowed shovels, looking to do their own drainage improvements.

A short convoy of an AMTRAC full of supplies, an ambulance, and a recovery vehicle ambled by. Several small units were out on maneuvers when the storm came. Some of them hadn't been heard from. While scouts drove out looking for them, this ad hoc team was assembled to take out what they might need.

I for one am glad we got in a decent storm while many men are still here in training. If one hit in combat we'd be much less prepared.

September 17, 1945 : Okinawa, Ryukus

Another storm peaked here yesterday. We prepared for it the same as last time. The storm was not the same as last time.

I'm in the Navy weather office here, partly to get whatever news they can offer (not much). Mostly I am here because they have a good wood frame building, with a roof that actually drains water away from the building. I am dry and warm at the same time for the first time in a week.

The meteorologists tell me that it has been raining from this storm for two days, that the wind peaked yesterday, and that the rain will stop in another day or three. I asked about the wind and they think it got up to a hundred twenty miles an hour. The previous storm they think was about the same strength, but the center of it didn't come within 150 miles of Okinawa.

Many tents were either torn from their rope anchors or simply ripped apart in place. The reader should note, the tent stakes in use here are not like what a civilian hiker has in his or her backpack. These are serious steel posts, driven into the earth with two-fisted hammers. Also the canvas of the tents is a heavy weave, and doped with sealant. The tents are tied down with taut ropes as thick as an adult finger. These are not trivial shelters. Still, the wind made them seem little better than a child's couch cushion fort.

A check in the base hospital shows that there were injuries, some of them serious. Two dozen or so beds are freshly occupied, in a facility serving about 10,000 men, and I have reports of similar results elsewhere. There is no word yet on fatalities, but it is still early and there are piles of debris to sort through.

I didn't have to go anywhere to observe damage to the fleet. From our battered tent camp (my particular shelter was one of the lucky ones), one can look directly down on Buckner Bay. Multiple transport and service ships are beached on the shore. A few have damage apparent even from this distance. I did go down to the bay to get better word. A tug captain tells me they're going to start surveying the damaged ships and pulling the relatively healthy ones back out in the water. He won't be the one doing it as his boat was smashed against a pier before being tossed ashore upside down.

September 21, 1945 : Okinawa, Ryukus

The weather has been clear for three days and things are finally pretty well dry. This morning I caught a big flatbed truck lumbering by my camp, moving very slow for having no load. On second look I noticed chains behind the truck running to a tired looking tank, which was missing a few details like her main gun. At a quick walking pace I caught up with the truck cab to inquire.

58

"We got a request for real targets," the driver explained. "That hunka junk is gonna wind up on a bazooka range." He didn't have to ask twice if I wanted to ride along. Army Sergeant. William Myers told me a bit about himself and his old life in Maryland, and about Private Wesley Dusek who was back in the tank working the tread brakes as needed to keep our tank on the road and out of some colonel's tent.

Under cloudy skies and with a refreshingly cool dry breeze we coaxed the tank through several hill passes until we came out onto a flat draw, about a half mile long and quarter mile wide. A handful of Marine Corps NCOs were unloading two jeeps and a small trailer full of wooden crates. We were waved through to drag our condemned prisoner by her chains to the far end of the draw.

Along the way I saw several splintered wooden posts and shattered boards around them, but no machine parts – I decided this must be the first bit of live bait at this fishin' hole. My new friends lined up the old tank as requested, unrigged the chains, and we hustled back to the firing line.

By then a short column of young Marines, marching since just after breakfast, came to a halt and formed up a semicircle for instruction. As the other NCOs organized weapons and ammo at three sandbag firing positions, the senior man, a staff sergeant I think, address the new privates.

He didn't have all good news for them. "You will NOT all get a chance to fire today. Other camps have higher priority for ammo, the ones who get to go into the fight before us." He sounded disappointed about both the shortage of explosives and not getting to go use them for effect.

The privates got a general primer on the bazooka ("M9A1 2.36 inch rocket launcher"), then paired off to drill through the two-man operation of loading a dummy round and dry firing. Every pair did that back and forth at least twice, three pair at a time. It took two hours for the thirty-some young Marines to get that far. Then, each pair got to live fire one round.

Hoots went out and big grins shown all around when the first rockets hit home. Sparks, flame, noise, and not a few flying chunks of former U.S. Army tank, M4A2 Sherman (zero mm gun), met their final resting place. Not every rocket found home, of course, and those shooters who missed risked getting fresh nicknames during the march back.

With the tank put permanently out of action several times over, and each pair having done a live fire drill, the instructors found there were exactly four rounds left. A question was put to the instructees, "How fast do you think a good team can put four aimed rounds on target? When you need to shut up an enemy gun, you need to make sure of it to save your buddies. So how quick can you make it happen?" After some murmuring a few answers rang out, "Three minutes!" to open, then a run down to "60 seconds!" before no one would go any lower.

The senior sergeant took dollar bets on that one minute over/under and told his privates to watch closely as two corporals took those four rockets to the center firing pit. I was volunteered to keep time, as the professional impartial observer. On my mark a martial ballet played out at a startling pace. I don't think anyone looked at the rounds hitting, as they were watching nonstop action in the gun pit.

The loader danced from tube side to ammo side of the gunner in nonstop motion, putting a firm hand on the gunner's helmet between each pass as a signal. I stopped my watch at 37 seconds, which was probably a little long as I watched the last round hit and the final bits of hot tank fragment fall back to the ground.

The column of Marines marched back to camp, a little wiser and about twenty dollars poorer.

You may look at news reports of battles, put a few of them together, and notice that veteran combat units are given many months off in between major actions. And you may wonder just what they do in all that time, while on public payrolls and dining in military mess halls. Well, this is it.

First of all, a division coming out of a long tough fight, like for the dirt under my feet here on Okinawa, has to deal with the fact that half of it is simply gone. Once the dust clears and the generals and clerks make sense of it all, there are a lot of holes to fill.

Some of the injured may be expected to return, but the timing is uncertain, and anyway most do not. Some men are promoted up out of combat roles, or transferred into other specialties. Some guys are simply due to rotate home, having fulfilled the current standard of combat duty (e.g. accumulating enough points).

The veteran soldiers or Marines, including those who were raw recruits just a month before and survived deadly on-the-job training, are redistributed across a division, to best use their supposed newfound leadership. Every unit down to the smallest fire team is affected by vacancies. So, boat loads of new guys show up to fill the ranks, each with nothing but a duffel bag full of gear and a thimble full of combat training.

A freshly reconstituted division begins training for the next assault before the veterans even get to change their socks from the last one. But it has to start from scratch. Riflemen learn to work in teams. Teams learn to work in squads, squads in platoons, platoons in companies, companies in battalions, battalions in regiments, and finally the whole division learns to work as a unit.

Maneuvers are walked through, then run through, then repeated with additional complications. Rifle men go from learning how not to get hit, to learning how to work together to concentrate brutal mixed firepower on a doomed enemy.

There is a rhythm to the buildup, and a necessary order to it. Senior NCOs in the divisions here don't think they're going to go into the fight any time soon[†††]. They only finished fighting for Okinawa in late June. They've been getting new gear and replacements in a slow trickle, and are doing mostly platoon and

---

[†††] They were right. Army divisions for Operation Olympic were all coming from the Philippines, where they had been refitting and training since the spring. The Marine Corps divisions involved would come from the Marianas and Hawaii, veterans of Iwo Jima plus the 2nd Division which had seen only limited action on Okinawa.

company size exercises, repeatedly "seizing" one of several nearby hills.

The Seabees and other support units have their own rhythm to the invasion prep routine. I said before that the construction battalions practically unpack whole airfields and naval bases from their luggage when checking in to each tropical resort on their Pacific tour. At some time they need to pack those bags, and on Okinawa they are doing that now. Crates of supplies, tools, and construction materials are beginning to accumulate, and the Seabees are staging them in the order they will be needed.

The 5th Marine division has an advance team here with the CBs[‡‡‡]. They are coordinating with the bulldozer men to get what they need bulldozed ASAP after the next landing. They also have some map books which have a guard attached.

September 24, 1945 : Okinawa, Ryukus

It is still raining. Don't worry, you haven't picked up an old column. It's just been raining here on and off, mostly on, for a month. As much of what passes for civilization here is a facade of cotton fabric and gravel underpinnings, management of water is a primary preoccupation when rainfall overstays its welcome. And this rain is well overdue to pay its final respects to its patient dinner host.

It was raining cats and dogs – and sheep and wildebeest and every other precipitous creature – all day today, and yesterday, and much of the day before. It's not going to let up for a while either. A few units were and are out on exercises. There are no war umpires to call a rain delay, not that we could see them in such nonexistent visibility. I was talking to a sergeant with a vehicle recovery team when he decided to go see if all the trucks and

---

[‡‡‡] Mention of the 5th Marine Division was originally censored. They were to be the reserve division of V Corps, going in to the beach at about the same time as the first non-Marine Corps support units. Coordination between those units would be essential in the flexible combat situation.

armor his crew played shepherd to were tucked away in their yard, or out somewhere getting stuck.

I spent most of the afternoon in the wood frame mess hall that has become the unofficial camp lending library (My stack of old home town papers were given up to the pile some time ago). It's a good place to see men come and go, and they usually keep hot coffee on. It's also a fine place to write, when not shooting the breeze with young servicemen.

By virtue of being in one place for a while, even though they are taxed by regular field exercises, some men have got a good bit of reading and writing done. One regular in our little library came by today looking for me. He wanted to pitch me on a book idea, before he went to the trouble of writing the rest of it.

I suppose that's a normal thing, getting an advance to write a book, for a known writer. I'm not sure if it will work for Marine Corps Sergeant David Carr. Here all the way from Philadelphia, Sergeant Carr has been getting a taste of home from Raymond Chandler novels. I'm just a newspaper man, working for a newspaper publisher, so I can't book anybody for a novel.

So here's what I said I'd do. The knockout intro to his new spy thriller follows. Publishers take note!

I knew she was trouble the minute she came into my office. My office is a tank. Address: Half a barrel of gas from where it was yesterday.

She was Korean, born to Japanese parents. Her father had been a big shot with some big shot company in some big shot business. She was an orphan now – and a spy.

The fighting to get here was fierce. At least they told me it was. We haven't seen any of it. Our job is to get this little lady to a dot on the map, then ditch her and pull back.

The whole operation, battalion size from the look of it, plus air support and artillery, was just for this little job. There's not an anthill of terrain in this sector that either side cares about.

We're in cramped quarters, but it's not her fault. She's tiny. The G-2 man with her however is big and loud. It's too bad he has to come back with us...

That's all you get for now, dear editors. Should you want rights on the rest, write for Sergeant David Carr, care of the 1st Marine Division. I for one am dying to see how he gets on with the Korean femme fatale, in the future tense.[§§§]

September 28, 1945 : Okinawa, Ryukus

I caught another USO show today, this time as a regular spectator. The core of the troupe is still made up of Arthur Zepp and the other talented people I met before. But today the headliners were Charles Ruggles and Mary Brian[****]. There was a lot of interest to catch this one. I almost felt bad for displacing an ambitious young private who had to move back away from the officers' rows.

Quite a lot of the combat elements here are not going to see this show at all. The unrelenting wet weather has cut into the training program for the fighting men. They are doubling up exercises while good weather holds. It was explained to me by a battalion commander, Major Walter Harris of southern Nebraska. While the troops do need practice in fighting through the elements, there are only so many times they can 'practice' hauling a jeep and her towed artillery piece out of waist deep mud before it just becomes another chore.

[§§§] [Editor's note, 2015 – We haven't found any 'Tank noir' sections in the bookstore lately, so we don't think any publisher took up Sgt. Carr's offer. If he had only written about cats, we could make a mint selling that book in today's market! – sdm]

[****] [Editor's note, 2015: An established film actor, Ruggles went on to make regular appearances in television shows from a self-titled sit-com to Bewitched to The Beverly Hillbillies. Brian had a prolific career in 1920s silent films, toured extensively with the USO, and largely retired after some television work following the war. – sdm]

The officers would rather move the men repeatedly through military problems. Attacking a system of fortified positions, especially several at once when they are positioned to support each other, takes a lot of well-timed team work. If one part is off tempo, friendly troops get caught in a crossfire and enemy gunners scratch more lines on the walls of their pillboxes.

In good weather, they can run through a drill like that several times in one day. Once the mechanics are second nature, the officers can look for an opportunity to have them try it in bad weather as an additional complication. But teaching it from scratch in mud and rain is horribly slow, and miserable for everyone.

I've noted how the rains keep our engineers busy. But remember that they have training to do as well. Once the routine busy work here is done, engineer battalions will be expected to support the invasion. Those battalions are growing with reinforcements, new men and new tools, just like the combat units. They need to train to work together, under fire and with lives depending on them.

Major Lawless and I hiked west over to the Army side of our island world to see engineers bridge a small river just south of Naha. The river already had a bridge. It had three in the span of a half mile in fact. One was semi-permanent, a metal framework propped up on rough hewn tarred wooden piers driven into the river bottom. The 6th Marine Division had built that bridge to support combat operations, reinforcing it during the fighting as trucks hauled many tons of ordnance over the span. The other two, spindly metal structures with no piers and thin wooden decks, had been laid recently by Army teams in rehearsals like the one we would see that day.

I checked us in with the most junior officer I could find who looked confident enough to make a decision (I've found that's the best way to get allowed in to a unit). Lieutenant Howard Kohl was fine with having reporters watch his team work. He thought pretty highly of his guys. Lieutenant Kohl ran well boring crews back home in Iowa, and felt this was the best work crew he ever had to do a job with. It may have helped that he could fine any of them with a word, or toss them in the stockade for the trouble of filing paperwork[††††].

Lieutenant Kohl said it was a great time to visit. There was to be an extra wrinkle added in today, which they'd been putting off with the bad weather and the attendant high river water that made it too dangerous. Hot pre-noon sun was only beginning to heat up the earth and air. The lazy little river ran from east to west. They would try to span it from the north over a six foot deep cut it had made in the land where the river ran straight and quick for a stretch.

At a whistle a gaggle of forty-some marginally uniformed men piled out of two trucks and spread out over the chosen work site. They ranged in age from teenage to forty-something. Another truck held sections of pre-fabricated frame work. One team of men got to work rigging sections to be lifted by a small tractor crane, which was then moving up into position between that truck and the planned span. The officers stood to one side pointing at nearby hills and depressions. The conversation I overheard was about what sort of security they would require to make a bridge here. Engineers are easy targets when up on the front line.

Two teams dug by hand to set the near side footers. Using the crane, the rigging team had laid out and connected the leading two ten foot long bridge sections and were rigging a third when the footer teams got their supports adjusted level with each other. By eye I figured they could cover this span with four sections, plus short on-off ramps. They could set the whole thing with two more lifts of the crane.

But then another whistle blew and everyone stopped to look. One of the officers jogged over to the crane and stepped up to the cab, telling the driver something over the sound of its compact diesel. The engine stopped as the officer stepped back down. The driver stood up, leaning out of the cab, with a dumb grin on his

---

[††††] I added that line for levity, but let me be very clear – without exception the men I have seen in support units near the front, who have to look at the soldiers they are supporting, are highly motivated and will move heaven and earth to get them what they need wherever they need it.

face. "This piece of equipment has been taken out of commission by 'enemy action'. You fellahs are on your own!" The driver crawled out onto the front deck of his mechanical casualty and sat down to watch the show.

It was a good show. Confusion reigned for just a moment, workmen not sure which tools they should be holding. The officers in this bunch knew what they were doing though, and they jumped straight into the job. All the interconnected pieces were broken down. Every man, officer and enlisted, took hold of a hot steel bar and they walked each piece to the river bank and onto the waiting supports. Beads of sweat and expressions of profanity flowed off the men as they forced their will upon the heavy steel.

There are integrated rollers in this bridge system, so each piece can be rolled out half way, the next piece attached, and the deck extended progressively. The anchor men waded across with their tools to work on the receiving side, coming back several times for more tools and bigger levers. The entire bridge would need to be manhandled once the free end of it got across to the other supports. Eventually two large driftwood logs were commandeered into service as pry bars, and the span was set and ready for a test run.

The young fellows looked overly happy running vehicles across. First one drove an empty jeep and soon groups were riding over on the truck with all their tools. They had completed a satisfying job. I didn't dare to remind them that their next job would be to come back and break down all those practice bridges.

October 6, 1945 : Okinawa, Ryukus

The last three days of clear skies have people's spirits up, but many of them are too tired to enjoy it. Army engineers and Navy Seabees have been working long days. Kit buildings are unpacked and erected for practice, and to verify the kit is complete, then broken down and loaded in assault ships. Bridging teams do the same, as I witnessed last week.

The pace is picking up, and equipment is getting packed on ships and left there. The common supposition is that we'll be going to work on an enemy held island soon, within a month. Command is tight lipped about it. They say the bombers that take off daily from here still have plenty of work to do before anything else happens.

Foot soldiers are not left out of the action. Units have been marching out into the southern hills and northern plains of Okinawa in regular rotation. Some exercises lately included multiple companies working together.

Good word came around this morning that everyone will be rotated through a few days of rest this week and next. Men started to make plans around it, be it laying around or putting together sporting matches. Moods dampened a bit when actual orders came out.

Tomorrow, after Sunday church services, the first batch of resting units are expected to report for a 'voluntary' blood drive. The rest period gained a new meaning, "It's not like they'd give us two days off just to be nice! No, they just need us to fatten back up after we get pricked."

Another implication was explained by the combat veterans to new guys and everyone else. Medical staff doesn't like to keep whole blood around for more than 21 days before it's used for a transfusion. The veterans presume that combat is expected in no more than three weeks from the first draw of blood.

October 10, 1945 : Okinawa, Ryukus

I am writing this on what may be the last piece of dry paper on Okinawa. It was found under a truck that rolled over into a small supply tent. That truck was the only thing which kept the tent in place yesterday. Hurricane force winds ripped up every other tent in sight.

We were told to expect significant rain two days ago, but it turned into an epic windstorm, much worse than what we saw last

68

month. Whole camps are totally wiped out. Ocean going vessels of many sizes are stranded in mud a hundred feet in from the normal shore line. Many ships were moved out into deep water, and they are still being counted. Some of them will never return.

The Navy weather station here had little to tell me. I didn't bother them too long, because like many here their office is now mixed into a field of rubble. Some information has come in by radio from Guam, where weather observing B-29s are based. They knew a typhoon was running through to the south of us. But for no reason, perhaps the whim of a bored Greek god, it stopped and turned north, growing stronger by the hour as it was nudged along by that neglected ancient immortal.

Anyone who was living in a tent, without exception so far as I have seen, is now homeless. Torn patches of wet green canvas littered the adjacent hillsides this morning. Now many of the larger pieces are laid out over stacks of junk, in the hope they will dry when the sun comes out again. Men spent all day salvaging personal gear and essential equipment, those who were healthy that is. Medics are scrambling to care for the injured, using what supplies they can scrounge.

Anyone who could not find cover yesterday was subject to abuse from a mad circus of debris. A storm is not dangerous to a person just from its wind and rain. Real damage comes when solid objects are wrested from the earth and mixed into the storm like rocks in a polishing tumbler. Examples are everywhere – a sheet metal bar wrapped around a utility pole, a long shard of wood stuck into the ground like an arrow, or a wrecked vehicle with damage all around from being rolled over the ground a dozen or more times.

The weather guys told me that officially winds got up to 130 miles an hour. They admitted that their instruments only go up to 130 miles an hour, not that I could check them on it as their wooden building is gone and their instrument tower is a twisted wreck.

The able bodied are working desperately to claw back their home from nature. Plenty of people here are not able bodied, so repairing the hospital for this part of the island is a top priority. It has some intact buildings left, but storage tents around it are shredded, leaving most of our medical supplies to the ravenous appetites of the wind and rain.

Everything is wet. Rain came down all yesterday, through the night, and shows no sign of stopping – ever. Insistent wind drove the rain into every crevice and under any cover short of a sealed ammo can. One of my former tent mates tipped over his foot locker and dumped out an inch of water.

For the time being I am camped in the one masonry building in our area, the photo lab. Wet bed rolls are spread over the floor of this building, wall-to-wall. Power is still out so we will have limited light after the 6 pm sunset. Some groups of men have fashioned shelters under jury-rigged pieces of torn tents, with scraps of wood laid out to make an approximately level floor.

All of this is being done on the fly by local groups and ad hoc units. Command structure is completely non-apparent, from this perspective. I suppose there simply is no text book military response to an enemy that hits everything at once, front, rear, left, right, and every supporting system. All order has to be reassembled from scratch, bottom up.

This corner of the giant Boy Scout camp that is Okinawa is at least stabilized by now. As groups each get their own situation under control, they are getting back to the jobs they do for other units. A crated field kitchen, earmarked for the upcoming assault, was uncrated and we even have hot coffee and warm food from cans. With my current situation up to tolerable, I too plan to get back to my job, moving around to see the situation at other camps. I suspect our field kitchen was not the only thing un-earmarked for the invasion.

October 11, 1945 : Okinawa, Ryukus

Buckner Bay is the new home to several dozen naval monuments. For example, some 50 yards in from the normal waterline sits a full size model of an American Sumner-class destroyer. I am sure it is full size, because it is the actual USS Laffey, DD-724. I found the Laffey with her bow pointed out to sea, and her stern jammed deep into the earth. She was leaned over a few degrees to port. The skin of her starboard side showed a long deep wrinkle, running vertically from mid height right down to the keel[‡‡‡‡].

Sailors were unloading gear and supplies from the dry and wounded ship when I got to her. I looked for petty officers to chat up and soon found one who was on the bridge during the storm. Radar man James Armstrong told me about the start of the adventure.

"We were told to stay in the bay, spread both anchors, and ride out the storm here. A lot of other ships left the bay for deep water, against orders, but we stayed. We could hear radio chatter from the ships out at sea, trying to ride out the waves." He gestured with his hands to mimic a struggling ship. "It was rough, especially for the big flat bottom boats, but they were mostly calling around to make sure other ships didn't get too close and collide."

"It got bad in here when the wind peaked. The water level went way up, and we dragged both anchors until one of them snapped off. After that it was a short trip to this spot here. We hit hard, a lot of guys got banged up. It's lucky we didn't flip over." He pointed at the nearly upright shipwreck. "We can still use the sick bay, and we've already taken in some guys from other ships that ran out of luck."

Those other less lucky ships line the beach and shallows. I quit counting at forty-something, with a long way to go. Some are capsized, others broken apart. Anonymous debris thoroughly litters the beach. I picked through some of it, trying to guess what any of it used to be. I stopped to find someone to tell about a body that graves registration hadn't found yet.

[‡‡‡‡] Since June of 1944 the Laffey was in hard fighting all over the Atlantic and Pacific, famously surviving six kamikaze hits off Okinawa. The unsinkable ship may have met her final fate, the blow perversely dealt by dry land.

Many piers and loading docks were damaged, by waves or by ships being smashed against them. The ones that are functional are working through a backlog of ships coming in from riding out the storm at sea. Each needs to offload her wounded, report missing men, and have damage assessed. Contact was lost with many ships. Scout boats are out looking for survivors, along with planes from the Marianas.

No planes are flying from here. Zero. I can't say how many planes we have here, but 'hundreds' does not cover it. Runways are being cleared of debris, but every single aircraft is grounded until each is inspected for damage. So far every bird has failed inspection, and they are cued up for work ranging from skin patches to engine swaps to outright scrapping.

A plane engine can be heard overhead periodically. I'm told we are flying limited CAP[§§§§] with long range fighters from elsewhere, just in case the Japs try to take advantage of our situation. I can't imagine what they would find worth bombing.

Most camps did as badly or worse than mine. Tents everywhere were merely fuel for the maelstrom. Many wood frame structures held, others became splinter-shedding projectiles. The fate of Quonset huts came down to how each was anchored. Those with concrete floors and footers, with the corrugated roof bolted down, are still bearing fruit where they were planted. The others are nothing but gravel floors drying in the sun, their sheet metal roofs now wrapping the adjacent hills like tin foil over a giant turkey.

Late today the first relief ship from the Philippines landed with new tents, fresh food, and other supplies. There was no shortage of volunteers to unload her.

As crates came off the ship, it was clear that most of the ship was pre-loaded with invasion support gear, probably meant for unloading on the third or fourth day ashore. Everything to make a small field hospital, minus perishables, came off first. After that was generic rigging, lumber, and small construction equipment

---

[§§§§] Combat Air Patrol

(our engineers jumped on a pair of weasels when they came off, putting them to use distributing stuff over the mud covered island immediately). After that came a whole mess tent and kitchen, and then crates of spare clothes, gas mask canisters, and assorted other needful things.

Ships like that will continue landing here and elsewhere around Okinawa, each of them subtracting from the store of equipment that was to support the upcoming invasion.

The advent of war and the need of conducting operations on the far side of oceans brought to light a paradox by no means new in military history, namely that armies may be immobilized by their own means of transportation. ….. The more vehicles were used overseas the more ship space was required for fuel, lubricants, spare parts, replacement vehicles, drivers, and repair crews, and the less was available for combat personnel, weapons, and ammunition. In March 1942 a plan was adopted to send thirty divisions to the United Kingdom for a cross-Channel operation in April 1943.

The Army Ground Forces on 2 April 1942 informed the War Department that forces would be available. The bottleneck was shipping. The number of United States troops intended for the operation had to be reduced.

Greenfield, Kent Roberts, and Palmer, Robert R.; The Organization of Ground Combat Troops, Center of Military History, United States Army; 1947; p 281

October 20, 1945 : Okinawa, Ryukus

We are expecting company soon! The entire 5th Marine Division is due here next week, in from their camp in Hawaii. We're trying to get the spare bedroom ready, but there isn't one. It's all-hands-on-deck throwing up new tents, and packing men closer together where they are already quartered. Several loads of air cargo were approved to get more tenting here and set up while the Marines are afloat.

It's no secret to the Japanese that a big storm hit here and probably delayed whatever it is we were up to. The same storm slammed directly into southern Japan straight from Okinawa. Operational details are still not widely known, but the men have been told this much: we were close, very close, to the next big assault when the storm came. Troops from halfway across the Pacific in Hawaii were almost ready to load up their ships and sail out. So after a short delay they did just that anyway. For the next big action, the 5th Marine Division will launch from here, the 2nd and 3rd from the Marianas.

I pitched in on the effort a few of the advance party Marines were making to prep for their buddies. Lieutenant Paul Bernard, Sergeant Thurman Price, Jr., and Corporal Francis Seeley were detached from the motor transport battalion to come here early. Their planning work was long done, so now the job was housing the unit until the final launching date. I wasn't obligated to offer up my labor, but I wanted to hear what they thought about the move. Tent ropes were drawn tight as the conversation got loose.

Corporal Seeley says he's been keeping up a tide chart, and watching the moon. He used to sail some off Baja California, the nearest ocean surf to Tucson, Arizona. Near the end of this month would have been perfect he says – high tide in the morning coupled with good moonlight most of the night. We could get ashore easiest and then have light to catch the infamous Japanese nighttime infiltration attacks. He saw the aftermath from many of those on Iwo Jima.

Since he spoke like he knew what he was talking about, we let him talk. He thinks the next decent chance isn't until mid-November. We would only have the counter-moon tide and less moonlight, but otherwise it's another three weeks before everything comes around perfect again.

I couldn't argue with the logic, but I offered up what I knew about the losses our Navy took, and wondered aloud how that might affect things. Many destroyers were banged up or grounded in the storm, but there doesn't seem to be any shortage of them. We are down three big carriers, which may be back in time, and at least two small carriers which will not. The big gun ships mostly did ok, riding out the storm at sea. But the flat bottom assault boats got roughed up bad. They don't have any good handling abilities in any rough seas. Eight of them are still unaccounted for, presumed lost. With the thirty-six large and hundred-some small transport ships wrecked or put into drydock here in Buckner Bay, that's over two divisions worth of boats gone. These Marines didn't seem too worried about it.[*****]

October 29, 1945 : Okinawa, Ryukus

As predicted, the end of October brought a big full moon through most of each night, and high tides in the morning. I have been taking nighttime or early morning strolls by the water to see for myself. I imagine landing craft bringing assault waves into this bay, my imagination aided by the sounds from our busy Navy airfield.

I didn't go for a walk yesterday though, as the weather was bad again, and will be for a couple days at least. Had we tried to attack in such weather, the landing would have been rough, our

---

[*****] I knew but couldn't discuss at the time that transport shipping was already the key limiting factor in the invasion plan. As it was drawn up, the first reserve division available could only be delivered on ships that had to go back from Kyushu to the Philippines, returning more than three weeks after the invasion start. The divisions would have to give up something if they were all going to go.

aircraft wouldn't be able to see anything, and the Japanese could move around undetected at night. It will be another good what-if for speculation after the war.

I have been spending my time lately with the newly arrived 5th Marine Division. They actually did come ashore in a mock invasion, driving AMTRACs ashore and hauling in a lot of gear. It took a lot of time to repack everything, but the only other thing they have to do is wait for the actual invasion.

A card game broke out last night in one of the enlisted barracks. That happens most nights anyway, but this one had very little to do with gambling. I was sitting in, mostly minding my ante, not wanting to take anyone's money but not wanting this bit of material to be too expensive (Editors are not fond of reimbursing wagers!).

The guys needed to pass the time thinking about something other than the impending unknown. We still didn't even know when we were going, nobody did. We had a good guess where, though, and talked about everything but that. Still, people will drift back to what they have in common, and this group from all over a dozen states had only two things in common – the United States Marine Corps and whatever adventure it ordered them on next.

Finally a readily agitated private from Detroit, Dante Iacoboni, spoke up. "They say the Japs spent eight or ten months, twelve tops, digging in around here {Okinawa}. It cost us three months and a giant ass-kicking to kick them out of this [expletive]. How long you think they've had to dig in on Japan proper?"

After a pause another veteran Detroiter, Sergeant Ora Inman, answered him quietly. "About a thousand years."

The senior man on the deck, Sergeant William Barnard, wasn't even playing, as he fastidiously tended his gear, like he did every evening. But he was listening and spoke up right away.

"Listen up fellahs. I'm not supposed to say anything, but the word is that there's a 'surprise' inspection tomorrow morning. Don't tell 'em I said so, but you might want to call it a night here and square away your gear now."

The players agreed readily that they'd had enough cards anyway. They had a quick round of the usual arguing about who had cheated using the markings on the well-worn deck and went to their respective barracks and tents.

There was no inspection today.

November 5, 1945 : Okinawa, Ryukus

Word came early this morning that all junior officers and NCOs were to report to a briefing immediately after morning mess. Reporters were not admitted. This left a lot of young men, and not so young civilians like me, unsupervised and without instruction for several hours. No one wandered off and no stunts were pulled that I heard about.

A few of the usual entrepreneurs went around collecting the usual wagers on what the next news would be. The action was on an over/under of the whole division pulling out in 72 hours. Nobody talked much beyond that.

The sun was high and warm by the time the captains came out and each got his company together, usually with a sealed folder of maps and orders under one arm. The men only got a few specifics. Advance elements of the next operation are already in the water, so they are letting everyone know to get ready. Some units have a specific exercise to walk through tomorrow. All are to be ready to move out in 48 hours.

A new frenzy of activity swept over many parts of the island. Men ran through lists of chores, most of which could have been completed long before. The sudden imposing deadline exposed all procrastinators. Letters home could be mailed, but would be held until the invasion was landed.

Long lines formed to ship armfuls of belongings back home. Personal effects, trophies, and mementos burdened the slow moving columns of apparent refugees. Some parcels were suspiciously close in size and shape to the more memorable signs and street markers that our engineers perpetually replace across Okinawa.

One fellow I met had only an old pair of tattered boots in hand. They were his first combat boots, veterans of three Mariana islands. He had a one year old son he'd never met. He wanted to be sure the boy had something to remember him by, whatever might happen.

Some of the men shipping out have been on Okinawa for several months. They had two days or less to reduce their personal effects to one duffel bag of material. Whatever homey touches they had accumulated in their tents or barracks had to go, by barter or disposal.

Special trash piles were started and soon were adorned with prints of the least favorite pin-up girls. Only the dearest images would wind up in wallets or combat packs. Hollywood producers might be surprised at which of their carefully promoted personas made the cut.

At night more than a few contraptions were added to the junk piles which might be recognized as liquor stills. They may have been moved discretely because of their prohibited distilling potential, or because most were made of materials pilfered from military stockpiles.

Before sunset I took a walk along Buckner Bay. Even without new orders anyone could have guessed that a big action was coming up. The invasion fleet hadn't started loading yet, but its companion attack fleet was at the piers in full force.

Spanning an inordinate section of the large bay, four of the biggest gun ships I had ever seen were lined up waiting to load on one-ton explosive shells and to fill their enormous fuel tanks. The setting sun behind me lit them brightly in front of their smaller escorts farther out in the sea. For a moment their dull gray hulls seemed to breath as they rose slightly in an ocean swell.

It was the entire Iowa class, with the battleship Iowa herself already at a pier. They are the undisputed kings of the Pacific ocean, and any other ocean they care to enter. With the pride of the

Japanese Navy scattered in pieces across the sea floor, they are the biggest battleships in the world.

November 6, 1945 : Ie Shima, Ryukus

I took my last chance to finish up an important bit of business before leaving Okinawa. Thankfully it was no trouble finding a ride over to the small island of Ie Shima, just west of northern Okinawa. We have small ships shuttling men to and from every occupied bit of dry rock as combat units form up and garrison troops take their places.

I wanted to visit Ie Shima for a particular, perhaps peculiar, reason. It is a small island with a small mountain and a small airfield, which the Army took with some cost, and many more Japanese died defending it. The same can be said now for many dozens of small islands in the Pacific. Ernie Pyle died here.

If you are reading this column you are probably aware of Ernie Pyle's enormous legacy. If you are reading this column instead of his, you probably also miss him. I read that Pyle was read in over 700 newspapers by 40 million people. I've no way of researching the point right now, but I can't imagine a writer in the past has ever had so wide a circulation or readership. This was at a time when newspapers may be just past their peak of power, as newsreels and radio broadcasts are taking a growing share of attention. Pyle may go down as the most widely read reporter and one of the most influential men of his day. Pyle would have wanted nothing to do with any such power.

Pyle made his name by learning about everyday Americans and sharing their stories. Tire treads and shoe leather were never spared as he criss-crossed the continent finding the big little stories that make us up. There was really nothing different about doing that on other war-infested continents. The subjects were living in the ground and getting shot at, but they were living just the same, each with an American story to share.

80

If you've ever felt empathy for a dirty cold soldier 5000 miles away, where you could really feel the chill in your bones as you reflexively scrunch your own shoulders to shrink down into a hole in the earth to hide from exploding artillery shells, it was probably because of Ernie Pyle. If you've felt the anxiety of an air base ground crew counting their damaged planes coming back from a raid, and the empty gut that comes when the count is short, it was probably because of Ernie Pyle.

I met Ernie on a number of occasions, but only briefly. A couple times we actually coordinated our activities, to make sure we were in different places and not in with the same type of unit (The Army usually tried to keep journalists from being bunched up in one spot anyway). He wasn't actually as unkempt in the field as he made out in his writing. Personal grooming and housekeeping in a combat area are tough, as he explained, but people do manage to make a suitable home for themselves wherever they are.

Here on this small island, which will fade again to anonymity once there are not fighter planes operating from its hard-won air strip, Ernie Pyle was in his usual place up near the front lines. Except the lines aren't so sharp in this desperate fight. The Japanese have employed many tactics to mingle with Americans, to inflict damage on the invaders where our heavy artillery and air power can't be brought to bear. In this case a single machine gunner hid out until the American lines went by. He had a good spot. After Pyle's jeep was attacked, it took a squad all afternoon to flush out the position. A simple wooden marker shows the spot where a well aimed burst killed Ernie instantly.

I will share one of my favorite Ernie Pyle stories, in case you missed it and because it's about my adopted southern homeland. Pyle was in Italy with a regiment drawn almost entirely from Tennessee and the Carolinas. The whole unit got paid, in cash, before leaving New York, collecting envelopes worth about $52,000 dollars. After a transatlantic voyage worth of poker games, in England that unit traded in their cash for $67,000 dollars of campaign currency. "Dumb, these hillbillies," was Pyle's dry wry end to the story.

November 8, 1945 : Okinawa, Ryukus

Waves of men have been moving toward the port at Naha all day. Some hitched rides on overloaded trucks, but most are on foot. Each overloaded Marine, with all his worldly possessions in his packs, on his belt, and over his shoulder, looks like a walking dingy green laundry pile.

I hooked up with a general services battalion. As a unit it exists practically only on paper, as a way to attach extra people to the 5th Marine Division. Many of the members have particular jobs to do, from external communications to coordinating special supply movements, but as many others are just ready reinforcements. They will be tapped to come forward and replace men who become casualties.

We passed columns of Army soldiers marching several miles to board ships in Buckner Bay. No one knows for sure why troops weren't all loaded near their own camps, but plenty of possible reasons were offered. Profanities added color to many of the suggestions.

Upon reaching the designated staging area, for most units the wait was on. Some piers still had cargo ships along side where assault transports were supposed to load. A few transports got moved to whatever free pier was open, and more marching ensued. My group waited, most men sitting on packs or laying out on the ground, until after dark.

Finally word came that we wouldn't load that day, but we weren't to go very far away. We were to be ready as soon as our ship came in. A few pup tents went up, and a couple guys scrounged wood for fires to sit around. Most men slept under the stars through the warm evening.

November 9, 1945 : East China Sea

It was almost noon by the time there was room at a dock for our transport, a new APA^{†††††} named USS Barrow. Pairs of Navy ensigns and Marine NCOs moved up and down our column making sure everyone was ready to move pronto once the ship was tied up.

The Barrow is a purely military ship, but actually more comfortable than some of the hurriedly converted passenger liners that were used as transports early in the war. A space that has bunks for a hundred men actually has ventilation for a hundred men, unlike the converted cargo holds of the civilian ships. The mess halls can take a steady stream of hungry servicemen at long rows of benches. Even the toilets are a production line affair – a relief to a nervous row of men all trying to relieve themselves at the same time before boarding assault boats.

An equally important boost to morale, and possibly to function of the units, is the better separation of "officer territory." Enlisted men no longer have to look over temporary dividers to see the officers dine from set places with waiters tending to every need, including cold dessert orders, while the privates bus their own trays of indistinct multi-colored food stuffs. The officers also have good dedicated working spaces, where I can attest they do spend long hours debating the best way to overcome the obstacles penciled in on their stacks of maps.

One thing that hasn't changed with the new ships is that troop ships are still over loaded. High-level planning documents show an allowance of 33,000 men for each combat division. The current T/O for a Marine Corps division has it at 19,176 men, fully staffed. The quantity of men and supplies attached to an assault division grows with every operation, as they learn about new

---

^{†††††}Amphibious transports of this type carry small boats on deck, which are lowered into the water for launch. Other types have large doors in the bow that open to let boats and amphibious tractors out directly into the water. Worryingly, our small landing craft with their bow ramps can't be loaded before lowering, because they'd buckle under the load until supported by water all under.

needs. It never goes down, and the increasing distance from US home ports only multiplies the problem[‡‡‡‡‡].

Since the Navy can't just stretch each ship to match new paper requirements, there are still men assigned "quarters" that are nothing more than a bit of shade under an assault boat up on deck. They get a good view of the sky at night, but will trade favors for a dry place to stick their butts and gear when rain comes.

The Barrow is rated to carry just over 1500 troops. With her 15 assault boats she could get them all ashore in three trips if needed. But most of our complement is division support or reserve personnel. They may not go in for a few days. I made a note to look and see if our boats get borrowed for use earlier on.

I'm bunked in a four-man room for junior officers. My roommates are all in a "joint" intelligence unit – Army, Navy, and Marine Corps. The Navy guys in the unit are the usual radio intercept, photo recon analyst, and map-making types. The Army officers in this bunch are liaison officers. This is an Army operation overall, but our sector is functionally all Navy, including Marines.

The Marines in the unit are mostly interpreters, most of whom will follow the ground troops ashore, in case there are any enemy POWs to interrogate. The Army and Navy officers will stay on our ship, which has 5th Marine Division HQ on it as well. Yes, there is plenty of flying brass to dodge on this trip.

Top man in our room is Marine Captain Gerald Holtom, from central California. He is one of the Japanese interpreters. He tells me they don't expect to be very busy. "The average rate of surrender or capture of Japanese troops at last count is barely one percent. It might have been better in the last surrounded pockets on

---

[‡‡‡‡‡] Table of Organization, the theoretical structure of a military unit. This is strictly for planning, readily excepted for different situations, and rarely realized even when they try, in the face of combat and logistic realities. One might think them the invention of frustrated fiction writers who are stuck on Pentagon planning staffs.

Okinawa or Luzon[§§§§§], but those dumb guys had been in combat under shelling for literally months and had no other hope of survival, or even of doing any damage.

"As it was we went hole-by-hole back over every square inch of Oki after it was 'secure' and it was hit or miss when we found Japs holed up if we could talk them out. If not we would just blow the thing shut and bury them alive." Holtom will go ashore not long after the initial assault. He isn't looking forward to the job ahead, but he's sure his part is both small and a good ways out in the future.

[§§§§§] It was; about 5% on Okinawa and 2.5% on Luzon.

There are many of the living who have had burned into their brains forever the unnatural sight of cold dead men scattered over the hillsides and in the ditches along the high rows of hedge throughout the world.

Dead men by mass production – in one country after another – month after month and year after year. Dead men in winter and dead men in summer.

Dead men in such familiar promiscuity that they become monotonous. Dead men in such monstrous infinity that you come almost to hate them.

Ernie Pyle, final column, published posthumously

Now that we are under way and the men have been briefed about their units' assignments, the invasion maps and orders are out in the open. Nothing but plain maps and individual unit orders will go ashore at first, for "operational security," but right now anyone in the officers' end of the ship can look over the entire plan for our corps.

We are in Fifth Corps (amphibious), with three Marine divisions, the 2nd, 3rd, and 5th. Two other similar size corps, Eleventh and First, will assault the island elsewhere.****** The augmented 40th Infantry Division is already ahead of us landing on some of the smaller islands off Kyushu. Another whole corps, the Ninth, is staging a feint far to the northeast, and there are an 'unspecified number of follow-on units.'

So far as I am told, until recently it was U.S. military practice to always call the day of an invasion, amphibious or otherwise, "D-day." (They also call the hour that it starts "H-hour.") Something changed in the last year, now that "D-day" has become something of a brand name.

Newspapers take D-Day to mean specifically the June, 1944 expansion of the war against Germany with landings on the Normandy coast of France. They already forget about the other fights which raged even then in all corners of Europe.

If they do that much in a year, I have to wonder what people will be told of this war fifty years from now. There might be just one D-day, which decided the whole fight in Europe. Never mind the massive land war in Russia, the back-and-forth turf wars in north Africa, or the painful struggle through Italy. In a hundred years they may just call it "The D-Day War"††††††.

Anyway, since Normandy and "D-Day" are forever linked in the public mind, the military had to get more creative. For the

---

****** Editor's note: Army practice calls for corps to be named by Roman numerals. We are printing them out to ease reading, especially when IX and XI corps are referenced together.

†††††† [Editor's note, 2015: Not if we can help it! – sdm]

invasion of Luzon in the Philippines they called it "S-day." At Okinawa, April 1ˢᵗ, which happened to also be Easter Sunday, was called "Love Day," much to the chagrin of superstitious or wry-witted soldiers and Marines who saw the setup of a bemusing but possibly bitter irony.

This time around our invasion of the island of Kyushu, set for November 15ᵗʰ, 1945, will begin on "X-day." That makes today X-4. I for one am glad we are back to a simple single letter.

If you've never seen a map with a whole modern amphibious invasion drawn on it, and I showed it to you, we would agree that it is a thing of beauty. It is practically a geometric work of art, and as such it is far removed from the messy brutal actuality of the thing it represents. I have seen a few invasions now and will testify to that.

On the map there are neat columns of small symbols, representing the AMTRACs and Higgins boats in their lanes of travel, with wide open lanes for vessels returning from unloading their precious deadly cargo. The columns are in staggered rows, each row representing an assault wave, each wave with a departure time known to the minute.

Crossing the many columns are open rows for fire support ships to cross back and forth, small rocket ships up front, destroyers farther back, and lastly big cruisers and battleships. There are lines of control, at which signal boats will organize the assault boats, form up rows, and send each wave at the appointed minute. Of course all of the lines are imaginary. And all of the close order is subject to compounding chaos once the enemy, and implacable nature, play their hands.

The columns are packed tightly and sent forward in rapid succession, to maximize the flow of forces onto the beach. In simple cold arithmetic, the more targets an attacker presents for a fixed number of enemy guns and troops to fire at, the more will survive to advance and reduce enemy positions. But when a boat in a tight column, between two other columns, is hit and disabled, those behind it are stuck. There is nowhere to go until boats running parallel get by. Of course enemy gunners know this.

November 13, 1945 : X-2

I feel like an old veteran at this now, if one can be a 'veteran' of watching other people do actual things. It is wrenching seeing new men go through this all over again. They don't know where to start, what to do, or even what to worry about.

Some veterans take new guys under their wing, walking them through preparation for combat. They talk mostly about physical prep – getting gear squared away and rehearsing their first moves. I've come to understand that such repetitive preparation is more or less a mental distraction for most of them.

Men have different ways of settling their minds before this kind of violent and dangerous endeavor. Some tend to equipment. Some seek out groups of people to hang around with. Some pursue solitude the best they can. In this great fleet it's not just men.

I found her at the rail, back of the ship in a quiet corner of officer's country. A small section of the ship was reserved for the women on board, nurses or WAVES or whatever role they were in. This one was a petite nurse, and happened to be the only woman on board. That's not supposed to happen, but it did, and they weren't going to hold up a combat ship just to move another woman over. Sailors and officers weren't allowed back here, but technically I was neither so I went snooping around one night.

I don't claim to be a psychiatrist. I don't have any sixth sense about human conditions. When I see a soldier by himself two days before a big attack I make an estimation, and have always been right about if it was good to talk to him or not[‡‡‡‡‡‡]. But this was a woman. I decided that I had no idea if she'd want company or not, but I did, so I walked up and talked to her.

The evening sun was almost on the water. Its direct and reflected light put a studio-grade golden light upon her calm face. Mrs. Cyrille Simms was a club singer in St. Louis before the war, while working her way through school. She volunteered to me being 24 when the war started. She finally signed up just a year or

---

[‡‡‡‡‡‡] The truth is, I always talk to them, and they've always appreciated it.

so ago, got her military training, tended maimed soldiers in Hawaii for a while, and was here for her first big live shootout.

With over 1500 men on this ship, doing everything from hauling equipment around to nervous pacing on dark decks, there was a likely need for medical attention in the week long span we could be embarked. Once all the men from our ship were ashore, she would go after them to a division field hospital, or transfer to a hospital ship if needed. Either location was expected to be busy.

She spoke idly about her adventures so far, while staring out over the sea toward a blank spot north of the setting sun. I heard tales of woe and loss, senseless loss, which if they had affected her she wasn't letting on. She was here to do a job, ready to see it through, and as matter-of-fact about it as the most hardened master sergeant.

She wasn't nervous. She wasn't apprehensive for all the boys she'd met who were going to get hurt. She was sad for guys back home, like her husband. He was a piano player, who recorded ad jingles and gigged the St. Louis jazz clubs. He had fruitlessly protested her decision to enlist.

I leaned against the rail nearby, just listening. I heard every word, but a detached part of me drifted off with the sound of her rare voice, the soft crush of waves against the hull, the warm evening light on her cheeks, and the gentle roll of our ship. Eventually she turned toward me, her bobbed blond hair swinging slightly either way before settling to the sides of her face. Strong Saxon facial features were highlighted by the low sunset.

"What do you suppose they think about at home? The guys who aren't here fighting, I mean. They must wonder, if they did the right thing."

I admitted I hadn't given it much thought, having plenty of guys on this side of the action to interview. "See that's just it," she continued. "Everybody's busy. I get that. But a busy man here, he does his job, and that's it. He goes to sleep, when he can, and gets up again, to get back at it, to stay in the fight. Back home, don't you think they have to do something more? I think every one of them, if they're worth anything, does a job then reminds himself why it's ok to just do that job and not be over here. They're

90

probably right, but still they have to wonder about if they're doing enough to measure up."

She turned back toward the rail and rested her weight on her straightened arms. "I worry about those men, the ones we'll have to see when we get back." Her formerly passive face was now furrowed with tension. I levered for the personal angle, asking about her husband in all this. "Oh, he's great. We write back and forth plenty, about all this in fact. He says I'm cracked up to worry about guys who have it easy stateside."

She grinned a little. "Still, he started working USO shows a few months ago, without any prodding from me. He's been playing the train and bus station in St. Louis. It's lucky for all those guys who are transferring over from Europe. He's pretty good."

I saw a cluster of sea birds on the water and changed the subject to small talk of nature and weather. With light failing I said good night and made my way back to the hot crowded gruff masculine parts of the ship, which was every other square inch of our overloaded people hauler.

November 14, 1945 : X-1

At this point I must introduce one section of non-contemporaneous information. That is to say, I didn't know all this at the time. And if I did know, of course the battle plans couldn't be published until long afterward. For aid of the reader I will present a map showing where all the divisions landed, and many of the key features and landmarks that would become important later. The locations of a few particular later events are also marked.

The primary focus of operations at the end of 1945 was to get as many troops as available onto Kyushu before winter set in. The troops available would be all the Army divisions MacArthur had used in the Philippines, and whichever Marine corps divisions were not heavily involved on Okinawa, the most recent operation.

Four multi-division army corps were set up, under a general command called the Sixth Army under General Walter Krueger. Planning staffs had labeled over 30 possible landing beaches on the southern third of Kyushu, naming them in alphabetical order from east to west by automobile brands. The final plan had us using eight of them in three clusters for the X-day assault.

The Marine Corps sent its 2nd, 3rd, and 5th divisions as the Fifth Amphibious Corps. They would land on the west coast, south of the city of Sendai. The First Corps, Army divisions 25th, 33rd, and 41st, would land on the east coast, either side of the city of Miyazaki.

South of that in Ariake Bay the 1st Cavalry Division, 43rd Infantry Division, and the Americal[§§§§§§] Division would land as the Eleventh Corps. Another corps, the Ninth, on X-2 has already made an elaborate fake landing operation toward Shikoku far to the northeast. Its 77th, 81st, and 98th infantry divisions can land as needed later. They are penciled in for a landing south of the Marines on X+3 or X+4. Ninth Corps also had the 112th "Regimental Combat Team"[*******], which could deploy independently. Incidentally, the 98th is an all new unit, the only one here with no combat experience.

Ahead of the multiple corps, the 40th Infantry Division, reinforced with the 158th Regimental Combat Team, started landing on the smaller islands south and west of Kyushu, to eliminate them as threats to the main fleet once it arrived.

What we need out of Kyushu most of all is airbases. You may have noticed, B-29 bombers are not small. They need room to stretch out those long wings, and they prefer wide long runways. In addition, there are supply depots and workshops and barracks for a million men (or more) to build. But Kyushu does not have an abundance of flat land to offer. It is woven from a coarse thread of steep ridges and volcanic peaks, interrupted only briefly by flat valleys and a few small plains. To get enough space for our uses, and secure it from Japanese long range artillery or sneak attack, we plan to push well into the hills north of the last set of valleys.

[§§§§§§] "Americans in New Caledonia", a division put together early in 1942 out of whichever regiments were available in the south Pacific.

[*******] An RCT is a regiment with extra units attached which would normally be part of a full division, so it can operate independently. Loosely defined, it could have 4000 to 6000 men.

As a layman looking at all this, the invasion plan at first looked like a focused application of awesome force, and it was impossible to see how such a large and well equipped invader could be turned away. But I had been at this a little while by then, and I did a little calculating. I'm sure real staff officers in many headquarters and Pentagon offices had run the same numbers many times.

Okinawa is about 5 miles across in its southern portion where we had four divisions abreast fighting stiff resistance for two months to advance about 15 miles, taking casualties all the way. Southern Kyushu is 90 miles wide, and we plan to land maybe 13 divisions. That would spread forces out almost six times as thin. Total area to be taken is well over 5,000 square miles. They talk about having 'maneuver room' and 'flexible force concentration' to overcome this. Time will tell.

Map – Southern Kyushu and Nearby Islands

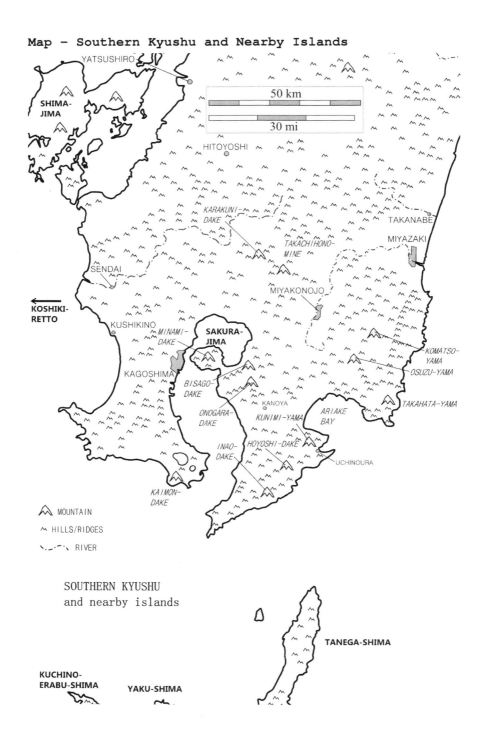

SOUTHERN KYUSHU
and nearby islands

94

Map – Southern Kyushu and Invasion Outline

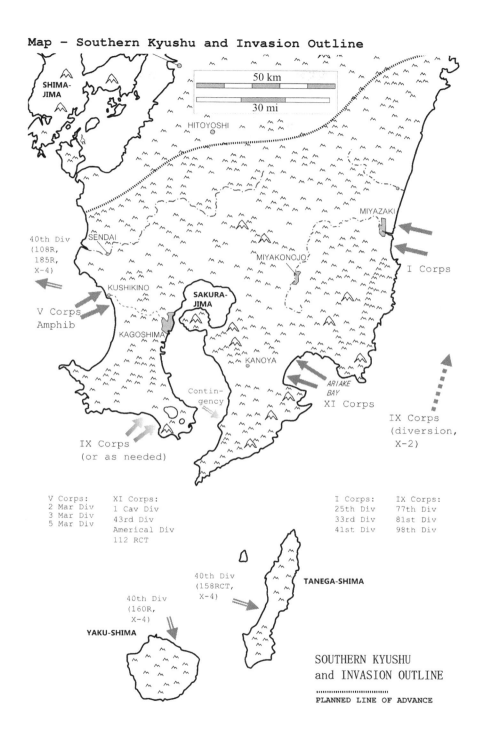

SHIMA-JIMA

50 km

30 mi

HITOYOSHI

MIYAZAKI

40th Div
(108R,
185R,
X-4)

SENDAI

MIYAKONOJO

I Corps

KUSHIKINO

SAKURA-JIMA

V Corps
Amphib

KAGOSHIMA

KANOYA

Contin-
gency

ARIAKE
BAY

XI Corps

IX Corps
(or as needed)

IX Corps
(diversion,
X-2)

V Corps:	XI Corps:		I Corps:	IX Corps:
2 Mar Div	1 Cav Div		25th Div	77th Div
3 Mar Div	43rd Div		33rd Div	81st Div
5 Mar Div	Americal Div		41st Div	98th Div
	112 RCT			

TANEGA-SHIMA

40th Div
(158RCT,
X-4)

40th Div
(160R,
X-4)

YAKU-SHIMA

SOUTHERN KYUSHU
and INVASION OUTLINE

PLANNED LINE OF ADVANCE

At its heart this martial art is first taking up the sword and then cutting down your opponent, no matter what is done or how it happens. Whether you parry, slap, strike, hold back, or touch your opponent's cutting sword, you must understand that all of these are opportunities to cut him down. To think, "I'll parry" or "I'll slap" or "I'll hit, hold, or touch" will be insufficient for cutting him down. It is essential to think that anything at all is an opportunity to cut him down. With martial arts in the larger field (where armies face each other), the placement of numbers of people is also a stance. All of these are opportunities to win a battle It is wrong to be inflexible.

    – Miyamoto Musashi, The Book of Five Rings

November 15, 1945 : X-Day — Kyushu, Japan

I don't like to think that there is anything fundamentally different for the average soldier between preparation for an amphibious invasion and any other long planned attack. The guys who can eat, eat. The guys who can't eat, give their chow to the other guys. Special church services are held. Gear is checked and re-checked. Blades are sharpened, rifle actions cleaned and oiled. Veterans do whatever they did last time, because it worked. New guys don't know what to do. Some sing, some sleep, most can't sleep and just stare at the bunk above them, where the next man is doing the same thing at the bunk above him, until they get to the poor guy on top who has nothing to stare at but the bare gray ceiling.

There are mechanical differences between an amphibious operation and an attack over land. For starters, amphibious troops launch miles away from the real starting point. The big ships lay well back from land until the final morning, for their own safety. The troops ordained to go in can't even see the objective but as a fuzzy line on the horizon until that morning.

In staged battles of old knights and footmen could look directly across the chosen field, and even see smoke from their opponent's camp fires. Even in the muddy fields of 1917 France, today's majors and colonels were lieutenants looking through field glasses (or periscopes) directly at the front berms of the enemy trenches.

On the way in an amphibious trooper is blind and helpless. There is absolutely nothing to do but crouch down in the assault boat and hope it doesn't get hit. Or get stuck. Or break down. The soldier has to take it on faith that all the sailors do their jobs, line the boats up right, move them in good order, and get them ashore where they are supposed to be.

Then the solider has to take it on faith that the reconnaissance was good, that the map is accurate, that the navy divers took out their assigned obstacles, that the naval bombardment hit what it was scheduled to hit, and that the first objectives for his unit are where they are supposed to be. Marching under a flag by trumpet or charging out of a trench the infantry man can see his own unit all the way, and the unit can do what it needs to do to stay organized. The unit is divided and helpless during the approach to a beach.

Incidentally, if terrain like a beach was all dry land and it was in a manual of military tactics, the manual would say "Do not under any circumstances attack here!" On a beach one is attacking uphill, approaching in the open, against prepared defenses on high ground, often with trees and brush covering them. It's a bad way in, but it's the only way in when one attacks an island, so this is our lot.[†††††††]

For this assault I've set myself among support staff and reserves. No one from this ship is going in on the first day. (They did lower a few of our boats, but I'm told those are just spares.) I've been around the nervous tension of men going in with the first wave before. I wanted to see how it is for the other guys.

There's plenty of that nervous tension here. In fact, I think it may be worse. For all the reasons above, the guys going in for the invasion have a sense of resignation to them. There's nothing they can do about the whole trip in, and to cope with that I think they detach a little. The men here don't have that. They have their own work to do, from minute zero on, and they all believe lives depend on it. Each man wants to be sure his part goes flawlessly.

Thing is, there's not much some of them can do about it either. I found one of the radio men, Ensign Gaston Morton, from Stillwater, Minnesota, studiously memorizing the lists of ships from our invasion flotilla and every other squadron and fleet on this job. "There's a slim chance I would ever need to relay a call for a destroyer on the far side [of Kyushu], and I could look them up in a minute anyway. But the only other thing I could do right now is clean and polish the vacuum tubes on the radio sets. What about you? What do you do when you're waiting around to start an important job?"

I'm not used to my interview subjects asking back! I told him that, first of all, I don't recall ever having a particularly

---

[†††††††] The entry for Nov. 15th up to here was pre-written and transmitted stateside in advance for publication on the day of the assault, along with breaking news of the invasion.

important job to do. But if I did, to pass the time waiting for such a job to start, I would probably go interview someone else about his job.

There was very little time left to pass, so Mr. Morris got back to his radio set and I got back to staying out of the way. About 5 am the pre-landing bombardment kicked off, starting with the very big guns. Our shelling of the shore in the previous three days had been done during daylight. Each ship could fix its position by visual cues on land, then work accurately through its scheduled target list. Tonight the moon had set just after midnight. The pre-landing bombardment was done in pitch darkness. It was just a rolling line of thunder with no particular target except the island ahead of us.

I went back and forth between watching the action outside and listening in on radio traffic. Layered groups of fighter planes could be seen weaving a curtain to the north. Boats and amphibious transports were loaded and launched toward control lines throughout the bombardment. The other landing armies were going through the same routine at the same time. Across the island on the eastern shore they were landing on either side of the port city Miyazaki, a straight bit of coastline similar to our objective here around the town of Kushikino. In the southeast they are landing on an ideal bit of long gentle shoreline, inside Ariake Bay. But, the sides of the bay are solid lines of steep bluffs and mountain peaks.

The first serious trouble came from Ariake Bay. Over the sound of our big battleships firing in front of us, my friend Mr. Morris tuned in the Navy frequencies for the bombardment group in Ariake. The pre-invasion bombardment did not have Navy gunships enter the bay until this morning. Army bombers laid several thousands of pounds of bombs per acre all around Ariake that morning, a repeat of what they'd done three days in a row at all the invasion sites.

In a surprising development, the Navy gunships found themselves in a shooting duel with land based guns which were not hit in the earlier bombing, and which chose to reveal themselves today. Calls went out for return fire on each new enemy gun. *We see the flash, in the shadows. Target square 99-11, grid S!* might be one call. Mr. Morris helped me find a few of them on a copy of the same map.

The Navy had help from ground-attack aircraft under a clear sky, but still lost a cruiser and a destroyer sunk, and other ships damaged. Some number of airplanes were also lost. They had to fly low over enemy held land to make rocket attacks on the back sides of hills.

Our boats over here in the west were starting to move forward and Mr. Morris and his mates got too busy to entertain me. Control boats checked in as each line formed up. This information was relayed to the bombardment destroyers so they knew when to get out of the way, or to continue firing and keep enemy heads tucked down under ground.

Radio calls came in at an even tempo, from firm calm voices. Those voices had made the calls before, as they've had plenty of chances to practice and perform this act of the play. *Boats at 2000 yards. Destroyers finishing last sweep. Boats at 1000 yards. Supporting guns cease fire. First wave still line abreast. Second wave moving on time.*

The voices wavered only a little as the enemy got in on the act. *Boats hit, beach Winton-3. Can you see the gun? First wave dry, Stutz beach. Taking fire, right of Stutz. Air control Winton, can you see it?*[*]

I stepped outside for a minute and looked down to the main deck. It was heavy with Marines, watching the action to our starboard quarter. They all had helmets and small arms with them, the daily uniform for today's duty, which was to stand ready as the reserve division and as targets for any *kamikaze* raid that might come in.

I looked toward the beach myself. It wasn't hard to find, being the source of a lot of noise and smoke. With my field glasses I could occasionally make out armored AMTRACs on the beach,

---

[*] In this area, the 3rd Marine Division was landing to the north on beach "Winton", immediately south of the town of Kushikino. The 2nd Marine Division was landing further south, on beach "Stutz", past a small river-fed harbor.

100

moving inland and to the flanks. I looked up to watch a Navy attack bomber fly overhead toward the fracas. Another plane followed twenty seconds behind the first. Between the two I heard a louder "chump!" from the beach. I looked to the beach again, and the wind cooperated with my field glasses, clearing smoke from my view. I saw two figures leap from a flaming amphibious tank. Other dark shapes around the tank were infantry who had dived into the sand and gravel when the tank was hit.

The two from the dead tank moved back toward another group of dark specs behind another two AMTRACs. I imagine there was much yelling and pointing, as the two amphibians split up, steering clear of where their cousin had been wrecked. The view was again obscured as that unit of Marines worked through their first live field problem of the day.

Some time later I went back inside to get more news from the other beaches. Across the island at Miyazaki the Army's 25th Division is getting fired on from the hills south of Miyazaki, but moving okay. The 33rd Division got ashore pretty easily and is moving into the city proper. Our aircraft are putting on a show over the open area north of Miyazaki, where good roads could carry in a swift counterattack.

In Ariake Bay the Japanese big guns have stopped firing on our ships, either by choice or by insistence of our bombs and rockets. The Army 43rd Division is still landing on the northern beach the best it can, maneuvering around half sunken wrecks, where rescue operations are still going on. They moved quickly through undefended low fields that could have been a killing zone. Their only trouble so far has been sporadic heavy artillery from deep inland.

At the south end of Ariake Bay the 1st Cavalry Division met resistance almost right away. As of mid-afternoon they have set aside some of their initial objectives and are pushing up into the hills south of their assigned beaches. Fire from these hills has gone from harassing to brutal and accurate as the Americans got close – too close for friendly support. The 8th Cavalry Regiment is drying out on the beach, to where many of them had to swim, minus equipment, when one of their first large transports got farther into the bay than planned and was shelled.

I am still appreciating my privileged place on a rear ship full of command and support staff. I know much more about what is going on across this beachhead than if I was ashore right behind the Marines and could never see more than a few hundred yard radius. Since there are three main beachheads, and other operations going on, I would know absolutely nothing about the other areas if I was on the beach in one of them. I miss being with the real ground pounders, and I'll get out there with them soon, but for now I'm in a very good seat to watch all of this unprecedented invasion at once.

Speaking of those other operations, they have been a mixed bag. The reinforced 40th Division took a number of the smaller islands around Kyushu, starting five days ago. Most are already secured. One of them has gone very badly.

It seems the Japanese chose to make their first-last-stand on the island of Tanega-shima, just south of Kyushu. Five days ago the 158th "regimental combat team,"a force of over 4000 men, was landed in the middle of Tanega-shima. Two days ago, after extreme casualties from attacks and counterattacks, the 158th RCT abandoned all offensive operations and dug in near their beach head, a vulnerable position sitting on a plain between two clusters of small mountains.

The 40th Division and the 158th RCT were tasked with taking and securing the larger islands off Kyushu. The regiments of the 40th are still busy securing those islands. Other combat divisions are landing and committed, and most shipping and fire support is committed with them. A plan to relieve the 158th RCT is going forward, but it means robbing units piecemeal, one transport ship at a time, however they are packed, from several areas of operation.

The 'reserve' corps, which faked a landing far to the north three days ago, will send its 112th Regimental Combat Team to land ASAP. The 1st Cavalry Division, which has four regiments to start with, will send part of the 5th Cavalry to stand by off Tanega-shima. Our own 5th Marine Division will lose a battalion of the 26th Marines the same way. Meanwhile, the few vessels still assigned to the 40th Division will pick up its 160th Regiment from the neighboring Koshiki-retto, put it on Tanega-shima, and put the survivors of the 158th RCT on Koshiki-retto. There are no facilities for them on Koshiki-retto, but there's simply no where else to put them.

I do not expect many readers to absorb all the detail of this improvised operation. I spell it out in detail to make clear just what a big wrench in the works it is. The Japanese are sure to lose the entire substantial force which garrisoned Tanega-shima. All their effort digging caves and camouflaging guns there will be overcome and eventually lost to time. But that price has bought them a large impediment to the complicated plan of their enemy, of an inestimable value.

Yet much of that plan still unfolds, on schedule. Yesterday afternoon saw the two lead divisions at each of the three main beach heads land two combat regiments. That much was according to plan. The plan of course assumes some resistance from the enemy, but that has been consistently inconsistent. Our landed soldiers and Marines got through the first mile and more inland finding only disorganized resistance. The worst were pairs of light machine guns hastily set up in the rubble and craters made by our pre-invasion bombardment. They are also being harassed by long range fire from inland mountains and high points to the sides of each landing beach. There is nothing to do about it but to push into those heights. Forces are moving and timetables are being adjusted.

This morning the weather brought low clouds with a chance of rain and heavy *kamikaze* showers. Before that a wave of suicide boats made out from the many nooks on Koshiki-retto, through a dim pre-dawn haze. The 160th Regiment of the 40th Infantry Division has been working to clear any threats from that island since X-4, together with Navy ships circling the jagged shore. Much ordnance has been expended against the rocks there, blasting any suspicious looking crevice which might hide a small ship. But there are a great many crevices and clearly some of the deadly boats survived.

Kamikaze planes were expected at the first bit of bad weather, but the risk from attack boats was supposed to be eliminated. Destroyer picket screens against incoming aircraft are well beyond Koshiki-retto from this invasion fleet. Just one destroyer and a few patrol boats were patrolling between our big ships and the island. The USS Charette claims five *shinyo* sunk, with another probable. That may have been most of them, but we know at least three more got through, because they found the cruiser USS Little Rock and my recent acquaintance the USS Red Oak Victory.

The Red Oak was back to her old job of at-sea re-supply of ordnance to Navy ships. The Little Rock had done her share of pre-invasion shore bombardment, and was to continue the job of delivering fire support after taking on more deadly packages.

The Red Oak Victory was parallel to the shore, less than two miles off, tethered to the Little Rock. Gunners on the Red Oak may have hit some of the attacking boats, but the Little Rock reports that two of them got close enough to blow big holes in the cargo ship's hull, possibly starting off secondary explosions in the holds, and put her under in a blink. It was all the cruiser could do to cut the transfer lines and get clear of the sinking ship so they wouldn't smash any swimming survivors. The Little Rock's gunners barely caught a glimpse of a final suicide motorboat gunning past the rolling wreck.

The boat closed the last few dozen yards to the Little Rock and its multi-hundred-pound bow charge ripped through the light cruiser's armor. I have no word on fatalities from below, but one machine gun crew on deck reported injuries from wood splinters and impact from one severed human hand.

The USS Little Rock is still afloat, after a scary stretch of fire fighting and damage control work. As the news came in, I sat in my corner of the radio room with an angry knot in my stomach at the certain fate of so many of my friends from the hard-working Red Oak Victory. Radio traffic continued its steady professional cadence. *Hold picket screen, do not adjust. Oakland to assist. Task two fleet tugs. Notify USS Comfort.*

Radio calls picked up urgency as two radar pickets ships saw a swarm of objects at the same time. A loose mass of objects came at cloud level from the direction of Nagasaki*. Dozens more stragglers spanned fifty miles behind the main body. It was just at first light, so our radar equipped night fighters were still on station. One at a time they braved the cloud layer to hunt by glowing scope. Flying singly in strict zones to avoid collisions, they would do little to reduce the pack.

Close flying through clouds is no picnic, even for veteran pilots. Our second line of picket ships reported at least one pair of wrecked planes tumbling down out of the clouds, probably after a mid-air collision. Minutes later the outer ring of destroyers in our invasion fleet opened up with radar-directed flak[†] at the approaching mob. Other ships joined in before I heard excited Japanese from one of the radios which had been silent.

I ran outside to look, brushing aside a scolding ensign, who shut the hatch behind me. Scores of Japanese planes dropped down out of the clouds. Two dozen Navy fighters, up and ready from the early radar picket alert, were inbound from the west to meet them. Once the forces merged it would be impossible for the ships' gunners to target Japanese planes without endangering American pilots. This rarely stopped American gunners under *kamikaze* attack.

One Japanese plane broke out, faster than the others, directly at my ship. I didn't run or even flinch. Its approach did not look like an attack run. The Jap plane streaked along low and level, shifting sideways just enough to be difficult to hit. The pilot was cool and experienced. I could see that his plane had no bomb. He did have two U.S. Navy "Hellcats" on his tail. The Japanese plane tore over my ship and I recognized it as one of the newest types, a

---

* Just off the provided map to the northwest, Nagasaki was a substantial naval and industrial city which had not been hit by American bombing until late August, 1945.

† By that time in 1945 many American ships' guns, down to heavy anti-aircraft pieces, were tied into radar systems which automatically aimed the shots.

Shinden, faster and stronger than the famous Reisen "Zero" that gave the world so much trouble through 1942[‡].

Behind the Shinden were the two American fighters, and behind those three older Japanese Navy planes were coming into view, each with an oversize bomb slung below. Our F6s were almost upon the dodging Shinden, and the lead Hellcat tore into it, throwing .50-caliber slugs through its structure and making the engine smoke. The Jap pilot pulled up into a full 180 degree reversal, adding a half barrel roll near the top, keeping up airspeed along the way.

The surprised American fighters started a long level turn to come around and finish their prey. But the lead Japanese pilot had done his job. His three followers stormed ahead free of opposing fighters. They weaved near wave top, daring Navy gunners to shoot so low they could hit other ships. Gunners did fire, from every angle, and shortly the left plane erupted into a shower of debris which scattered over the water. The other two bore on, absorbing minor hits, engines screaming.

Just 300 yards forward and to port of my ship was the transport USS Montrose, also carrying elements of the 5th Marine Division. Like us she was still full, waiting for the division to get orders ashore. With barely a dozen yards to spare, gunners on the Montrose found the right plane in the remaining suicide pair, causing it to break apart, but it was too late.

Most of both planes plowed into the side of the lightly armored transport, the bomb from the damaged plane impacting somewhere below the water line. In a dramatic flourish the injured Shinden pilot finished his flaming dive directly into the superstructure of the rapidly listing transport.

The Montrose sank in eight minutes. The Third Battalion of the 28th Marines ceased to exist.

[‡] One could hardly avoid learning to spot planes and ships. Recognition charts were pasted everywhere, and decks of playing cards were handed out with aircraft profiles on them.

November 17, 1945 : X+2 — off Kyushu

Rescue parties combed the nearby sea through steady rain all yesterday afternoon. It was a grisly duty and did nothing for the frustration of the men who want only to get off these boats and get the job done on land.

The invasion fleet here west of southern Kyushu is centered around bunches of large amphibious assault ships, which are grouped in rows of loose semicircles stretching out from the beach. The closest are now about a mile off shore, discharging the last of their men and equipment for the 2nd and 3rd Marine divisions. Behind them are engineers in bow-ramped landing ships loaded with support equipment from fresh water haulers to tank recovery vehicles. Further out, two miles back I estimate, are us combat reserves and the heavier support units.

On either side of the big transports, destroyers are seen roaming continuously, split between looking for trouble from land, sea, or air. Three old battleships circle slowly just south of us, waiting with a few big-gun cruisers to fill fire support orders like loud burly short order cooks at a raucous 24-hour diner. I can't see them but know that even more destroyers and smaller ships patrol further to the south where a peninsula off Kyushu points out into our right side.

With better weather today, a thin overcast, a substantial armada of small carriers just west of us sends regular runs of light bombers overhead for ground support. From still farther out, to the southwest, a fleet of large carriers is rotating waves of covering fighter planes that we can hear somewhere over the clouds.

The outer defense of the whole fleet is two lines of destroyers to the north and west. They patrol about thirty and fifty miles out, to give the best chance of detecting and hopefully putting a dent in waves of attacking bombers and *kamikazes*. At Okinawa those picket line destroyers took a beating, as Japanese pilots tried to take them out before advancing on the main fleet. The destroyers were usually alone or in pairs and paid a heavy price for the alerts they gave the fleet.

Yesterday off Kyushu the destroyers were left practically alone. None of them reported more than two enemy planes diving on them and none of those hit. The whole flight, estimated at 100 to 150 enemy aircraft, came hunting the bigger ships in the invasion flotilla. Chasing fighters claimed some kills. Ship board gunners claimed many more, probably some of the same kills. Many suicide pilots crashed before making an attack run, or missed and put their planes into the ocean.

Still we took over twenty hits in one day. The Little Rock, Red Oak Victory, and Montrose took six of those hits. A transport supporting the 3rd Marine division was hit and lost, but most men got off. Another cargo ship, a whole airfield-in-a-box, was abandoned in flames just behind her, sunk as a hazard late in the day. Behind the landing fleet two of our escort carriers took hard hits. They will finish this battle in Okinawa if they stay afloat long enough for the tow to Buckner Bay.

Early in the day the 5th Marine Division sent one battalion south as a reserve for the Tanega-shima fight, and now it has lost another permanently. Staff officers are generating stacks of paper to reassign veterans to head up replacement companies. Over a thousand raw Marines, fresh from basic training, will be absorbed into the division, and it will have no opportunity to train them before it gets ashore.

Once the orders come down, our small boats will be very busy moving men around between transports. So I took the opportunity to get a ride in to the beach while I could. Late in the afternoon I climbed over into a Higgins boat, under the occasional shadow of a heavy shell streaking in to a requested coordinate. Fighting on the beach was mostly out of sight by then, but the sounds of modern war echoed out to fill the air over the entire fleet.

An ethereal calm settled over the battle as a novel apparition materialized. First a rhythmic slow strum, like off a cracked old out-of-tune cello, began to fill the quiet instants between rifle cracks and mortar tube 'whoomps.' Then the battle stopped altogether as the first helicopter anyone there had ever seen came into view.

The curious non-flapping bird moved quickly across the water, seeming dangerously low over the trundling transport boats, but probably well above them. Our own heavy guns had stopped

108

firing to clear its passage into the center of our beach head. The helicopter slowed as it approached the shore line, lowering to a hover just above a deliberate clearing amongst all the debris of war, about 100 yards from the water.

It dropped to the ground and its body came to a rest, rotor still spinning almost too fast to make out the blades. Medics moved confidently under the blades, as if they'd practiced the maneuver (I assumed they had). Some critically wounded Marine was loaded in behind the solo pilot. The noise of the rotors picked up its rhythm before the medics were even clear, and the nature-defying aircraft was up again, moving the precious cargo to a hospital ship out in the fleet.

Another helicopter was already heading in to the beach. The hole in the combat noise caused by the first whirlybird began to close. Small caliber guns opened up on targets of opportunity, such as an individual Japanese soldier or American Marine who had stuck his head up to catch the side show. Larger Japanese guns, including some that had been hidden and discretely silent, began to bark as the second helicopter came close to landing.

Our medics worked fast to load the next injured man, and Marines shot back to silence the new entrants into the battle, but the Japanese guns were pre-sighted and quickly found their mark. The second helicopter was ten feet off the ground when it exploded into a shower of hot metal scraps and one screaming dying engine.

The pilot and injured Marine were lost. What had been the 2nd Marine Division's first main aid station fought through flaming chaos for another hour. Helicopter medevac operations will not start again until every hill in view of the beach is secure.

November 18, 1945 : X+3 – Kushikino, Kyushu

Late yesterday afternoon I made it safely ashore, keeping my feet dry the whole way. Engineers are already working their world-shaping magic, which so far includes small piers, a fresh water plant, and a basic vehicle repair shop. At least it's supposed to be a basic shop – I watched mechanics using a hand pulled crane to swap the engine out of a 2½ ton truck, which was missing half its rear axles, into one which took an anti-tank round into its engine block.

I checked in with a division intelligence tent, making some very busy major vaguely aware of my presence. I hung around until near dark, picking up details of the operation on land. The 2nd and 3rd Marine divisions have made steady progress, against steady resistance. Someone thought our forces here would sweep quickly north into Sendai and almost as rapidly across this peninsula into Kagoshima. Infantry commanders noted several opportunities the Japanese would have to frustrate that plan. So far the Japs have taken advantage of almost every one.

There were no fixed fortifications anywhere in range of our naval five inch guns. This is partly because every visible structure, and many imaginary ones, in that radius from the shore were thoroughly obliterated by a redundant schedule of bombardment. Mostly it is because the Japanese didn't bother. A few obvious coastal guns were set up for our large scale target practice, but I'm told that on closer inspection of the ruins the guns were already relics.

Our bombing from ships and planes did leave a predictable mess of shell craters and fallen timbers, which the Japs were ready to use. The map guys figure they hid out of range of most of our guns, then ran forward as soon as the shelling stopped with whatever light weapons they could carry. They had sixty something minutes to get forward and improvise positions for riflemen, machine guns, and small mortars.

Our Marines took only sporadic mortar fire on the beaches, which was met promptly with counter-battery fire or air attack. Advancing inland they soon got into sustained machine gun duels. Smoke from burning timbers limited visibility in many areas. This cut risk of sniper fire from all the facing and surrounding hills, but it led to numerous squad-level engagements at point-blank range. The advance of our veteran troops is certain, but halting and bloody.

Those hills are the second big opportunity for the Japanese to add drama to this play and looking at the maps it seems they will have plenty of dates for repeat performances. Defended hills never

110

come just one at a time. On western Kyushu they pop up in threes and fours, like pimples on a teenager over-excited about a big date.

A single obstacle like a lonely hill can be overcome by application of firepower from multiple angles, friendly forces supporting advance of their brothers. But when the enemy has a cluster of three natural forts, they support each other instead. An attacker has no safe lane of approach to any one hill, as his would-be supporting forces come under fire from the other hills. Taking any of them requires attacking all of them at once, with artillery, airplanes, armor, and every available foot soldier.

It means stopping every day to plan out a big operation for the next morning. If that operation fails, then stopping again to collect the wounded, bring up reinforcements, plan another bigger attack, and try again in a day or three.

On top of the problem with the many small hills, there are a handful of scattered enormous volcanic peaks that dominate the Kyushu landscape. They offer practically unlimited visibility to telescope-equipped observers. Yesterday the 8th Marines probed their way down the road toward Kagoshima. Once they got beyond some magic line, very large artillery shells fell in with the advance parties, and the operation pulled back. The big rounds came from somewhere to the east, and aircraft will start making observation runs that direction when the weather improves.

Lastly, word has come from aerial scouts that Japanese units are moving down from the north. Our landing has, as expected, triggered a Japanese plan for reinforcements to move to where they are needed. It was also expected that our air forces would pummel any enemy forces trying to move in, but the weather has limited that to a few harassing attacks near Yatsushiro and Hitoyoshi.

With dusk approaching, 2nd Division HQ sent a jeep bound runner out to check the disposition of all its units before nightfall. I hitched a ride along to see for myself.

Our driver was Corporal Don Blue, who said he drove a county snow plow back in central Michigan. His slick-road experience paid off, since days of intermittent rain left the winding dirt roads we had to use persistently hazardous. This section of

Kyushu is composed entirely of similar rolling hills, covered in modest evergreen trees or cleared for small terrace houses and farms.

Back near the beach everything had been completely leveled – buildings, trees, and anthills. It was perfect desolation, oddly beautiful as the smoke cleared revealing its special sort of purity. Further inland some of the hill faces are partly denuded, from shell impact and fires kicked off by incendiary bombs, but the spread of fires had been damped by regular rains. A constant smell wafts through the winding valleys, mixing churned earth with burning pines, gunpowder, and occasionally cooking meat.

Going forward most of the narrow road way is bracketed by a three or four foot high stone wall to one side and a similar drop-off to the other. Traffic knots are inevitable, even for ambulances trying to haul men back to the beach front.

Navigating through it all in the other front seat was 1st Lieutenant Martin Myers. By map, temporary signposts, and a few hollered exchanges with knowledgeable looking men on the ground, we reached each regimental headquarters. Lieutenant Myers conferred with the XO of each unit to get a face-to-face run down of how they were doing and what they needed. He would take back any priority written items for HQ or division intelligence.

I wandered around outside at each stop, taking in the action. Everything up here, just a mile or two from the very hot front line, is transient. It could fall under attack at any time and will probably move again in a day or two. Yet still there is an insistent order to each outpost. Engineers were busy making a clearing to expand a tent-bound medical aid station. A kitchen unit marked out space to work, with a dedicated lane for trucks to pull in, load up, and haul hot meals as far forward as they could be served.

With limited light to drive by, we hustled back while Lieutenant Myers caught me up on the rough details of his scouting mission. "We're about four miles inland, all along a fifteen mile front. Third division is holding at the edge of Sendai and cleaning up the chunk of land left of them out to the sea." He pointed on a map to the lumpy peninsula that was defined by our beach head and the wide Sendai river. "Second division here is holding the same way, already stretched out thin and waiting for the Fifth to land before making another move."

I asked how well off the units were, as we pulled over to let a line of ambulances get by. "Truth is," the Kansas City, Missouri native admitted, "they're pretty banged up. Everyone's reserves are already committed. We plan a morning rush to lock up the first good line of hills."

He pointed again at the map, touching contour bubbles in a line southeast from Sendai. "That bunch of hills will be a great place to be once we take it. Thing is, that works both ways. The Japs here are dug in on all sides and not budging. Every move we make to dig them out is spotted and opposed. These guys so far seem lightly armed, but they call in some heavy stuff from the hills behind them."

Glancing back out to sea the Lieutenant added, "The Navy has been hot and fast with fire support, but the Japs hide on the reverse slopes most of the time and there are so damned many trees we can't spot them until too close most of the time." He made a sweeping gesture at the forested hillside next to us. "Even if we had enough rounds to level all the trees, it would make an impassable pile of logs, a sniper behind every one."

Once the immediate objectives are taken, the Marines will have fought uphill about 1300 feet from the sea. I noted that beyond the first prize ridge line sits another. After that the hills become mountains that have names. Here on Kyushu there is always one more hill beyond the one you just conquered, and it's always just a little higher.

Back at the division tent city, I found my way back into the intelligence "office," through a double entry which kept their work lights from leaking out. I settled in near a recent acquaintance, Captain John Clifford, sitting up in a canvas chair next to his work area. A simple chair is a rare luxury in a combat area. I take them when I can.

Captain Clifford showed me some of the things of interest which had been brought back from the local area. Clerks were typing up reports on them tonight, for courier and radio relay to the other corps. "The town behind us was totally deserted, and I mean completely. This was no last-minute evacuation. It was long planned."

I asked how he could be sure. The locals could simply be ordered and obedient people, as we've been told.

"We don't have the actual plan, but we found this." He put an empty brown cloth satchel on the folding table next to me. It was torn along one edge and dirty with dark earth all over the outside. "The owner of this is dead, one of the last to leave apparently. Our artillery caught up with him. Here is some of what we found in the bag." He picked up an unmarked folder from next to an analyst who had moved on to type about something else in the pile. Tipping the folder open with one finger, he snapped up the first three sheets of paper from within, then closed the folder and set it back. "This is a fighting manual, with pictures and instructions for various home-made weapons."

I held the first two double-sided pages, which were run on a production press. Simple silhouette figures held clubs and spears and small bombs in various poses, next to blocks of Japanese text. The last page showed groups of people working together, bombing then stabbing then bludgeoning other hapless faceless rifle-toting figures.

"This last page is just a list of names, with a few dates." He handed me the handwritten sheet. "The names are in groups, each next to a larger name, which is written in more formal address, a group leader we think. A character next to each group corresponds to one of the weapons in the other instructions." He sat back for a second to let me digest the connection.

"The people here, the civilians, they're not just told to not trust us, or to resist us however they can. They've been trained and organized." Captain Clifford added, almost under his breath, "The enemy army here has grown by two million."

114

Map – Details from Army Maps

The maps drawn for this book only hint at the terrain on Kyushu. Following are samples from actual battle maps prepared for the invasion in 1945, land just south of the Marines' landing beaches and Sakura-Jima.

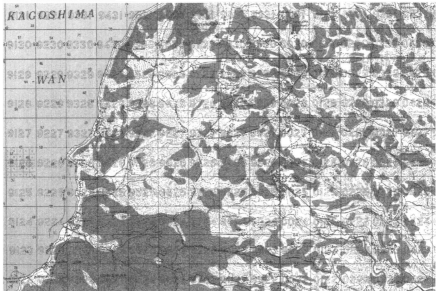

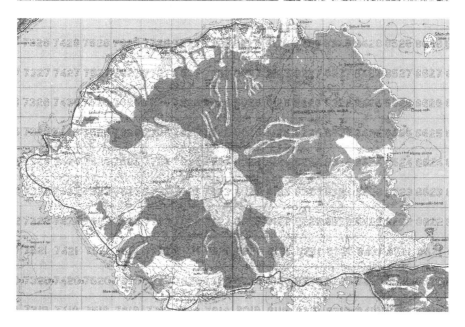

116

November 19, 1945 : X+4 – Kushikino, Kyushu

While I was with the G-2 men last night, I got caught up on developments and rumors from the other beach heads. Either side of Ariake Bay our forces are driving hard into the hills from which Japanese fire still makes landing treacherous and the best beaches unusable for support functions. South of Miyazaki they have the same problem with fire from the hills. Around the city they have dealt with urban fighting and a large counterattack.

The entire 1st Cavalry Division is now committed to fighting south of the Ariake-Kanoya pass, toward Kunimi-yama and its supporting cast of slightly inferior peaks. At the north corner of Ariake the 43rd Division has been doing the same job, over an unending spread of smaller but innumerable hills. Combat units of the Americal Division are all landed, taking up slack in the middle and helping the 43rd.

It had been brutal, taking fire from the mountains to each side and from deep inland, fighting up into the nearer mountains, and dealing with sparse but dug-in enemy to the front. After three days of fighting, the 1st Cavalry Division is beat up to the tune of maybe 2000 casualties. The 43rd is spent, having sent a full quarter of its infantry back for some level of medical attention. The Americal Division saw action immediately in the central plain northwest of the bay, and had to detach a large force to secure the right flank while the 43rd regroups in between.

Out on the smaller islands the 40th division is well along securing their assigned minor patches of homeland Japan, except on the heavily defended Tanega-shima. There the 158th RCT has been relieved by the 112th RCT, detached from Ninth Corps. The 112th made a big push into the south of the island, while the 158th is stuck in the middle, hoping to not get jumped again. They were going to be evacuated, but shipping is just too tight. They and the 112th are stuck until the fight there is done and ships free up to evacuate the 158th – or bring in still more reinforcements if the Japs in the north end of Tanega-shima don't fold soon.[§]

---

§ The 160th Infantry Regiment was going to go to Tanega-shima, but after suicide boats snuck out from the island it had 'secured,' it was to stay and go over the island again in greater detail.

117

Miyazaki is overlooked by mountains close to the south and tall bluffs farther inland to the west. A sizable plain stretches out to the north, dotted with small towns and villages and many level roads. The 25th Division has fought tooth and nail to claim the first peaks of the mountains in the south. After taking the near slopes, with ample Navy gun support, they are stumped by defenses on the reverse slopes, supported by more Japanese forces on the next hills. On Kyushu there is always one more hill, and somehow it's always a little higher than the one we just took.

Rain has frustrated efforts to hit the back sides of ridge lines from the air and to observe enemy movements. Overnight Japanese infantry and a stunningly large tank formation advanced on the 33rd Division, which was in a semicircle west and north of Miyazaki. They engaged while it was still dark, after a large artillery barrage. The barrage was not a random pattern, it was directed against particular parts of the division camp. Forward supply points were a sore loss, and medical tents were not spared.

At the sound of tank engines flares shot into the sky and a giant carnival shooting gallery opened up. The main road from Miyakonojo, and several parallel to it, ran directly into the 136th Infantry Regiment. Division armor was not positioned forward, so the ground pounders fought with small towed guns and bazookas against the tank columns and their infantry support. While many tanks were flaming hulks lighting the night, others got right into the American lines, spewing machine gun rounds up and down the line. At first light a short American retreat was organized. Ammo was in desperate supply, especially anti tank rockets.

While it was still dark an estimated two thousand* Japanese infantry emerged practically out of the dirt directly in front of the 130th Infantry, right of the 136th. Fighting too close for artillery or even mortar support, the forces fought with field guns, rifles, knives, and rocks through the morning. Both forces bled heavily.

In the end, reserves were engaged, more ammo was delivered, and American lines are back where they were yesterday. Dozens of Japanese tanks are a field of charred scrap. The

---

* It was closer to three thousand.

attacking Japanese infantry retreated at mid-day, leaving more than a thousand bodies behind. But the American 25th and 33rd divisions are inoperative, having pushed the medical chain to its limit and beyond. And they are no closer to the heavy guns hidden inland which keep them up at night and much worse.

The 41st Division landed at Miyazaki today, which is good news for that beach head, but while they were landing, reinforcements for the other divisions had to wait. Combat units here in the west are now all ashore, and just in time for reinforcements to start coming in after them.

There is one road to Kagoshima. Today the 27th Marines tried to use it. The Japanese decided it was to be a toll road. The Marine regiment did not bring exact change. I am here in the division hospital with several hundred of its travelers.

The division did not consult with me before sending the regiment out, so I did not get to ride with them. For better or worse I have plenty of people to interview here who were out there just a few hours ago. Private Donald Cameron I found sitting on an improvised bench outside, with a clean bandage around his upper right arm. His uniform jacket sleeve was cut off at the shoulder by medics. He'll be fine and has his first war story to take back with him to Charleston (the West Virginia one) after the war.

Private Cameron was in the back of an AMTRAC in the lead column. The column had six tanks up front, a dozen or so armored tractors behind them and an assortment of trucks behind that. Other columns probed down side roads looking for opposition that might jump the rear of the main group. He stood up and gestured as he told me about it.

"They told us we were going to go fast, and we did. We slowed down every half mile or so for scouts in jeeps and half tracks to beat the brush ahead of us, but if any Japs were waiting for us, they kept quiet and we motored on through. We had just got through a small city at a river junction. I even saw a couple kids wave at us, no grown-ups though. Then when we got into a big bend they lit us up." Private Cameron sat back down as he told the end of his story.

"I hear there wasn't much left of the vehicles in front of us. Some mortars got set up behind us pretty quick and they laid in suppressing fire and smoke for us. My squad set up a line along the bluffs and tree line either side of the road, others went up to bring back wounded. It took us an hour or two to get everybody loaded again and pull back."

A bunch of small hills were taken today in support of the run toward Kagoshima, and a surprise (to us) Japanese tank company was almost eliminated, but not much else was gained, and the 5th Marine Division has a lot of new vacancies to fill.

Several officers helped me put together the bigger picture of the action today. The road to Kagoshima city runs to the southeast out of our Kushikino beach head, then cuts due east through our front lines and across this peninsula to Kagoshima Bay. The plan from the start of the invasion was to cut across quickly after landing, trapping Japanese forces on the peninsula. The 8th Marines, of the 2nd Division, made probing attacks in that direction over the last two days, but was turned back. With the 5th Marine Division ashore, it's 26th and 27th regiments were tasked with making the big push to get across. (The 28th is still reorganizing after losing a whole transport at sea.)

The American Ninth Corps started landing two divisions on the south of this peninsula this morning. The clock is ticking to push across and cut off Japanese forces between there and here, before they get a chance to pull out, if that's what they want to do. We may never know if the Japanese were prescient or lucky, but so far they have set up defenses that perfectly oppose what the American Sixth Army wants to do.

The 27th Marines were to make a mechanized assault down the road to Kagoshima, led by tanks and armored tractors. The road lays mostly along a string of wide valleys with a number of natural choke points. The 26th Marines moved out at dawn to attack as many of the adjacent hills as possible and if not take them at least tie up any Japanese in position to fire on the road.

Our tanks and trucks would outpace the foot soldiers, but it was expected that well spotted artillery and air support would extend the reach of those infantry. Yesterday's low clouds and rain did not break as predicted, so that didn't all come together.

Japanese fire discipline kept their positions hidden until too late anyway.

The latest Sherman tanks here have generous armor up front, to go with a new hard hitting main gun. It's thought that the Japanese have few remaining field guns that can punch through our tanks from the front. But today they let the American column pass by before snapping shut their trap. The road takes a long northerly U-bend following the flood plain of a meandering river before heading southeast the last four miles into Kagoshima.

With good sight lines across the relatively wide open mud flat, the armor column moved quickly around the bend, almost ahead of its scouts. A jeep mounted machine gun fired into a suspected enemy position to the inside, and that was the cue for all the Japanese guns to open up. It was also the cue for a squadron of Japanese tanks to charge into the flat from the east.

Stationary guns cut into the American column behind its tanks. Some AMTRACs exploded in place, others took multiple lesser hits as they sped off the road toward the bluffs and trees, shedding Marines as men scattered away from the tracked targets. Our tanks turned toward to the Japanese positions, to put rounds on them and to present their thickest armor to the enemy. But there were no safe lanes. Multiple positions with Japanese heavy anti-tank guns were spread out on either side of the river valley. Two of the lead six tanks took disabling hits through the side, and more small caliber fire as Marine tankers tried to move their injured mates out through escape hatches.

By that time the Japanese tanks were spotted, at least a dozen. Or two dozen, depending on who you ask. Our armored squadron turned back up the road to face them with the remaining four Shermans. So far in this war the Japanese have not fielded a tank equal to even our medium weight Sherman M4. Today was no exception. The American tankers met their counterparts head-on in open tank-on-tank battle, which they could hardly have expected on any other Pacific island before now.

The Japanese machines screamed forward to close distance and fight the American steel at point blank range, the only way their smaller guns stood a chance. Half of their number were destroyed before closing within 400 yards, but they still outnumbered the American quartet. In an exhibition of old-fashioned jousting, tanks ripping past each other just inches away, whole strips of sod and clouds of dirt were slung skyward by the desperately turning machines.

Two more American brutes were disabled, one losing a track and another burning from a round that punched through from behind into the engine compartment. Still, by plain count they had the best of the stubby Japanese mules, making scrap of most of them.

With four or five running tanks left, the Japanese turned to withdraw. They were chased by our last two stallions, who gunned down another two enemy vehicles before the Japs slipped into the next narrow chasm and turned out of sight. The Marine tanks held back, stopping momentarily to decide the next move. A tanker from the one which lost its track described the scene to me, Sergeant Cliff Buckley. He and his driver had found cover under a small river bridge a quarter mile from the last healthy tanks.

"From a hut beside the road on the left, and out of some trees on the right, eight or ten guys came charging out. Four of them had thick satchels hung across one shoulder. The others fired rifles from the hip back toward us, drawing fire away from the satchel guys I guess. By this time we had a couple machine guns set up and plenty of Marines lined up along the riverbank like cord wood. They cut down all the Jap rifle men and dropped two of the satchel guys. But the last two got right up to the side of each of our tanks."

"Both charges went off almost at the same time. They sent bits of tread three hundred feet. One guy got his charge under the tank enough that it was tossed up and almost flipped over." That tank had one survivor, if he wakes up again.

The Marines took a beating today, rolling the dice on a quick thrust. But that first deep drive into enemy territory had one sure bright spot. We picked up a flyer who had gone missing. He was taken prisoner by the Japs just yesterday. They hadn't decided where to send him yet, so he was still near the front, and got away during the initial confusion of our attacks.

122

This afternoon our intel guys debriefed the young photo recon officer, Lieutenant Jorg 'Georgie' Gjerde of Duluth, Minnesota, who had been in the back seat of a twin engine plane that went down with mechanical trouble just short of our lines. He managed to escape, but only after being interrogated by a Japanese officer and his translator. Our instructions to any captured pilots have for some time been to cooperate fully and tell their captors everything they know. They'd talk eventually and the guys we send forward aren't told much to start with.

The interrogator had asked, 'Just how many soldiers will the Americans attempt to land on the Japanese home islands?' Georgie says he answered immediately, without a blink,

"All of them."

November 20, 1945 : X+5 – Tanega-shima

I left the Marines behind this morning. They will assault Sendai, Kagoshima, and hundreds of named and numbered hills without me. There is much else to see in this enormous multi-faceted operation.

With too many transport needs to accommodate them individually, the Navy has regular shuttles running between the various fleets of the invasion armada. I caught a landing craft out to a transport and picked up a re-purposed utility ship like transferring at a downtown bus station.

With a Navy medical team aboard we sailed around the southeast tip of Kyushu toward Tanega-shima. A flotilla bearing Ninth Corps could be seen huddled near the shore, discharging the 77th and 81st Army divisions[*], which would fight north to meet the Marines, securing the whole west side of Kagoshima Bay. The date of that meeting will be determined by an unknown number of Japanese defenders caught between the two American corps.

It took almost six hours to reach Tanega-shima. I got to know my fellow travelers along the way. Commander Dr. Anthony Federowicz is leading a group of seven volunteers from hospital ship USS Sanctuary. While their ship is certainly busy, the two RCTs on Tanega-shima are in rough shape, and their field medics have been working without rest for days on end. The conditions are primitive, and they get shot at and have had aid stations nearly overrun by night attacks.

A call went out for volunteers on clean calm hospital ships to go get dirty for a while. Lead nurse Chief Evan Fields tells me half the ship volunteered, so this group was chosen by lottery. The group of seven is from eight different states, spanning the continent from Maine to Oregon. Pharmacist's Mate Paul Atha was born on a Kiowa reservation nineteen years ago in Oklahoma. We sang him happy birthday over the sound of our ship's engine.

---

[*] The rookie 98th division of IX corps had been sent to help out at Ariake Bay, where XI corps had all they could handle.

Each person in the medical team had a heavy foot locker with him, and other boxes and crates, all barely luggable by one man. I needled them about their excess baggage but Dr. Federowicz corrected me. "All we have with us is the clothes on our backs. They've been tearing through medical supplies on the island, so we brought our own tools and all the consumables we could carry."

Our ship tied up at a temporary pier off the south end of the American beach head. It was supposedly the safest place on the still hotly contested island. I unloaded crates for the team, as they were put to work immediately loading injured soldiers onto another boat. I followed bedraggled corpsmen and stretcher bearers to the aid station the stretchers were coming from. Their dirty green uniforms were damp with sweat in the mid afternoon sun. Just that morning they had been dry for the first time in days.

The aid station is nothing more than three twelve foot square tents. Under clear warm skies the tent flaps are wide open. One can watch four teams of surgeons working two of the tents, wading through loose bundles of dirty uniform pieces and bloody gauze on the ground at their feet. As I passed stretcher bearers took one case off the last table, carting him over to a quiet corner of the loosely organized compound. There laid rows of poncho covered bodies, some with a stake at the head holding some memento left by comrades who were still standing. Stretchers were in short supply and not left with the dead.

For a moment the bustle and flow of the scene reminded me of a casino with popular table games. Gamblers come in and out, each trying his luck. The doctors and nurses are just dealers and croupiers, they have no stake in the game, however they might cheer for the lucky and anguish over the losers. The House is death itself, and the house is doing terribly well, paying out absolute loss to losers but only meager victories to the winning gamblers.

The surgeon from that losing table stepped out into the sun, resting his weight on his knees for a moment, staring passively at the well worn dirt trail in front of his work place. After a routine cleaning of the operating table corpsmen brought another priority case into the tent. The surgeon joined his team in the third tent to change his apron and gloves and move on to their next case.

125

The 158th RCT is still here, what pieces of it are still together. Shipping simply wasn't available to carry them away after the 112th RCT pulled in and started unloading its gear and equipment. Spreads of men living in small tents and tent-covered foxholes radiate out from a loose cluster of primary buildings on a high plain about a mile in from the beach. Their engineer detachment managed to erect two Quonset style buildings, with raised gravel floors. Checking in with the regimental HQ, I got the lay of the camp.

Over half of the regiment's combat soldiers are not here any more. It has reorganized itself into two battalions, each with two light companies, not that it expects to deploy into the fight any time soon. It has no armor left, having lent its last tank squadrons to the 112th RCT. Another two independent companies are set up just to defend this camp, from fighting positions on three sides of it. The 112th only claims to have secured the south end of the island yesterday. Men here are ready for survivors to pop up and make a final charge, as they did at Iwo Jima days after that island was "secured."

Poking my nose around through the camp I found what passed for the command post of the new Baker Company, Second Battalion, 158th Regiment[†]. A few NCOs sat across from the command tent, on a ring of stumps, logs, and lumber scraps serving as benches. One wooden plank was laid up against a log to display hand written lettering, "Enlisted Mens' Club." Conversation was easy among the corporals and sergeants who came and went during my brief visit.

They weren't exactly primed to talk about the vicious fighting of the last week, but on my prompting Albany, Oregon's Corporal Ken K. Kean, who they call "Kreak," went first, telling me about his view of it.

"We landed easy enough. Our gear came in behind us, this camp got set up, and then we pushed out north and south. It looked

---

[†] Incidentally the 158th is a integrated unit, with more races and ethnicities than are found in most of our combat units. I don't care to list them all, and the men of the regiment would rather be known simply as the best jungle fighting force in the world, the "Bushmasters."

a lot like the job on Luzon [in the Philippines]. First battalion went south, third went north. I was with second, the old second, waiting back here until the Japs gave us trouble." A couple of the guys got up, lighting fresh cigarettes and pacing behind the improvised benches.

I asked where the first trouble came from. "It came from everywhere, all at once. They let us get close to the hills, north and south, and opened up with everything. Our guys were under small mortars and our tanks were hit by field guns." He pointed up toward the distant small mountain range. "Big artillery from somewhere farther back joined up as we pulled back. It was all dead on target."

Sergeant Henry Brockell, a rare Montana man, had something to say about the support they got, waving his lit cigarette for emphasis. "The Navy didn't give us shit. Jap artillery covered the whole island, right down to the beach, and all we had was two old cruisers to shoot back at them with. The planes couldn't find [the enemy artillery positions] either so we had to march right through and dig them out ourselves."

There was no safe haven on the island. Japanese artillery was spotted onto American troops during the day and raked the beach camps in patterns at night. Small groups of enemy soldiers came out at night to cause havoc in the American lines. One night a much larger group came out from the south and nearly got to the water's edge.

The fighting got easier once the 112th Regiment came in, possibly because the Japs were running out of ammo and artillery shells. It was still tough brutal work, but it was methodical clearing of a dug in enemy which Americans have practiced so thoroughly on previous island strongholds.

With limited daylight left I excused myself and hiked back to the beach, to catch the last "bus" to the next temporary town. Tomorrow I expect to be with the fleet inside Ariake Bay, where we now have four divisions locked into combat in a huge ring around the bay.

November 21, 1945 : X+6 — Ariake Bay

Yesterday evening my shuttle boat, formerly loaded with rockets for the initial shore bombardment, pulled up to the transport USS Hydrus. The Hydrus was serving as the command ship for the 43rd Division and was sitting outside Ariake Bay, over a dozen miles from the beaches. None of the commands have gone ashore yet, as fighting is still very close to the beach.

I was the last person left on the shuttle. Looking at the many other ships farther into the bay, I had a word with the coxswain and asked if I could be taken closer to the action. "Fine with me, pal, I've got no where to be until the morning."

The sun was well set as we came up to the USS Athene, just two miles from shore. After some 'lively' discussion, a net was lowered for me to climb aboard by failing twilight. My only luggage by then was a half-empty duffle bag, so I was on deck quickly and the shuttle got away while she could still move without hitting something.

The officer of the deck was sore at me for coming on board in the dark with no notice. After a hearty handshake, he got to his business of chewing me out. I was told there were no officer's quarters available, but I was free to hunt for a bunk below deck. The Athene is another large attack transport, with capacity for 1500 officers and enlisted. Walking past at least two half-full state rooms I made my way below to meet my new ship mates.

Soldiers of the 98th Infantry Division are younger on average than the other units, and those guys are barely in their twenties. The 98th is all new, made up of recent enlistees and draftees. It was seeded with a few old salts, and those sergeants were hovering over their charges, checking that everything and every man was ready before his unit went in for the first time.

The men on Athene would be the last combat units of the division, which had started ashore on X+4 and already seen some combat. While technically combat reserves, developments on land meant this group would probably be tested right away. Orders to load up were expected in the next day or two, and everyone was on four hour ready notice.

128

I was greeted by the youngsters as something of a celebrity. With no combat stories to share, they tried to make me the interview subject. I insisted that I did want to hear their stories, what they did back home and what brought them here. "An A+ draft card!" yelled one wisecracker from the rear of my small audience. Private David Ruby of Jersey City stepped forward between rows of bunks where men had gathered, at my urging. He used to be a big city bicycle courier. His company begged to keep him on, as "essential war equipment," but the draft board saw it differently once he was of age.

I talked to various men for over an hour, signing a few books and newspapers. One fellow traded his Army fatigue cap for my Navy service cover. Lights out was called and I had no trouble sleeping in a middle bunk, in a hot stagnant corner of the cavernous bunk room.

Restless men were stirring well before dawn, and I got up with them. There was no muster or reveille or inspection for the Army soldiers, but there was coffee to drink and bacon to eat before the mess lines got long. I was out on deck before the first glow of sun light hit clouds in the east. The sky gradually lightened as I took in my first good look at Ariake Bay.

The bay is almost a perfect square, eight to ten miles on a side, set with one corner pointing north. On the northwest side of the square a plain rises up gradually out of the water, only a few dikes and short ridges to obstruct movement inland. The seaward edge opens to the southeast. The northeast and southwest sides of the square are immediately hilly, right from the waters' edge, with a line of 2000 foot high peaks rising up impatiently in the southwest.

An occasional dull thud or distant crack sounded out from the front lines on land. I was standing under a lashed assault boat to stay out of steady rain, two cups of coffee in me, when the sea all around erupted with gun fire.

Radar directed five inch guns were quickly elevated from shore support positions to fire at aircraft somewhere in the dark rain clouds. I saw scattered flashes of light from land where anti-aircraft batteries had been set up. They must have been firing blindly, following whatever the Navy guns were doing.[‡]

Sailors on the Athene ran all directions toward battle stations. Soldiers moved down into the holds, where they were instructed to wait out any attack. I ran, field glasses in hand, toward any ladder I could find that took me up higher for a better sightseeing location.

I got to my best vantage point, forward and several decks up on the superstructure, just as the medium anti-aircraft pieces across the invasion fleet came alive. All guns were firing to the northwest, over land. Whatever the threat was, it was coming from the interior of the island. In my binoculars I could just make out flaming planes falling out of the sky, one and two at a time. A few flew down out of the clouds under power, still over land – over our lines. Pulling up and turning clumsily, surprised at the lack of water and naval targets, each was chewed up by ground fire shortly after coming into view.

Ships in the fleet began to slew their AA batteries different directions, as the radar targets came almost directly overhead. Some guns were at maximum elevation before the first live planes came diving out of the sky. Just as those planes came diving, more planes, slow and low flying, were spotted coming out over land at tree top. Patrolling Navy fighters, helpless to intercept the cloud-covered waves, shot out to intercept those low flying bogies while they had a chance.

Planes diving out of the clouds had a short window in time to find a target. They had no fighter escorts, all were suicide bombers. Most were probably inexperienced pilots flying old planes, but there were hundreds of them, and they were right on top of the fleet.

Kamikazes came down so thick that for a time it looked more like part of the weather than a contrivance of man. American gunners kept up a furious pace of firing. The hardest part of their job was choosing which target to work on, out of so many deadly

---

[‡] [Editor's note, 2015: Tuttle was probably wrong here. Compact land-based anti-air and even counter-battery radar was available to the Army units. – sdm]

130

options. Airplane wreckage and small oil slicks littered half the bay before the first of the suicide planes found success.

I watched myself as the destroyer USS Kidd was hit twice. The old cruiser USS Chester took three impacts amidships and was still burning at noon when she was abandoned. But the focus of the onslaught was clearly the transports. Most of the troops were already ashore, but our heavy support equipment was largely still waiting on the water. In close sequence I saw a heavily laden cargo ship and two tank landing ships next to her put down with multiple impacts from one well-disciplined formation of suicide planes. Behind them the tanker USS Kishwaukee, loaded with aviation fuel, lit up the eastern sky brighter than the sun after just one near vertical impact drove straight through the ship, flooding the sea with burning fuel.

After an intense few dozen minutes, the assault from above and over land was down to a few stragglers, aircraft which got up late or got lost. One at a time they were easy prey for fighters and Navy guns. Then an alert went out about more planes coming from land to the northeast. Practically out of the ground around Takahata-yama another thirty-some planes launched toward the rear of our fleet.

My first clue to this was the sound of guns behind my ship. I ran to a railing further back and got my field glasses up to see tiny shapes approaching our big ships on the horizon. The tiny shapes were old float planes and even some fabric biplanes. They had less than two miles to close on the nearest large American ships, whose destroyer escorts had cheated west during the earlier assault.

One at a time I watched the tiny shapes fall from view, splashed by defensive gunfire from the big shapes. The race was on to see how many were splashed before the big and small shapes met. A new sound from above, a screech, wail, and furious rumble all at once, made me look up again. A unique shape came out from the clouds, two miles due north of the ships inside Ariake Bay.

It was a small aircraft, with no propeller but a flaming jet bursting continuously out from the back – a rocket-propelled suicide plane. The sound of it was as if the air itself was crying out in agony at being torn through by this cutting flame. A few guns got rounds near the plane, just as the rocket motor exhausted its fuel, but most were behind the wickedly fast craft. While the small rocket planes look nimble, they maneuver sluggishly and this one made a terrific splash not within 200 yards of any ship.

I turned back out toward the mouth of the bay, just in time to see another *oka* suicide rocket splash harmlessly into the open sea between us and the support fleet outside the bay. By now the slower planes were into the fleet. By dumb luck, the first ships they found were close together, the tanker USS Chiwawa and the escort carrier it had been servicing, the USS Windham Bay. The small carrier was besieged by suicide pilots, no doubt joyful that they could go out taking down what they thought an American capital ship. Both ships went down fighting, but they are down for good.

A final few *oka* broke through the clouds as the last land based *kamikazes* finished their runs, together closing in on their final fates. Most of each found that fate in feckless open water, but two prop planes and one rocket plane came together almost at the same time, joining fates with the USS Hydrus. I had begged off of staying on the Hydrus just last night. Her crew and complement, including the command of the 43rd Infantry Division, did not have that choice.

Our ship had rescue boats in the water before the attack was even over, as did most others. I spent the rest of the afternoon gathering reliable information about the attack, picking it out from rampant rumors which ran from Japanese frogmen boarding American carriers to a secret Japanese fleet of new battleships simultaneously blasting the British fleet to the west near Formosa.

No one can account for the large number of *kamikaze* planes that came from somewhere, or everywhere, on land. Long range Army fighters had been above the clouds and did intercept the *oka* carrying bombers early in the attack. But those bombers were escorted by the latest Japanese Army fighter planes with the best pilots we've seen in years[§]. Our Mustangs were kept busy by the fighters for a long time. They scored some kills, but many

---

[§] It was pointed out to me that once Japan gave up training new pilots, it freed up all her instructors to join the fight, with their personal aircraft. Veterans of all of Japan's years of conquest were then in the air again.

Japanese bombers got into the clouds to hide, waiting for the appointed time to release the human-guided rockets, however bad their blind navigation would be.

I got what I could in the way of a clear picture from sailors in the radio room. The other fleets around Kyushu were also hit this morning, with a variety of 'special' weapons. The coordination was superior to anything the Japanese have pulled off since 1942. The radio men heard next to no traffic about it, but of course here on the Japanese main land they can readily communicate by land line and courier.

Late yesterday spotter planes saw explosions in the water, far to the north, near the bays that make up much of northwest Kyushu. We mined all the straights coming out of those bays, so the explosions were chalked up to our mines doing their job.

The easiest way to eliminate a mine is to run a ship into it. The ship may be lost, but the mine is also gone. The Japanese have a multi-thousand-year seafaring tradition. They have many thousand old ships and barges sitting around. It seems those old ships were put to use in deliberate mine clearing.

In dreadful weather, behind their sacrificial screen of mine-clearing barges, a flotilla of small boats moved out from some parts of Nagasaki prefecture. We think they must have been refueled at sea by some larger ship, a submarine perhaps, to make it all the way south to our fleet off Kushikino. Pushing through choppy waves in the dark, many must have been lost. We don't know how many started. We know that at least twenty got past the destroyer screen and five of them found targets in the pre-dawn light.

The hospital ship USS Comfort is gone, among the first hit. A *shinyo* hit her amidships, opposite the side where a *kamikaze* had slammed into the ship at Okinawa. The small boat's charge ripped open a hole well below the water line, dooming the ship to a slow sinking. A nearly empty transport moved back to assist the Comfort and shield her from further attack, which was clearly necessary. That transport took two more impacts, one may have been from a small suicide submarine, and wound up sinking faster than the Comfort.

Many of the able bodied had time to get off the Comfort, but she was laden with wounded and staff who would take great personal risk to try saving their patients. I'm told the Comfort also took a full third of our refrigerated whole blood supply with her. Marines fighting on land will have no blood for their injured but for what modest quantities can be rushed over.

The fleet off Kushikino also got attention from the same *kamikaze* mob that attacked Ariake Bay. Those planes came out of the clouds with farther to go over U.S.-held land and had no laden transports for immediate targets. Still they made their mark. Another of those unladen transports was sunk in shallow water, where it will impede traffic to the beach. A diesel tanker lost her load, and her life, into a sea of fire almost as big as the fireball I saw. The biggest fireworks came when the ammunition ship USS Firedrake, turning madly to dodge diving planes, was hit anyway and ran into one of her escorts. It is not expected that more than twenty survivors will be found between the Firedrake and the destroyer USS Orleck that was next to her when several tons of ordnance lit off in one giant eruption.

Only a token number of *kamikazes* attacked the fleet off Miyazaki. None of them found a target. That fleet did have a substantial problem with suicide attack boats. The southeastern shore of Kyushu is a rugged collection of steep ravines that greet the sea with a multitude of small and large river mouths. It was expected that ground troops would need heavy fire support when the time came to fight through the ravines, and it was ideal territory to hide small attack boats and midget submarines. The U.S. Navy placed warships along that coast just for those contingencies. A bit south of the invasion fleet was a stout line of destroyers, with the new heavy cruiser USS Guam.

The Guam's 12" guns can pulverize shore targets, including suspected boat hiding spots, and she was doing that for the last week. This morning the surviving boats came out to get revenge, rushing past American patrol boats close to shore with a few losses. They had a much shorter trip than the boats from Nagasaki. Our lead destroyers said they came out from the shore in well-ordered close waves. The destroyers fired as quickly as their guns could come down from airplane hunting, but the boats were fast. Half of the first wave bounced over the chop clean past the lead destroyers, and were mixed in among them. A small periscope was spotted in the mix more than once. Two destroyers took single hits, but like most combat ships they controlled the damage and stayed in the fight. The Guam however took more than she could control. Three *shinyo* exploded close to her port side, making significant holes in her armor, and a more serious hole was opened to starboard by an opportunistic torpedo. She stayed level and took two hours to sink. Most of the crew got off, but there was no saving their ship.

I have only mentioned the large ships lost which I got names for. There were others. Many more ships took non-fatal hits, and they will be out of action for some time. The fleet has taken a beating far beyond anything in living memory, perhaps back to the Spanish armada of the 16th century[**]. All told, just today we have lost for ever at least: thirteen large and nine small transports, four tankers, one hospital ship, four destroyers, one cruiser, one escort carrier, one heavy cruiser, and tens of smaller ships. The search for survivors will continue at first light, but the final body count is sure to be well into the thousands.

With the loss of ammunition, blood, fuel, fire support, heavy equipment, and transportation, the impact will be felt by troops on land very quickly. The 98th Division is immediately without much of its heavy equipment, and the 43rd is headless.

Japanese forces on land facing Ariake took advantage of the suicide attacks, either as planned or opportunistically. A text book attack drove parts of the American 43rd and 98th divisions back a quarter mile or more. Jap artillery, infantry, and even tanks – moving around in the open under heavy cloud cover – worked together to push through temporary U.S. field fortifications. Losses were heavy on both sides, but the Japanese won the ground.

Late yesterday a small convoy of empty assault ships drew off, heading south. They had delivered some of the earliest waves of soldiers and equipment onto Kyushu. Now, having been cleaned out of anything useful, they are going back to the Philippines. There are reserves of some number ready for us there if we need

---

[**] I looked it up later. By any count, American naval losses at Kyushu had well surpassed what the Spanish Navy lost in 1588.

them on Kyushu. There were no spare transport ships for them, and now there are even fewer.

The Navy told me at the outset that shipping is the critical constraint to everything here. Much of it is still tied up bringing men and equipment across the Atlantic from Europe, or is still loading on the other side of the Pacific. We had only enough room in the holds of every ship in the western Pacific to move what we just did at one time onto Kyushu[††]. Storms and suicide attacks have put a big dent in that number of ships. Things will clear up once new and redeployed divisions come over on their own troop transports. The Navy has plenty of ships, just not here.

November 22, 1945 : X+7 — Ariake shore

Rescue parties scoured the bay starting at dawn. My ship did not put out any rescue boats. Today the young men aboard went ashore into combat for the first time. Most of the fellows I bunked with are in one platoon of Able Company, Third Battalion, 391st Infantry Regiment, part of the new 98th Division. I stayed with the platoon as nannying veteran sergeants double checked their gear and gave final quiet encouragements.

Out on deck the platoon was addressed by its commander, 2nd Lieutenant Buck Cooper, who was as green as any of the draftees he commanded. "Once the boats are away, keep your head down and focus on your objective. The boats will land together. You will form up into three squad columns. You will advance two hundred and twenty meters to the second dike." He pointed stiffly at a point on his map that everyone had already seen ten times. "Stick with your sergeants, keep together, and wait for instructions once we get to the dike."

[††] Most soldiers didn't know it, but they were supposed to have much more heavy equipment, including new tanks and armored transports. Transport tonnage had to be trimmed every time cargo ships were hit or storm damaged. The big heavy stuff was an obvious target for the planners.

At first light I went to load the boats with 'my' new platoon, but the eager young looey‡‡ stopped me, "You need to find another ride, old man, this unit has a job to do and we'll be moving fast." I put on my new Army hat, pulled it down snug, and slipped in with the soldiers of the other boat for his platoon.

The 391st Regiment was to land this morning and move right through the 390th, relieving them on the front lines next to the 389th Regiment. They were not expected to push forward, just hold the line, in the center of the bay. To the right of the 98th Division was the 43rd Division, which had been fighting hard on the right end of the beach and into the mountains north of the bay.

The Americal Division wound up split, part of it pushing past the 43rd to quiet Japanese artillery in the hills northeast of the bay, the other part holding down the far left end of the beach. The 1st Cavalry Division was working hard to get into the taller mountains southwest of the bay, and they pretty well had the first line of major peaks under control.

After a week of fighting, all the units which had been in it from the start were pretty well stalled, with enough manpower to hold a line but not to make a serious offensive. Our forward units ended yesterday as little as four miles inland from the beach, after falling back late in the afternoon. That's a thin margin to be building facilities on the beach (of course the engineers were anyway). While the mess in the bay was still being cleaned up, we were trying to get the last combat units and first reinforcements in quickly, before the Japanese could regroup.

But the Japanese had already chosen yesterday to move in fresh troops, under cover of lousy weather, and set up for a counterattack. Before dawn our lines were hit with a rolling artillery barrage, of every caliber from half ton shells to small mortars. After first light came waves of charging infantry, supported by tanks rolling across the open roads of the plain which slopes into Ariake Bay.

I heard about all this later, as troops heading in this morning were not told. The boats for our platoon motored in at a

---

‡‡ "Looey" is a term of endearment for lieutenants, especially new 2nd lieutenants who don't know a damned thing.

relaxed pace, not being on a D-day-style time table. We went in through a light rain, but the water was calm. So when our boat was rocked everyone got up to look. A destroyer escort, the USS Robert W. Copeland, pushed by us at twenty-something knots. Quickly overtaking her were the fast destroyers USS Heerman and John C. Butler.

Our small boats recovered their easy stance as we watched the destroyers cut ahead. They pushed close by other rows of landing craft, sending each group bobbing and turning for a long moment. The three destroyers slowed only when they must have been inches from running aground. Each turned almost parallel to the beach and took under two minutes before starting to fire five inch shells, at a curiously low angle.

Soon our view of the gun ships was obstructed by other landing craft, then by larger landing ships already at the beach. Next we hit sand and our boat's ramp came down in a foot of water. I lingered back while the requested columns formed up and started to move forward. I waded out of the boat and caught up with the right column when they all stopped. We were standing in ankle deep mud, on a flat that was probably flooded with salt water on a regular basis.

Lieutenant Cooper was standing up, front and center, looking at his map. Everyone else crouched down and scanned the land around us. It was a long mud flat, no first dike, no second dike, no dikes at all. A quarter mile ahead a few smashed buildings could be seen among rows of scorched brush and small trees. It looked like the U.S. Navy had been here, but not like where we were supposed to be. Three artillery shells landed in close succession about 500 yards to our left.

I slogged up to the lieutenant, re-introduced myself, and took over holding the map for his sergeant. Stammering angrily, but complying, he handed the platoon sergeant his compass. The sergeant and I took bearings on three distant peaks, drew lines on the map, and the sergeant pointed our location to Lieutenant Cooper. (Sergeant Mitchell Zenesky had found his way through woods in western Massachusetts many times.)

We were supposed to land just to the left of a medium size river mouth near the town of Hishida. We had instead been put just to the left of an identical medium size river mouth near an identical town about two miles northeast of Hishida. Since both towns were recently serviced by said U.S. Navy, it was unlikely that any bridges remained over either river. There was nothing to do but move inland, or stay there and wait for a Japanese artillery pattern to sweep the beach.

After some discussion among the sergeants, the platoon moved up into the deserted coastal town. Bits of abandoned American equipment, some obviously damaged, some looking like the owner was coming back any minute, littered the gravel streets, but the town sheltered no people. Our pace was quickened when one very large shell ripped through the remaining upper floor of a formerly grand two story masonry building, exploding just left of where we had been two minutes before.

We continued through the town until it tapered into a single dirt road leading uphill due north toward a wide steep ridge. Soon we saw a cluster of intact buildings and instinctively went for them. There we finally found elements of the 98th Division, sheltering in buildings under the near face of the ridge.

Lieutenant Cooper didn't complain when I followed him and his sergeant to find the HQ for which ever unit was there. It was our sister company in the 389th Regiment. Their Captain Charles Harrison, of New Orleans, Louisiana, said it was good to see us. His modest Cajun drawl was welcoming.

"We were holding the line with rifles and mortars. I was told to expect no heavy artillery support, and to get in line to request armor." I told him about the loaded LSTs that went down in the bay yesterday. "Well that explains it. Still, we're holding, or we were last I saw. My company came back here to get a rest while our reserve unit took over. So, what are y'all doing here?"

Lieutenant Cooper explained in schoolbook terms about variable force vectors and combat adaptability and was interrupted by the captain, "So, ya got lost! Well welcome to the party in any case. I suppose you want to find the rest of your unit. I'll tell you what I know, and you can grab extra ammo here before you move out."

As the officers talked, runners went to grab boxes of machine gun ammo and rifle clips which were passed on with a quiet "good luck." Conversation was interrupted several times by low flying aircraft, each time a single Navy fighter-bomber, flying low under the persistent clouds.

We got directions to head roughly west on a local road. It was covered by a line of hills to the right, out of enemy view, until the point where we should meet our own division. For the next hour we marched, still under assault packs, until nearing the end of the last protective ridge.

We faced a broad shallow valley. Nothing moved in the valley, except the occasional cloud of dirt kicked up by an exploding artillery shell. Across the valley I could make out American soldiers and trucks, moving back southwest along the base of the hill which defined the valley between us. Vehicles had struggled to move over the soaked earth, more than one was abandoned in axle-deep mud. An occasional heavy shell streaked from left to right, probably from our Navy gun ships. Smaller rounds moving from right to left, from Japanese cannon and mortars, could not be seen until they exploded.

Lieutenant Cooper wanted a better look. He took a sergeant a ways up the hill next to us to get a better view to the north. He stood up tall at the crest, pointing and talking while looking through his binoculars. One minute after that the earth shook all around us, trying to swallow the entire platoon. Veterans instinctively threw themselves against the adjacent slope. Sergeants and corporals screamed at their charges to follow suit and get cover behind the hill.

The violence of heavy exploding shells defies description in terms any adult knows. The whole earth, the fundament upon which all our plans begin, is ripped apart and shot in all directions. To understand when something one has always relied on to suddenly be gone, one must try to remember the helpless fright of a small child. Almost anything can be terrifying to a person who hasn't yet learned about the supposed permanence of the world around him.

The large artillery that terrorized us thankfully diminished quickly, but soon after it high trajectory mortar rounds fell close

140

behind the hillside. We gathered up into a decent line and crawled up the ridge line toward the top, but not exposing ourselves like the looey, who was still curled up in a ball near the crest.

A quick roll call showed we were short seven men out of 58, including one squad sergeant. A "volunteer" was tasked with crawling down to check for injured men that could be dragged to safety. There were none. Among the ambulatory were several with severe cuts or embedded shrapnel. Our two corpsmen got to work on them, but there was no further support after what they could offer. No one else knew we were there. We were on a small nameless hill behind and between the mating edges of two regiments' front lines.

Correction, the enemy knew we were there. Every few minutes for the next two hours a mortar round exploded a short distance behind us. Someone was keeping tabs on us, even as they put continuous pressure on the main lines. Frequent bursts of distinctive American machine gun fire could be heard to left and right, even as we saw groups of soldiers pulling back across the valley to our left. The lieutenant risked a peek over the hill a couple times to see the same thing over our hill to the right. American forces were pulling back, in good order it seemed, but still backwards.

I took a turn next to the lieutenant, sticking my head up in front of a small bush he hadn't thought to use as a back drop instead of the bright gray sky. The long hills to right and left of us were split by a half mile wide gap, through which a keen eye could see Japanese units moving.

Jap tanks and trucks littered the landscape. Some were intact, just stuck in the mud and abandoned. Others were burned out on or just off one of the narrow elevated roads that bisected numerous farm fields. A mile of flat farm land ran out beyond the gap, stopping abruptly at a wall of small hills, which fronted more walls of small hills, which repeated into the mist. In those hills the Japanese must have gathered waiting to spring a large counter attack under clouds that would deter our planes. It was all the better for them that the day came when we had advanced right to those hills. They engaged the lead American units at close range and kept contact as the Americans pulled back.

The lieutenant decided that we were stuck where we were, at least until daybreak. Sergeant Zenesky said that we should move back at night, but Lieutenant Cooper stood firm. I took it upon myself to hike down to where our dead lay. I borrowed a pack shovel from a fellow who wouldn't be needing it, and helped PFC John Grandfield dig a foxhole for the both of us. I didn't mention to anyone that I also picked up a .45 pistol and tucked it into my belt.

We spent the rest of the afternoon huddled under ponchos from light rain that had never quite stopped after the storm yesterday. There wasn't much to see but the occasional lone attack plane flying under the clouds. More than once during the day a small group of *kamikaze* planes came down out of the clouds. One larger group had an American fighter pilot close behind chewing them up one at a time until he ran out of ammo. We don't know how many got through or how much damage they did.

November 23, 1945 : X+8 — inland from Ariake Bay

Last night our three squads technically took turns being on watch. I don't think anyone slept. The Navy put up star shells overhead continuously and sent explosive shells farther inland sporadically. By the sound of it, to the left and right ahead of us, the Japs continued to press into American lines during the night.

Japanese artillery, some of it very large, hit American positions with painful accuracy. It was always a small pattern from each gun to one location, never more than three or four rounds. The vets with us say it's because they move the guns each time, between different pre-sighted positions or back into a cave, before we can register good counter-battery fire on it. Ample return fire was issued by American guns in any case.[§§]

I didn't dare stick my head up over the crest of our hillside home, for fear of being highlighted in the high contrast light of a

---

[§§] [Editor's note, 2015: Secret at the time, early anti-artillery radar systems were in use on Kyushu and may have located some of the Japanese guns or mortars in fewer shots than they could expect. - sdm]

142

falling star shell or large gun blast. The battle soon came into view anyway. The ridge across from us to the west was entirely U.S. Army owned when we got here. Through the night flashes of light from rifle muzzles could be seen at various points on the near slope. After some hours more rifle flashes came into view along a line farther to the right.

At times a machine gun would briefly paint the hill side with streaming tracers, in either direction. But those bursts did not come from one place for very long, as the show attracted robust return fire. We had a few tanks in the valley by then, and when they could find a target they let loose three or four at a time. Still. the whole light show was slowly moving to the south – the front line on that side was moving behind us!

I found the lieutenant at the top of our hill, looking out from the shrub-sheltered spot I had used earlier in the day. Lieutenant Cooper it turned out was from Columbus, Ohio. He worked as what they call an "adjunct lecturer" at a college there. I wondered aloud how the other units were holding up in front of us to the east, but he was already on it. He had sent two guys on a scouting mission, to swing around our hill on the east and ask directly.

After an interminable wait, in which each rifle crack and shell blast seemed to get closer to our blind position, we heard that night's password being yelled in the dark. "Mellow fellow!" came the call, closer and closer as our scouts closed with us. The pair ran right up into the middle of our camp without stopping. "Sarge, we got to move! Like, now!"

Private Joe LaFleur caught his breath as Sergeant Zenesky asked the other man, Corporal Max Jacobs, what was going on. "That unit up ahead of us, it's part of the 389th like we thought, but it won't be there but another two hours tops."

The lieutenant had come down by then. Prompted for details, Corporal Jacobs explained, "They were advancing out in the open in front of that hill when the Japanese attack came yesterday morning. They got shot up with all sorts of crap, artillery and mortars, and started pulling back. Then the Jap infantry came…"

"While they were taking back the injured and dead!" Private LaFleur interrupted. Lots of our guys got left out there, a lot of medics too. The Japs brought tanks, lots of them. They couldn't even drop mortars on them with our guys so close." Corporal Jacobs quieted his companion with the back of a hand on his chest.

"At any rate, they're pretty well toasted up there, and they're pulling back." Corporal Jacobs turned to point at a road to the east of us. "Before dawn, a bunch of trucks will come up to take back the men and whatever gear they can save. A rolling barrage, courtesy of the Navy, will cover as they pack up and load out." He turned back to look over our temporary home. With a wry grin he added, "It's a good thing we went over there. They might have blasted this hill too to cover their flank."

With that news, we made quick work of packing up. Stretchers were improvised of boot laces, sticks, and ponchos to move our dead and injured. It was three miles back to where we were supposed to be in the first place, just in from the beach.

First light showed that the day would start with a clear sky. This would allow American air power to seriously flex its muscles for the first time in many days. The Japanese must have decided this would be their last chance to push their big counter-attack through[*]. My unit had just started marching south under a pale pre-dawn glow when they Japanese started their own rolling barrage. Their guns were unrestricted in volume of fire this time. Some of the guns put out smoke, and the Americans soon found out why.

Out of the smoke from every highway, local road, and dirt track for a ten mile wide span Japanese tanks rushed forward in groups of ten or more. They were followed closely by trucks with infantry and mounted machine guns. American defensive lines were badly jumbled after a string of daytime ambushes, nighttime actions, and retreats. The long hill I was watching overnight was encircled, its remaining garrison brutalized. The tail end of the

---

[*] Much of this section was assembled in later days from interviews too numerous to detail.

evacuation column we learned about early in the morning was caught and pulverized.

American commanders had gathered a good number of tanks in the valley near our overnight camp, for our own counter-counter attack. But they were hit hard by the Japanese morning barrage and could not re-organize to meet the first Jap thrusts.

Farther to the east, the 43rd Division thought it had finally won a good fighting line in the mountains north of Ariake Bay. The division was exhausted and resting, not ready for more action until reinforcements came in. But as the beach front units fell back, the 43rd found itself hit hard in the flank where it had no sound defenses. Japanese mountain units it had been facing joined in the attack and the division was hanging on to its hard won hills by fingernails.

Southwest of Ariake Bay the 1st Cavalry Division had been making steady, if expensive, progress pushing up into those taller mountains. As the beach head behind them was pinched, they had to pull back, turn around, and prepare to fight in a new direction.

The Japanese offensive did not play out on a broad front. By design or by circumstance it formed into a focused thrust toward the center of Ariake Bay. Their mechanized forces moved steadily down parallel roads toward the water, helped by the work of our engineers who had cleared and patched roads and replaced many blown bridges heading inland.

This was no frenzied banzai charge. The Japanese moved quickly, but fought from cover and applied combined arms to reduce our hasty defenses and keep American units moving backward. It was all by the book, right from the latest war college papers[*].

Progress for the Japanese was terribly expensive. Their vehicles were easy prey to the growing variety of field guns packed by U.S. infantry. Long range naval fire was not an option for us with the Japs intermingled among American forces, but the destroyers which had come in close yesterday had positioned themselves to put direct line-of-sight fire on key roads and passes.

---

[*] I had a lot of time to read on Okinawa.

In one surreal scene a Japanese tank commander brought his team of four tanks into a side-by-side line just a mile from the beach. They began to fire on the destroyer John C. Butler. The destroyer lined up her 5 inch guns and dueled mano a mano with the armored squadron. The destroyer won.

The latest *kamikazes* had only a limited impact, but one of their successes was to hit the destroyer Heerman, just once but low near the water line. The Heerman, no stranger to a tough fight, beached herself to keep from sinking and kept up fire support against targets on land.

American planes raged through the sky all day. Many of them went up with oversize rockets built for crushing hardened concrete bunkers deep under many feet of rock. I saw first hand one of those giant rockets slam into a Jap tank, practically re-smelting the entire steel monster, redistributing its constituent elements back into the earth from which they came.

Troops on Japanese trucks soon learned they were also priority targets. They quickly dismounted, by choice or by explosive force. The Japanese attack eventually slowed to a foot soldier's pace. They kept coming though, merely tightening the focus of the attack. They were driving right through the middle of the 98th Division, the least experienced large unit in the invasion, whether they knew it or not.

My particular platoon of the 98th eventually made it back to a low long hill one mile in from the beach, where the 391st Regiment had regrouped to set up a fighting line. The acting commander, by that point a Lieutenant Colonel, had thought we were long lost and had set up the line without us. We were sent all the way back to the short dikes by the beach – right where we were supposed to have landed – to be the true last line of defense.

Our Lieutenant Cooper, having learned much in the previous 36 hours, quietly gave instructions to get our machine guns set up and assigned rifle teams to support them in sectors. The platoon faced open farm plots, where fresh water crops were grown between the dikes, and had excellent fields of fire over the barren wintertime plots.

Aircraft which had been flying everywhere overhead became more focused over our area. By early afternoon we had an air show just for us. Single engine Navy fighters and twin engine Army bombers flew in a parade from over the bay, past us on the left and on to targets directly inland.

We could follow the battle just by timing the passage of aircraft and the explosions of their bombs or rockets. The interval between the two got smaller and smaller, until it was under a minute. Then the planes stopped coming.

Motion was seen in the brush across one of our assigned farm fields and a machine gun on that side let loose a burst of five or six rounds before a sergeant yanked the gunner back. "Mellow Mellow, or whatever the hell! It's us!!" the brush called out. A mixed group of about two dozen dirty American G.I.s emerged and hustled over the flat under an all clear sign from that squad sergeant.

With just a few words shared about the situation, they settled in with us, some taking firing positions, others collapsing into shapeless heaps of whatever makes up an exhausted American soldier. The next disturbance in the brush would not get a warning shot.

I am sure that there were deafening sounds of war from all around us, but as we waited for the enemy to approach, focused intently on the open space immediately in front of us, I can't recall anything but cemetery-grade silence. That silence deteriorated slowly. A cyclic mechanical squeak grew louder over the span of a minute and was joined by the grumble of a badly muffled engine. A Japanese tank, surely one of the last, breached the tree line and rolled down off the road into a soft farm field just 150 yards west of my platoon's left end.

We had no heavy weapons to deal with the tank but had plenty of softer targets in short order. First walking, then running, thirty or forty Japanese infantry came out from the brush into our field. Other groups of men made better speed running down elevated roads that broke up the fields every quarter mile. Riflemen and machine gunners from our side fired wildly into the approaching infantry. They were still green and our non-coms had their hands full keeping young machine gunners from melting their barrels.

There were no friendly troops to our left for a good gap, farther than I could see. We were it. The tank on that side noticed the same thing and sized up my platoon as a target. It turned toward our flank, churning up dark brown earth as its gun came around toward one of our newly dug gun pits. Japanese soldiers crowded behind the tank, covered from our rifle fire.

I ducked into my hole, as did everyone around me, expecting the tank to fire. A loud noise came from that direction, but it was not the sound of a Jap tank gun. I popped up to get a look, just in time to see a second round from the USS Heerman crush the far side of the Japanese tracked gun. The tank was a flaming ruin, and its escorting infantry took cover behind the next raised road behind the tank.

In the distance I saw tracers from another distant American machine gun, firing back toward us. The Japanese had found a place of no refuge, so they ran, in all directions. Our rifle men picked off many of them on the run. One young Japanese solider chose to run directly toward the water. He had only fifty yards left to go. No one fired at him, maybe because it would mean firing straight down our own lines, maybe because he was a singular poetic sight.

The young son of Yamato, just 200 yards from me, was certainly a teenager. His plain uniform was ill-fitting but new and barely dirty. He ran toward the water single-mindedly, oblivious to the presence of hundreds of enemy soldiers. Lieutenant Cooper jumped out of our hole and ran toward him, pistol in hand.

The Japanese soldier reached the waters' edge and dropped to his knees. He reached out with his right hand into the water, catching his weight on his rifle, butt in the sand, with his left. He closed his hand upon a fist full of Ariake Bay, that one fist full being all of what he and his comrades had reclaimed for his country and his emperor.

At once the sea reached out and swallowed up the man. Heavy machine gun rounds from the Heerman splashed in front of the loyal soldier in a line of boiling craters which was walked into

148

the shore. The man was obliterated, his body torn to shreds by multiple .50 caliber slugs. The butt half of his rifle was thrown directly at Lieutenant Buck Cooper, hitting him broadside. Our "looey" got a broken arm from the impact and has a souvenir to take back with him to the hospital ship.

November 24, 1945 : X+9 – Ariake shore

It will be said in shorter histories, if they're long enough to mention it at all, that the American Sixth Army "won" the battle of Ariake Bay. I am not sure at this time, just a day after the event (I presume it is over – time will tell!), if that is true. We are still regrouping and counting our losses. We still hold the bay, and we killed or maimed large units of the Japanese army. We also suffered mightily, and we are 8000 miles farther from home than the Japanese. In strategic military terms, our forces and equipment and supplies are all terribly precious, clinically more so than those of the Japanese.

As I write this, parts of the 1st Cavalry Division and the Americal Division are sweeping across the beachhead from southwest and northeast respectively, to 'clean up' any remaining Japanese units and re-secure the lodgment. Our 43rd and 98th divisions are being pulled completely back to the beach. The Americal and 1st Cavalry divisions have had to give up hard won mountain territory to pull back and defend the beach.

Engineers have watched much of their handiwork be undone. For now their only job is to dig graves. Dead Japanese are going into group graves, American soldiers into individual marked sites. It's not the engineers' job to count and compare the two, but they do. The unofficial count shows us putting about the same number of bodies under ground for both sides, over 6000. Intelligence men will have the official count of casualties, which will include the number of injured G.I.s who have been taken out of the fight.

Those intelligence men have had a chance to go through items taken off dead Japs and to interview the few who were captured alive. All or parts of four Japanese divisions were thrown against us, on top of the two divisions that had been defending Ariake Bay in the first place. Two of the new divisions here were long time veterans from fighting in China – how they got here is a question for another day. Also in the mix were two whole tank brigades, independent units which are supposed to have hundreds of vehicles each.

The G-2 men can't tell me just how much of each of those enemy divisions were committed to the attack or how many got away into the hills ahead of us. There's only one sure way to find out, and I'm afraid American curiosity will demand that we push ahead to find out.

Around Ariake Bay there is only the 1st Cavalry Division and the Americal Division to hold almost forty miles of front. Most of the 40th Division, having secured the small islands around Kyushu, is to land here today and tomorrow. It remains to be seen if all the divisions here remain standing, between personnel losses and equipment that was sunk in the bay.

I slept soundly through last night, oblivious to star shells, night fighters, and the occasional bit of Navy gunnery chasing the retreating Japanese. The platoon I was with during the attack wound up camping in the open, right where they ended up. The healthy ones are rotating in as stretcher bearers and on clean-up details. I left them to their duties after mid-morning goodbyes and went for a look around.

I first had my own small chore. I found the local dump for 'spare' equipment, which is mostly the personal gear of dead soldiers. I turned in the pistol that I had borrowed, checking it in with an older sergeant. He looked at my "CORRESPONDENT" patches, down at the gun, then back up at me. "Are you sure you don't want to hang on to this? I won't say a word about it if you do." I assured him that I could get along without it, and there will be plenty of weapons laying around without users should I ever need one again.

Walking northeast along a shore road, I moved over several times for trucks and tractors to push past going the same direction. A mile from where the fight touched the water, more landing craft were unloading soldiers. An LST let new tanks into the sand. The 40th Division was coming ashore at Ariake and none too soon.

150

A bit further north I found the object of interest to all the rushing engineers. Japanese forces had come close enough to the small commercial harbor at the northern tip of the bay to put observed artillery into it. The piers were a mess, and the few heavy cranes it had were wrecked. On my cargo ship ride last summer they explained to me that landing ships are cool, with their drive-off ramps, but to unload high volume supplies from regular cargo holds we need big docks with big cranes. I was looking at the only cargo cranes on this part of the island. Engineers had fixed them up after we landed, never got to use them, and now have more serious damage to deal with.

Moving the other way on the coast road in a steady stream were war-weary soldiers and trucks. One truck was barely half full of tired men. I knew it was full to capacity with stories to tell, so I hitched a ride.

Benches along either side of the bed were occupied by men sitting upright or sideways or variations in between the too. At the front on the right side was the only officer. First Lieutenant (provisional) Manchester B. Watson had his feet up on the bench and was sound asleep, possibly dreaming of his hometown of Greenville, South Carolina. "He ain't slept in five days," Private Johnnie Garrett told me, along the way to mentioning that he and the Lieutenant were from the same town.

On the flatbed floor was a chaotic assortment of equipment, from cases of grenades to post hole diggers. I picked up an ammunition belt that had all of 13 cartridges left in it. Private Garrett explained, "They told us to grab whatever equipment we could and move out on the first truck that came for us, after we carried back injured and dead all morning. Everyone took up exactly one armful of junk, tossed it in, and got on board." Some of the men were asleep sitting up.

Behind us was towed a small artillery piece, an Army 105 mm, I think. I asked around and learned everyone on the truck was with the same infantry platoon. "That's not ours, and we couldn't tell ya where its crew got off to. Nothing but empty crates around it when we found it." Corporal Judson McBrine of Newport, Rhode Island continued, "The driver couldn't stand to leave it there.

Whoever left it took the breech pin with them[*], but otherwise it's in good shape."

For the rest of the trip across Ariake Bay I heard competing stories of ocean fishing from men of the unit. Most of the 43rd Infantry Division was from New England, and anyone who wasn't a commercial fisherman was a keen angler, or at least talked a good game. There were nineteen men on the truck. I asked about the rest of Lieutenant Watson's platoon.

"This is it, the whole thing." The new voice was Staff Sergeant Clifford Blais, who's accent from Providence they tell me is different from the Newport man. I can't tell the difference. "They sent two trucks to bring us back, and said a third was coming. We sent the second away and the third one is probably still looking for someone to carry."

I moved up front with the Sergeant, the ranking non-com on board. We talked quietly as he filled me in on the experience of his unit so far. They were among the first ashore and had been fighting in the hills north of Ariake Bay since the first day.

Their regiment, the 103rd, had no trouble getting to the beach. Other parts of the 43rd Division had to maneuver around shipwrecks in the shallows and took sporadic but accurate heavy fire from hideaways in the hills. The 103rd Regiment rushed on toward its second day objectives right away – up into those hills.

All of this was perfectly predictable to the defenders, so the American charge went right into a trap with multiple rows of teeth. Little American artillery had made it ashore yet, naval support was limited by the angle of the hill slopes to the bay, and air support was limited when anti-aircraft guns became priority targets for the Navy attack planes. The infantry had to knock out positions one at a time with rifles, grenades, and a few bazookas.

Obscured by smoke from bombardment and brush which had survived the bombardment, Japanese positions did not reveal themselves until American troops were at close range. Each one

---

[*] It was normal practice if equipment had to be abandoned to wreck it or take away some key part, so that a gun or tank could not be captured and turned around for use by the enemy.

152

generated casualties that had to be carried back to the beach, as a plan was improvised to regroup and take out the new enemy pit or pillbox or cave.

They kept at it for five days, repeatedly taking out small networks of enemy positions and seizing small objectives, until the last hills with direct view of the American beach were under American boots. A halt was called there, not that it mattered. Sergeant Blais said they were spent. They couldn't take another ant hill, let alone the ever larger mountain peaks in front of them. Word went up and down the line that every other unit was in about the same shape.

In the course of fighting off the large Japanese counter attack of the previous days, they fell back twice, taking many casualties back with them. Fighting was hand-to hand during one early morning charge. Some small units elsewhere in the division were wiped out to a man on the worst day. But other Army units closed up those gaps, recovered the dead, and retreated in some semblance of order. This was a veteran division, and had been for some time.

During it all they had a panoramic view of the large and small *kamikaze* attacks on the fleet. They were powerless to do anything about it, and their guts were kicked out every time a transport or cargo ship took a bad hit. That was their guys, their food, their tanks, and their ammo. They didn't find out until two days after that the entire command of the division was sunk. "We all dug holes a little deeper that night and re-counted what ammo was left."

November 25, 1945 : X+10 − Ariake shore

Yesterday afternoon, not long before dark, we pulled into camp near the southwest corner of Ariake Bay. I went hunting for a communications and intelligence unit, leaving my riding companions to find themselves a spot in camp. Engineers are overwhelmed with damage control and combat support functions. They did not set up an organized camp for all the men who were sent back.

153

On a first-come basis, half of the original assault force of Eleventh Corps has claimed bits of a sprawling agglomeration of small tents and big tents, and lean-tos made against damaged trucks and tanks. Motor transport companies have, out of necessity, marked out a few narrow roads through the farm fields and fallow plain near the shore here.

I found a communications group for the 98th Division set up in a building of the town that used to be north of the jumbled camp. The building only used to be a building, as it had no roof and barely three standing outer walls. A large tent was set up inside the walls, where loose bricks and timber had been pushed aside into piles, on which sat soldiers smoking or eating from cold ration cans. Three men were raising an antenna pole up into one of the two remaining corners of the building, improvising some way to lash it there.

I found the inside of the tent quiet, three young officers laying down or sitting in the far corner, half asleep, waiting on the new antenna. The senior man, Captain Duane Pepple, of Snohomish, Washington, was checking the larger of their two radio sets against a book of settings and frequencies when I sat down across a folding work table from him.

He too had time to kill until they could transmit again. They had little in the way of paper reports to deal with. Division commands were only just coming ashore, and regular staffs would pick up the backlog from the last couple days once they got set up. Since I was up front with small units lately, I had no knowledge of action in other divisions or on the other beach heads. News sheets had come all the way forward with baseball scores from New York and speeches from London, but we knew nothing about the situation two hills over. The Captain caught me up with the bird's eye view.

Around Ariake little could be done while the Japs held hills overlooking the bay. They could spot artillery from bunkers and caves onto green and gray targets with the first-shot accuracy that comes from practicing with a fixed gun. The big Japanese counter-attack came just after we finished working through the hills, but then we had four divisions stretched out all the way around the bay. The 1st Cavalry was in the south, the 43rd in the north, 98th in the middle, and the Americal Division split up to fill gaps. The Jap attack drove right into the thinnest parts of the line. The most badly beat up small units had been pulled back toward the beach, and they were also run over.

The 43rd Division is being pulled out, entirely. Its losses of officers and equipment can't be replenished fast enough to make it worth feeding its idle units until that time comes. Its healthy men will be redistributed to other units, which are thirsty for veteran replacements.

The 1st Cavalry is the one division here to have four regiments, most others switching to three before the war. This may have been a compensation to the division for losing its horses in favor of trucks and scout vehicles. But that compensation is over. The 7th Cavalry Regiment is being split up, too expensive to rebuild while other units are too depleted to function. If it remains an active regiment, it will materialize somewhere back in the States as the regimental colors are presented to a column of new boot camp graduates.

The 40th Division is still being landed, charged with defending the whole middle of the line while everyone else prepares to move back into the mountains around Ariake Bay.

In the west, the Marines did take Kagoshima and Sendai, experiencing tough urban fighting, and attacks by civilians, after a week of slogging through a maze of defended hills. They scarcely hold either city though, as every night and some days heavy artillery from vantage points looking down into the cities hit known key points in each. The 2nd and 3rd Marine divisions hold the Sendai-Kagoshima line, having taken in multiple waves of reinforcements to keep the advance going, ten miles in ten days.

South of Kagoshima the 5th Marine Division has been making painful progress down the five mile wide peninsula. It is a ¾ scale model of southern Okinawa, but there is only one Marine division instead of two Marine and two Army divisions working to clear pits and caves and tunnels which defend each other. All of it is in range of Navy guns, and I don't doubt that it's quite a show when they light up a stubborn hill. Engineers got to work in earnest on an airfield behind the Marines yesterday, sure that it's now out of Jap artillery range. It should boost by half the volume of ground support flights they can run on a good day.

South of the Marines, the 77th and 81st infantry divisions made good progress at first, pushing through open flat land west of Kaimon-dake, which was undefended. The small mountain was expected to be a tough fort and the Navy was almost disappointed at not getting to blast at it. The Army divisions are now coming into hilly territory and finding the going considerably slower and more bloody.

In the east around Miyazaki the story has been mixed. In from the beach is a plain almost ten miles deep. American spotters can observe all of it and direct Navy guns on any part quickly. The Japanese did not try to fortify it. Miyazaki itself was largely deserted, save for bands of scared or angry civilians who did not evacuate with the others. Some of them attacked American soldiers in small groups, to limited direct effect but it makes our soldiers ever more wary.

South of Miyazaki the 25th Division did the tough job of taking hills close to the beach, which overlook American camps. There the Japanese did defend, and it was all the 25th could do to take the first line of mountain ridges before digging in to rest. Miyazaki will become the first developed place we really hold on Kyushu. Its port and airfields will be opened up 'soon.'

Early on the beach head at Miyazaki faced a dress rehearsal of the big counter attack that just finished in Ariake Bay. They figure that parts of "only" two veteran Japanese divisions drove into American lines, supported by about fifty tanks. The attack at Ariake was more than twice as large.

One thing that has everyone surprised is the number of Japanese tanks that have been thrown at us. Intelligence men are optimistic that we've already seen most of what they can muster, but when pressed they have to admit they just don't know for sure. Movement of troops far to the north has been seen by our aircraft when weather permits. When weather does not permit observation, Japanese reinforcements can move without aiding our insight.

Another surprise was the scale of organized attacks from civilian "companies." Yesterday as American units reorganized

156

around Ariake Bay, part of the 40th Infantry Division moved to thicken up our lines to the west, almost into Kanoya. They were pinned down by fire from a mountain to the north and its foothills, then gangs of people came out at them from the city. It was a coordinated attack, and a new terror for the soldiers who've prepared for so long to fight only other uniformed soldiers.

November 26. 1945 : X+11 — east of Kanoya, Kyushu

This morning I made my way across the great American bivouac on Ariake Bay to the west where combat units were still re-securing that part of our lines. Driving rain started early and did not let up all day. The only people moving in camp were those who chose their sites badly and were moving to relatively drier ground. Dry weather the day before had allowed some men to get clothes and bodies washed. Some uniforms were still out on improvised clothes lines and were probably just about dry when the rain started.

A few people had important jobs to do, and jeeps and trucks navigated through and around muddy holes in the narrow unimproved roads. I tried to stay out of their way, not having a particularly important job, nor any particular preference for being splashed with mud.

Along the way I passed a low lying field which had been given over to a vehicle scrap yard. Rolling machines of every variety had been driven or dragged there when it was still dry. They covered several acres, with barely room to walk between the rows. Today young privates in ponchos waded through ankle deep mud with hand tools, including a portable blowtorch, hunting the new relics for usable spare parts.

My own feet were soaked, after I used up my own luck avoiding deep puddles and clenching mud along the road west. I had managed to obtain a good poncho and one pair of dry socks back in camp, but the socks were soaked again already, along with my uniform and courier bag, my only luggage for now.

After a couple hours of miserable slog, I was made to feel better in comparison to the more miserable men I was there to find. Soldiers of the 1st Cavalry Division had found no rest in camp, no change of socks, and rarely even a flat patch of land to lie down on for the last ten days.

I checked in with one battalion CO and got up to the front to see his soldiers. From mortar men in back, machine gunners up from them, and riflemen in fresh dug (and poorly draining) holes on the line, they had stories similar to what I got out of the 43rd

158

Division. The 1st Cavalry Division had been fighting up into steep hills, in repeating lines, for over a week. Then they had to give up much of what they had won. The Japanese rush had caught parts of the division from behind. Its other regiments had to turn around 180 degrees, come down out of the mountains, and fight on the beach again.

From there I walked just across an imaginary line to the domain of the 185th Regiment, of the 40th Infantry Division. The 1st Cav will move back into the hills now that the 40th is here. The 40th just got here and saw action right away moving in to cover the side and rear of the 1st Cav.

I spoke with some of the soldiers about the large attack by civilians. There wasn't much chatter at first, but after the first few fellows started I couldn't get the stories down fast enough.

Probing into the outskirts of Kanoya, keeping close to ready cover should heavy artillery start again, lead units found the trip lever of a trap. Regular Japanese army soldiers opened fire from cover to the north. It wasn't very effective, but it made most of the regiment stop moving and find cover while they could set up a response. Fire from the north stopped and immediately American rifles on the left were engaging with a mob running in from the west. Comments on the action ran from wild to tragic.

"Civilians? That's a laugh. We found Jap Army papers in with them. They were regular units with regular orders, no ifs, ands, or buts." "I watched dames in kimonos get torn up by our rifles, then saw one explode! She had grenades or something under the dress – if it was a she." Other men were closer to the fighting. "We got a lot of 'em, but they just seemed to grow more on the spot. I emptied two clips, clubbed one guy, and knifed another before I took off… Not everybody made it back."

In the end, the American line held, but they say about two hundred more of our men are gone, half of them for good. The burial detail has made room for five hundred Japanese, and they think that may just about do it. Facilities are being assembled to lock up the survivors, pending interrogation to sort out any regular military left among them.

One of the American soldiers I met waited until we were practically alone to talk, near nightfall. Corporal Joe Simpson and his foxhole buddy were finishing their hole, adding touches of home like shooting ports, a grenade pit, and a dirt shelf for extra ammo. I was saying good night to whoever I could before heading back. I almost walked away when I heard Joe say, almost at a whisper, "She was just a kid."

"Who was?" I stopped and turned back toward the hole, ready for a story.

"It was just yesterday, not two days ago when the civvies attacked. We were all still pretty jumpy, I guess. I know I was. My squad drew patrol duty, I was the tail. We had to scout through the next abandoned village to make sure it was still really abandoned."

Corporal Simpson turned to face that direction as he talked. "We got to the center square and sarge said that was enough, so the column made a right turn, meaning to circle back and get out of that creepy place. This girl, a teenager maybe, came out from one of the last standing buildings on the left."

"Joe, it's alright! You don't have to..." his hole mate interrupted.

Joe didn't turn to address his buddy as he cut off the other soldier. "No, no, it's ok. The man came a long way for a story, he's going to get a story." Simpson looked down at nothing and continued. "She started out kinda slow and awkward. Looking back I suppose she was scared and nervous, but so was I. I know I will never forget that face."

"Her face was like a china doll, sitting up on a shelf in my kid's room. I don't know anymore if she ran at us or I ran at her. Her face didn't change at all, with a bayonet in her gut. It was the same damned peaceful perfect stare. A flower... a fucking flower. She had a flower in her hand."

I've made up Corporal Simpson's name, and not given his home town. I had a word with his CO and sent a note to a friend of mine at his local newspaper. Corporal Joe Simpson will have a good man to talk to when he gets back to his good home town.

160

November 27, 1945 : X+12 – Kanoya, Kyushu

It is nearly dark, which in late November means about 5:30 pm local time. Nightfall means little out here, where few people have slept consecutive hours for many days.

This sector of Kyushu, all taken through the Ariake Bay beachhead, has been free from large nighttime infiltration attacks, thankfully. Instead, with most of what we hold still overlooked by rugged heights, we get night time artillery barrages from well sited positions firing on pre-registered targets. Most nights the barrages are spread out harassment, just to keep us awake.

Others have written about the sound of incessant artillery, and how men, especially desperately tired men, can tune it out and get decent sleep in their cozy holes. It seems the Japanese commanders have been keeping up with the literature on the subject. The nighttime artillery focused on American troops and equipment has been just that – focused. The rounds are either spread along the lines, or the obvious places one would want to set up overnight defensive lines from our side of things, or concentrated on an actual cluster of tents or an equipment dump that was observed setting up during the day. The timing is stubbornly inconsistent, but few that I talk to think it's random.

There are always precautions against making light at night which can draw enemy fire. In this position the rules are especially strict. There's no hope of getting a double tent with a blackout lock set up this close to front, let alone a single tent. Everyone is dug down into the earth, as far as they can get into the rocky hillside. I am rushing to get my notes written out before complete darkness overtakes the southeastern face of this mountain.

I am with the 40th Infantry Division, near Kanoya on the first (southern) slope of the multi-ridged mountain they call Onogara-dake. Yesterday our 108th Regiment moved through Kanoya to be the first Americans to touch the precious waters of Kagoshima Bay†. Today the division's other regiments, the 160th

---

† I was reminded later, by my own notes, that the 5th Marine Division took that honor the day before, after vicious street fighting through Kagoshima city.

and 185th, attacked up the first ridge face of Onogara-dake and now hold it. It was not cheap – a steady parade of stretcher bearers still working their way down the hill is ready testament to the price – but there was a prize in this box of explosive Cracker Jacks. The position of one very heavy gun that has been firing on the beach, and everywhere else for a dozen mile radius, was taken and silenced for good.

It was known that some of the Japanese navy cruisers and older battleships have had their gun turrets removed, since for a year now it has been all but impossible for a Japanese capital ship to leave port and succeed at any military purpose. Not that our submarines or bombers or navy gunners care about the purpose – they are attacked and sunk on sight. Several Jap ships have been put down in harbors while already toothless relics. It was supposed that the turrets were melted down to make other more needful things with the steel, but some wondered about the guns.

Major Benjamin Davis of the 160th Regiment staff tells me it was an eight inch gun, they're not sure how old. It's larger than anything the Japanese army lugs around[‡], and dragging it up to its hole in the mountain had to be a mean feat, along with fitting out the hole. The gun could be taken back in out of sight after firing. "We didn't see the cave, which we think was hand dug, until about 200 yards away. It was already abandoned, but a pair of machine guns was left waiting for us to approach and check it out. They had the thing on tracks, with a manual traverse that was slow, but worked. It was right under a natural brow in the hill, with brush around it, some of it drug there recently. The whole thing looked like nothing but a dark spot on the hill, on a sunny day. Oh, they had other shallow painted fake cave entrances scattered around it. One of them we pounded with 155s and rockets for days, just a hundred yards away – for nothing."

The bad news, from the sound of some previous nights' artillery barrages, is that the gun has friends. There are more eight inch diameter projectiles stacked up next to smuggled guns in artificial caves under ancient mountains ahead of us. This one had

---

[‡] I'm informed that the Imperial Japanese Army did have some mobile extra-large howitzers, but they were much shorter than the fixed guns we fought against.

absolutely nothing left around it. There were no leftover rounds. Either the Japs timed out the schedule of firing exactly to the day a US division would overtake the position, or they took what was left back to the next fire-breathing hole in the ground.

November 28, 1945 : X+13 – Kanoya, Kyushu

After a brief stay with the 160th Regiment, which included a 'routine' overnight raid by Japanese soldiers, I came back down. I put in a one-way turn as a stretcher bearer but insisted that I be tasked with a dead soldier. It's big pressure to take an injured man under your arms, who is counting on you to navigate rough trails in bad light and worse weather. I have seen men dropped, and stretcher bearers in tears as they continued on in shame.

I made my way to a dot on the map a little southeast of Kanoya, a small town at the base of steep hills that rise up into taller mountains to the south. I had an appointment.

It was something of a request, from somewhat high up. I was overdue to chat with some top brass, I figured, so I said yes. I got into the 1st Cavalry Division's rear camp by mid morning. I was welcomed with a place at the head of the line for a lukewarm shower, presented with a fresh (Army) uniform, and had lunch with some junior officers who had done the same drill before me. Each of them said the same thing. They had a day or so rotated off the line but were expected to be up front and ready by nightfall tomorrow.

A bit after noon I was directed to division headquarters, in the former town post office and shown to the office of Brigadier General Connor Colt, currently XO of the 1st Cavalry Division. General Colt was on a wired telephone as I came into his otherwise empty office. He motioned for me to take a seat without breaking his sentence.

"I know the Air Corps is nervous about sneak attacks, but that's why they're supposed to bring along security men." He listened for a moment, while smashing his half done cigarette into a brass ashtray with stout fingers, crushing it with much more force than necessary. "You're damn right, we'll get it done! If that's what Corps says needs to be done. But you tell that pinhead flyboy – I'm going to put the division cemetery right between his runways!"

General Colt caught himself about to slam down the handset, set it down easily instead, and stood up. His broad 6'2" frame made the modest Japanese bureaucrat's desk look like a scale model. He reached out his hand and with half a smile welcomed me[§]. His thick black hair did not betray his fifty-something years.

"What you just heard was probably the last 'discussion' about what this division does next. Though I'd hardly call it a discussion. The decision was made in Guam weeks ago, I'm sure." He sat down again and lit another cigarette. "The Air Corps, they want a big air base in Kanoya, sure. They want to be certain the base is secure, I get that. But to make sure, they want us to make it happen, by clearing out every nook and cranny of all the mountains south of here."

I recalled how other air fields, like at Iwo, had been overrun long after combat troops had 'cleared' the area. I asked what was so hard about it, as I pulled out my pad and started taking notes. "When we landed, someone had to push up into these mountains," the general pointed behind him with a fist and thumb, "so the Japs couldn't put spotted fire on to the beach. That job fell to us. Then they put random fire on the beach and we had to drive in even further. Then we got hit from behind (because nobody at Corps knows what they're doing!) and we had to turn around and clear the beach – again."

He leaned forward more, pointing a finger at nothing for emphasis, "Now they've taken away a regiment, told us to reorganize on the fly, and stuck us with a big dirty job. They've always been out to get us! They always said the First was oversize, and top heavy [with senior officers], but this division has had the flexibility to split off units of any size, send them out for every other dirty job, and always got it done." His pointing finger thumped the desk for emphasis of every phrase. I was starting to

---

[§] He also cleared me to repeat the conversation I had overheard.

164

understand why I was invited to this interview, instead of the other way around.

General Colt sat back in his chair, hands folded across his sternum. He paused to draw an easy breath. "We've already broken the back of the resistance here and soaked up troops and artillery rounds that they can't possibly replace. If Jap stragglers ever did manage to hit the airfield, they'd only do it once. They'd be mowed down in the open, damaging a few planes at most." He sat up again and continued gesturing, pointing loosely back toward Kanoya. "We offered to set up a mobile ready response unit, regiment size, who would patrol to defend the base. But no, they insisted on a whole division to lock it up airtight, or we go in and clear it out. Corps sure as hell is not going to leave a division sitting here, so we're going in to take the next however goddamned many mountains."

He leaned forward and thumped the loose stack of maps in front of him. "It took us two weeks and several thousand casualties** to get five miles in. Now there are twenty miles to go." General Colt got up and paced across the small room as he finished his cigarette. "They offered us the 112th and 158th RCTs [off Tanega-shima], to land inside Kagoshima Bay. We can't support them there, but the Navy is supposed to come in and blast the place."

He crushed out the cigarette then apologized for not offering me one. I accepted and lit it as he asked, "So where are you going? What would you like to see next?" I said I'd like to see a warm fireplace and a cold glass of bourbon some time soon. With a hearty chuckle he moved to the far back corner of the room to light a small gasoline heater.

"Sorry, I don't have any ice," he apologized as he reached into a lower desk drawer for a small half empty bottle of young scotch. We shared it without glasses next to the tiny metallic hearth. It was not cold out, but 60 degrees at night is uncomfortable when everything is damp all the time.

** 3,342

I answered his previous question agreeably, to both of us, as his operation was the most interesting thing coming up that I knew about. I would go along. The 1ˢᵗ Cavalry Division probably did deserve some attention. It was just massively realigned, in the field, while absorbing many badly needed replacements, and pushed into a tough assignment on short notice. Pass or fail, it was about to be tested like never before.

Map - South-central Kyushu

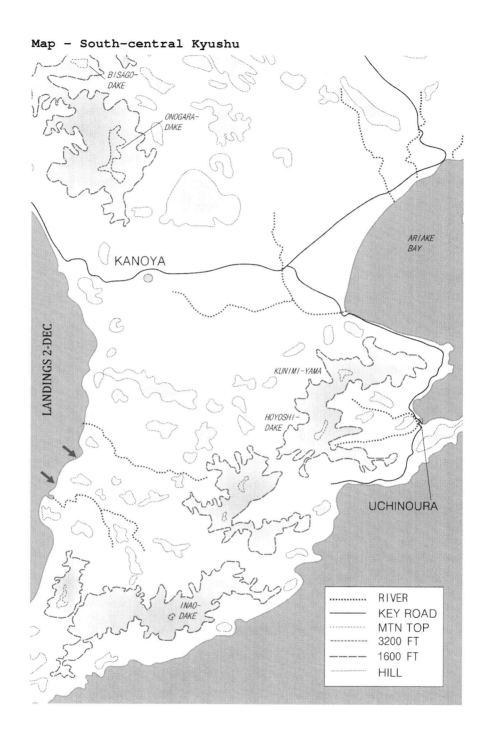

BISAGO-
DAKE

ONOGARA-
DAKE

ARIAKE
BAY

KANOYA

LANDINGS 2-DEC

KUNIMI-YAMA

HOYOSHI-
DAKE

UCHINOURA

INAO-
DAKE

....	RIVER
——	KEY ROAD
....	MTN TOP
- - - -	3200 FT
—— ——	1600 FT
....	HILL

The central southern part of Kyushu is a mountainous peninsula which points acutely out into the East China Sea. It defines the east side of Kagoshima Bay and one shoulder of Ariake Bay. 18 miles wide at the first foothills, it tapers south by southeast 25 miles to a sharp cape which is the southernmost point of Kyushu. Except for a steep east-west pass about halfway through, the peninsula is a continuous sequence of named mountains, joined and divided by long ridges which run in a variety of directions. Small and large rivers cut through every valley. All of them ran high in the rainy season we met on Kyushu.

Yesterday afternoon I was taken by jeep up dirt trails which only a very stubborn driver can make usable by motor vehicles. The 8th Cavalry Regiment took most of the 2500 foot mountain Kunimi-yama and had been camped in spots on and around it preparing for their next move. This morning I went down the east side of the mountain on an even worse trail.

Like all the mountains in the area, it's far more than one single hill. From each peak that gets the name, there are a cascade of smaller peaks, divided by uneven valleys. The land is practically impassable. Beyond a few logging roads, there is no organized access. So American soldiers have been practicing with ropes and climbing gear, and engineers are ready to tie up cable hoists right behind them.

Through this land, the 8th was to move forward, roughly southward, in a continuous line, gather up in the next long broken valley, and attack up the next set of slopes. The east end of that valley holds the small fishing city of Uchinoura, which sits in a small bay at the southern tip of Ariake Bay. I was to ride with an armored column that would take the coastal road around the mountain, ride into town, grab the one good river bridge there, and secure it so our infantry could be supported into the next ridge line.

Our side of the operation could expect good naval support from the small bay. Farther inland the infantry would rely on close air support. Clear skies afforded unrestricted air operations, for once.

When I first arrived I was delighted to find the British reporter Major Peter Lawless, my tent mate on Okinawa, with us at the top of the mountain. We caught up on what each had seen during the 'big show.' He was a late comer, having only got a cast off his arm two weeks ago, after getting it broken pitching in to rebuild on Okinawa after the last storm. He went into the eastern beach head at Miyazaki on about the fourth day.

Major Lawless said he saw the 25th Division do the same thing we are about to do, on a smaller scale, a couple times. They have a long sequence of steep ridges to deal with down the coast. They could get naval support, like we were to have, but were exposed the whole time coming down the steep face of the ridge they held before even starting to work up the next ridge. It was difficult, and deadly when the Japanese chose to make it so.

Among dense trees in a rare flat spot we shared a crowded tent with an assortment of young officers, catching whatever sleep we could before getting up before dawn to pack up. We would have only about ten hours of daylight to work in. As soon as there was just enough light to see ten feet, our jeep was off.

Major Lawless and I shared the jeep with its driver, Corporal Donald Bignall, and an interpreter, Captain Doyle Dugger. Captain Dugger picked up Japanese the hard way, in schools the Army rushed to set up at the start of the war. He said the foreign language options at a small Catholic college in southern Indiana didn't venture much beyond Latin, Greek, and German. Corporal Bignall learned some Chinese swear words growing up in San Francisco, and is sure any Japs we meet would understand them just fine.

We all cursed together, in every language any of us knew, as our jeep was tossed down the old mountain trail, more by happenstance than by steering and throttle. Supposedly a scout of some sort had run through here before the operation was approved, but we had our doubts. The mountain was not our only problem, as there were other vehicles ahead of and behind us. We had to stop short on several occasions as the jeep in front got set up for a tricky turn, praying that the one following us got the message in time.

Finally we came out through a tiny deserted village onto the coastal road. The sun was uncomfortably bright over the ocean, as we emerged from two hours of navigating through an evergreen forest. We moved back along the road to find a place in the attack column that had formed ahead of us. Driving in the dark all night, a few tanks and at least forty armored scout cars had come along the coast road from yards near Ariake Bay and Kanoya.

The gravel road was in good condition but barely one good lane wide in stretches. It took some time to find our place toward the rear of the large company. We had time though. The mechanized column had five miles to cover. The infantry beside us had less distance to cover, but they had to go up and down almost as much as forward. We were to wait until a bit after noon, or the first time the infantry made contact, to shove forward.

It wasn't even 11 am when the call came, reinforced by the sound of attack plane engines and distant explosions[††]. Everyone put out his cigarette or scarfed down the ration he had opened, engines fired up, and each vehicle got up on to the road.

We moved at a modest but steady pace. The objective was to get into the town and take its bridges intact before the Japanese might think to blow them. We could have just rushed in first thing in the morning but that would have left a bunch of trucks sitting in a valley with no friendly forces in any of the surrounding hills. It could easily become a two-bit carnival shooting gallery for the Japanese.

At any rate, we had no trouble the whole way in. Twice that I recall we came upon an occupied house. Children of the house looked at us curiously, while one grown-up stood by holding up one of the pamphlets we had dropped earlier. The pamphlet said to do exactly that if one wished no trouble. Gunners in every scout car eyed the families nervously, our calm interpreters talking to them notwithstanding, but we passed without incident.

The road offered postcard-ready views of the bay, but steep retaining walls and thick evergreen brush limited visibility inland and made for short sight lines around every turn. The column had few combat options should it be fired on, and everyone was

---

[††] It turned out to be a false alarm. The infantry did not make contact with enemy soldiers their entire way down Kunimi-yama. But a den of Japanese "raccoon dogs" was dramatically displaced.

nervous. Eventually the lead tanks moved one at a time over a creaking old bridge by some river front houses and they could see down into Uchinoura. The road forked soon after, and we waited a moment while a detachment was split off to run inland a ways. It would circle the city where a line on the map promised such was possible.

Looking inland I could see up into the valley that defined the day's objective. A few columns of smoke on the near side rose up where bombs or Navy shells had burnt out some trees. On the far side a column of pale green smoke pointed to an unlucky location that a solider had tagged with a rifle launched marker grenade. A moment later an aircraft engine was heard, growing louder for a few seconds until drown out by the shriek of two dozen rockets cutting through the air. They made impact around a point 20 yards up and 15 yards right of the green smoke, or however a controller on the ground with a radio had adjusted close air support fire.

Another plane was inbound, but then we were off. The column came to life and we moved quickly into the coastal city. It was barely 1 pm. We were well ahead of the infantry, which couldn't be seen anyway through the forest carpeting the mountains to our right. We had exposed ourselves and there was no good option but to take the town quickly. The town sits in a soft flat river delta, with steep hills beyond the north and south banks.

Being near the rear of the column, our jeep was still coming down as elements to the front fanned out to scout every street for trouble. Single tanks cut down alleys barely wide enough, each followed by three or four scout cars, until we were out of tanks. Dismounted infantry ran down the sides of each street, stopping at each corner, looking up into the few two story buildings for snipers or hidden guns.

There was no trouble. The town was deserted. A single stray dog, about 40 pounds with short solid brown fur, ran up excitedly to greet some of the first men on the main road. Only cool nerves kept the animal from getting shot. The men ignored it and kept moving.

Our vehicle rolled into town, with a few other jeeps and supply trucks. Behind us was only a rear security detachment, which would stay up on the coastal road. I stole a glance out toward the small bay and saw the Navy at work. Three destroyers sat in a line, bow-to-stern, guns pointed inland, waiting for jobs. Ahead of them two minesweepers were doing their methodical work near shore, escorted by patrol boats.

Overhead two Navy attack planes circled, dark shapes under the white winter sun. At once I was home in the American country side, watching hawks soar over farm fields and open woodland. Some birds would spiral up higher and higher, simply flying for flying's sake. Others cruised lower, actively hunting for prey that revealed itself below.

Our planes had so far found very little prey. Even the earlier rocket attack was probably against a fallen tree limb that one of our spotters thought might be a poorly hidden gun barrel. We had made no contact and heard no sustained fighting from anywhere inland.

The column stopped again just as our jeep got down into the town. I encouraged Corporal Bignall to move us up closer to the front. He obliged the best he could, finding room on the narrow streets, until there simply wasn't any way around the other vehicles. Ahead, the northern part of the town ended and there was only one road leading through a narrow bit of land where the river ran parallel to the ocean beach. After that narrow piece, the streets opened up again into what could be called downtown Uchinoura. The city ended abruptly where the river took in another tributary, turned left, and ran out to sea under a wide stout bridge.

Discussion and pointing was going on to the front of the column. I hopped out of the jeep, grabbed my bag, and asked if anyone else was going up with me. Major Lawless' seat was already empty. I turned to find him twenty paces ahead down the road. I jogged a bit to catch up and kept running as he picked up the pace to get up front.

Instructions were being given on how to re-divide the column. After we moved into the downtown, a hill in between the two rivers would block off support from the vehicles that split off previously. A trail forked off toward the hill, to the west, over a good foot bridge. Dismounted troops would cross the bridge and check out a row of small buildings at the base of the hill. Others would fan out into the twenty or so city blocks. The armor and remaining manned scout cars would jump straight through and take the main bridge out of the southwest corner of the city.

Shortly everyone moved forward again, keeping good order like the veteran unit they were. Every alley was checked, no one had a blind spot that wasn't covered by someone else. In a matter of minutes tanks and cars and soldiers were on the river bank, where it cut off the city on its way out to sea.

Without breaking stride, two lead tanks rolled onto the bridge, followed by two armored cars. Riflemen and gunners on the north bank eyed the south bank warily. Astride a road parallel to the river was a long cluster of houses and fish processing buildings. Behind those buildings the land again rose steeply into the next forested mountain ridge.

Up to that point we had not seen a living soul since entering town. Upon leaving town they came out to see us. The first tank rolled off the far side of the bridge and turned immediately to face the first buildings on its left. People of all different sizes and attire ran out from behind several buildings, thirty or forty people in loose columns from every alley. Some brandished sticks and clubs, others carried satchels or old suitcases. The lead tank opened up, its machine gunners ignoring spears and clubs in favor of people carrying likely bombs. The second tank pulled up close alongside to join in.

On top of the bridge two scout cars paused to bring their four machine guns into action. From under the bridge another eight or ten figures crawled unseen over the far railing. Soldiers who had dismounted were immediately in hand-to-hand combat, rifle butt against club. That gang of civilians also had bombs, and they were only feet from the armored cars before being spotted. At least three charges went off, in close succession. The last explosion tossed one scout car, armored, model M3A1, fifteen feet into the air. Men, guns, and pieces of each were tossed in all directions. The remains of the chassis came crashing down next to a splintered hole in the bridge deck, and the entire thing went smashing through, taking several bridge girders with it into the fast running water below.

Our tanks had beat off the mob attack, the lead tank taking only superficial damage from one explosion. But they were now stranded. The hill in front of them came alive with small arms fire against American soldiers around the bridge, who were still getting up from the blasts that wrecked the bridge.

The American line on the near riverbank returned fire, a hail of bullets ripping into the brush and trees opposing us. Without prompting one or more Navy ships to our left added to the fire with automatic cannon. No one could see the enemy under the dense shade of evergreen trees, the low winter sun behind them. But an intense volume of fire was distributed over the entire hillside.

Shortly the bigger Navy guns began to walk a pattern of five inch explosive shells along the hill. The circling attack planes were circling no longer, having been released by their ground controllers to come lend a hand near the shore. They strafed in long passes near the river, after loosing rockets into crevices higher up that Navy shells could not get into.

Under smoke from the bombardment, and a deliberate smoke screen, the tankers disabled their vehicles and got back across the river along one remaining truss of the tattered bridge. All the injured and most of the dead were recovered, and this special task force of the 8th Cavalry Regiment pulled back out of downtown Uchinoura, to the relative safety of "uptown" Uchinoura[‡‡].

November 30, 1945 : X+15 — Uchinoura, Kyushu

By mid afternoon yesterday the mechanized column I was with had set up camp in the northern part of Uchinoura. We had hours to wait for the line of infantry in the mountains to advance southward down into the valley that ran inland to the west of us. A couple cases of bad sprains or broken legs came out from the forest and soon jeeps were making runs inland to collect other injured men. They would be classified as non-combat injuries, but it was

---

[‡‡] There are actually several named villages packed together in the river delta feeding Uchinoura-wan, apologies to the proud residents for my simplifications.

military necessity that had their units climb down 2500 feet in one short day.

Military necessity will have them climb up a similar slope tomorrow, wearing the same assault packs. It has been decided that all these hills need to be swept of Japanese defenders, thoroughly but also in a hurry. We found none on the way down, but the group I was with definitely engaged with some at the first uphill face.

In the skirmish yesterday we lost six dead and eight wounded, and four vehicles. Fifty some Japanese died, mostly civilian. An American security detail went up through the valley before the infantry got down, busting into all the small houses, searching for any more bombs among the few remaining scared villagers.

Technically losses were light for the ground gained yesterday. The commander of the column I was with felt encouraged. "We hit nothing but small arms and an angry mob. If that's all they have left, we'll be on the point in two days. It's a shame we can't use the bridge. It'll be that long before engineers say they can even start fixing it." Major William Gill pointed beyond where we lost the bridge. "Another good road runs through there and along the coast. We could have double timed it around whatever Japs are here and close in on them from all around."

The major will continue on with his troops on foot, joining the line with the rest of the infantry. Luckily they have climbing gear to use. Navy landing craft came in yesterday through the bay we had just secured. They brought food, ammo, spare gear, and medical supplies, which it was thought we would need. Two boats waited to carry away all those injured in the climb.

While we encountered no heavy arms yesterday, overnight the Japanese announced that they still held at least one good size gun. On two occasions, about midnight and two am, a spread of three shells exploded in our camp. They came from at least a couple miles away. Few men had dug holes, most of them camped under a clear sky next to their vehicles. There were only a couple minor injuries, but everyone woke up and scrambled when the first shells hit. If anyone got to sleep, they were awake again when the second barrage came. That was probably the point.

Before the echo of the last explosion died out wagers were being called out in the dark about exactly what size gun it was and when, or if, we would find it.

Before dawn we were moving around. Men helped each other adjust packs. A few rookies got a crash course in ropes and climbing gear. Our driver from yesterday, now a common foot soldier, asked if us reporters were going along. I let Major Lawless answer for me as he handed me a backpack and helped me adjust it.

No one had time for hot food, even those of us close to the beach. It was impossible to truck anything in to the guys further inland, down trails not fit even for mules. They were getting by on ground water and whatever was in their packs.

I was to march with a full infantry company out of the task force I was riding with yesterday. We were to continue up the road that 'our' bridge led to. The road cuts across the tiny pinky-finger peninsula that defines Uchinoura Bay, two miles at the widest and about four miles long to the tip. About a hundred of us would move out into that peninsula, down a trail which runs over its high points. We had to climb a thousand feet up the road, but once we turned onto the trail it would offer only a few hundred feet elevation change.

To the west as far as could be seen, and well beyond that, tired soldiers began to march south again and up. We followed along, just behind the rest of our company, which would head west when we turned east down the little finger. Another patrol went up to beat the brush on the hillside which ambushed us yesterday, but it was almost certain that the enemy had pulled back after bruising us. They were more concerned with booby traps left behind than active opposition.

Progress was easy, but slow and cautious, through the morning. Thick cloud cover came in to block the direct sun. It was a comfortable 70 degree day, perfect for hiking, except for the occasional flying bug in the form of a supersonic rifle bullet. Organized resistance was nowhere to be found, but individual snipers held us up, or worse, several times during the morning. I found out later that units in the other areas had the same problem at

176

random, but in our area they were specifically watching the road, waiting for us to pass.

The first sniper shot an old sergeant through the chest. The third nearly took off the head of a rookie PFC. By mid-morning it was common practice to put a shot or two into any tree that could hide a gunman, and there were a lot of trees. Side parties scouted down any promising looking trail and into any threatening patch of brush.

In a couple hours we had moved two miles in and up to the crest of the road. I walked to the front and could see out into the peaceful open ocean south of all this mess. The majority of the company fanned out and moved west, up toward the next peak, another thousand feet up. My group went the other way, starting down a clear trail to the east.

The official Army map clearly showed a trail continuing on out to the tip. Every person in the column wondered aloud, in a colorful palette of language, just what the map makers had seen that we couldn't. We had assumed they used aerial photos and perhaps old file maps made by locals before the war. The analyst who drew this map may have used old horoscopes.

The trail went plainly enough to the first hilltop, where a small clearing would have been a pleasant camping spot. Today it held a captain and two lieutenants arguing about which false trailhead in front of us actually went anywhere (none of them did, it turned out). Finally they agreed to navigate by the contour map, which seemed accurate enough. We moved out line abreast, stubbornly hacking through patches of brush, to find each local high spot. No enemy were sighted, and we took no fire, even though we were making a good bit of noise, with nothing else to mask it.

About noon I did notice appreciable traffic of aircraft flying into the hills behind us, accompanied by distant thunder from exploding bombs and shells. So there was some action. Around one o'clock we were on another high spot about half way out, and a quick lunch break was called.

Out loud I ordered a hot salami sandwich with fresh pickle and a double martini. A couple guys laughed at my wisecrack so I sat with them for our lunch of cold canned rations and crackers, with vintage canteen water.

We formed up again and continued before anyone could get too comfortable. The point narrowed, so we had less area to cover, but it also got more steep. Men were walking sideways on steep slopes, ducking under branches, wary of both twisting an ankle and of being shot at from some anonymous tree top. In several places ropes were tied to make hand holds. In another two hours we were near the end and closed in on the last high spot, at the very tip of the bony peninsula.

The entire lead squad stopped, knelt down, and waved for an officer to come forward. I followed. They had come to the edge of a U-shaped clearing. The open end of the U had a clear view of the ocean. At the center was a short rectangular concrete building. It was clear even from directly behind that the front side of this reinforced pillbox had been smashed by very heavy artillery or bombs.

Supporting squads were moved out along the sides of the clearing. From the closed end the first squad advanced in line toward the wrecked fortification. A few of them had rifles shouldered, ready for trouble. Others were mostly casual, sure that the emplacement was long abandoned.

A shot rang out and an American soldier in the center of the line was down. With a bloody shriek the first Japanese soldier anyone had seen up close in days ran out the back of the bunker directly toward the American line. He fired a rifle from the hip, and got off two more wild shots before return fire cut him down. In a few seconds at least twenty American .30 caliber cartridges were snapped off toward him.

The Japanese soldier, an older corporal, fell first to his knees. He reached into a jacket pocket, which drew three more shots into his abdomen. Before he died he drew out a small crumpled rising sun flag. It fluttered open freely as he fell forward. By chance his hand caught it again on the way down. His lifeless fingers involuntarily clutched the flag, its bright red streamers flowing out across the ground next to the bleeding body.

Our man who was hit by the first shot was back up, a corpsman dressing his right shoulder. The rest of the American squad inched closer to the pillbox, ready for more trouble. There was one opening in the back of the squat twenty foot wide structure. A call went back for a flame thrower and extra grenades. Then voices were heard from inside, calling out in Japanese. It did not sound aggressive.

No one on the American side paid the voices any attention, but shortly a stick appeared with a dingy white strip of cloth on it. Next to the strip was fastened a piece of paper – one of our flyers with instructions for peaceful civilians. A call went back for an interpreter. The flame thrower man came up and got his tools ready at the same time.

The interpreter who came up happened to be my acquaintance from earlier, Captain Dugger. He moved up ahead of the lead squad, insisted that the flame thrower be taken back out of sight, and got to work.

We took three prisoners, one Japanese Army regular and two conscripted locals, and they readily shared their story. The dead corporal with them had been in charge of the gun they were there to man. It was a coastal defense gun, which could fire out into Ariake Bay. It was an old gun, but it could do serious damage to our fleet and was not hard to spot in a concrete bunker with no cover. So of course the American Navy destroyed it long before entering the bay.

The gun crew was camped away from the gun, as instructed, before the invasion. They had no other instructions, and no one communicated with them as the invasion took place. The Japanese corporal insisted, violently, that they stay and do their duty. He was not shy of berating or even beating his subordinates. They had no supplies, but for what food the young army private had gone down into town to forage from abandoned homes.

I walked out to where their wrecked gun had once had a magnificent view of our magnificent fleet. It had a postcard perfect view across the wide bay. The fleet in front of me, and all around me, was even larger than when the invasion started. The men here, cut off from any friendly forces, must have been intractably depressed, at best resigned to their fate. The American fleet had to

179

be bigger than anything any of them could imagine – because it was bigger than anything in all of history – and it was here for them.

December 2, 1945 : X+17 — west of Hoyoshi-dake

I was up early this morning, after a decent rest. Two days ago the 8th Cavalry finished clearing Kunimi-yama and its adjacent ridges, with light casualties, mostly from tough mountain climbing. I rode back to division headquarters with a line of jeeps carrying minor injury cases. The jeeps had come up loaded with food for the men who had been living out of assault packs for two days. They were the only vehicles we could get over the remaining bridges along the way.

I got in two nights on an actual mattress, up off the ground, up off the floor actually as it was in a real building. The 1st Cavalry Division took over a deserted small town, and made use of its every remaining facility. As did I, resting up after two weeks of running around the island between sleeping in holes and tents.

Over lunch I made a point to find the communications crew, to get second hand news about the other fronts. Across Kagoshima Bay the 5th Marine Division has been making slow grinding progress to the south, pushing to meet two Army divisions moving north. The 81st Infantry Division moved quickly past Kaimon-dake, but got into rocky terrain full of old mines, all of them occupied with armed squatters. It still sounds like a repeat of southern Okinawa, which the 77th Division remembers all to well. The 2nd and 3rd Marine divisions have made halting progress, ridge by ridge, past the Kagoshima-Sendai line. They are stretched out along a 20 mile front, finding resistance at every point ahead of them.

In the east around Miyazaki, a breakout has proved elusive. The 25th Division has made slow progress across the steep ravines south of the city. The 33rd Division controls the plain around the city north to the next major river and inland to the start of the mountainous forest that covers all of central Kyushu. The 41st Division wants to drive down one of two passes from Miyazaki to Miyakonojo. If they can meet units from Ariake Bay there, it would cut off any Japanese troops in the eastern mountains.

This is no secret to the Japanese, and intel suggests a whole top-notch division from up north was sent down just to bottle up the passes. Parts of the passes are now called the Devil's Infield and Outfield. Relentless heavy artillery opens up when Americans get into those sections. Air operations finally started at Miyazaki yesterday, which will send additional scouts and hunters against the hidden steel carnivores.

The units around Ariake have their hands full. The 40th Division is parked on the near slopes of Onogara-dake, living like goats. The 98th Division is still rebuilding itself on the plain just in from the beach. The Americal Division has taken to the hills northeast of the bay. None of those units can do anything substantial without getting help. They won't get it until we finish here on the rocky point south of Kanoya.

At first light I moved up to the front, to the west near Kagoshima Bay. By jeep and tractor it took two hours to move the last two miles up ancient mountain trails. Our engineers already made obvious improvements to the road, which we only held as of four days ago, but the passes had surely never been attempted by motor vehicles before we got here. Not a few old cavalrymen have remarked how their horses would have been worth the trouble of hauling tack and feed here instead of spare parts and gasoline.

This morning I became attached to the 99th Field Artillery Battalion, which was tasked with supporting the 5th Cavalry Regiment. Shortly after I got to an artillery position the two regimental combat teams from Tanega-shima were to land inside Kagoshima bay. Once they got in, they would either push forward as the 5th Cav supported, or 5th Cav would advance while the RCTs supported. It depended on who found Japanese resistance first. Everyone found Japanese resistance early on.

The RCTs were to land on a flat straight bit of beach, in between two medium size rivers about three miles apart. A small town sat around each river mouth. Inland from the beach the land rolls up into wavy lines of cypress covered hills, which lead into ever steeper ridges which finally converge into the three thousand foot high Hoyoshi-dake. I found an eagle's nest view of the whole area as I got onto the outcropping where the artillery had made a home. Engineers had cleared 'shooting lanes' out of the forest, after a head start provided by Army bombers. Rain from low clouds cut visibility somewhat, but I could still make out roads and small houses five miles south across the river plain.

182

My riding companions this morning included radio-equipped spotters from infantry units who would need support down below. Sergeant Herman Parsoff came over early from the 158th RCT. "I honestly don't know how they got the regiment ready to make another assault," he offered without prompting as we looked out from our perch. "When I left they had got it organized again [into three battalions], but we only picked up a couple hundred replacements. I figure another thousand is what it would take to really fill all the jobs.[§§]" Sergeant Parsoff knew a bit about doing sums, as a grade school math teacher in the Bronx.

Across the southern river that brackets the landing zone, there are a number of freestanding small peaks. All of them were smoldering mounds when I first looked out through my binoculars. Big bombers had made runs at night, punishing the whole line that could threaten the landing. All morning a handful of attack planes circled under the low ceiling, making runs against anything that still stood up from the charred earth. Dozens of acres of forest were denuded, and in spots fires still burned, just beginning to be damped by the steady light rain.

Similar patches to the east of us had been bombed and torched, in preparation for the planned day's advance. It's impossible to level the entire evergreen forest, even if we really wanted to do that. But there are only a few feasible passes through those brutal ridges, and that was where the 1st Cavalry Division needed its blind spots reduced.

Near ten a.m. I saw the first Navy ships come into Kagoshima Bay. We were sure the Japanese had mined the bay, and for good measure we had mined it too. In previous days minesweepers made careful progress northward, escorted by gunships and aircraft, watching for Japanese guns on land. A few fixed coastal guns had been destroyed without firing a shot. Any hidden guns kept quiet – until today.

Overnight the sweepers, and Navy divers, had cleared any last obstacles to the beach. They got away safely, and it was not

---

[§§] The 158th RCT got over 750 replacements in the previous week, but took on two thirds of those while on transport ships, with no chance for practical exercises with them.

until the first troop transports appeared that a cluster of Japanese guns revealed themselves. A line of destroyers ran close to the enemy held shore as the transports sailed behind them. Four miles south of the beach a freestanding ridge proved to be where the Japs had dug in defenses. From my distant view I could tell fire was coming from at least two places on land. Navy rifles and diving aircraft responded quickly. The Japanese gunners were sure to be extinguished where they stood. But the lead ships were hit hard by the pre-sighted artillery.

Converging fire caused multiple explosions on the lead destroyer. It was afloat but dead in the water, drifting in its own oil slick, clearing the way for fire on the advancing transports. A lumbering LST went down quickly, probably laden with heavy vehicles. The full size transport next to her took accurate hits near the waterline, fore and aft, and sank just slowly enough to get half of her boats in the water. Another transport's captain will be credited for getting his flooded ship across the bay to land held by American forces, where it was beached and men could simply walk off.[***]

The engagement lasted barely ten minutes before the threatening land mass was smoking from end to end. Around me everyone was watching the action, helpless to do anything else. By then the distant ridge was shaking from the impact of massive shells that must have come from a battleship laying far from sight outside the bay. Any survivors would have to be deep inside their jagged fort, if the Japanese had taken time to carve tunnels into the burning rock.

Destroyers worked over assigned targets around the landing beach as the transports got assault boats loaded and lined up. From our left, to the east, dull thuds could be heard echoing out of the mountains. Either the other parts of the 1st Cavalry Division were starting early, or the Japanese had tired of waiting for them to come. The booms grew closer over the next twenty minutes. Radios behind us came to life, and each operator double checked

---

[***] The 1st Battalion of the 112th RCT was then divided, a third of it on the wrong end of Kyushu, another third being picked out of the water.

184

that he was on the right frequency to get any requests meant for him.

Landing craft were still getting lined up in the bay when visible artillery hits could be seen exploding on hills barely a mile to the south east. For whatever reason, someone had started shooting, and the whole land based part of the attack was starting early. Two attack planes which had been circling near the beach turned together and accelerated inland, flying low under the hovering cloud layer.

In front of us was all enemy held territory, with an unknown population of soldiers and equipment. They definitely had small anti-aircraft guns. We couldn't see the machine gun bullets coming up, but black puffs from flak shells peppered the sky in front of the American aircraft. The trailing fighter, behind and to the right, lost most of its right wing in a flash of burning fuel. The plane spun madly, and I could finally see its broken outline, the one gull wing of the Navy Corsair flailing with sudden lack of grace as the plane twisted through the air into a nameless hillside. The lead plane banked left and climbed sharply, cutting a spiral up into the sheltering clouds.

Finally orders came in for my artillery unit to hit targets near the beach. I watched boats come in toward the beach, alternately covering my ears with one hand until someone lent me a pair of good earplugs. Our 105 mm guns walked a pattern down the northeast sides of the hill masses that overlooked the beach from the south and east. Other guns put fresh craters into the towns that bracketed the beach. Recent experience with civilian mob attacks made villages wholly expendable.

On the crumpled plain below our position I could occasionally make out vehicles moving slowly along the larger roads. There were friendly infantry in the trees nearby, clearing out brush and treetops of snipers. The snipers down there weren't the sort who get off a couple good shots then move to another spot. The Japanese soldiers left behind tie themselves up in a tree, from which they will fire until being spotted, then shot and killed, and left hanging in the tree. It is desperate, and sad, and highly effective at slowing down the American advance.

By mid afternoon the RCTs were largely ashore, having broken firm but thin resistance at the beach. They were a mile inland into the first high ground. Below and to the east of me the 5th Cavalry had gone over two miles. Then both groups hit tough resistance at the same time. Both had to get across a river and through a narrow pass at the same time. Both were engaged separately and couldn't support the other. Each had to work it out independently.

Artillery fire from my hilltop perch shifted from covering the RCTs to bailing out our own division. Radio traffic picked up to an overwhelming pace, as requests came in, were prioritized, then cancelled or reprioritized. More than once a major countermanded a captain, or a colonel overruled the major. Ultimately it was orderly and professional, but tense and chaotic in the moment.

My view had been obscured while friendly units were down in valley roads, but I could see more of them as they maneuvered around their problems. Both regiments pushed up onto hills to one side of the passes they needed, but in opposite directions. A spotter next to me was the first to catch Japanese moving in the gap between the forces.

Without orders, we put artillery into the river valley behind the 5th Cav, where Japanese troops and a few trucks could be seen moving in between masses of trees. They chose to attack the cavalry regiment in the back just as it was itself attacking up a serious slope. Japanese squads came out of the trees in scattered groups, finding holes to fire from and charge out of, too close for American artillery to get at them.

Impacts from some Japanese field guns hit the American held hillside as I heard a voice beside me. "Mind if I borrow those for a minute?" General Connor Colt himself had made the trip up to see the action. I let him look through my field glasses while I took a wide look around myself. Navy destroyers were conspicuously close to the beach, where landing craft were still coming in with combat troops and the first support teams. The destroyers had nothing to shoot at, with the action too close in all fronts. To the south I saw fresh plumes of smoke all across the horizon, where the 112th RCT at least had a few planes supporting it up close.

The general made a few comments to his aide and turned back toward our guns. I got my binoculars back this time. He gave final instructions to the artillery captain before heading back out.

"See what you can do about the Jap artillery down there, and for gods sake don't let them retreat. We didn't want to have Japs wedged in between us, stabbing us in the back, but while they're here we might as well kill them."

December 3, 1945 : X+18 — west of Hoyoshi-dake

I spent the night up on the high point where the 99th Artillery Battalion had drug its guns. They were to keep watch over the plain below and be ready for any support calls. Fire support was unlikely at night, with American lines jumbled and the enemy very close.

Fighting had continued past dark, under a moonless sky, lit only by an occasional star shell glowing through the clouds. The dawn showed that overcast skies would carry on for some time longer. The 5th Cavalry had eventually stabilized their situation to the east and the 112th RCT was doing okay in the south. Word came that the 158th RCT, which had landed on the beach north of the 112th, would move out to clear the gap between the other two regiments.

I had no trouble getting a ride back down the mountain, as a parade of jeeps and weasels was hauling ammo a few rounds at a time up to the artillery, which they would need to paint the terrain ahead of the 158th. It was a bit of a trick to find a way over to the 158th, but I didn't want to miss seeing them in action. A signed and inscribed copy of the division's daily newsletter, and a signed note explaining my driver's absence, got me a young private willing to 'borrow' an MP jeep for the hour it would take him to shuttle me over and get back. Private Joe Pezzotti, of Queens, New York, was no stranger to camp pranks, or to getting in trouble, from what he told me on the ride over.

187

The coast road was well secured by then; we moved quickly. We had no difficulty finding the 158th HQ, as it was at the geometric center of a sprawling patch of chaos. Men were generally well ordered, sorting themselves out by unit, but equipment was coming ashore for the first time. It had to be assigned on the fly to the largely improvised combat units. Some headquarters staff were reduced to traffic cops, pointing trucks and tanks different directions while flipping hurriedly through stacks of paper on heavy clipboards.

I directed myself down dusty streets, freshly cleared by American engineers and found the new-old second company of the new-old second battalion. Sure enough, a couple of the NCOs I'd met on Tanega-shima were still with the unit, working to form up their groups of men into functioning units. A third of them were brand new, some only recent boot camp graduates. Any of them who had been through any further skill training were practically respected vets.

Sergeant Henry Brockell had three teams of his platoon doing last minute runs through on the two machine guns they actually had. His lead gunners were veterans now, and their assistants had been trained, but the runners had never so much as picked up a box of ammo let alone fired a burst.

The regiment was due to move out at eleven. At one thirty the first tanks finally moved out, leaving four hours of good daylight to use on the short December day. Smoke and dust were kicked up in lines ahead of the columns as artillery worked to pave the way.

We had about five miles to go to clean up the patch of enemy held land between the other regiments. The bumpy terrain had decent roads, which ran in parallel through small river valleys or along the high ground in between. The forest was interrupted only by infrequent farm clearings and frequent smoking artillery craters.

I rode along with a column on one of the high roads. They had thought to land armored bulldozers for us, tanks with fixed angled blades on front, to shove felled trees aside. Those vehicles led each column, followed by a regular tank or two. Truck borne soldiers learned quickly to hunker down, as snipers and an

188

occasional small artillery round harassed the American advance. Our own artillery answered any Japanese gun that dared to fire more than a couple shots, betraying its position to observers or spotter planes.

Early on my column rolled through a derelict crossroads village, formerly the trading post and community center for some number of local farms. We had not seen any Japanese troops yet, but just past the town another band of civilians came out to fight. These were all young men, perhaps all the angry youth of the battered town. About fifteen of them waited for the tanks to pass before running out from brush where the road fell off steeply into a small ravine. They were all cut down by volleys of fire from nervous truck mounted soldiers, but one of them managed to lob a burning bottle of gasoline into one of the open trucks. The Molotov cocktail smashed open among the American GIs. The column stopped to reorganize so the burned men could be moved back.

Scattered snipers and one solo machine gun nest were the only resistance we saw the rest of the day. Many snipers were picked off early, as they were dealt with by tanks or truck mounted machine guns which raked any promising looking tree, whether a man was spotted there or not. Still, troops had to be sent on foot down every side road and into every standing building, so it was slow progress. Near nightfall, barely five pm, orders went out to make contact with adjacent columns and form up a defensive line overlooking a small river three miles in from the bay shore.

Rain started again as men were pairing up and digging fighting holes.

December 4, 1945 : X+19 – Kanoya, Kyushu

During our advance yesterday the 5th Cavalry Regiment and the 158th Regimental Combat Team had somewhat tightened up the gap between them, leaving only a closely watched pass to the southeast for any Japanese to attempt a retreat. This left a less than two mile square patch of enemy held territory in front of us to clean out. The Japanese would not wait for us to clear the pocket.

Before midnight a few American soldiers heard noises in front of them[†††]. Flares went up, followed quickly by rifle shots at charging shadows. I was camped barely 200 yards behind the front foxholes of my adoptive company, close behind the smallest battalion mortars. The mortars fired, and I could just make out struggling figures in the light of the burning launch charge. The rounds landed and the same figures were sharply silhouetted by the bright flashes. Enemy soldiers were in amongst our lines!

Fighting was hand-to-hand, practically silent compared to the exploding mortar rounds tossed liberally by both sides. My foxhole mate was a supply truck driver from Des Moines. We had one M1 carbine and one fighting knife between us. I declined the offered knife, having learned to shoot years before but never learning the first thing about knife fighting. My hand went to the spot on my belt where I had tucked a .45 pistol just a week before. There was nothing but cotton and leather to grab now.

Some men ahead of us left their holes, running back from the line. Most yelled out the nightly password, others did not. Some of each were gunned down by their own scared comrades. Fighting continued in rages and fits through much of the night, as individuals or groups of soldiers came upon each other in the darkness.

At first light there were three more young soldiers in the cramped hole with us. One of them had been injured by jumping into the hole right on top of my original companion's knife where he had stuck it in the dirt.

The scene before us was a battle line still held by the 2nd Battalion of the 158th Infantry Regiment, but it was hardly a prize. Smoldering brush covered the southern skyline with smoke. A sickly smell of cooking meat mixed in with the burning pines to slip past the closed eyes of anyone who tried not to look at the carnage.

American soldiers got organized and walked forward in a careful line, medics close behind. They stepped over dead bodies,

---

[†††] [Editor's note, 2015: Secret at the time, a limited number of early infrared night-vision scopes may have been in use, to detect a night sneak attack. - sdm]

making sure the Japanese ones stayed dead, as they moved down to the river bank. The water ran fast, about four feet deep in that stretch. It had been a slow fording for the Japanese and many were caught there when the shooting started. A brown uniformed body floated past, face down, spinning slowly as the current carried it along toward the bay.

It is believed that the Japs in the pocket sent every last man into a final rush, realizing they were practically surrounded. My company counted almost a hundred dead in front of it; other units report the same. They also report each of them sending back about the same number in casualties, a third of them dead.

Ultimately the 158th did what was asked of it, again, but paid a high price, again. It was pulled back, again. I rode along as they moved out, listening to soldiers take a personal tally of their buddies – who made it, who didn't, and who knows.

We drove back through lines of the 5th Cavalry, which was walking forward to fill in the line as we borrowed many of their trucks. The rest of the 1st Cavalry Division had taken the mountains they were after, receiving casualties from the terrain as much as from scattered resistance and lingering snipers.

South of the new front line the peninsula tapers and forms into two parallel ridges. Only so many units can be concentrated into the last few miles of combat advance left to go. Beat up units are coming back to Kanoya and camps around Ariake Bay to rest and rebuild before the next violent action.

I have not slept in three days. Whatever quarters I can find around Kanoya, however primitive, will take me in for a very long nap.

December 6, 1945 : X+21 – Kanoya, Kyushu

I got some of the sleep I needed in the last two days, but only in short bits. Japanese artillery has been obscenely consistent at disturbing American camps. Most nights they only throw a few long range heavy shells, spread out well behind our lines. Direct damage is slight, but it forces everyone, from mechanics to cooks, to prepare holes and to shelter in them frequently.

Sometimes, when they can see some unit or facility of ours, and bad weather keeps us from easily finding their big guns, they do make a material impact, killing men and tearing up American units with a sustained barrage. Of course we have large gun batteries set up to return fire, but the Japs have not often given them a good chance.

If life in our camps is made difficult by enemy artillery, for troops up on the line it is truly brutal. Soldiers and Marines in many places have been on static lines for a week or more. On these lines the Japanese deliver regular volleys of smaller artillery and mortar fire, which can reach down into the deepest protective hole. The barrages are often followed by infantry charges or preceded by sneak attacks.

Life under artillery fire is an inestimable and unrelenting agony. One is sleep deprived, lonely, scared, and above all helpless to do anything about it. There is no rational response. Some flavor of functional lunacy is required to carry on, be it bitter hardness or detached resignation. Cases of shell shock accumulate when a front is static – one more reason commanders are anxious to maneuver and push forward again.

It is certain that life on the Japanese side is even worse. For every scattering of shells they send, we are carpeting whole hills and valleys. We fire patterns of shells at the taller rocky mountains deliberately on schedule at the same time each day and night. The barrage is not meant to catch anyone by surprise. It is meant to reinforce the idea that we can do this at will and without end. Japanese there are probably hiding deep down in well stocked caves. It's fine by us if they simply stay there.

Ernie Pyle wrote that in Italy some artillery men figured that we were spending about $25,000 for every German soldier killed. They wondered what would happen if we just offered each of them that much cash to surrender instead. Pyle didn't think much would happen.

I put the question to members of a supply company here. They spent some time doing some serious accounting. Their total came to $127,200 for each Jap. They agree with me that few of them would surrender for even that lofty ransom. We are going to have to go get those Japanese soldiers the old fashioned way. Toward that end the first large reinforcing unit, a whole division, is due here from the Philippines in the next few days. There is no word yet on where it will go.

Of course we are not the only team bringing in reinforcements. Attack planes intercepted a column moving southeast into Miyakonojo during a break in the weather. Rain has picked up steady since then, and there's no telling where that group went. Many times our planes have seen and attacked vehicles caught in the open around Hitoyoshi. We can watch the roads, when the weather isn't too bad, but there are certainly many hidden footpaths through the great forest north of the Sixth Army.

I got news from the other fronts, but there is little to report. All our lines either hold good positions or advance slowly one-hill-at-a-time against tough and clever resistance. The static lines are spread out thin. To concentrate forces on new objectives we need the divisions which are fighting in the two arms of Kagoshima Bay to finish their jobs, rest up, and move north.

December 7, 1945 : X+22 − Kanoya, Kyushu

Infantry in the field have little use for calendars. The day of the week means nothing to a man who is on the job all seven days no matter what and hasn't seen Sunday church services in months. Prayers out here are whispered on the schedule of artillery barrages and frontal assaults, not according to the program in a hymnal. The day of the month is immaterial to a soldier who pays no rent, though it should be cheap for accommodations consisting of a muddy hole and half a tent.

Those few here who do still keep track of what day it is recognize this as Pearl Harbor day. December 7th, four long years ago, the mighty Imperial Japanese Navy launched the surprise attack that ultimately brought us here. It would seem fitting for us to present them with an unpleasant surprise today, a little 'thanks for the memories' token of appreciation.

But I don't think there will be any surprises offered in this part of the world. We assaulted this island with a quarter million combat troops, thousands of trucks, and hundreds of tanks over three weeks ago. Our naval guns and army artillery have pulverized in detail thousands of acres of Japanese home territory. I think they know we're here.

One surprise for them might have been that the Air Corps is operating out of the large airfields in Kanoya, but I'm told that won't happen until tomorrow. We have been flying ground attack fighters from small improvised strips near the beaches since early on. Engineers get busy on the larger permanent airfields as soon as they are taken, but regular air operations can't commence until the field is out of enemy artillery range and the threat of night infiltration attacks.

Kanoya has the biggest prize airfield in this area, but it lies in a valley between what a civilian might call 'beautiful mountain backdrops,' or the military calls 'commanding heights.' Those heights must be cleared of unfriendly sightseers before the field is safe to use.

The 1st Cavalry Division has nearly flushed out the last resistance in the rugged peninsula to the south. The 40th Division believes it has a firm hold on the near sides of the dominating Onogara-dake, a 3600 foot jagged mountain that I imagine will be featured on postcards sold at Kanoya if it ever becomes a civilian airport.

So the plan is by this time tomorrow to have aircraft of many types able to land at Kanoya, quickly turn around, and rejoin the fight. Each captured or improvised airfield that opens up in a combat zone gets put to use like this as soon as it's safe, and often before that. I can tell you several reasons why and why it's important.

The first and most obvious thing is that the hours flying back and forth from a far-back air base to the front don't have to happen. An attack plane can make many short trips in a day instead of one long one, delivering its presents to a greater number of naughty boys on the ground. A patrol fighter can spend many hours circling a patch of sky, or fight until its guns are empty instead of the gas tanks.

194

Sometimes people look at a map which says that target such-and-such is now in range of aircraft type so-and-so and they think 'Great, that's a done deal now! It's practically ours already.' But it they stop and do the math they'll realize the severe limits of operating at range.

If a plane has say 12 hours endurance, as they call it, and it's five hours away from the target each way (assume it's the same both ways for simplicity), the plane can spend no more than two hours "on station" over the combat area. If you need to have constant coverage, and let me tell you the boys on the ground would really appreciate it if you made that happen, it now takes a squadron of twelve planes just to keep two at a time where they can do any good. Flying at great distance is what they call a "force divider."

A subtler point is the drain long flights have on the airmen. It's physically taxing and a unique mental strain. I've seen this in every flying unit, but the problem was most acute with the long range B-29 pilots I visited in the Marianas. A squadron leader in one wing, Major Ralph Praeger of Great Bend, Kansas, explained it to me. "A bombing mission from here might be 8 hours out and 7 coming back. All of that is over wide open deep blue ocean. There's very little to do but think about the risks, how on every large mission a few planes don't come back, and for no known reason. They just don't show up.

"Getting shot at over the target area is one thing. It almost seems fair [the Japs shooting back], I think some guys look at it that way anyhow. The rest of it though, it's just nerve wracking." Indeed it isn't fair, one little (relatively) aluminum skinned bomber up against a humongous piece of fickle nature like the whole Pacific ocean.

The B-29, being a complexity-no-object state-of-the-art machine, requires plenty of maintenance after a long flight. If you ever get a chance to see a cutaway of one of those 18 cylinder supercharged radial engines that power these bombers, four at a time, I recommend it. It's a thing of beauty, but remember that all those parts have to keep working together dozens of hours at a time, without service or inspection, for a loaded bomber to do a job.

Now, if you get a chance to see a cutaway of a bomber pilot, I do not recommend it, because it's pretty messy. He's also a lot more complicated than that radial engine or even an entire bomber. Bomber crews sleep for a whole day after a big job. After an all-day mission they typically aren't asked to fly again for three days or more.

Another reason we want close land air bases sooner-than-possible is the way it opens up the Navy's aircraft carriers for their best uses. Navy and Marine Corps flyers love supporting ground troops, but they also love their ships. The majority of the sea based fighter planes here have been doing air defense, and as we've seen the fleet itself is the thing most in need of protection. The British sent every carrier they could muster, but their planes are 100% tasked with protecting their own part of the fleet.

The impatient airmen I talked to today, watching their new home air base being roughly finished, explained that the carriers would be free to move around more once the Army lets them go. One thing they would like to do is go hunting for small airfields and harbors the enemy suicide planes and boats have been coming from. Shooting Japanese planes on the ground and boats at anchor would bring us back to symmetry with December 7, 1941.

It's been a grand show[‡‡‡], but I will not be sad to see the Navy pull up its circus tent and take the show on the road, with a different program.

[‡‡‡] I was not in close touch with Navy intel right then, but the last good count I had gave the *kamikazes* credit for three cruisers, four escort carriers, eleven destroyers, twenty-three large transport ships, and scores of LSTs and smaller ships sunk or towed away useless. Almost nine thousand Navy sailors went down with them or died in explosions and fires on surviving ships.

December 8, 1945 : X+23 – Miyazaki, Kyushu

I got confirmation that the first reserve division, the 11th Airborne, is heading in and will be landed at Miyazaki to help First Corps finally break out. It was always possible to bring in the 11th in an actual airborne operation, but landing them by ship allows much more heavy hardware to come with them. They have traded their wood and fabric gliders and parachutes for extra armor and artillery.

I figured wherever they went would be the scene of the next offensive action, so I moved that way to go along. I got a lift out into the fleet and transferred around to Miyazaki for a dry-foot debarkation onto a good functioning pier.

I got my first good look at the southwest shoreline of Kyushu. The stretch just north of Ariake Bay could be called rugged, but the stretch north of that, closer to Miyazaki, defies English adverbs. Scandinavian languages may have a word for the shape of the coast, as it looks something like postcard pictures of Norwegian fjords. Deep parallel ravines cut into a long giant ridge, some of them carrying sizable rivers. A couple of the rivers have laid a small delta plain at the ocean edge, to which small towns cling, perilously close to falling into the ocean.

American troops have been trying to jump across some of these ravines for weeks, and their smaller nooks held suicide attack boats that took out the heavy cruiser Guam early on. My transport gave the coast plenty of space, allowing a pair of patrolling destroyers and their team of smaller boats plenty of room to work.

We unloaded at the middle of a long pier in the well functioning harbor of Miyazaki. We had to wait for a line of tanks to rush down the busy pier. At the end a ship was letting them off directly to drive one at a time to the shore. These were our new model of heavy tank[§§§], much bigger than the Sherman. I had only seen it before on promotional tours in the States.

[§§§] The M26 Pershing tank had better armor and a bigger gun than the M4 Sherman. It was also slower, burned more fuel, weighed 30,000 lb more, and was three feet wider than the venerable adaptable Sherman.

197

After the tanks were on their way, the pedestrians with me walked toward the shore. I walked the other way, right to the ship which had just let out the new tanks. Seamen were stowing rigging and getting ready to put up their ramp and get the lightened vessel ready to leave. I bothered a pair of them for a minute with standard questions about their ship.

Then I asked what they thought of that new tank. The sailors looked at each other quizzically for a moment, then one of them decided he had an answer. "I'll tell you what I think of that tank – it had better be good." Seaman Second Class Duane Surber re-hung the chain he was stowing and pointed up into the hold. "Those things are so big, we can't quite get four of them across on the main deck. We could squeeze Shermans in five wide. We can't carry barely half as many, and now we have to go all the way back to Manila to get more." A big dent in the right bow door illustrated his next point, "That long ass gun is a problem, too." My question answered I let them get back to work and made my way through the city.

Boats carrying the 11th Airborne Division can be seen letting them off onto the beaches north of the river Oyoda-gawa which bisects Miyazaki and makes its harbor. The harbor doesn't have anywhere near the capacity to bring the whole division in, not in three days if it tried.

By this time tomorrow the division is expected to be established in the forest east of Miyazaki, between the 25th and 41st infantry divisions. The 25th has anchored the southern side of the front since X-day, gradually working through ridgelines and hill clusters to push the front line ten miles out from the city. The 41st has been in the west and made multiple attempts on both of the mountain passes which lead to Miyakonojo. It was met with a coordinated Japanese response each time.

The 11th Airborne will now be the vanguard and attempt to take the passes. The 41st will cover its right, preventing Japanese from rushing in like they did to the 41st when it was mobile. The new division also allows all the units northwest of Miyazaki to shift right and close up ranks, opposite the rugged forest from which large counter attacks have come.

Most of the people I came in with were headed to the main airfield at Miyazaki, just south of the harbor. It had been operational for the U.S. military for about a week. That day heavy rain had grounded everything on the field. I had no trouble finding an idle airman to give me a ride inland.

Miyazaki is a hub of transit and commerce for the region. It is built up in a modern way, with good multi-lane roads. Other areas on Kyushu would have been swamped by fifteen or twenty thousand men trying to get inland all in the same day. Here it was a normal metropolitan rush hour. We joined a steady stream of trucks and cars and even tanks rolling down the paved roads.

The division headquarters was to start out in a town about 10 miles up Oyoda-gawa. We stopped there at a crossroads next to a bridge to the north side of the river. A signpost at the intersection had nailed to it at least thirty hand-painted planks giving directions to different U.S. Army units and facilities. A pile of discarded planks on the ground spoke to the transient nature of those destinations. Most vehicles continued on straight, to where the 11th Airborne Division was to take positions in the jagged hills which consumed the western horizon.

We went over the bridge into town. Since the division was expected ahead of time, engineers had the chance to do it up nice. Nice in this case meant looking like an Army camp somewhere in Nebraska. Every building on the main drag had been taken over and labeled with a prominent sign in English, tacked up over whatever Kanji writing was there before. Other signs gave directions, and still more signs listed the ubiquitous local rules and regulations.

I thanked my driver, checked in with the division, and drew quarters in an old hotel. I think it was actually a local cathouse, but I didn't see the madam.

December 9, 1945 : X+24 – west of Miyazaki, Kyushu

First Corps wasted no time taking advantage of the newly arrived 11th Airborne Division. I learned today that overnight units all along the front around Miyazaki packed up and moved in the dark. It was expected that units would move left or right to make room for the 11th and tighten up their lines. Instead every unit attacked diagonally into a new position, forward of where its neighbor had been.

Before dawn the largest bombardment of this island to date opened up across the front. Big battleships, some of them borrowed from the other beach heads, came right up to the shore to fire at long range or at high angles into inland valleys. The 11th Airborne Division was still moving into position as parts of all three other divisions were moving in the dark, overrunning some frontier outposts of the apparently surprised Japanese.

Much of the territory seized was vacant no-man's-land that had been established over the last weeks of fighting. To the northwest, brief foothills lead up into deep mountains and river valleys with frequent waterfalls. Those foothills are now being dug into by the 41st and 33rd infantry divisions. To the south the 25th Division jumped another artillery-riddled river valley to smooth out and shorten its line.

For it's part, the 11th Airborne got organized in view of the two passes down to Miyakonojo and made a charge at the hills around them. They took minimal losses, seeing almost no resistance, compared to the withering fire the 41st Division took in the same area. The American front line is now almost a perfect semicircle 15 miles in radius out from the center of Miyazaki.

I learned about the operation only by chatting up another fellow down where hot showers had been set up near the river. Soap still in my ears I toweled off and jogged back into town in my week old dirty uniform. In short order I was hitching a ride further west on the back of an armored bulldozer.

On the dozer with me was a two-man chainsaw team and their two-man chainsaw. Corporal Vernon Starr, of Eugene, Oregon, informed me that Lumberjack is a real official U.S. Army specialty, job number 329 if you want to sign up. "They actually came out recruiting us, and it's a good thing." He didn't look away as he thumbed toward the forest. I didn't look either. It didn't matter which way he pointed, there was nothing but forest filling every horizon and most of the sky.

200

"Normally we want to think ahead on a tree line. They have to come down a certain way, in a certain order, for the lumber picker to drag them back and get them to the mill. Out here they want us to fell them just one direction – the hell outta the way!" We are rolling through what the Japanese have designated a national forest. They are here to reduce it, more than just a little bit.

The forest between Miyazaki and Miyakonojo does not have hills and mountains as steep and high as in other places, but the hills run into each other with no order and no interruption. It is dense terrain and almost impossibly thick with tall evergreen trees. Other areas we had fought in had only a few roads and trails. The forest preserve had no roads at all, until now.

There are exactly two reasonable passes through the forest toward Miyakonojo. It was not surprising that the Japanese defended them, but the scale and stubbornness of the defense has been a big problem. Going around the forest proved unworkable, so now we are going through it.

Engineers have been working since we first secured this part of the forest, and for some time while it was still contested, cutting roads through. Where they can manage it the roads run arrow straight, "To make shooting lanes if the enemy comes out at us." Our dozer climbs and falls as we pass from one high spot to the next.

Most hilltops have a clearing with some kind of camp on it. We passed communications, kitchen, and medical groups in order until we got to the first combat units. A new artillery base was still being cleared as men bedded in a pair of our truck-size 155 mm guns****, sisters to another pair not far away. Incredulous about how they got there, I asked. The answer was a derelict tracked tow vehicle shoved off to the side. Of the six tractors they used to bring up guns and shells, three of them were torn up and didn't make it back. That one was abandoned in place up there on the hill.

**** I didn't think to ask where the 155s were from. The 11th Airborne Division would not normally train on guns that big, but I'm sure they'd be happy to learn.

December 10, 1945 : X+25 – Miyazaki, Kyushu

Here again I have inserted a bit of material that I did not have at the time. Any reporters who were around headquarters of First Corps were invited to a press conference after the big push on December 8-9. When I got back from my time in the field with the 11th Airborne Division, I was given an edited 'transcript,' which inlines the questions and reads more like a speech. Major John McKee, of the communications company for First Corps Headquarters, led the invitational meeting.

Thank you for coming in, I know we surprised you all today. At least I hope we did! We gained some good ground yesterday, and we think it was a surprise to the enemy, at least. General Smith has asked me to be as candid with you as possible. In kind, as usual we ask you to be discreet with anything we talk about here regarding future intentions.

It can't have been any surprise to the Japanese that a whole division came in to Miyazaki starting on Friday. There was a chance they would try something before we got settled[††††], but we beat them to it. On the big map you can see that every front line unit moved up as they shifted over. It may not look like much, but we now hold the local high ground all around. We could hold there forever if we had to.

Of course we have no intention of holding. We are going to take the whole valley [greater Miyakonojo] and move on into the forest north of Mount Karakuni. We have to.

Let me back up for a minute to last October, when we lost two hundred ships to the storm. Something had to give. We couldn't bring in a dozen divisions with what was left. We could have waited another two months, instead of two weeks, for more ships but that would put us into next spring by the time this island is ready to support full-scale bombing of Honshu, for the invasion of Tokyo itself.

Yes, that's the next target, and the Japs know it. Anybody with a map knows it.

[††††] We found out much later that actually the Japanese had pulled back, being exhausted from the many previous skirmishes outside Miyakonojo.

If we can't land at Yokohama until the summer, we'll be fighting there into the typhoon season. Plus they just get more time to dig in, making it take even longer. No one wants to be fighting through next winter. So we have to get the job done here quick.

Most of you have been up into the hills with the troops. It's not tank country, contrary to what some generals drew up back in Australia. Lacking transports to get everyone and everything here at once, we went with everyone. Troops first, tanks later. Most previously fielded tank battalions came along, but none of the new heavies.

Yes, yes, we could have used heavy tanks here and there. But that's always been the problem with armor – it's never right where you want it when you want it. Or all the support vehicles couldn't keep up and the armor can't keep going for very long. It was debated hard, let me tell you, but it was decided that the infantry could get by with the new field guns you may have noticed. Anyway, the heavy armor is here now, and it's going to keep coming.

We're going to clean up the mountains this week. Then we are going to tear right through the central plains, right up to the central forest. These last obstacles [Sakura-jima, Karakuni-dake, and a ridgeline between Karakuni-dake and the marines' front line] will be surrounded and pulverized.

We didn't get the air cover we hoped for, with the nutty weather. But now our soldiers are going to bring along their own support!

In the next few days the 11th Airborne Division will be into Miyakonojo, and the 98th will come up to meet it. Then we'll have all this [mountains east of Miyakonojo] cut off. By then the marines[‡‡‡‡][§§§§] can converge with the 40th over these rocks [Sakura-jima and Onogara-dake] and the 1st Cav will move around to meet the marines and stitch up [Kagoshima] bay.

[‡‡‡‡] Army press style did not include capitalization of "Marine".

[§§§§] [Editor's note, 2015: It still doesn't. – sdm]

The session continued through details of the medical and supply situations, and the imminent arrival of the first USO shows on Kyushu.

December 11, 1945 : X+26 — west of Miyazaki, Kyushu

Night before last, my tree clearing companions went off to their job site, connecting some of the many hilltops we own here in the forest northeast of Miyakonojo. I got off near a field artillery battery and was directed down smaller and smaller machine-cleared trails to find front line infantry.

Charlie Company, 3rd Battalion, 188th Glider Infantry Regiment, 11th Airborne Division, welcomed me in to their un-named hilltop HQ. The artillery behind them had rated hill "number 260." This unit would not have a named home until they took a taller hill across the valley, hill "number 367."

Company CO Captain Arthur Leonard told me a bit about the trip forward. "We practically hiked straight in. We took up old positions the 162nd [Infantry Regiment] held and then another couple hills past that." He pointed back up to the mortar squad behind them that I passed on the way. "The Japs had pulled out. All we saw were two snipers, and we're still looking for booby traps here." He drew a wide circle around the camp which had been a Japanese infantry camp facing the other direction. Captain Leonard said the land here isn't too different from where he used to hunt in the Alleghenys east of Pittsburgh.

Platoon Sergeant Walter Strauss, also of Pennsylvania but more accustomed to the flat Erie lake shore, was standing next to us and pointed out the sandbag berms his men were set behind. "We even got to reuse the Jap sand bags. Except they left grenades jammed under some of them." That drew a couple chuckles from some shovel-hefting enlisted men, even though the first grenade caused two casualties. "I've sent back three medical cases so far," the captain explained. "One of them was a bit of grenade shrapnel in a guy's butt, but another was a twisted ankle his buddy got diving from the grenade. He tumbled straight down the steep end of the hill, arms swinging like he was swatting off bees."

The unit was digging in for the night. Some gentle encouragement from the sergeants was required to get the holes textbook deep, as they had yet seen no enemy soldiers nor any artillery rounds. I had drawn a bedroll and extra blanket to camp under as winter weather was finally being felt on the temperate island. With clear skies the temperature would get below 50 and stay there until the sun made its brief appearance the next short day.

Artillery was heard that night, to either side of us, less than two miles away. They were short barrages, but of heavy caliber from far away. We never heard the sound of the launch, which would have followed some seconds after the report of the exploding shells in the passes east and west of us. Some small villages sat in the river valleys that made up each pass, but all were deserted save for a few American sentries.

Before dawn the third watch roused everyone and men fumbled to gather their gear under a moonless sky. At the pre-appointed time, artillery and mortars from several distances behind us began their almost daily ritual. Flashes of light walked up the hillside opposite us, and on many other faces up and down the American line. When we couldn't see the flashes any more, the explosions were on the back sides of the objective hills, and it was time to move out.

The company advanced in two waves of squad columns, in a chevron formation. At least that's what the captain told me it was. I went out behind the second wave in any case. The next peak was about three-quarters of a mile away, but we had to go down about two hundred feet and up three hundred to get to it. Our side was a single slope, but the opposite side was broken and wavy.

We had some light by then. Groups of men moved in and out of the remaining clusters of trees. Previous artillery fire had roughly cleared deliberate sight lines, which were good for us to spot the moving enemy, but of course they work both ways. Half charred felled trees were a nuisance everywhere.

A half hour passed before the first shots were fired. A few rifle shots went up into trees that could hide a lurking sniper, but a submachine gun was preferred to rake the tree tops. Forty minutes of careful hiking, two or three stumbling steps down, followed by a rifle-ready scan of the opposing hill, had the front wave at the bottom of our hill. Runners reported adjacent companies all on track and no trouble to the sides. The lead squads advanced again, up the next hill.

Columns drifted apart some in the twisted terrain, and lieutenants made adjustments to keep us lined up and to cover blind spots. The point of the advance was moving directly toward the crest of "hill 367," groups of men trailing it left and right in a vee. They paused at the last trees before a clearing at the top, letting the line come up more even. Then the whole line moved forward over the top.

There was nothing there. Absolutely nothing, but a Japanese trash pit. Even the trash was clean of anything useful, like any scrap of metal from shell casings to food tins. Corporal August Disparti had transferred from a field artillery unit, saying it reminded him too much of working big stamping machines on night shift back in Chicago before the war. He said the hill top had been a Japanese artillery position.

"The tracks leading off in the mud [it had rained there a lot until two days ago] could be from any kind of wagon. But look over here." A pattern of impressions in the dirt was repeated three times in the clearing, down in semicircular pits four feet deep. "They had guns here, spade and side arms spread out like so." He folded his arms out like some artillery pieces unfold. "You can still see where they drove a long bar into the mud on this one. I bet the guns were jumping all over in the muck."

Where we had come from was the infantry camp in front of these guns, just as we were lined up the night before in front of our own artillery. The captain surveyed the gun pits and deep holes on the back side of the hill where their crew had weathered our barrages. He also noticed loose piles of drying cut branches piled to one side.

"They probably had these guns hidden pretty good, protected in the pits, and maybe not even in the pits when they weren't firing. For whatever reason, we didn't take them out, by air or artillery. Now they're gone, and we're going to see them again. We were too late."

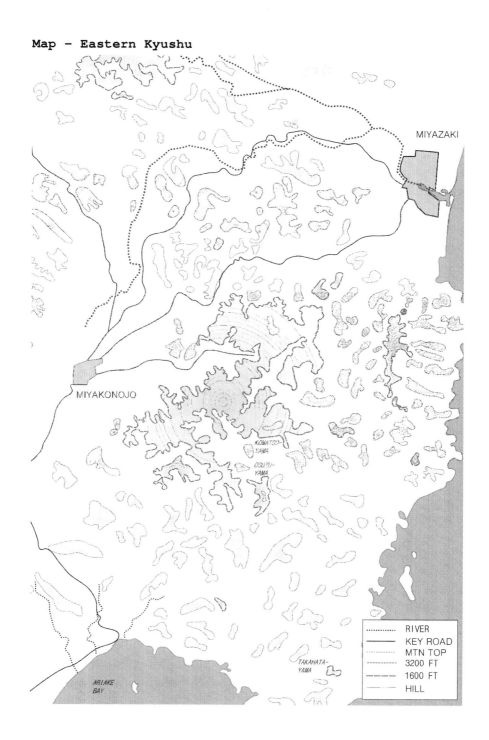

This morning we executed another textbook advance, securing another two numbered hilltops. The previous afternoon was spent with patrols moving around the hills we took yesterday, connecting with adjacent units and combing the spaces in between for any traps or Japanese hideouts. It is slow work, for a unit trained in mobile quick strikes, but essential.

Two days ago, on the first night 'on the job,' B company of our same regiment had two Japanese soldiers materialize out of the darkness from behind. Two men were found in their foxhole with their throats cut as they slept. The next hole was awake, and a short firefight left both Japanese dead and another American shot.

This company had easy going the first two days and may have gotten complacent. Today we were nearing the end of our bumpy trailblazing through the forest, almost to where the two natural passes into Miyakonojo come together northeast of the city. We hit our first real resistance in the afternoon, and it cost us.

The last bit of the day's objective terrain was a jumbled mat of misshapen hills and winding shallow ravines, southwest of where we broke camp that morning. Contour lines on the map of this patch almost draw out rounded letter shapes. One squad ran out of high ground to scout over and moved down into a curving ravine for a while. They rounded a turn, and patient Japanese gunners waited until all dozen men were through before opening up. They were about 300 yards away and downhill from where I stood on a high clearing, the company command post for that hour.

The squad was immediately pinned down and cut off. No one could see them down low and around a bend, not even the adjacent squads. The sounds of at least two Japanese light machine guns and cries of "corpsman!" amply illustrated the situation. It was the middle squad of the middle platoon, whose lieutenant was trying to move the others to assist. But mortar fire, of mixed sizes, dropped in around the trapped men, keeping their help at bay.

Captain Leonard got involved, sending another platoon around to the left, staying low through the next couple ravines, to put eyes on the enemy machine guns. A radio man dialed up our own mortar section, ready to relay spotting to them. On the right, where we had no friendlies for some distance, the heavy weapons section set up machine guns to cover the gap while the company worked through its current problem.

Above us in the bright clear sky there were layers of fighters and attack planes circling, waiting for targets. The Captain cursed aloud, "We were supposed to have an air controller down here by now! God knows where they all are."

The sounds below changed as another two Japanese machine guns started to fire. A squad of the other platoon was now pinned down like the first and soon bracketed by mortar fire as well. From somewhere to the west, small and medium artillery rounds began to pepper the whole area occupied by the company, heaviest around where the machine guns had set up.

It was a trap, a perfect ambush, and we were all the way in it. Holding still ensured being gradually consumed by artillery fire. Pulling out meant abandoning two dozen trapped soldiers. The captain stood up and yelled out, "Airborne! Give 'em hell!!"

The radio man called in our situation as Captain Leonard ran forward to the platoon rears. This would be quick, but not a mad charge forward. He drew up a play like a sand lot quarterback, and his veteran unit snapped into action. I got down as close as the scattered remaining brush would still allow me a good view, which was about as close as I dared.

Two .30 caliber machine guns were marched along on the right, continuing to move so as to not be static targets for the mortar spotters. The gunners fired from the hip, each aided by two ammo handlers, sweeping the top of the high ground opposite where our men were pinned down. It was a long crescent shaped ridge, flat on top, bare in patches from many rounds of bombardment. The enemy machine guns could not be seen, but they had to be in that ugly rock. Our roving machine gunners were exposed, but they were suppressing any infantry that might be ready to protect the machine gun pits.

The surviving platoons, save one reserve squad, hustled forward, crouching low. Explosions kicked up dirt around and among everyone. They dodged between clusters of surviving brush and along hill sides, until they could see the problem.

The ravines our boys were stuck in curved together into a vee shape. The vee pointed directly into the arcing hill, across a small flat. Guns dug into the hill could fire down both lanes. A higher ridge some ways west afforded visibility to enemy spotters observing any approach into the trap, or anyone trying to flank it.

Captain Leonard crawled with the center most squad, on the high ground in the point of the vee. From there one could make out the Japanese machine gun positions, more by muzzle flash than physical features of the emplacements. Mortar and artillery rounds began to close up on the platoons as Japanese observers figured out where they were all clustered. The captain stood up and fired his .45 pistol at the enemy hill.

On that mark everyone rushed. One of our machine guns to the right began to rake the hill side, joined by three BARs. Two bazookas fired rockets from the left toward different Jap guns, both near misses. The Japanese gunners didn't flinch at the direct fire. They had nowhere to hide or retreat. One immediately swung over to where the bazooka rockets had come from, tearing up one of the teams.

American smoke grenades began to fill the air in front of the machine guns. The Jap guns fired continuously, sweeping the whole flat, for a full two minutes. Certainly their guns would be melted quickly. Artillery fire from the distant ridge began to land near the crescent hill, undeterred by the presence of friendly forces. Aircraft began diving on the taller ridge, by direction or from seeing our plight themselves. The Japanese artillery men would have to close up shop and hide.

Most of this C Company of airborne infantry was across the flat in a minute. The hill was curved enough that the two end machine guns could cover each other, and they did, each cutting down the first two GIs who tried to take out its partner. New attempts were made from above, and by grenade and Tommy gun eventually all the pillboxes were shut down and cleaned out.

There were four gun houses in the hill side, one hot machine gun in each. A mix of cave digging and reinforced concrete made up the S-shape of each. They did not interconnect, and there was only one way in or out of each. Once engaged, the soldiers inside would turn back their enemy or die trying. Foxholes for infantry had been dug on the back side of the hill, but the occupants had left some time before, possibly when our bombardments started in earnest, leaving the trap unprotected from behind.

Captain Leonard saw to the wounded and requested vehicles for their evacuation. Word came back that it would be a while. Other units also hit trouble and Division was addressing their needs 'in turn.' The captain fumed quietly for a while. "We took 15% casualties today [15 dead, 27 injured]. All I'm asking for now is a couple damned jeeps."

The company set up a new perimeter, loaded injured on the AMTRACs that finally came, and enjoyed a bitterly satisfying light show as the looming ridge to the west was battered by American ordnance through the night.

The company I am with has had two days of "active rest" since getting ambushed and beat up. Yesterday the unit was technically in combat as a static "fixing force." The ridge which hit us with big mortars and small artillery was to be assaulted and cleared out. Another battalion of the 185th Airborne Infantry Regiment would run over it lengthwise, from north to south, while we covered it from the east.

Immediately west of the ridge is the Oyoda river, which carries on into Miyakazi. Our bombs and shells had ripped apart any and all bridges over the river, making retreat of the Japanese guns and equipment impossible. This bunch we intended to destroy where it sat.

Through intermittent rain we watched the attack unfold. American GIs made methodical advances down the ridge. Riflemen advanced in loose lines, watching every rock ahead for movement. Men with grenades and flame throwers sanitized every hole as it was located. Squads on the back side found almost no resistance, but were shook up by scattered long range artillery from far west.

Large tanks rolled through the valley between us and the ridge, supported by their own infantry. Many times a patient Japanese sniper or hidden machine gun cut down an American soldier at can't-miss range. Just as many times the Japanese shooter, and a large chunk of the hill around him, was obliterated by an American 90 mm high explosive shell.

With plodding certainty, the ridge was secured late in the afternoon. Our sister companies counted their losses and dug in for the night. They discovered very little inside the small caves and revetments in the rock. Numerous broken field guns and carts were found on the back side, smashed as the Japs tried to pull out at night under our steady artillery fire.

The bridges were indeed gone, but a number of stout wooden rafts were found down stream, having been cast off once the Japanese were done hauling their guns over the river. Again we had let some get away.

212

Today my company made one more move, south a bit into an area already cleared by another outfit. We are on the last stretch of high hilly terrain before the broad flat valley which holds Miyakonojo and her surrounding towns. I can look directly down into the outskirts of the city. In the afternoon winter sun it might normally be a picture perfect sight.

Today the sky is overcast in a soulless gray. The wet earth is bare and muddy brown where bombs have leveled most of the trees. Ahead of us the deserted inland village is black, still burning in places where an artillery barrage was directed on a formation of Japanese troops. Or it may have been a few lost cows; we don't seem to care much either way. Shells are cheap to us and so are quaint Japanese villages.

Now that we own the southern pass through the mountain forest, big supply trucks and heavy weapons are moving through (the northern pass is still overlooked on one side by Jap held bluffs, which direct heavy artillery onto it as needed). We could push down into the city and meet our brothers from Ariake Bay any time now. Except they still haven't broken out at Ariake to start up this direction.

We don't know what is holding up the 98th Infantry Division, but the elite of the airborne division here have plenty of ready excuses for the green unit. Taunts range from, "I lost my pacifier!" to various gynecological afflictions that might trouble men of the other division.

We want to lock up any Japanese still in the mountains between Ariake Bay and Miyazaki before they too escape. They still hold a two mile thick line of mountains and ridges which includes the 3100 foot high Komatsu-yama. The Americal division has been holding the line north of Ariake, but is stretched across fifteen miles of mountainous front. The 25th Infantry Division is now joined by this 11th Airborne Division, driving south from Miyazaki.

December 15, 1945 : X+30 – east of Miyakonojo, Kyushu

Almost as I wrote about the possibility, the Japanese did
start moving a large force out of the mountains south of us, into
Miyakonojo. Once out of the forest, they could stay in the city,
putting us through expensive brutal urban fighting, or pass through
to make a new defensive line in their choice of rocky volcanic
ridges west of the city.

Under a dim gray moonlit sky one spotter plane braved
ground fire to fly low over the area, almost under the star shells
that went up occasionally to light the Japanese held corridor. I
could see it in glimpses, appearing in the light just ahead of the
steady sound it made. It found an organized column of burdened
soldiers, caught in the open next to their own shadows under the
artificial light. The plane drew fire immediately from the exposed
troops, but instead of evading it turned to make another run, even
lower, while requesting more pyrotechnics.

Flares went up all across the line. One of our radio men
tuned in calls from the plane. Men, trucks, ox carts, even armor –
all were moving out, in organized columns using the one good road
into Miyakonojo. The column ran at least four miles up into the
mountains. Their only cloak was the cover of night, and we had
torn it from them.

Captain Leonard broke nighttime rules and allowed himself
to use a flashlight on his new map. We had moved off one sheet
onto the next late yesterday. Radio chatter shifted from spotter
plane reports to artillery coordinates. Working the map grid, the
captain soon identified the road in question. There weren't many
roads to pick from in the mountain forest south of us.

A quick conference with the lieutenants and platoon
sergeants resulted in word going around to get packed up and
ready to move. We had no orders, yet, but the captain read the
situation for himself. It was about two miles over rolling high
ground to the road, which led into the northeast corner of
Miyakonojo proper. Beyond the road the land rose rough and
steeply. If the Japanese were engaged in the narrow river flat
around the road, they would have no choice but to either come up

214

to fight us or to flee on foot into the rugged forest, abandoning any heavy equipment.

Up to now, here and on most Pacific islands, the Japanese have owned the night. They either infiltrate and sneak attack or make big rushes. American tactics have usually been to hunker down at night and let the Japs come. But some American divisions in Europe had success attacking at night. It's already been seen that someone high up in First Corps would like to demonstrate the same success.

Captain Leonard took up the radio handset to be sure HQ knew just where we were, and that we were ready for anything. Before he got in a word, the call came down – everyone was to be ready to move in 90 minutes.

Ten minutes later, at minute M-80, a spectacular light show took over the entire horizon in front of us. Near simultaneous dull booms from behind us were followed seconds later by bright flashes and much louder noises in front of us. We had a good viewing spot, up on a clear hill top about 600 feet higher than the valley target. We couldn't see the explosions directly, but could locate each flash in the building smoke and mark it on the map. The captain helped me follow along, as each battery laid in a blind pattern across its assigned grid square.

The barrage of small and large Army shells was well under way when the Navy joined in. We were over 15 miles inland, up in the mountains. The Navy salvos would be 14 and 16 inch monsters from their battleships. Some of the one ton shells could be followed well into their high arc, as a loose trail of burning propellant and powder bag followed them. At the end of that rainbow would appear a phosphorescent white dome, lighting ten times as much sky as the smaller explosions.

The end of our wait was a nervous twenty minutes, as the barrage line walked out of the valley, right up towards us. With ten minutes to go we could see the explosions directly, and the noise was becoming uncomfortably loud. Most men gave up spectating for a place back in their foxholes.

With two minutes to go the world again fell silent. The appointed minute came, and we moved out.

The instructions for us, and every other company on the line, were dead simple. We were to advance due south, strictly in an assigned lane. Everyone was to keep the same pace, crossing each imaginary line on the map at the same time. We would move into the valley, each unit clearing out what section of the winding valley road it came across in turn.

Captain Leonard figured we could mange the terrain ahead with modest difficulty. He was worried about men to our left, where three severe peaks broke up the landscape. It would be impossible for them to move in clean lines at any speed. And if they tried to work around the mountains, they would have to navigate in the dark to regain their place in the larger line.

We made our way down the face of our hill and picked through the forest below for a quarter mile before heading up again. It was relatively easy going under the mature forest canopy, where even the dense evergreens had thin lower limbs. Progress slowed in patches of shorter brush and was dead slow where our artillery had made a quick demonstration.

Felled limbs and shattered trunks littered the woods. In the harsh light of our star shells broken trees were levered aside or simply climbed over. Some weren't stable and shifted or rolled under the weight of a scrambling GI. We suffered a casualty when one man had his leg broken under a falling twisting log. It cost us two men when his lieutenant detailed another man to wait with him until first light when he could be safely moved.

A distant rumble suggested that an American armored column was moving down to our right, out of the forest hills, into the outskirts of the city. It was confirmed by the sound of a series of small cannon shots from the same direction. Division was pulling out all stops to trap the Japs ahead of us this time.

We had started about 10 pm. It was just after midnight that we ran head on into the company to our right. That wasn't supposed to happen, so another fifteen minutes were spent going over maps, arguing about which wavy contour line was which by artificial star light. The line got squared away, and we were off again, moving due south with only the near ends of our units in earshot of each other. We had only a mile to go to be at the road on our left (it ran northeast to southwest in our assigned zone).

216

With a half mile left we found our first band of Japanese, holed up behind a small knob, about 200 feet in elevation above the road bed. They had sentries up, but were still surprised to see us. A few shots rang out in either direction as everyone got down and took positions. The firefight was brief but fierce. A dozen Japanese rifles and one light machine gun fired non stop toward where we had first made contact.

Our captain moved a whole platoon quietly around them, and the position was pummeled with grenades. We wound up with prisoners, though some of our men wanted nothing to do with them. Up close in the bad light I could see only two uniformed Japanese soldiers. With them were ten or fifteen frightened civilians, most of them women.*****

We continued through toward the road as trees and brush thinned, partly due to our artillery and partly due to the farmers of the river valley. Impressive swaths of land were cleared and terraced for farm plots. Three to five foot stone berm walls divide and define the land, and make good firing lines. Distant artillery to our left signaled some trouble that way, as no shells were coming unless requested.

The platoons broke lines to work with the terrain overlooking the road. The map showed clusters of small buildings along the road in front of us. There were none. There was barely a road. Everything was rubble and craters. A few small fires glowed sourly, their light somehow a different color from the happy campfires of our youth.

On a cue I never noticed, squads advanced in unison to check the buildings on the near side of the road, or whatever corners of them still stood. On the road in front of them, and in the fields across the road, an assortment of wrecked vehicles were found, at least ten in the short stretch I saw. Some were crumpled black slag, having burned furiously until they had nothing more to give long before we got here. A couple were barely scratched,

---

***** Later inspection of the site turned up eight dead Japanese soldiers and twenty to twenty three dead civilians. Counting of the bodies where grenades had gone right into their huddle was difficult. The remaining rifles had been manned by local civilian boys.

apparently pulled off and abandoned in good shape by fleeing soldiers.

Across the road were a few more damaged farm houses, then a low field led into the river that fed the fertile valley. Half of the company moved together across the road and among the other houses. A shot rang out as the first soldier finished picking his way around shell craters to the south side of the road. He fell back into the last crater as dozens of other rifles came awake.

Men fell back in twos and threes until whole squads were together again on the north side of the road. Some of them were hit along the way. Enemy fire was coming from behind terrace walls on the far side, which led down into the next farm fields. American GIs tucked in behind cover on our side including stone garden walls.

I felt for a moment like it was the Revolutionary War, where Nathaniel Green's few regulars lined up against Cornwallis' British Army out in farm fields. Except now we were the redcoats.

I was separated from Captain Leonard and the other officers. I don't know what decisions were being made, but I knew we were too close to call in artillery. I knew we had lugged at least two bazooka tubes and some rockets for them down with us. I knew this because the men lugging them had complained about it the whole way. They were sure it was a waste.

Most of the enemy were sitting behind a terrace wall; there was nothing but solid earth between us and them. But a few were up above ground, behind one surviving garden wall. I watched that spot, and sure enough, it was the point of our eventual attack.

Seven bazooka rockets slammed into the wall in thirty seconds, followed by BAR and rifle fire into and around the wall. A squad rushed the wall, through its new openings, and into the courtyard behind it. They couldn't have known that there was nothing behind it. The house inside was demolished and there never was a back wall. They had no cover and walked into a new Japanese shooting gallery.

In the dark there was no way to switch over to a 'plan B,' but we had men trapped forward, and we were committed. Soldiers poured into the false gap, as the whole rest of the line advanced

218

evenly. It could have been one of the infamous desperate Japanese charges on Guadalcanal.

Except we did overrun the enemy lines, wiping them out hand-to-hand at the end. Captain Leonard cancelled any idea of continuing on, fording the river and pushing up into the hills on the other side. He had had enough for the night. It began to rain heavily as his company located all its wounded and tried to make shelter.

Once sound of the battle died away, numbing cold demanded everyone's attention. It was carried by rain through every layer of clothing. Men sought improved shelters through the night, mostly in vain.

By morning light we surveyed the wretched scene. The village had been abandoned for some time, its people either fleeing or being taken into labor by the military. Last night American artillery had converted the town into a hellish obscene landscape, with twisted burnt military hardware for its statuary. On top of all that a bloody battle had been fought, in the dark at close range.

To look at it, it's inconceivable that anyone would want the place. Surely the burned out and leveled homes will stay that way until nature overtakes this place. But in reality we can be sure that proud villagers, those that survive the war, will return to this place, remaking it one shovel full and hammer strike at a time.

This company is hurting. It took another 20% casualties, on top of previous losses. A trickle of vehicle traffic is picking its way up and down this road we now own. They say most other units hit thin lines of resistance like we did, some taking similar casualties. In the darkness units ran into each other or got separated. They hit trouble at different times. The artillery we heard came down dangerously close to one unit that was making better time than their neighbors, who had tougher terrain.

Burnt and shattered Japanese vehicles line the road side for miles in either direction, but many more people were certainly with them. Other civilians were found, mostly older females. The consensus scuttlebutt is that a lot of Japs took off on foot into the next rugged hills, soldiers and civilians together. They could still try to make it out to the west into Miyakonojo, or dig in and fight in the mountains.

I have been with the 185th Airborne Infantry Regiment. It will set down in place to lick its wounds, while the 511th Airborne moves through it and carries on the attack. I am going to let them do just that, without me. I said my goodbyes and hitched a ride on a slow moving AMTRAC. It was supposed to be heading to our armor column that advanced toward Miyakonojo overnight.

December 16, 1945 : X+31 — west of Miyazaki, Kyushu

The trek inland on our newly taken road was bumpy and halting. Shelling and close fighting had left craters of missing road and put piles of debris where there was good road. We rode through one farm village where the infantry platoon there paused from grilling up a couple abandoned farm pigs to help clear us a path. Clouds were thick, and the ground was muddy, but the rain had stopped.

The driver of our AMTRAC was Staff Sergeant Reggie Dunklin from the division's engineer unit. His job today was to drive along the new front, courier some critical mail, and survey what else needed to be done. Sergeant Dunklin had cleaned up hurricane damage with the family dock company near Mobile, Alabama, but the mess we made of Kyushu so far was much worse.

By ten o'clock we left the forest and entered a crossroads town at the outskirts of Miyakonojo. The mood there was tense, as Airborne infantry were still moving from house to house, or rubble pile to rubble pile, securing the area. They'd fought in spurts through the night, finding resistance from every block of the town, which had not been 'serviced' as thoroughly by our big guns as other villages. They gave us directions back through their lines to meet the new armored front.

We turned north at the village center and passed between American watch posts, through a low gully and down onto a low plain that sits northeast of Miyakonojo. As we entered the plain from high ground a fantastic and contrasting scene was laid out spanning our view.

A pastoral scene of irregular farm fields, meandering roads, and quaint village clusters spanned the broad vista and ran out into the next mountain range. The postcard-ready scene was marred by only a few smoldering shells of buildings. The picture was dominated however by ranks and columns and mobs of armored vehicles of every type, right in the foreground. Their dark shapes looked to have been added over the classic painting by some brutish amateur.

The road was straight and smooth as we rolled (Is rolled the right word in a tracked vehicle?) by the lead group of tanks. Nine of the big new Pershings sat in an arc, bisected by the road. Other formations sat astride other roads and in every other important position. We stopped with the first group so Sergeant Dunklin could get any requirements they had.

What they needed was the other three tanks of the unit. Two were left along the way with mechanical trouble. The problems would normally be quick fixes, but most maintenance facilities are still on the other side of the mountains. The tankers will have to hold here until heavier support facilities come up closer. Armor doesn't like sitting still, where it's more of a target than an aggressor.

The third tank was banged up pretty bad by an anti-tank mine at a crossroads in the town behind them. Mines have been rare finds here on Japanese soil, though a lot of time has been spent looking for them. Last night they took a chance on a quick thrust and found some the fast way.

Our vehicle was converted into a rough-terrain ambulance. We would take wounded along with us, back through the mountain pass to somewhere near Miyazaki. The armored unit sent two sedated stretcher cases back with its corpsman, and I gave up my seat to Lieutenant Donald Schupp who had been in the mine-damaged tank. His right leg was pantless and heavily bandaged, but he said he'd been hurt worse playing college ice hockey back in Mankato, Minnesota.

Continuing on we passed light trucks carrying men and supplies, and armored AMTRACs hauling fuel and ammunition. Behind those we came into a thick patch of new-style heavy artillery. The big 155 mm Army artillery piece has been fit onto a large tracked chassis and armored all around for near-front-line combat. It's not a new idea, but this was the newest model. They call it a "self-propelled howitzer." It looks fearsome from the front. But behind them I counted at least three support vehicles for every big gun, hauling shells and fuel and supporting infantry around with them. So the armored artillery still has a soft spot.

We got past just in time not to be deafened by a handful of registration shots. The howitzers would be there a while, behind the tanks they supported and which protected them.

The first medical post of any substance we passed flagged us down and asked directly, "You hauling live or dead?" We had live injured, so they did not try to burden us with dead to take back. Lieutenant Shuppp explained that they hit little resistance during the drive but were taken under by snipers from several buildings along the way. Those buildings are the ones I saw burning.

The last town before we would turn onto the mountain pass was the market and transit center for the area. Its market center backed up to a rail depot where people and goods could be sent in to the city or out to the coast. Bulldozers were working in teams to remodel the city, which had been heavily blasted by earlier bombardments. We drove parallel to the tracks for a ways before turning east back into the mountains.

Sergeant Dunklin drew a line in the air where the railroad continued into the next bunch of hills. "We've got teams on those tracks already, trying to get them open. There's a railroad tunnel through the last mountain. We blasted one end shut before we even landed. The Japs blew up the other end when they pulled back." Our vehicle lurched forward down into a washed out hole in the old river valley road, then motored up the other side.

"We'll need that rail line to ever move enough crap in to support that armor. This road by itself could never be enough."

December 18, 1945 : X+33 – Miyazaki, Kyushu

I got a chance to rest, get cleaned up, and get caught up. The Army communications office fed me the standard news, the same words all the rear echelon reporters had sent back in their identical reports days before. Little of it was real news.

The material substance of the situation is apparent to anyone who looks out over the giant hive of activity throughout Miyazaki and the territory all around it. New buildings pop up whenever one glances away from a clearing for more than a second. Men and vehicles hustle day and night to move materiel, pushing most of it immediately south and west to where First Corps is still making its current push. A regular stream of vehicles head out to fetch casualties. They move slower coming back, either to be gentle on their live cargo, or because their cargo is such that there's no reason to hurry anymore.

The only thing that mattered in the news I was fed was confirmation that the situation is the same for the other corps. Both have one big push under way – the same ones they had going when I went to the front a week ago – and are largely sitting still on their other fronts. Real news would be if things were going much differently elsewhere, for substantially better or worse.

11th Airborne Division Headquarters was still established in Takaoka on the Oyoda river. They are anxious to pack up and move forward through the mountains. All of its combat and support units were already clustered near the new front.

I made my way on foot the five or six miles from Takaoka back to Miyazaki. It had been cloudy and cold, but dry for two days. The main road was wide and paved, but the pavement had seen better days. Our heavy trucks were the heaviest thing it had ever seen, and steel tank tracks claw obvious scratches at every turn.

Miyazaki itself, largely untouched by fighting, was a fully functioning modern city. People went about their business like in any other business district. They just happened to be all young men in matching uniforms.

I got to the far side and found the Navy had an expansive presence. Being the only port of any substance we hold on Kyushu, the Seabees had been hard at work improving and expanding it. In just two weeks since I first came through two old canals that branch off the small harbor were dredged out for larger ships to tie up. They offload using new cranes that must have come in kits right from the U.S. mainland.

The Navy also has a new airfield, wedged in between one of the canals and the main airport. I passed a short line of small rail cars being loaded with 'beans and bullets' on my way to the Navy

224

complex. They bore entirely Japanese markings. I hoped our engineers could read the dials on the curious looking locomotive.

It was my good fortune to run into a familiar face. Navy Captain Lee Clary was still doing photo interpretation, and now he was doing it right here on Kyushu, for Navy attack plane and bombardment missions. His group was in a top corner of one of the few two story buildings in the neighborhood.

Their windows offered a good view of waves crashing into a long beach which ran from the airport up into an artificial breakwater the engineers were still busy extending. Across the harbor, past a tangle of tugs pushing big ships into tight berths, trucks could be seen lined up out of sight waiting for the ships to offer up their precious loot.

Captain Clary's team had the good fortune to be situated above an officers' mess. It could be busy and noisy, but we had fresh coffee to drink while catching up. It broke the chill I had from walking over under a gray winter sky.

We traded stories of our trip there so far. He had been stuck on Guam until only recently, summarizing reports on Army bombing missions and photo intel for Navy use. The fleet may have used his work in their many raids on Japan, but he never got to see any of that. He finally got to Okinawa just as a waypoint before coming to Miyazaki.

Now he is almost on top of the action. His group helps plan attacks and sees photos from each job usually the same day. He's both exhilarated and exasperated about it. "It's great to get the instant feedback. But too often we do the same job, days in a row, and never get a result." He mentioned a few examples and got out pictures for two of them. "I wasn't here at the start, but as soon as I got off the boat they took us up to look at this mess." He sat back down and set a large photo between us, turning it to lay the same way as the actual land it depicted.

"Japanese emplacements right here around the city were easy to see and pick off, by ship or plane. But just over there," he touched the photo and pointed to the southwest, "they set up big and small guns and man traps cut into all the steepest rocks. They couldn't be seen from a hundred feet away, unless they were firing right at you." He touched a pencil to several circled spots on the photo. "We're learning to pick out some tells that give away the positions, but it's still a guessing game."

The second photo he took out was a current problem. In the middle of Kagoshima Bay is a large steep volcanic island. Sakura-jima they call it, though it's not an island any more, having connected to the main land just a few decades ago. Some of the heavy artillery that has punished American forces came from the volcano, of that we were sure.

Army and Navy flyers have taken many turns bombing the island, from every attitude and elevation. New photos are taken after every run. Planes were lost almost daily until a focus was made against anti-aircraft pieces in the old craters. The dark volcanic rock has still not betrayed the big guns it hides. At least one position was quieted for a while, much to relief of the 40th Infantry Division, but it came after a giant combined barrage and carpet bombing. They can't say which shell did the job, and now the Japanese gun is again back in action most nights.

On the topic of action on the other fronts, Captain Clary gave me a better update than I could ever get from the official summaries.

In the west The 2nd and 3rd Marine divisions remain stretched out between Kagoshima and Sendai. On a few occasions a regiment or two was able to advance over the next bunch of hills. They would dig in there, get reinforcements when they came, then chew through those reinforcements in the next advance. The 2nd Marine Division is lined up along a road about mile and a half in from the Sendai-Kagoshima line. The 3rd Marine Division is in a arc around the outskirts of Sendai, its 3rd regiment filling all the land north of the river which leads out of Sendai to the ocean.

The 5th Marine Division just this morning started what should be the final big push to meet the 77th Infantry Division and the 81st Infantry Division south of Kagoshima. All their units have been absorbing supplies and reinforcements as quickly as they could be offloaded onto the beaches – all to advance a few hundred feet a day. A Japanese division headquarters was overrun two days ago. It is hoped that material from there will tell us what the rest of

226

their defenses are like. I wonder what use it would be if the answer is that they're just more of the same as we've already seen.

The 1st Cavalry Division did finish clearing out the peninsula south of Kanoya. It cost another two thousand casualties, plus whatever the RCTs took helping finish the job. While they rest, the 40th Infantry Division stubbornly pushed over Onogara-dake and up the near sides of Bisago-dake. They got help on the left and right from the 112th Regimental Combat Team and part of the 98th Infantry Division, respectively.

There was no shortage of artillery and air power in the 40th Division's fight, and four days ago it reached historic ferocity. The front and back sides of Bisago-dake, and Minami-dake behind it for good measure, were dressed up and down by ordnance of every size. Army heavy bombers dropped loads perilously close to friendly troops. Tanks and self propelled guns ran up the bay shore road to get a word in. The Navy came farther into the bay than ever before, with bigger ships. Again they traded fire with land batteries that seemed to prize waterborne targets, losing one destroyer but smashing the enemy guns which exposed themselves to cause it.

The bay shore could not be held, as the night invited accurate pre-spotted artillery from the island. But the last mountain ridge before the north end of the bay was under American GI boots. Like everywhere else on Kyushu, it was expensive, and the unit that took it will not be able to attack again for a while.

East of the 40th Division the 98th Infantry Division spans the rolling plain south of Miyakonojo all the way to the eastern mountains. It has made only halting advances since being moved up from the beach. In the mountains north of Ariake Bay the Americal Division is also stretched across a long span, this one mountainous. They have kept pressure on the Japanese there, but can not make major advances.

This morning the 11th Airborne Infantry Division pushed through and finally met the Americal Division. The 25th Infantry Division to its left now has any remaining Japanese in the mountain forest trapped between it and the Americal Division. The enemy there is confined to a single deep river valley which lays between Komatso-yama and Osuzu-yama.

The 41st and 33rd infantry divisions remain stretched out west and north of Miyazaki, mostly in the foothills of the severe jagged bluffs that overlook the city plain. They trade artillery and probing attacks with the Japanese on an irregular basis. Everyone lives in holes, and no one stays still for very long, lest a unit become a target for an overnight artillery program.

As soon as you open your eyes, you are wrong.

– Ancient Chinese proverb.

December 21, 1945 : X+36 – Sea of Hyūga

Repeated stretches of alternating damp cold field living followed by a dose of hot showers and soft beds have gotten me sick. I have to wonder if simply staying up front in a dirt hole would have hardened me up and staved off any illness. At any rate the morning before last found me taking up a bed at the new First Corps hospital.

The hospital used to be a school of some level, perhaps a small college, in the northwest part of Miyazaki. The school's entire campus, at least four multi-story buildings that I saw, was taken up by the hospital. Additional temporary buildings filled the grounds. Parked trucks served as storage sheds, ringing the campus out to the stone terrace wall which surrounds it, a ubiquitous feature to most plots in the area.

They were busy with injured and sick men coming back from the front, but not overwhelmed. In Miyazaki they had every facility established that a hospital could offer in the most modern city and over a thousand beds to use. The other beach heads were not so far along, having fought longer through less developed territory to push the front away from the shore.

While the hospitals such as this one are equipped for almost everything, they still send men further back at every chance. There are only so many beds available, and they must be kept clear for any rush of combat casualties.

My affliction was likely to be short-lived. I was welcomed to stay and fight off the unspecific viral infection they vaguely diagnosed. I asked for a favor, if it wouldn't displace a fighting man on his way back. I got sent 'upstream' to the Navy hospital ship anchored off shore.

A seriously injured soldier would take the same trip. He would move from the battle front through a succession of larger and larger aid stations and field hospitals until it would be decided if he needed long-term care. (Early on the final field hospitals were actually assault ships landed on the beach.) From there the chain runs through fleet hospital ships, to hospitals on Okinawa, to the

Philippines or Marianas, then back to Hawaii or all the way to the U.S. if the soldier is likely to be discharged.[†††††]

It is now routine to see one or two helicopters ferrying a few of the most urgent cases out to hospital ships. They fly as far forward as we dare send the delicate aircraft. Several dozen transport planes have been reserved to airlift badly injured men directly to the best facilities for them, however far away. Mundane cases like my Japanese variety of influenza take the slow road.

On the way to a pier by Army ambulance I finally found out what had become of the civilians I was sure had stuck behind around Miyazaki. No matter how urgently an evacuation is ordered, or however violently an invader arrives, some stubbornly stay behind. They always have.

A dense neighborhood, almost a small town in its own right, was completely fenced in. High barb-wire topped runs joined small guard towers to make a well observed perimeter around the town. Any Japanese encountered by our forces nearby had been moved there. No one presumes to know which among them will live peacefully around American occupiers and which would plot attacks. So they all get boxed up together. From outside the fence the town looked sad and isolated. Cold winter rain complimented the setting.

Viewed inside the fence the Japanese city went about its normal business as if nothing was unusual. We drove through the middle, as American MPs patrolled the main street where a few shops were open for people to trade for what they needed. The people had little to do but volunteer for supervised work parties organized by the Americans, who also provided everything stocked in the stores.

I took a survey of the men in the ambulance, those who were conscious, as we had one sleeping stretcher case. Each man had a story to go with his wound, and I'm sure most will get practice embellishing the story in coming years. Private George Roscoe got a Japanese bayonet in his thigh during night fighting.

[†††††] Ernie Pyle gave an excellent description of the whole medical system on land in Brave Men. The process continues out to sea, and all the way across the ocean.

He has the bayonet to take back to Philadelphia with him, as his own blade found the torso of that attacking Jap at the same time.

Other injuries ranged from indiscriminate shrapnel and machine gun wounds to one fellow who was shot in the rear end. He insisted that the Japanese sniper got behind his unit, explaining his case while laying front down on a stretcher. One man in a complicated arm splint was quiet until I finally got him to explain his injury. The arm had been broken in three places and two ribs underneath it. It was a severed human leg that had smashed into him. The leg had come off of his own platoon lieutenant when one of our own artillery rounds fell short into their camp. Conversation for the remainder of the trip was limited to a few poor attempts at morbid humor.

We boarded a small boat at a regular pier. It was not necessary to load injured over sand into a landing craft like early in the invasion. The boat got us to the USS Sanctuary, and we were moved aboard. I had nothing to do but sit back and be tended to, so I let the efficient team of orderlies and nurses run through their well practiced routine of processing me in and getting me set up comfortably on a clean ward bed just below the main deck.

A few hours rest got me felling pretty well and even getting back a bit of appetite. Something in the cocktail of pills I was given may also have helped. I found my shoes and jacket and got up to explore the ship a little.

Just the smells of the first dining hall I found proved to be too much for my stomach, so I drew a cup of coffee and kept going. The rain had stopped so I took a short walk outside down the main deck. My queasiness had perfect timing. I looked out to sea just in time to see another great fleet lit by the low sun behind me in the west.

Two of our Iowa-class battleships, I couldn't say which, cut out huge chunks of the horizon. We have many big ships here in the Kyushu invasion fleet, but nothing like those. The Iowa and her sisters have heavy cruisers as escorts the size of the biggest battleships left here for shore bombardment. They appeared to be moving slowly, gliding across my expansive field of view, but I knew that they were steaming north at a speed the old ships could never match. They had re-armed at Okinawa and were heading

232

back north to rejoin the big fast carriers to attack Japanese land targets.

Winded and achy from just that short bit of sightseeing I returned to my bed for more rest. My illness needs to know that it has a deadline. I was tipped off that I need to get back with the Army troops near Kanoya in the next few days. I wasn't told any secret plans so much as updated on what the current situation maps look like.

Two days ago the last Japanese hideouts in the western arm of southern Kyushu were finally cleared out with explosives and fire. Yesterday the 25th Infantry Division converged with the Americal Division in the eastern mountain forest. Massive artillery shelling filled the last occupied valley, followed by the quieter but more desperate sounds of vicious close fighting until that valley was also cleaned out.

There is just one stubborn pocket of Japanese resistance left behind the long American front. It is right in the middle of Kagoshima Bay.

December 22, 1945 : X+37 − Sea of Hyūga

Bed rest on a clean comfortable hospital ship is a wonderful thing, when needed, but it's infinitely removed from what I came here to do. This morning a novel type of suicide raid was visited upon Miyazaki, just a mile away from my floating bed.

Weather was dreadful all day, a heavy frost was quickly washed away by dark cold rain that lasted all morning. Few people were out on deck, but I heard from a couple of them that there was a spectacular show. Follow-up with Navy staff on board confirmed that the show was destructive and tragic.

Japanese Army bombers joined the *kamikaze* wing this time, covered by a few of their newest top-line fighter escorts. The bombers came down out of the clouds in four or five waves, mostly dead-on target. They were hunting fixed locations on a land mass which would be well familiar to them.

They say our fighters actually intercepted and damaged most of the Jap heavies, but the mass of each bomber, and its substantial payload, isn't deflected by a few machine gun bullets. High explosive and incendiary bombs, wrapped in plane parts, first hit on and around the facilities in Miyazaki harbor. The largest old wooden pier burned for hours. One newly built metal causeway was cut in half by a recently erected metal crane which fell through it into a freshly dredged corner of the harbor.

The Japanese were lucky to find a laden tanker car in the main rail yard. The odds were good since there is almost always a tanker loading there, to bring fuel forward to our thirsty heavy armor. Some hundred thousand gallons of gasoline lit the city for an hour, consuming untold other buildings and equipment with it.

At least one road bridge was cut in two. A number of the more densely occupied building blocks were also hit. The Japanese seemed to know just where the key facilities were set up. First Corps headquarters was barely missed. Medical staff on my ship are anxious to get word about the hospital complex, which had a falling bomber explode just outside the largest building. The building was badly damaged and may not be usable. Dozens of patients and staff were killed.

I was more motivated than ever to get back into the action, but all I could do was write about activities and conversation on the hospital ship. There is little for men to do on a ship like this but to one-up each other with combat stories, or try to chat up the outnumbered nurses. I held a losing hand at either game, so I caught up on news from far away.

Home front news which should be encouraging was bemusing at best to men deployed here. A rush to demobilize and kick start the peacetime economy was both exemplified and fueled by boat loads of servicemen returning from Europe. Tokyo Rose[*] reminded us often that guys at home had a head start on taking all the good jobs – and good women. I myself couldn't help

---

[*] Japanese radio broadcasts meant for American troops usually featured a female news reader and propagandist, along with popular music and other features. The women were collectively nicknamed Tokyo Rose.

but scan the major newspaper mastheads for new editors and feature columnists.

On the political front all eyes were on the mess in China. It was always a mess, but this was something new. We were happy when the Soviets invaded China and Manchuria in early September, because it would tie down Japanese units that we wouldn't have to face. But once we found half of the Kwangtung Army[*] here on Kyushu, no one was sure what to think.

We understood then how the Japanese fell back so fast. Men reading the papers with me wondered aloud how the situation could have devolved into a four-way land war. They couldn't see how the Chinese communists could hate Russian communists that badly, or how Chinese nationalists could so readily turn from fighting the Japanese.

It should surprise no one that a tough Siberian winter slowed down the Russians, least of all the Russians. Old Man Winter saved Moscow itself from invaders multiple times in living memory. I'm sure the Chinese also have a name for him. Ancient legends in China are considerably older than Russian folklore.

Speaking of winter, it arrived late but definitively to Kyushu. Lately inland locations can expect frost most mornings and biting cold on clear nights. Whole cargo ships full of cold weather gear are arriving direct from California, later than planned but just in the nick of time. I plan to catch up with one and get myself kitted out better when I head back over to Ariake Bay tomorrow.

---

[*] The Japanese army in Manchuria, which had been fighting on the mainland for over a decade. It had the most experienced and effective divisions in the Japanese military.

December 23, 1945 : X+38 – Kanoya, Kyushu

Sakura-jima is a castle. Kagoshima-wan is its moat. There is one drawbridge, a narrow causeway to the southeast corner of the fortress island. Jagged mountains at the center command a view over lumpy lava fields that slope down to the water for a mile or more to east, north, and west. Short needly pine trees and thin brush cover patches not as recently thrown under searing liquid rock[*].

Minami-dake, the dominant peak, rises steeply from the south to a volcanic crater 3600 feet high at the rim. Lesser peaks and craters step down from Minami to the north. The approaches from shore are generally rolling gentle grades at first, but at the base of the mountains proper the land shoots up in crooked knife-edge ridges. Hot steam and ash rise frequently from vents in the active crater. It all looks exactly like some ancient dragon built this place for her keep, then abandoned it for us puny mortals to squabble over.

In the next day or two we will assault Sakura-jima. Our units who venture too close to it, be they Army, Marine Corps, or wandering Navy ships, have been set upon by artillery hidden in the rocky heights. Our airplanes have taken out many of the guns, but sometimes only temporarily. The dense volcanic rock is a natural cover deeper and harder than any of the concrete shapes we destroyed close to the invasion beaches.

Some number of very large guns on the island have brought trouble for us more than ten miles away. They never fire a great many rounds, but they are deadly accurate. Since we still do not control the bay, not coincidentally because of the island mountain guns, Japanese spotters have slipped out by small boat to observe our camps.

After Marine guards found and shot up one Japanese scouting party with a precious radio, two others have been captured with nothing but note paper. Once American camps are

---

[*] The island is an active volcano. It only became connected to the mainland during a giant eruption in 1914. In 1946 another large eruption covered over much of the eastern sector.

made before dusk, they can note locations of the more important looking tents and have plenty of time to get coordinates back to the gunners before dawn.

This morning I checked out of the floating hospital and was shuttled by three different boats over to the docks in Ariake Bay. The Army has regular land transport running now, like the Navy set up at sea. I took a scheduled green canvas topped 'bus' west to where units are camped around Kanoya.

After clearing out the point south of Kanoya, the 1st Cavalry Division and the 158th Regimental Combat Team went into camp to rest and rebuild. North of them regiments of the 40th Infantry Division and the 112th RCT made a tag-team assault over the giant ridges centered on Onogara-dake and Bisago-dake. Some time soon they will be leap-frogged by units here who will assault Sakura-jima.

The 98th Infantry Division covered and supported the right side of the advance over Onogara-dake and Bisago-dake. It is now stretched out over the plain south of Miyakonojo into the eastern mountain forest. The Americal Division finished its part of clearing out that mountain forest three days ago and is in bivouac back near the beach to heal up.

Across Kagoshima Bay the Army and Marine Corps finished up at the same time. The 81st Infantry Division is now in camp down near the beaches beside Kaimon-dake. The 77th Infantry Division and the 5th Marine Division are taking in reinforcements near Kushikino. They will be back on the line soon.

Miyakonojo and the large plain around it remain in Japanese hands. First Corps is anxious to take it, but they are going to need help and Eleventh Corps still can't give it until they scratch the giant itch caused by attacks from Sakura-jima.

Incidentally, on my way in I made a point of touring the big air base at Kanoya. My guide told me all about how much American engineers have already built up and expanded the facility and how many cargo flights and attack runs we can make out of it every day. He pointed out some of the new aircraft types and their latest weapon upgrades. I was there looking for one thing.

I didn't see any cemetery in the infield, as promised by General Connor Colt. I did see a prominent sign, posted between the first main runway and a parallel taxiway. An arrow under its words pointed to the southeast. "Courtesy of the 1st Cavalry Division. First Team Cemetery, 3000 yds."

December 25, 1945 : X+40 – Bisago-dake, Kyushu

Today might become known as the Christmas D-Day. Parts of two divisions assaulted the giant thorn in our gut this morning, and are heavily engaged with the oversize pricker. I had an excellent view from a 300 foot tall hill just across a narrow land bridge to the southeast corner of Sakura-jima.

The 26th and 27th Marines launched at first light on small boats from Kagoshima to the western shore of Sakura-jima. Before that, elements of the 5th Cavalry slipped across the land bridge, along two miles of the south edge shore road and into the deserted town of Arimura. As the sun rose all units would come under fierce directed fire from the heights before them.

Before dawn I moved up to be with the forward observers for the 8th Cavalry Regiment, which stood ready to move in beside or through the 5th. The weather was clear, and in the dim morning light I could see gunpowder flashes from the mountain as Japanese guns on the dark sides of each sharp ridge took aim on the landing Marines.

Marine close air support planes were up early though, and rockets were soon let loose against any gun that dared light itself up in the shadows. The Marines had slipped a few radio-equipped spotters onto the island overnight, ready to guide in our planes using pre-arranged terrain marks. The part of the bay I can see does not have any Navy ships in it. The wreck[*] of the USS Hazard

---

[*] The Hazard had been minesweeping just ahead of gun ships which were supporting the fight for Bisago-dake nine days before. She took gun fire, and her captain got her to the nearest shallow water where it is thought her entire crew got off. They were behind Japanese lines and taken as prisoner. Their fate was unknown until the recent armistice.

can still be seen at low tide, where she tried to beach on the south shore of Sakura-jima to save her crew.

The sun rose over the few hills that push into the area occupied by 5th Cav, and Japanese spotters began to find plentiful artillery targets. Whichever guns could fire without inviting immediate response from attack planes made life miserable for the cavalry men. The 5th Cavalry didn't have far to go to reach the base of Minami proper, where they could find some shelter, but very little heavy equipment made it up with them.

I watched as small groups of men dashed over open lava flats to seek cover in small ravines and depressions. Japanese machine guns had been sighted down most long low spots. Squads pulled back out of them under cover of smoke screens.

The smoke made things difficult for other units. Smoke works well when pulling back or moving sideways, but it blinds men trying to advance. Eventually they must emerge from the smoke, in an uncertain location, and likely in the sights of enemy rifles.

Japanese mortar fire from deep pits was distributed liberally from the mountain down to the shore. Navy fire support could not get down into such positions, and aircraft took risks flying low enough to find them. Attack planes dove against the mountain, playing chicken with the unblinking rock. A few were damaged by ground fire on the way down and didn't or couldn't pull up in time.

By last light two battalions of the Army regiment were pressed up tight against the base of Minami-dake. They waited for darkness to move casualties back and bring up more equipment.

Marines on the west plain had made better progress. They landed through a pair of deserted fishing villages and moved over a mile up hill across a lumpy lava plain. The lava field makes an easy approach to the mountain, mechanically, but it offers little cover from enemy fire. They were exposed, though in the morning the dark side of the mountain dared not fire its larger guns into the lingering night that clung to the western face.

By mid morning the Marines had found cover at the base of many bluffs and ridges well inland. They took only 'ordinary' casualties for an amphibious assault, but that was better than would be expected for running across a hard surface into the face of a jagged mountain loaded with defenders. By early afternoon progress was halted. Enemy fire made it impossible to move anything across the lava field to the covered positions up front.

The entire afternoon on both sides turned into a machine gun duel. Marine and Army positions were then in small arms range of Japanese positions on the mountain. The front lines were still very thin, so to get other teams up they sprayed the anonymous rocks ahead with rifle and machine gun fire. The Japanese who were not forced into cover by all that shot into the open areas that they knew the Americans had to move through. The entire world as can be seen from here is divided up into many unsavory pie slices, each of them the field of fire of a traversing machine gun. The team who can serve up more slices wins.

Writing of pie reminds me that this is still Christmas day. I hope all my readers did get a good warm slice of apple or pumpkin pie, or whatever kind of dessert suits your holiday traditions. The 8th Cavalry Regiment and I will be eating in the dark from cold ration cans. They got some special rations up, including whole hams and cooked turkeys in large cans. We did the best we could to share the odd feast with no place settings. Watches have been drawn and everyone is dug in, ready for the possible night time counterattack.

December 26, 1945 : X+41 — Bisago-dake, Kyushu

Clear weather today allowed us to attack again with good naval and air support. It also allowed us to clearly see the messes made overnight and to clean them up before advancing.

Last evening much of the 5th Cavalry was dug in on the south side of Sakura-jima. Only a thin corridor on the south shore connected it to friendly forces on the main land. Early at night no flares or star shells were lit. In total darkness the 5th Cav would try to move more men forward, as the 8th Cav put its first units onto the island over the small land bridge.

Japanese defenders of the island fort also took advantage of the moonless dark. Over a hundred Jap soldiers crawled over the young lava field east of Minami-dake and got in among the Americans trying to establish themselves on the island. A thin line of American GIs guarded the road. They couldn't dig into the surface rock, so were laying in any depression they could find, looking for dark shapes against the even darker sky.

We know at least a hundred came down, because that's how many Japanese bodies were counted this morning. They did outsize damage. The 5th Cavalry Regiment this morning loaded wounded into several Navy assault boats to be taken away. The road back to Kanoya was too littered with wrecks and full of others trying to come forward.

Once the Japanese made contact, a few flares went up. The Navy joined in with long lasting star shells over the whole front. This invited heavy fire from the mountain on units which were caught in the open, trying to rearrange themselves in the dark.

The mess left the 5th Cavalry parked while the 8th attacked through and right of it today. The two Marine regiments on the west side also advanced. The fight moved into the sharp edged sides of the mountains and ground to a bloody crawl.

Each spiny ridge must be taken in turn, but none of them are worth anything in isolation. The sharp top crease offers little safe ground to hold, and both sides can be fired on by the adjacent enemy held faces. There is little cover to use and no chance to dig positions into the bare rock. Every effort forward soaks up a great deal of manpower and firepower.

I was still observing from a high spot overlooking the island's land bridge when an officer from a 1st Cavalry Division artillery unit joined me. Captain Condon Terry's guns were somewhere on the shore of the island in front of us. He came back to "watch the show."

In a slight north Texas drawl the captain told me what to watch for. "This is the only job going anywhere [on Kyushu]. The Army needs that rock taken out; it's the last thing keeping us from pushing north." He paused while a dense chevron of attack planes came in low overhead. "Here it is! It's on now."

The planes let loose volleys of large and small rockets, each pulling up and turning to the east as it got light. The rockets all impacted some ways up hill from a line of colored smoke being made by American troops. Before the rocket planes were out of sight regular bombers came across the line from the southwest, laying iron bombs into points higher up, including the main volcanic crater. Loose anti-aircraft fire tightened up as the formation passed. The very last plane, of about two dozen older B-17s, poured smoke from the left side for a mile as it slowed down behind the others. It tried to turn with the formation and that wing simply fell off into the bay. The rest of the plane joined it just short of the American held shore.

Captain Terry was still enthusiastic about the display. "That's going to happen every two hours on the dot, so long as weather holds." He checked his watch. "They'll give it another four minutes for smoke to clear then my artillery will start working the hill. Twelve minutes after that, everybody advances, the Marines too."

As he called it, guns below us barked out fresh ranging shots. I heard louder booms to the left and looked to see Navy destroyers and a couple cruisers in the bay. They were not about to miss this party. "Everything is pre-set and timed out," the captain continued. "There's naught for me to do but sit back and watch. An artillery man doesn't hardly ever get to see his own work!"

Late in the afternoon one of the Navy LSTs which had been used weeks ago as a temporary beach-front hospital ship was moved to a small dock on the southwest corner of Sakura-jima. Army and Marine Corps units had met there this morning, including engineers. The small floating hospital was full to capacity as quickly as it could be loaded. The engineers were still clearing space and setting up a large aid station. Scattered harassing artillery fire reminded the engineers and doctors that their position was still at risk, but it didn't look like it had been singled out by Japanese spotters.

Our own observation planes several times have caught small boats bringing supplies or reinforcements to the north side of Sakura-jima. Everyone is reminded that taking the island volcano quickly is tantamount to taking it at all.

242

December 27, 1945 : X+42 – Minami-dake, Sakura-jima

Minami-dake and the slightly inferior peaks which it sheds off to the north rise up from Sakura-jima steeper than anything we have dealt with on Kyushu. The peaks are braced by knife edge ridges that radiate out in many directions, separated by steep valleys with impossibly tight bottom crevices. The mountains look like rough round versions of classic cathedrals with spire-accented great flying buttresses.

American tourists might one day visit to take pictures of the natural architecture, but they better hurry. The Americans here this week would just as soon demolish the whole thing, and they may have the means and motivation to do it.

Extra motivation came from a long artillery barrage that walked across American rear lines overnight. Thick clouds and light rain moved in late yesterday. The Japanese took advantage of the relative cover from air observation to open up many large guns for unrestricted fire. They were repaid in kind many times over by ground-directed American return fire. The Japanese guns may also be close to being lost to the American advance, we will find out soon.

Shells landed along and beside the coastal road all across the south and west of Sakura-jima. It may have been spotted, but could have been simply laid along the road where an invader has little choice but to set up all supporting facilities. That detail we will probably never know. Everything from small artillery batteries to large supply dumps were hit or disturbed. The field hospital I mentioned yesterday took a murderous couple hits, which found barracks tents of both engineers and the medical staff which was to take over from them.

Our stubborn advance yesterday was ultimately successful, in taking ground at least. The 26th Marines and 8th Cavalry finished the day holding all of the south half of Minami-dake. They settled in for the night in relatively secure positions. Only the very top main crater was left to directly threaten them. The crater was fed a regular diet of American mortar shells through the night.

There was nothing else to see from my viewing position on the main land, so I made my way onto the island. It was a record slow two mile trip.

The only road onto the island and into American base camps was beaten up and overburdened. A mob of fresh troops, new equipment, and odd personnel like myself were trying to move onto the island. As many injured, tired, or broken men and machines were trying to move the other way.

All along the shore road burned vehicles, or pieces of them, had been pushed onto the black beach or over ledges directly into the water. In two spots along my way engineers had no choice but to close the road for some time while cratered sections were cleaned up, and whatever temporary structure or fill was available was put in to make the road usable for a little while longer. Ambulances were cleared through but then everyone else had to wait.

A few men pushed through off road on foot, but overnight rain made that sticky in some places. In sandy places those men will have picked up abrasive grit that they will be chasing out of their boots for days.

Everything was compressed into a narrow band at the base of the mountain. Since there clearly wasn't enough capacity over the one road for all the division services to support its two cavalry regiments – and the Marines, which had only small boats connecting them to Kagoshima city – the facilities had to set up on the island. An artillery battery worked across a narrow alley from a field kitchen. A medical aid station was uncomfortably close to a pile of fuel drums.

Eventually I got through to the one substantial town on the south shore. It was a cluster of poor looking buildings, two blocks deep from the shore, formerly prospering in whatever fishing and commerce happened through its few docks and piers. North of the town was a gentle rocky slope, almost a plain. In it was a quiet spot, relative to every other clear area, which were all being put to immediate use.

I walked up to find the quiet area was a temporary cemetery. Poncho covered bodies laid in neat rows. A crude signpost at the far end of each row I guessed must categorize the men there by branch and unit. A small team of men was unloading an assortment of vehicles at the far corner. The vehicles were lined up almost back into the town, each bringing over bodies that had come down the mountain or been discharged from a medical station.

I walked between the rows to where the team was working. Looking closer it was clear that some of the old ponchos on the ground covered only a portion of a human body. There were five men working the yard, rotating who was off as pairs of them carried each new case. They had a few stained stretchers to use. I offered my services to the chief NCO there, to make it an even six men working.

Staff Sergeant Bill Allen looked me over for a few seconds, unsure if I was serious I suppose. Few men volunteer for the job, even the drivers who bring over several corpses at once. I was paired with a young Army corporal and we got busy clearing their backlog. Footing was tricky in some spots, the day's rain putting wet rocks or slick mud under foot, and making them hard to tell apart.

Corporal Warner Thompson hails from Fairfax, Virginia. Most of his infantry unit is doing back-line jobs like this one. Their part of the 5th Cavalry was hit hard and probably won't do much until it can get off the island to rebuild. We talked about his experiences in the fight, and about life back home, and pretty much everything except what we were doing.

Finally he broached the subject, by way of a standard soldier's gripe about getting a lousy job. I asked how long he'd been at it. "This is the third day. They had us stack 'em here almost right from the start." Getting ambulances back and ammo forward took priority on the narrow road.

I asked if he ever started counting them. "Start? Hell, I can't stop." We had just finished placing one body at the end of a long row. Corporal Thompson stood arms akimbo as he allowed himself a wide look around. "Last night I tried to sleep, and it was like counting sheep. They just kept coming, one at a time, all night."

We had walked back to the front and were reaching down to grab another stretcher when he said, "I guess it's alright, the counting. If I look at them as a bunch of numbers I might not remember them one at a time." He pulled the cover of the next body fully over its face which had been half exposed. "That would keep me up worse."

I finished with the team only when they were relieved near dusk. All through the afternoon we had heard explosions and seen smoke from the top of the mountain and beyond it. The line of vehicles delivering dead had shortened for a while but by sundown it was longer than when I started.

December 28, 1945 : X+43 − Minami-dake, Sakura-jima

Fighting to take or keep Sakura-jima raged out of my sight all yesterday. I pieced together a general outline of the action from bits of second hand reports. I also got myself up to the front again so I could see the next action.

Yesterday morning before dawn the 27th Marines charged into the main crater of Minami-dake, after the briefest mortar and artillery prep. Their surprise attack couldn't have been any shock to the few Japanese left in the crater, who had been left there to die, taking as many Americans with them as possible. This final clash is what they had lived for as warriors. For them it was the *sho-go*, the final decisive battle.

Marines crested the rim and met only a thin line of poorly equipped, and mostly already injured, Japanese soldiers. Word is some of them may have been local conscripts. At any rate they had only a few rifles and limited ammunition for those. Those who had a good spot to hide waited to fight Americans by bayonet or knife.

It was assumed that any dead Jap was booby trapped. They were left behind for others to check out and disarm. This meant the Marines could not use the fighting holes those bodies were in, even though they were the best positions, dug deep into the inside of the crater rim. Across the crater other Japanese, with better weapons, were still dug in and alive. Marines in the open took rifle and machine gun fire from every direction. A few Japanese field guns

246

even got in on the action, firing their last rounds from small bunkers before being overrun.

By smoke screen, mortars, artillery fire, air support, tenacity, and not a little sweat and blood, the 27th Marines eventually took the entire crater. The 26th Marines kept up outside the crater, leapfrogging itself over several spiny ridges on the west face. On the east face the 8th Cavalry had a harder time moving over a much wider stretch of haphazardly broken terrain.

A mile wide lava field, the youngest part of the island, provided scattered obstructions but very little cover to the advancing cavalrymen. Some Japanese positions still in place on the northeast face of Minami-dake could fire across the whole field. No Navy guns or established Army artillery could hit back at those positions. The cavalry regiment pushed forward anyway with what air support could be provided under unbroken rain clouds.

The first elements to complete their dash across the open lava field came within sight of an occupied coastal village. It was the only occupied settlement anyone had seen on the island. American soldiers were met well outside the town by a group of civilians, one of whom spoke passable English. The people hoped to avoid seeing their town pulverized by American artillery and bombs[†].

A little snow fell late in the day, just as I caught up with the 26th Marines. I let someone important looking know I was there and made camp on a damp cold slope with Charlie Company of its Third Battalion. We were almost 3000 feet up, barely a mile from the shore. I don't think anyone had a flat level spot to lie down on, except for the lucky few who found a spot on the rock soft enough to dig into.

[†] Division artillery orders reviewed later showed that the town was saved with less than two hours to spare.

There is a small cemetery, barely marked, on the short plain east of Minami-dake. A small river runs between it and an abandoned temporary city, running out into the still inner shallows of Kagoshima Bay. On one side of the river Korean slaves and conscript civilian workers for the fortifications on Sakura-jima were camped. On the other side they buried their dead. Digging in the gravel and dark sand near the water would have been immeasurably easier than cutting through solid rock on the mountain.

The G-2 men of the 5th Marine Division have been through the remains of Jap fortifications on the island, the ones that weren't blasted shut by bombs and rockets and hand-placed satchel charges, and they tell a tale of woe for the builders. Innumerable pits and caves were cut into the steep rock faces with hand tools.

These defenses are not as interconnected as with the tunnel systems we found in places like Iwo Jima and Okinawa, but the number of positions is staggering. Firing pits for infantry were everywhere. Among them were double-L shaped rooms for teams manning machine guns or field pieces. None of them could be resupplied or reinforced once we were on Sakura-jima. All of them were there to protect the crown jewel of this hand chiseled gem set.

A tunnel with parallel light rail tracks cut high up through the volcano, running around the entire west side of the main crater. Two of the now infamous eight inch naval guns were mounted on carts for the track. Either gun could be moved to either end of the tunnel, or into the center where we found a small workshop and store room.

At those tunnel ends, heavy doors of welded scrap iron and old steel plate, salvaged remnants repurposed instead of melted down to make new shapes, closed up the tunnel when the guns were pulled back. The two doors sat under bony protrusions of rock, like the mountain itself was scrunching its furrowed brow at the headache caused by all our commotion outside. The Japs even thought to tack small round bands to the face of the doors, where fresh brush could be tucked as camouflage. They were practically putting up Christmas wreaths.

248

The southern end of the tunnel still had tools and iron scraps and empty gas canisters for a cutting torch piled to one side. That position was silent for several days after we bombed it, but it seems they got busy with repairs right away. It's not like they had anything else to do.

The rough count so far shows about 3,500 American combat casualties to take Sakura-jima and Minami-dake. We think the Japanese military dug in there numbered about 3000 total. Practically all of the Japs are dead, whereas most of our boys will live, but our combat power is still reduced by a ratio on the losing side of 1:1. We can't afford many episodes like that, when we are fighting so far from home, in the foyer of the Japanese home land.

The entire 5th Marine Division, what is left of it, is moving back to camps near the Kushikino beach where they first arrived. Actually, much of the division is already there, in the field hospitals. Most of the 1st Cavalry Division is doing the same, retiring to camps near Kanoya. The 2nd and 3rd Marine divisions are taking up reinforcements as fast as they can be landed, and I can't see how the 5th will be back in the fight any time soon.

The 12th Cavalry Regiment is still on Sakura-jima cleaning up. It has taken on some of the healthy equipment and people from the retiring parts of the 1st Cavalry Division, making it almost an independent unit. Updating my well worn pocket map, I can see how a commander will be tempted to deploy the 12th Cav just that way very soon.

December 31, 1945 : X+46 – Kushikino, Kyushu

When the assault on Sakura-jima was complete the Marines and soldiers who had won her had one job left to do. I moved along with the 26th Marines as they swept back over and around the mountain island. They advanced in one big line, each slouching tired shoulder practically touching the dirty arm patches of the next man. The wave of men moved in fits as parts of it stopped to work.

The job was to tag any possible booby trap for later demo teams, and to double check every hole in which a Jap could still be hiding. The ubiquitous flame thrower men followed close behind the main line, like impatient semi-mechanical grim reapers.

I went around the mountain with a group in the middle. It had little work to do, out on the rolling lava fields. Marines nearer the shore had a few holes and old buildings to clear. Uphill from us the others had a tough time.

All the impossibly steep spiny gullies they'd fought through they had to climb through again in closer detail. Sleep deprived men and climbing ropes are a testy combination. I caught bits of profane arguments echoing out from many valleys.

They were thorough, in a fashion. Every rat hole, however shallow, swallowed a grenade or three. Any hole that turned or went deeper than a glance could fix also got a long pulse from a flame thrower[‡].

Eventually the sweep was done and in low afternoon sun the Marines loaded the same small boats which had brought them over. Originally the boats had needed four trips to bring every one across, including their equipment. They needed just one sortie to take the regiments back.

Their injured had already been moved across or out through the Army hospital chain. The dead were still being collected. Most of the ammo which had come forward had been expended and much of the equipment used up or destroyed.

[‡] Portable flame throwers only had a few dozen seconds of fuel to begin with. Several times the men got a sit-down break waiting for more heavy canisters to be hauled up.

Most of us rode from Kagoshima across to the original beachhead on an assortment of motor vehicles. I was in the back of an open two and half ton truck. The ride was quiet, since most men fell asleep sitting up. One fellow was still wide awake and had a point to debate with anyone who had one eye still half open.

Private Sam Singleton of Beaufort, South Carolina, asked repeatedly, "We won, didn't we? I mean, we took the island right, so we won?" Most of the others pretended to be asleep. A couple told him to shut up.

Finally a very young three stripe sergeant engaged the private, explaining that yes, we took the ground and were here to talk about it, so we won. The corporal looked back at the line of trucks behind us and said, "Yeah, that's what I thought. I guess we did win, but still, why does this feel like a retreat?"

I looked the column up and down again and decided he had a point. The line of trucks didn't look much like a victory parade. For starters it was not half the size it should have been. It looked more pitiful than conquering under the darkening winter sky.

We entered the Kushikino beach head camp still a mile away from the water. It had grown tremendously since I left it a few weeks before. Our truck was directed up a recently clear-cut hill to a high camp overlooking the small harbor town south of Kushikino.

Rows of new wooden buildings took in the entire 26th Marines in two such camps. The 27th went a little further into another new camp near the sea wall. The 28th Marines were still in older tent camps, where they had been since it was sure they would not be needed on Sakura-jima.

This morning I went around to size up the 5th Marine Division – after taking advantage of a real bed and pristine officers' mess hall. I was keen to reconnect with any of the men I met during my previous time with the division. Finding them was a ghost hunt.

Most barracks were full of young recruits, privates with the last few weeks on Kyushu containing their only combat experience. Even some of the NCOs were fresh from the States, having earned their stripes in post-boot-camp classes instead of on burning Pacific islands.

Finding little but sleeping babes in the barracks areas I went through the medical facilities. The hospitals around Kushikino, and there were a great many, were by then many miles back from the front lines. Their thousands of beds were filled by men with some days to a couple weeks of recovery time expected. Urgent surgeries were performed further forward. Men with longer to go in recovery were sent further away, like Okinawa or Guam.

Military hospitals at this level are quiet places, sighing softly in lonely resignation. The buildings, of whichever construction, house men with permanent damage at some level. Most of those men will be expected to stand up and jump into the fight again.

Visually the most obvious cases are men missing appendages or whole limbs. Those do not accumulate here, as they are sure to be sent home and discharged. They leave when they are ready or when the hospital is full.

The men stuck here are those with non-vital flesh wounds, small fractures, various illnesses, and cases of 'shell shock.' I did not see any of the psychiatric patients. They are kept separated, and practically isolated. The infant science of psychology can not yet provide firm guidance about which patients can be left in an open ward.

By plain numbers the majority of the 5th Marine Division had been through these buildings or was still in them. The official tally of casualties was well into five figures. More of them would go home than would return to service. I didn't need the exact number, I knew that of the dozens of men I met before I could find exactly one.

Master Sergeant Cliff Buckley had been promoted at some point during the drive south after the Marines took Kagoshima. He was top NCO for the whole tank company of his battalion. "We kept trying to concentrate armor to rush past hard points [in the Japanese defenses]. But dammit, there was always another position behind the one we attacked."

Sergeant Buckley was in a room by himself, just off a long ward in the original hospital for Kushikino. His right leg was bandaged from hip to ankle, where they were still working through burns over most of it. He sat up and talked animatedly, enabled by whatever drugs were listed on the chart below his bed.

"I pushed them forward, even when I knew better, into that furnace. All day long, just like they asked. Dumb sonsabitches… Finally I had to get up front, just to help them pull back." He started to diagram the battle with his finger on a flat sheet, but I had already got the gist of it from officers higher up. Under pressure to speed things up, the division had several times given up slow methodical advances for quick maneuvers to surround the next hill. Trouble was, usually the hill had support and right away the maneuvering force was itself surrounded.

"…and that's when the rockets hit," the sergeant concluded. A few of a Japanese bazooka knock-off had made it to Kyushu. Sergeant Buckley's tank eliminated two of them, the hard way. He was lucky still to have both legs.

January 2, 1946 : X+48 – northeast of Sendai, Kyushu

Yesterday the 81st Infantry Division established itself on the right end of the American lines across western Kyushu. Everyone else cheerfully slid left to make room at the big dinner table. The move was planned for many days, though one could barely tell from Fifth Corps headquarters.

Radio and telephone calls came in streams and bunches, asking for last minute instructions or missing necessities. Outside the camp buildings a traffic jam rivaled that of the worst Boston business day lunch hour. Vehicles were looking to connect with one of the few roads forward. The corps had limited daylight hours to get everyone in place, but they largely got it done.

By the end of the day they consisted of, from left to right, the 3rd Marine Division, the 2nd Marine Division, the 77th Infantry Division, and the 81st Infantry Division. The line started with a semi-circle around Sendai which blended into a southeasterly line to the northwest corner of Kagoshima Bay. The four divisions together covered about 25 miles of front with around 40,000 fighting men.

Theoretically all the divisions would be set up the way they like to be before going on the offensive. New help moving in meant each unit could have a meaningful reserve behind the front line. I didn't expect they would sit still like that for long, so late in the day I caught a ride up to the left end of the line, with the 3rd Marine Regiment, of their namesake division.

The new year arrived yesterday with little attention paid in this quarter. Most of the several hundred thousand people on this side of Kyushu were busy moving house. There might have been some parties set up further back, but up on the line not much happened but a quiet toast from 'special' canteens[§].

You might think it unnecessary to remind men in a combat zone that fireworks are a bad idea. They should be thoroughly bored with explosives of any size. Still, they were reminded to maintain noise and light discipline on the lines. Some men didn't get the message.

I know of at least two incidents where soldiers or Marines made up firecrackers and small rockets. As each of them carried several pounds of lethal ordnance every day, such toys seem especially ridiculous. But right at midnight cracks and pops went off in several places. Flares went up, either joining the party or so sentries could see what the commotion was. Thankfully Japanese artillery did not join the party.

Checking in with a new unit can be a chore, or an opportunity. I'm always looking to get unvarnished information, from whoever might have it, and people seem to think that I am a bottomless source of such information from anywhere outside their own area.

Major Bill Merritt, of the HQ battalion for the 3rd Marine Division, lapped up whatever I could remember about action seen by the other corps. He seemed disappointed that things had been relatively uneventful for Fifth Corps (as much as fighting

---

[§] A special beer ration had been arranged for everyone, but it was only partially and haphazardly distributed during the big move.

254

generating over 25,000 casualties could be considered uneventful). They had fought tooth and nail to gain what they held, but there were no big enemy counterattacks or fancy flanking maneuvers on their part.

In turn I got his best version of what was happening in front of us. All the units from here to Kagoshima held good high ground, won by stubborn attacks with considerable costs. All looked out across broad valleys or short plains to where the land rises again into another long series of hill groups and ridge lines.

The next planned action was to be perfectly straight-forward – attack everywhere, all at once, using every mortar, gun, aircraft, tank, howitzer, bazooka, rifle, and knife at hand. "Nothing fancy, just meat and potatoes, and lots of it." I kept my fork and napkin handy. I expected the dinner bell to ring soon.

Sure enough, before first light an earthquake on par with anything this volcanic island has felt in millennia woke me out of the hole I had taken for the night. Thick waves of bombers had come in from over the water, bombing inland objectives by radar[**]. Some bombs may have fallen short, but I couldn't confirm the details.[††]

The 3rd Marine Division was working up the coast so it would get ample naval support. Small islands near shore gave up huge mounds of themselves as heavy shells made sure they would not present a hazard. The barrage picked up breadth and intensity as it moved inland.

I watched the bombardment from a small high spot with some of the artillery spotters. The bombardment was to spare the roads ahead, for our own use. Corrections were called backed several times after they watched the making of a large pothole through their specialized telescopes.

[**] [Editor's note, 2015: At this time they may have had use of a secret system of land-based radio beacons. It has been theorized that mis-use of this system led to several bomb drops far off target. – sdm]

[††] An element of four B-29s dropped their full loads right through camps of the 77th Infantry Division. Officially 89 men became casualties in the incident, most of them fatalities.

The division was established in a prosperous small coastal city northwest of Sendai, where a navigable river met a small harbor and a train line. The Marines were to drive another two miles north to the next such nearly identical town.

What drew me to the Third is what it would do next – nothing. The 3rd Marines would be the first large unit to reach the planned "line of advance." The line is to run generally northeast from there all the way across Kyushu, about 90 miles. Some number of the combat divisions will dig in there and defend what we took, while bases are prepared to support the invasion of Tokyo itself.[‡‡]

The Marines met little organized resistance today. The knobby terrain had only a few good roads connecting local villages. The Japanese had well disguised but uncoordinated traps set at most intersections or choke points. As usual, the American advance could not be stopped, nor could it move quickly. Ambulances had no trouble keeping up. They made numerous round trips.

Fresh artillery craters made convenient ready fighting holes for Japanese who chose to use them. Under clear skies their use was made short lived by patrolling attack planes.

One group did attack an American convoy in force, jumping it when it got ahead of its infantry. What was described to me as a "wretched half civilian mob" ran from dugouts where they'd been in camp near a small lake. They had nothing with which to damage American tanks or armored tractors and were cut down or simply run over.

By mid afternoon it was almost quiet where I stood, incidental battle sounds being almost two miles away. I rode up a little ways with an engineer unit, by train. They were already moving rail cranes and tie setters forward to repair the tracks which would go on to support our forward lines.

[‡‡] Naturally, this paragraph could not be published at the time and was not even submitted to wartime censors.

The morning had started clear and cold. The setting sun in the west lit fire to columns of dust and gun smoke to the east, where hard fighting continued to rage.

January 5, 1946 : X+51 – Sendai, Kyushu

Not all units fared as well as the 3rd Marines when the new offensive started three days ago. The 3rd quickly took the next town ahead of it. Marines dug into the heights around the town while engineers worked below. As they got settled in I hitched a ride back into Sendai for the night.

There I found no shortage of loaded ammo trucks or empty ambulances starting round trips forward to the 2nd Marine Division lines. I rode an ammo carrier, which was less likely to have wet blood stains inside.

AMTRAC driver Corporal George Shanahan told me what had happened, from his perspective. "I've got a pretty good idea what's up from where they send me. I was moving artillery rounds before this push started. All day after that it was all bullets, and I took them right on into town." Much of the 2nd Marine Division had been fighting through the river junction city of Miyanojo [a place different from and much smaller than Miyakonojo].

The city sits in a mile wide plain, braced by branching river valleys and high ridges which divide them. Japanese small artillery in those hill sides harassed Marines in the city and even took out some of their tanks.

"Four of us tried to go in as a convoy on the first day," Corporal Shanahan said. "Mistake! I got us past one intersection, into a narrow bit, and there they lit us up!" Japanese guns disabled his second vehicle and obliterated the third. Roving American planes found some of the offending guns, punishing them promptly. The supply train was spread out to one vehicle at a time from then on.

We crossed a small but fast running river several times as we wound our way out to the front. Most standing vehicle bridges were temporary ones laid down by American engineers. We passed several small foot bridges, ancient structures of classical oriental design and ornamentation. Their limited capacity was all that had saved them from bombardment or sabotage as the land around them was contested.

Corporal Shanahan gunned his engine to push us around or through patches of mud on the abused road. We neared Miyanojo from the south as I noticed fresh columns of smoke on the small mountain to our right. The steady rain, which had started two days before, would put them out quickly, but just then the hill was still being fought over.

Engineers and artillery men were already working to push big guns up to the marginally secure near end of the mountain's long top. Saws and bulldozers cleared steep lanes while trains of tractors were chained together three at a time to pull one gun at a time up the wet slope.

We approached the outskirts of the city proper and were immediately pointed down a small side street to clear the main road. A steady stream of vehicles came through the other way, moving out of the town to the southwest. Finally a quartermaster man approached to find out what we had and to send us somewhere useful.

The 8th Marines had spent all the previous day fighting into the city. They got to the river which divides Miyanojo and found all its bridges gone. Any reasonable place to ford or place a temporary bridge was targeted by Japanese artillery. In fact, every part of the plain holding the city and its adjoining towns was vulnerable to fire from big guns hidden in mountains that push up abruptly about eight miles north.

Most of the 8th Marines was going to move back some and try to circle around on the left, under cover of some smaller hills. The 6th was to continue fighting from hilltop to hilltop on the right. We were directed to a new supply dump back a bit, between the rears of both regiments.

I was invited to stay on with the Marines after the tractor was unloaded. I looked up at the muddy hill slopes all around, noted that the rain didn't look likely to end, and decided to ride back instead. I'd already been sick once, and I was feeling what they meant about a thing being a 'young man's game.'

We paused in our empty vehicle to let several loaded ambulances pass. I also knew that the Marines would get through that branching valley under deadly fire the whole time. My queasy stomach may not have been only remembering the flu.

I tucked myself in near the 2nd Marine Division HQ. I picked up more news on the advance and arranged to move over again to the Army side in the morning. Before dawn I was moving again and was dropped off right among the 77th Division Headquarters.

I entered one important looking tent and found staff officers huddled over local maps, noting positions of subordinate units and updating strength and supply tables for each. More senior officers were working around a smaller table. They had laid out another map, not of Kyushu, but of southern Okinawa. I was familiar with the area, from watching men train there. These officers knew it better, from watching men die there.

The 77th and the 81st infantry divisions had yesterday been repulsed, with tough losses. They were trying to jump from one line of anonymous hills and high paths over onto a larger set of named peaks and ridges. The 77th had tried the same thing on a smaller scale on Okinawa and also failed on the first several attempts.

Dead and injured were still being collected from yesterday, but the new attack would not wait. They were to go again this morning, with a new plan based on old lessons. Rain was predicted to continue for a third day, but that too was just like on Okinawa.

The Navy was called in to Kagoshima Bay to support with big guns. Once the attack started they would not fire on the mountainsides which our soldiers were attacking. They would plaster the reverse slopes, where it was expected Japanese defenders were only shallowly dug in. So long as they stayed hunkered down, American teams could work methodically through the valley between the two high lines.

Noise of the renewed assault was thick and loud by the time I went up with an observer from the headquarters unit.

Engineers had worked through the last two days and nights to clear rough roads through and over the forested hills. Softer parts of the road were corduroyed with felled logs, brutal riding in a round-wheeled jeep. We came out onto one of the sharper peaks, dodging a hard working bulldozer to make the top.

Heavy tanks and larger self-propelled guns had been established on most such local peaks, owing much to extreme engineering effort. More than one had been left stuck, or had simply fallen right through the edge off of a waterlogged embankment.

Our tanks would be static guns for the day. They could depress their guns better than the heavy howitzers, firing directly down into the valley. Down in that valley mixed teams of tanks and liberally equipped infantry worked along the valley at a dead slow pace. They could rarely be seen.

Usually we could only track American progress by the smoke and dust made by their magnanimous application of firepower. When one of the smaller tanks came forward, there was no mistaking the sight of its long range flame thrower scorching a substantial patch of the mountain.

The opposing ridge was rugged and wavy, with many deep crevices in the near side. Each crevice was treated as a new objective, soldiers climbing up the near edge, before tanks turned into it as the men moved around the edge. Steady rain kept visibility short and footing haphazard.

Japanese guns waited for good targets and opened up only when the side of a tank or a cluster of men presented themselves, which was often. The Japs took a toll on the approaching soldiers and armor, often firing from close range where the covering guns on our side of the valley could not safely engage them. More than once the American GIs simply backed up and waited for friendly guns to pulverize the threat, before rushing the position with grenades and charges.

By night fall about half of the opposing ridge face had been cleared out. As many armored vehicles were lost into the mud as to enemy fire. We rode back down on a tracked vehicle, not trusting the jeep to make it.

Officers at headquarters were reasonably pleased with the early reports. Gains were on the good side of modest, but casualties were reasonable for a change. They were less happy with news from the Navy. The cruisers sent in for support had only brought enough shells for that day's planned bombardment. They would need a day to go load more and would also want orders from higher up to keep pouring so much ordnance into one area.

Division officers worked out what to do next as I went to find somewhere dry to sleep.

January 8, 1946 : X+54 – north of Kagoshima Bay

An Army communications officer went fishing deep into Navy territory yesterday. I caught him on the way out with his partial haul. He was collecting reporters, baiting them with promise of an important event to witness. I bit.

1st Lieutenant Millard Wells drove his own jeep, which he succeeded in filling with three reporters. I rode in back with Bob Bellaire of Collier's. John Elliot sat up front as the Australian representative.

It took some time to get back near corps HQ, continue southeast on a good secure (and freshly rebuilt) road, and finally get up to the front lines near Kagoshima Bay.

We turned the drive into an hour long press conference. Lieutenant Wells shared what he could about the larger situation. Fifth corps had top priority on everything for the current breakout – ammo, air support, even toilet paper stocks were advanced to keep the divisions 'moving.'

Some divisions of the other corps were catching up on laundry and USO shows. Rumors said that Bob Hope had left on a boat from the Philippines and would be on Kyushu soon.

Before our big push in the west the focus had been on getting First and Eleventh corps together in the Miyakonojo plain. Lieutenant Wells struggled to find words to describe the urban fighting in what was left of Miyakonojo. The city center was all rubble and ash. He described Japanese use of the ruins as "improvised fighting positions" but I gathered that they had planned and practiced for such dirty work.

Our new heavy armor was largely useless inside the trashed city. Terraced farms all around the city sheltered many shooting lanes for what antitank guns the Japanese could muster. While our attack planes ruled the sky, Japanese soldiers kept their pieces moving. They rarely stood to fight in place, where they would be fixed by a radio equipped support controller.

The 98th Infantry Division had done much of the urban fighting. It was then tasked with closing up the middle, between

262

Miyakonojo and the east shore of northern Kagoshima Bay. We know now that the top flight troops left over from the big Japanese counter-attack weeks ago had pulled back to dig into the rolling hills west of Miyakonojo.

Those Japanese made a thorny briar patch out of that land in the middle. After rooting them out, the entire 98th Division was again sent back to recover and rebuild. The Americal Division and both regimental combat teams took over the turf won by the 98th. The 98th passed through the 40th Infantry Division which had been rebuilding since taking Onogara-dake and Bisago-dake. The 40th was nearly at full strength again.

Out of First Corps the 11th Airborne Division had been poised to jump out of Miyakonojo, using the good roads running north out of the city. With the 98th no longer on their left they had to spread out and dig in. To their right the 41st Infantry Division had stood ready to support. The 25th and 33rd divisions lined up northwest of Miyazaki, still just outside the next mountain forest.

What Lieutenant Wells had gathered us to see was the planned meeting of American units at the north end of Kagoshima Bay. Once connected there, the American front would finally be one unbroken line all the way across Kyushu.

He described the shore there as dense with small cities. They were well situated as a hub for commerce, closer to inland parts of Kyushu than any of the larger ports. Industrial development of the coast was sparse, but in aggregate it was something worth taking.

Intelligence suggested the area was still well populated with people. The lieutenant didn't know why, but it was another reason we had not and would not thoroughly bomb and shell the area before moving in.

We drove right to the water's edge north of Kagoshima city. Lieutenant Wells pointed northeast across the bay. "That flat land runs north all the way into the next really big mountain [Karakuni-dake]. The 12th Cav already tried to get across once and got lit up by big artillery. Then them and the 158th [Regimental Combat Team] got shelled at random all night after pulling back."

I asked the lieutenant if there was anything we were going to do about the long range artillery before they moved out again. He hesitated a moment then answered without looking away from the road ahead, "Not really. Heavy bombers will carpet the mountains, but they did that twice already."

This morning found me situated with forward observers for the heavy mortars of the 322nd Infantry Regiment. We were staked out on a small hill, hurriedly cleared of brush, looking down into one of the coastal towns on the north end of Kagoshima Bay.

Behind us was a similar town, one held by American forces for many days. That town had experienced tough urban fighting, followed by heavy artillery fire from the recently pacified Sakura-jima. It was less than a ghost town. Its few charred remaining buildings offered no outline of the former city streets. Paths cleared by American engineers went straight through, with no thought to the original map.

The town ahead was pristine. One could imagine people getting up for work that morning, and children running off to school along the quiet safe streets. In fact, a keen eye could pick out heat and faint smoke from cooking fires down below. I didn't think they had made enough breakfast for the ten thousand guests they were about to get.

We wanted the town intact. Artillery, mortars, and even a few Navy gun ships in the bay stood by anyway. The 12th Cavalry had a similar objective, coming into the very next town from the east. (Coordination between friendly forces would be critical as the regiments converged!)

The attack began quietly. The loudest thing to be heard was the strum of a tank engine. The 81st Infantry Division had taken some of its allotment of heavy tanks. They led the way down any streets wide enough for them. Older tanks worked narrower through roads. I stole a look through a big range-finding spotting scope. I could make out infantry working down every alley and checking every building.

More than a mile of easy but careful progress was made by noon. Only a few cooperative civilians were discovered along the way. Just past the city center everything changed. Lead tanks were ambushed by bomb laden attackers, or hit in the side by anti-tank guns hidden in buildings far back from the windows. The attack was almost simultaneous on all streets in a north-south line.

The Japanese soldiers and fighting civilians there may have been considered expendable, or on a suicide mission entirely. Japanese artillery of every size rained down on the city and its people. A valley running almost due north of the city plain runs directly toward the high foothills of Karakuni-dake. That valley hid positions for guns of every mobile caliber.

The 12th Cavalry hit a similar trap. The valley running north out of their objective pointed directly at Karakuni-dake, and they got heavier rounds from guns that had to be fixed into the mountain.

Men of the regiment tried to adjust and move around their burning tanks, only to find that side streets near the trap line had been mined. While they struggled to move, support calls came in.

Two blocks north of green smoke, let em have it! That caller was asked to confirm just how long a 'block' was in his area. Navy guns began firing, hopefully against more precise target descriptions. I watched as much as I could through building smoke and haze over the city and to the north where we were sending return fire.

A different kind of explosion was heard in the bay. I turned my binoculars that way and saw most of a burning destroyer. Much of its rear quarter was missing. Destroyers and two cruisers which had been anchored for shore support were trying to move again.

I couldn't see their attackers but learned later that we had kicked open a hive of suicide speed boats. They had holed up in the last bit of Japanese held shore on southern Kyushu, finally finding a prize as we closed in around them. They were quickly chewed up after the first one found its target.

Both the 322nd Infantry Regiment and the 12th Cavalry Regiment had to collect injured and pull back. The 12th Cav was banged up worse. Both will try again, soon, after and during a tremendous bombardment of the enemy positions that punished them today.

I had to give in and admit it – I was sick. Whatever I had caught which put me on a hospital ship a couple weeks ago never quite went away. I had shied away from tough living since then, never feeling quite up to it, but finally the bug caught up with me again.

Field hospitals were very busy this time, and they wanted to send me far back, even off the island again. This time I begged to stay close to the front. They compromised by shuttling me eastward over to where the land based facilities weren't so busy with broken fighting men.

It was a jarring ride, even though our engineers have improved roads in the center of the island appreciably. A splitting headache, dry cough, and rumbling gut can turn the smoothest road into rough seas. I woke up miserable this morning on what I'm sure a healthy man would consider a comfortable bed, in the 40th Infantry Division primary hospital.

My roommate was feeling much better than I was. He had been there two days before me and was well over the bug that had laid him down. Master Sergeant Harold Elliot whiled away much of the afternoon telling me stories from Dodge City, Kansas. I wondered how a patch of table-flat farm land could hold many good stories, but Sergeant Elliot was good teller of tales. I didn't mind his monologue one bit.

I didn't have much stomach for combat stories, but Sergeant Elliot wasn't trying to tell any. He was one of the top NCOs in the 40th Infantry Division, and easily senior among them. He had been with the unit since just after World War I, when he enlisted too late to be assigned for action in Europe. He hadn't left California since 1920, until 1942.

The 40th had trained in Hawaii, then done clean up work on Guadalcanal. After that it was one of the key spokes in MacArthur's great 'cartwheel' across the South Pacific. They made assaults on New Britain, New Guinea, and many of the toughest parts of the Philippines.

Sergeant Elliot was with the division for all of it. He described his service and made sure I knew how proud he was of his only outfit. Eventually conversation came back around to the current situation.

"Can you believe it? Another whole division coming at us, and a pretty good one they say." I'd heard about more Japanese being spotted moving south, but that we only had a few aerial spotting reports to go by.

"Ha! Those intel guys talk a good game, but don't you think we'd put guys out there on the ground if we could? Ok, maybe I've said to much, but some of my old boys went on to special forces. We catch up when we can. That's all I can say about that."

"Anyway, it means more grinding away out there." The sergeant's face lengthened as he connected the news with the future. "There's no way forward but to kill the bastards, and they're not just going to line up for us to knock them down."

Finally he asked, "Don't you ever get sick of it? Tired of writing the same story every time?" He hit a nerve. It was exactly what I'd been brooding over for days.

After every pitched battle I had to come up with a new way to say, 'Things were destroyed. Men are dead.' I had been at it for years. It seemed important, telling people what an awful spectacle I had seen. But somehow I still had to entertain them. I had to keep readers from becoming as numb as me and turning away from it all.

Sergeant Elliot perked up and leaned over closer at my account. "That's exactly what I mean! I wanted to hear it from a civilian." He confessed to me as a new found kindred spirit. "Honestly, there's no solid reason for me to be laid up back here. I've been a lot sicker than this and stayed out on the line with my boys."

He sat back against the metal headboard again and looked around the room, as if to make sure it was still just the two of us. "I'm just tired, sick and tired of it all. Personally, I could get out there and fight forever, out on the line. In fact I was sure this was a job you just do until you get killed, no exceptions. But since they gave me those fifth and sixth stripes," he pointed at his hanging service jacket, "all I do is feed good men into this… into that machine out there. It adds them up, spits some back out, and nobody knows how it decides."

"And so what? So goddamned what?? These mountains, they don't care. They'll be here long after all of us. The ocean? It could swallow us all and not notice. Even the cities we think we destroyed, they'll all come back. They won't care one whit that their old people are dead, and if the new people are a slightly different color."

The old master sergeant about had me convinced to resign, to give up and buy a struggling grape orchard somewhere. Since I didn't have enough saved up to do that I continued the argument. We talked until well past the second lights out scolding from the floor nurse.

There was never a doubt that the sergeant would return to 'his boys.' He was part of the best chance they had to accomplish something, however indifferent the mountain might be to it, and to get back home alive. It mattered because they mattered.

We were people. Ultimately all we could worry about was people[§§]. The ambivalence of the birds we would have to live with, however many of us lived to hear them sing again back home.

I was suddenly impatient to leave my sick bed again. It felt like me getting out to witness things would help them along, just a little bit faster.

[§§] It didn't seem salient at the time to mention that our conversation included the fates of Japanese people. We wanted the war to be over for them, too, however much some of them didn't want it to end.

Yesterday a sand snake crawled by just outside my tent door, and for the first time in my life I looked upon a snake not with a creeping phobia but with a sudden and surprising feeling of compassion. Somehow I pitied him, because he was a snake instead of man. And I don't know why I felt that way, for I pity for all men too, because they are men.

Ernie Pyle, June, 1943

It felt good to get back to the front again. I was there with my boys. Yes, they were my boys, just as much as they were Sergeant Elliot's boys, or their mothers' sons, or their nation's best men. Three days of physical rest had afforded me a mental reset worth more than the physiological recovery.

I woke up later than usual, well after other men were stirring. I was ready to see this thing through, more ready than I was even at the first landing. To paraphrase Miyamoto Musashi, 'The only blow which matters is the last.' I didn't plan to miss it.

Steady rain muted the sounds of war, but distant artificial thunder reassured me that it continued, and both sides were still determined. At my leisure this morning I went to look for a ride forward. I hooked up with an ambulance this time, not minding the dark red stains under the rear door.

The truck, painted dark green despite the prominent white and red crosses on all sides, carried me up a progressively worsening series of roads until we got to the very front units of the 40th Infantry Division.

The division's 108th Infantry Regiment was about two miles north of Miyakonojo. It had fought its way there, clearing out deep rows of twisting hills. The hills were hundreds of feet tall, but they looked like stubble on the chin of the great mountain mass another mile to the northwest. The compound mountain, including Takachihono-mine and Karakuni-dake, lofted multiple peaks which all topped 4000 feet.

American units had lined up in a semicircle south of the great mountain, about a mile out from the base. They all had fought to get there, through rough terrain and resistance which took advantage of it. They all were punished with artillery fire from the mountain on a regular basis, especially if they tried to move through any of the flat areas which surrounded it. Heavy smoke screens laid over the mountains at times covered American movements, but also obscured the Japanese positions.

Another arc of good roads and developed towns circles the mountain to the north, lying in a broad flat valley. North of them the land rises abruptly into a dense rugged forest, full of beautiful waterfalls and invisible firing positions.

The men I found in the 108th Infantry were preoccupied with digging, rain or not, to make their home livable under the bombardment. To their right was the whole 11th Airborne Division, ready to swing around the great mountain on those good roads to the north. Beyond that other divisions were preparing to drive into that high forest. A mirror image of those maneuvers would happen to the west of Karakuni-dake.

A few officers of the 185th Infantry Regiment were up with the 108th. The 185th would move through the 108th when the next attack came. The 108th was depleted from working hard to get into their most inhospitable home, which was no place in which to rebuild. The 185th had priority for reinforcements.

I talked with a few of the traveling minstrels to hear their song. They are happy to be going on the offensive again and glad that the 185th has just a short way to go to make contact, pushing almost directly into the big mountain. I wondered aloud how that could be an easy job, by any standard.

"Look out there to the north, what do you see? Nothing." I had barely got my binoculars out when Captain Gordon Peck answered his own question. "It's a big straight flat, for the next mile and a half and then more of the same turning west." He drew a map in the air. "The 11th [Airborne Division] has to get through a long gauntlet before even turning up against the mountain."

"Over there," he pointed to the northeast without looking, "The 41st [Infantry Division] has almost as far to go, out in the open, before it can even begin to help the 11th." He let the ephemeral map fall away and stood arms akimbo. "Sure, they're going to gobble up a lot of ground, but it might swallow a lot of them along the way." The officers continued discussing their plans while I looked for a drier place to stand.

A shock wave greater than that from any explosive shell ripped through American lines just after noon. All forward units, everywhere on Kyushu, got orders to pull up and move back to the previous good fighting line, not less than one half mile back – immediately.

The move had to be completed by nightfall. Also, every man was to check the state of his gas mask. Officers were to plan inspections of masks by no later than 9 am the next morning.

Whatever sort of uncomfortable shell-wracked muddy crap holes those men were in, they had fought for them. They were offended at the idea of pulling back. They did so anyway, but complained loudly to the wind, which should have turned red at the profanity it heard.

Field kitchens served men where they could before packing up, but some simply dumped a whole hot meal. Junior staff officers scrambled to figure out where people were, or were going to be, or simply to find room for everyone when units suddenly wound up on top of each other.

Still, the men assumed there was some marginally rational reason for the order (despite all previous experience with Army orders). Suppositions started with some use of chemical shells by the Japanese elsewhere on Kyushu, to wild stories of plague infested rats being loosed by the OSS.

I fell in with a heavy weapons platoon, making instant friends by offering to haul two cans of machine gun rounds. Once back to roughly where they would wind up, everyone sat down waiting for final orders from the battalion. Their commander, Utahan Lieutenant Levi Pace, took stock of the gas mask situation. Of 47 men active in the unit, ten had a mask with them. Six of those had a good filter canister.

A gas mask was on the fingers of every soldier on the morning of the initial landing. No one knew what to expect of Japanese tactics when Americans first invaded their homeland. Two months later, after zero need for them, most gas masks had been 'misplaced' as men lightened their combat load. The changeable filter canisters could be hollowed out to make cooking vessels or many other handy things.

The lieutenant tasked three men with running, as fast as they could, back to division depots for more masks. They were too late. Rear units had been there first, leaving only what supply men kept in reserve for barter. As night fell the platoon counted a lucky thirteen working gas masks, and had IOUs to fill with several division quartermasters.

Map - Central Kyushu

RIVER
KEY ROAD
MTN TOP
3200 FT
1600 FT
HILL

HITOYOSHI

KARAKUNI-
DAKE

TAKACHIHONO-
MINE

MIYAKONOJO

January 16, 1946 : X+62 — north of Miyakonojo

I had completely forgotten what silence sounds like. In the last two months the sounds of combat had been a steady constant. The intensity varied only between loud and ear-splitting. From any position one heard artillery shells either being fired or exploding on impact – or both. Engines of trucks and aircraft filled the air between every echo of every distant rifle crack.

This morning I heard a bird. All of the mechanical noises were temporarily muted. Sounds of combat were not heard anywhere on Kyushu in those few hours. Lastly I noticed that there weren't even any distant aircraft engines.

Without fail since before X-day American fighter planes had been flying long figure eights high over a line well to the north. Even in bad weather at least a few planes did combat air patrol up there, to detect and impede any Japanese air attack. Their constant drone was the last steady lullaby for sleeping soldiers on the quietest nights before today.

A second bird answered the first. I listened to their conversation as my current camp woke up. The sounds of clanging canteen cups were eventually joined by the first mechanical sound of the day. A jeep, driven fast and hard, stopped at the edge of our camp. It gave instructions to the nearest man and sped off again.

"If something big happens, don't look at it! Stay low, keep ready, and wait for instructions. Pass it on!" Some men wondered aloud what it meant. Some asked why it wasn't simply radioed out. Those who had gas masks double checked them. Many moved their foxholes to spots with a better view of the Jap lines.

A little before nine am the fighter planes came back, in force. Three broad waves came in from the south, at three different altitudes. They continued many miles north, to at least their old regular patrol line, then turned east or west out to sea. The lowest group took some anti-aircraft fire, at least one plane going down deep in the Japanese held forest.

About 15 minutes later the soundscape changed again. Twelve B-29s came in high from the southeast. They were almost over Kyushu when the formation broke up into five pairs and two

275

lone sentries. The pairs each turned level toward a target location. The solo observer planes corkscrewed up even higher. I noticed another pair of bombers trailing the twelve, coming in a few minutes late behind them.

I stole a glance around and saw that everyone, to a man, was watching the unusual bomb run with me.

They say it was 9:12 am local time when the first bomber released its load and triggered the others to follow suit immediately after. Some men say they saw all five bombs in the air. I for one caught only a glimpse of the first giant steel ball just after it was released. I watched that pair of B-29s turn and dive steeply, right toward my vantage point. The other pairs pulled the same maneuver, leaving in whichever different direction would keep them best clear of the coming blasts. The first pair passed back overhead still diving, engines ripping madly at the air to pull the bombers away from danger. The high flying sentries continued to orbit over the area, a little to the south.

I was eyeballing the two laggards, which had passed the first pair on their way out. A great flash lit them up, brighter than a clear noon sun. Instinctively, though against instructions, I turned north toward the source of the light. In close succession, above the hills and trees in between, another four flashes lit up across the horizon. Each was similar to how the blast from a big navy 16 inch shell lights up the night, but this was in broad daylight.

An ethereal dome formed and spread out around each blast site, visible only by its effects. Cloud layers alternately formed or vanished as the dome passed. Walls of dust and smoke pushed out along the ground around each blast, quickly visible over the near faces of the mountains north of us. A flattened ball of burning air raised up over each of the sites I could see, shedding and re-swallowing smoky clouds as it roiled up through the hole each bomb had made in the atmosphere.

I remembered the late pair of bombers and picked them up again roughly over Karakuni-dake. The laden one had released its bomb and they had turned together to the east. Due north of my location they caught the first blast wave. Both planes suddenly jumped forward and up, while banked into a right turn. With their full profile facing the shock, they were hopelessly damaged

276

instantly. Closer observers say one plane lost most of the right wing before being sucked directly into its partner. Debris rained over the 11th Airborne Division's former staging area.

The last bomb detonated high over Takachihono-mine, barely two miles from the former front lines of the 40th Infantry Division.^{***}

I wrote some time ago about an 'earthquake' from artillery bombardment. I thought it was modest hyperbole, but it was not remotely close. Today a real earthquake moved the ground under our feet starting a few minutes after the first bombs went off. A great crack from each explosion was heard, followed by continued crackling that took some time to soften into an echoing rumble. Some men thought they felt the wind shift for a moment.

Men began to talk over the sounds, some of them excitedly whooping, some asking what it meant. The company captain had already gathered his officers and they were pointing at the burning mountains and marking up their maps.

Each explosion had been capped by a flattened ball or rolling donut of smoke and fire which rose steadily over a perfect column of hot smoke and steam. The ball shape stayed together until almost out of sight high in the sky. By then a great haze had spread over the entire horizon. Fires raged around each blast zone. A slight wind carried the smoke to the northeast, away from us and mostly across all the Japanese lines.

We sat tight as instructed, as wild conversation bounced around between foxholes and all the way back to command tents. I went back to see what the officers thought of it all. I noticed that my eyes felt dry and itchy, way in the back where I could never scratch. It was a familiar feeling, like how they would get sunburned on long summer lake days. I noticed other men rubbing their eyes, one keeping his shut firmly while holding a tight grimace.

---

^{***} The last bomb was supposed to explode near ground level on the north face of Karakuni-dake, where it was hoped it would crush many of the fortifications dug into the mountain. Hurrying to catch up, the late plane dropped its bomb over the wrong mountain. It is thought that shock waves from the other bombs triggered the altimeter-based fuse.

Battalion command was set up in a tent a half mile back from the bluff top camp. Inside two men worked radios through every frequency in the current book, and got nothing but wild static. A few officers were talking over a map table, wrapped up in tense conversation.

A decision of some sort was made, and some of them left. I approached the table and engaged the senior man. Lieutenant Colonel Ken Olson commanded the battalion. "If you're wondering, no, I don't have the slightest idea what happened or what we're supposed to do. And yes, I'm furious that they would blind side us like this."

I looked over the marks on the largest map. "This is about where each bomb went off," he explained, "each atomic bomb. We know that much, but only from what anybody can read in a science magazine." A two mile diameter circle was drawn around each spot, which might be the effective kill zone of each bomb, but that was their marginally educated guess.

"Here's my current problem." Colonel Olson laid out a local map. "We have a patrol out there. They were supposed to observe this road, camp overnight and scoot right back." He outlined the path out and back. "Someone thought they saw Japs moving out there. I approved the scouting operation, despite the pullback order. I can't stand being both blind and chained down back here."

He wasn't sure what they were going to do about it, but the other officers had gone out to gather up the best equipment they thought might help and assemble a team to go find the missing men. I was about to leave when another courier came in. I'm not sure how difficult it is to drive a jeep in hood and mask and gloves, but that fellow had been doing it all day.

The colonel got four carbon-copies of a typewritten instruction sheet to pass out to his companies. It provided little new information and reinforced previous instructions: We should have seen six atom bombs go off, near listed landmarks (if one didn't go off as planned we were to steer well clear). Blowing smoke might be dangerous if it came our way. Fresh water supplies should be topped off immediately and not refilled from anything downstream of the blast areas. Any Japanese soldiers which might either attack or surrender should be treated like lepers and not directly contacted.

One bit of firm news offered was that the 6th Infantry Division was landing that day, bringing special equipment and technicians with them.

January 17, 1946 : X+63 – north of Miyakonojo

Forest fires burned through the night, keeping a hazy glow above the northern horizon. Morning recon plane flights say that quarter to whole mile diameter areas were burned out. The bombs made clearings in the trees more thorough than area bombing and shelling could accomplish with thousands of rounds.

Light but steady winds had carried smoke and ash to the northeast. This put it all back over Japanese lines or empty rugged forest. Another reminder went out that fresh water sources from the high central forest, which was most of the supply for our lines, were not to be trusted.

By this morning radio traffic was largely back to normal. A few radios had simply quit working after the blasts, mostly ones that had been set up with units far forward. The battalion I was with was not the only one who had sent scouts forward against orders.

Our own scouting patrol finally made it back, escorted by a larger rescue patrol which had gone out after dark. Word is that they made contact with some Japanese. Both sides surprised the other in the dark and exchanged ineffective fire for almost an hour.

The original patrol had been up on a small ridge, looking out over the plain east of Takachihono-mine, when the first bombs went off. They got down behind the ridge but it was right in line with the last bomb and offered little protection from its flash. Their radio was completely shot.

They reported scattered Japanese activity all over after the bombs. Positions up on the mountain all came alive ready for an expected rush. The American patrol hid for the day, planning to slip back at night. They would have come back fine without the rescue party.

I got all this second-hand. Both patrols were taken away into quarantine as soon as they got back by members of the 6th Infantry Division. That division did land yesterday, but not as a unit. They broke up into teams which went out to most American front line positions.

Teams of the 6th carried an array of bizarre looking equipment. They had portable radiation detectors, hand held units with shoulder bag batteries. Some machines rolled on two-wheel carts. Another looked like an industrial vacuum cleaner (which it was – it sucked up soil samples to pass through an enclosed analyzer).

Other odd contraptions could only be hauled on dedicated trucks, some of which looked hurriedly improvised. Men of the division tell me some civilian 'eggheads' came along. They stayed back near the beach, along with lead-lined gunless tanks which can roll out into the blast areas directly once we get there.

Bundles of new personal equipment came forward with the specialist teams. Whatever sort of closed-skin gloves could be assembled in the Pacific came up, be they leather, rubber, or plastic. Rubber overshoes went out to the forward most units as available. Many more men finally had a working gas mask. On a dark cold day new drawstring hoods were welcomed as another warm layer.

The new gloves were not as warm as the woven gloves most men had, so that was the first of their many complaints. The overshoes lacked traction in the wet mud that was certain with the next rain. Most new items were quickly modified by veteran field soldiers, fingers cut off for trigger fingers and ear holes made by crude knife cuts.

Orders went around to prepare for a night advance. We were to quickly get back the margin we'd given up to be clear of the bombs. I was pointedly asked to stay back during the action. I had no objections.

January 18, 1946 : X+64 — north of Miyakonojo

They told me the night advance went well. It wasn't news to me. After so many cycles of day and night combat, the distant sounds of gunpowder-driven fighting tell the story to an experienced ear before any map gets updated. On the cold clear night sound traveled far and could be located pretty accurately.

Through the night I mostly heard sporadic bouts of small arms fire to the north. Usually it started with the distinctive noise of Japanese machine guns. Occasionally a single rifle crack echoed without a response. Ahead of us only a few Japanese had tried to come up and take advantage of positions left by the American 108th Regiment.

Some miles to the west booms of larger artillery were heard with regularity. The 81st Infantry Division had a harder time taking ground back, as what they wanted was still under the sights of guns dug into Karakuni-dake.

Only the faintest sounds of small artillery came across the Miyakonojo plain from the east. The morning didn't reveal any telltale smoke columns. I finally went all the way back to 40th Division Headquarters for whatever news they were handing out.

There wasn't any canned news on offer. Everyone was improvising, including the communications staff. Official word is that strict operational security meant that field units couldn't be told anything about the bombs in advance. Everyone was in on-the-job training. Skipping the press people, I caught a regimental XO, who was just leaving after trying to get information himself.

Lieutenant Colonel Walter Radicowicz was frustrated. "If someone had a plan for this operation, I've yet to see it. Officers at the corps HQs were given a whole two days to prepare for the bombs. I don't know how much they were told or allowed to tell their own units, but they didn't give us much."

Colonel Radicowicz said on days like this he wondered if it would have been better to follow after his father, a retired tool builder in Detroit, who was un-retired to build forges for the very tanks lined up along the road. He caught me up on other general news as we walked back toward his unit.

"Not that planning would have helped with the surprises that came up so far. Out east they're stuck, but for different reasons. The 33rd [Division] has its hands full taking in refugees and surrendering Japs, all of them pathetic with burns and disease." The easternmost atom bomb blast had found a valley full of sheltering civilians and the remains of some low-ranking conscript Japanese Army units. "Right next to them the 25th [Division] hit the teeth of the stiffest defense they've seen. The bomb there was practically a dud." It went off too low, on the wrong side of a small mountain, protecting Japanese on the back side. "I suppose the Japs think it's gloves-off now. They're not going to hold back now."

It's been assumed that Japanese artillery rounds were being conserved, both to save their supply and keep the guns from being easily spotted. Such restraint might not continue if they believed more giant bombs might come. They might perceive their last chance to punish the American invaders.

Another potential relaxing of restraint raised concern. For whatever reason, the Japanese military had not used chemical weapons against American armies. If they had any handy, it would be natural to use them in response to the atomic bombs. This was another reason for the gas mask situation getting recent attention.

I asked what we knew about the Japanese reinforcements that were still coming in. The colonel was hesitant to answer, but it was clear I already knew something of it. "We missed them entirely. And that's all we know. Nobody can come the way they did again. The entire city of Hitoyoshi was wiped out, as planned. But the Jap division had already moved out, taking anything useful with them."

Colonel Radicowicz paused mid-stride, remembering, "Oh, we hit another smaller city the same way, over there." He gestured west with a nod, hands on his hips. "It didn't mean damn thing either. They can't move through that town now either, but the Jap 77th [Division] is already dug into their line facing the Marines." The Marine divisions, and coincidentally our own 77th Infantry Division, had to fight the same battle over again to regain the previous line. It was easier with the practice, but still an unwelcome chore.

282

Everyone was supposed to spend the day consolidating the line and getting ready for another morning push. It was time to take advantage of the great bombing. Teams from the 6th Infantry Division would be with each front line unit, watching for radiation and other dangers on the new frontier.

January 19, 1946 : X+65 — Takachihono-mine

A steady light rain developed overnight. It came with a sense of foreboding, partly because we had already been told it would continue all day and lead into heavier rain the next day. Slightly warmer air moved in with the rain. Still every man was a bundle of standard-issue and improvised layers under his dark green poncho.

Yesterday Colonel Radicowicz had directed me toward one of the companies of his 160th Regiment. It was to move over some foothills of Takachihono-mine, in a spot we thought was screened from the guns dug into Hitoyoshi-dake behind it. We would have no armor, which was saved for units with more need for the support, but it was still expected to be one of the safer jobs of the day. We also would not have a radiation monitor team, for that days planned advance was believed safe.

The days were finally starting to get a little longer. As the gray sky started to lighten we moved out past American front lines, climbing down a ways to cross a short flat. It was open rocky terrain and everyone felt self-conscious in our fashion ensembles of wet dark green.

The company advanced slowly in one double line up to the next hill, across the valley American troops had been watching for so many days. At the base three patrols split off, one to either side and the third moving up to the peak. The patrol I was with advanced cautiously around the right side of the hilltop. Just over the crest we found about a dozen shallow fighting holes. Abandoned shovels, packs, and a few rifles were left there in and around the holes. Also in the holes were three dead bodies.

It looked like the Japanese had moved up to that line the day before, or the previous night, and made a temporary fighting line. There was no fighting so the soldiers there had died of existing injuries. Outwardly they looked bloated, as if they'd been dead for days. A few odd large sores were visible on the head and hands of a couple of them. The private next to me tipped the helmet off one with the point of his bayonet, and clumps of thin dark hair came off with it.

Our senior sergeant growled out a quiet reminder about booby traps, and we left the bodies and materiel there for others to clean up. We advanced slowly through the rocks and leafless brush down the back slope of the hill. Over the next four hundred yards we found six more bodies, soldiers in ragged uniforms, some with whole limbs wrapped in dirty bandages. Most looked like they collapsed while crawling on all fours, away from our lines.

We had gotten ahead of the center patrol, and it was there from our left that one live solider came stumbling toward us. He moved out from behind the dark boulder he'd been leaning on in a staggering half-awake walk. His pathetic form did not carry a gun, and no one fired at him. His uniform was dirty like the others, but straight and neat, topped with a sharply creased brown cap. He had been their commander.

The young officer raised his sword with one wavering arm. One could see from twenty feet away that it was a cheap stamped steel model. The Japanese were mass-producing them for every new officer to make him feel like part of the 'warrior elite.' His jaw fell and the sores in this warrior's cheeks opened to expose the tortured flesh inside his mouth. He attempted to yell but only made a raspy mewl. He was almost upon our left column.

The point man on that side froze, horrified and mesmerized by the almost inhuman apparition. At the last second he raised the butt of his rifle and deflected the sword's feeble blow. The imitation samurai blade was slowly raised again, and a Thompson barked out a long burst. The second man in the patrol line put his slugs all clean through the officer's wrecked body. That lifeless body fell at once into a disorganized heap of parts, barely recognizable as a human corpse.

Press Release, January 17, 1946

FOR IMMEDIATE RELEASE

HEADQUARTERS, UNITED STATES ARMY
FORCES IN THE PACIFIC

Yesterday the American Sixth Army
entered the annals of history. A new
age of warfare, or perhaps the end of
warfare itself, was begun. The most
fundamental force of nature was
unleashed upon our enemies, in the
form of six atomic bombs.

The unprecedented destructive power of
these new devices has been laid upon
the fighting forces of Japan, deployed
in the field against our armies. Know
that they can also be used against
productive centers and the cities
around them, but this will always be
our last resort.

Not only will the bombs employed on
Kyushu break stubborn resistance
there, they will freeze all plans of
aggression by America's adversaries,
now and long into the future. A new
age of peace has been born of fire.

At this moment more atomic devices are
being moved to Kyushu, from where all
of east Asia will be in range of their
terrible wrath. We call on Japan and
all belligerents in China to cease
hostilities and honor previous
territorial agreements.

 - General Douglas MacArthur, Manila

Postscript

Thank you for reading my book.

Regular news readers know what happened on Kyushu and across the Pacific after January of 1946. I'm sorry that I wasn't there to tell you about any of it. Many readers wrote in asking just what became of me after the end of Kyushu Diary.

I had plenty of company in the evac hospitals of the Philippines, all of us minor radiation poisoning patients. After the first day's advance into new atomic bomb territory, more susceptible men began to complain of nausea and headaches. By the end of the second day many small units were called back.

Each man was stripped and had a shower, if he was still standing. Great piles of uniforms were collected for burial or dumping at sea. They processed us through separate medical tents, full of nurses covered head to toe in improvised protective getups.

Now that we are a few years removed from later events, a follow-up summary might be helpful to some readers. I hesitate to color my own observations with "historical reflection," but I will make an earnest attempt to keep it straight and simple.

Early signs of low-grade radiation sickness did not stop the American army from launching a large attack on the third day after the big bombs fell. Two divisions tried to swing around Karakuni-dake on the east. Coincidentally the Japanese tried a thrust around the west side of the mountain. Both assaults were tragic wastes.

The atomic bomb meant for Karakuni-dake had gone off too high and done nothing to its fortifications. The Americans moving around it were caught under massive fire from three sides, pulling back through a driving rain without many of their vehicles. The Japanese on the other side of the mountain charged into American lines which had been static for over a week. They made no progress and were punished by naval support from Kagoshima Bay.

While a few Japanese units were hit hard by the atomic air blasts, the bombs didn't come close to breaking resistance across Kyushu. Each bomb could have killed men out in the open for just over a mile radius, much less if they were well dug in. The front was over 100 miles long in mid January.

American scientists were sure lingering radiation effects would make life hell for Japanese on the downwind side of everything. We have only fragmented accounts from survivors who stumbled down into American camps.

Official casualty numbers for the American Sixth Army on Kyushu before the atomic bombing came to just under 101,000, almost exactly one third of them being fatalities. The Navy says 33,042 sailors were lost. Casualty counts for the time just after the bombing remain secret. Those who counted medical transports leaving say they added up to just over 20,000 evac cases.

American observers estimated Japanese military casualties at over 150,000, most of them dead. With the recent peace treaty we may finally be able to compare estimates against official Japanese numbers. It will take longer to get any idea how many Japanese civilians were killed during the fighting. The city of Hitoyoshi has already gained infamy as the first populated city to be "nuked." The paucity of firm information we have about what happened there only adds to its legend.

I wouldn't say anything definitive about MacArthur's public proclamations after the atomic bombing, except of course that they got him into a great deal of trouble. Historians will debate if it was right for Congress to save his job. They will probably say he was responsible for keeping the Soviets from seizing Hokkaido.

The new treaty may seem to settle things, but remember that much is still unresolved. American and Japanese negotiators have only begun discussing an American withdrawal from Kyushu. Korea remains divided, with the British sector sought by all the Chinese factions. It seems everyone wants it except the British.

I leave it to professional historians to debate the merits of all the decisions made which brought us here. They will argue for generations what should have been done, how things could have been different, and 'was it all worth it?'

My simple account I leave as a plain record of how it actually was.

Walter F. Tuttle
January, 1952
Charleston, South Carolina

Thank You

The reader is kindly requested to leave a review at their online retailer. Reviews help other readers be matched up with a book that might interest them. They also keep people from being disappointed by something which wasn't what they expected.

Shawn D. Mahaney may be found at:
www.facebook.com/pages/Shawn-D-Mahaney/939977792720310
twitter.com/sdmahaneysc
www.sdmahaney.org
riverratsc.wordpress.com/
and may be contacted directly through the project web site,
http://www.xdayjapan.com/

For a much lighter read, consider a farcical tail of a hard-boiled detective squirrel,
http://www.amazon.com/Farewell-My-Legume-Private-Detective/dp/1500278785

Glossary – Military Structure and other 1940s Terminology

Unit sizes (may vary widely by nationality, branch of service, and situation):

These are for US infantry of the period (Marine units were built about the same). There are parallel structures for armored units, support units, and even naval fleets and air forces,

– Fire team, four riflemen
– Squad, three fire teams,
– Platoon, three squads
– Company, three squads, plus heavy machine guns and small mortars, 250 men
– Battalion, three companies, plus a heavy weapons company, 900-1000 men
– Regiment, three battalions, about 3000 men
– Brigade, seldom used, can be a specially reinforced regiment or two regiments
– Division, three regiments, plus artillery and support troops, 15-20,000 men[†††]
– Corps, multiple divisions, typically three, plus command elements
– Army, multiple corps. The Sixth Army under General Krueger on Kyushu had thirteen divisions in four corps, about a quarter million troops in combat units.

The rule-of-three that guides these structures was new to most armies in the 1930s, but quickly adopted by most contemporary forces.

Unit names:

The formal name of a military unit often includes its specialty, e.g. 40th Infantry Division. But unless there is confusion from duplicated numbers, it may be called the 40th Division.

[†††] For planning purposes in amphibious operations a 'division slice' was used, including together those under command in the division and all support and ready replacement personnel behind the division, which could grow to over 40,000 people.

At that time, the standard permanent large unit was the regiment. Regiments are often called out only by their specialty, e.g. the 3rd Marines, 511th Airborne, or 185th Infantry.

People:

Many people, military and political as well as celebrities, would have been immediately familiar to Tuttle's readers, but perhaps not to a reader seventy years removed. We outline a few here:

General Douglas MacArthur – commander of all US Army forces in the Pacific theater. MacArthur was an incontrovertible genius and living legend, and he knew it. He was disliked by many for his outsize public persona and overt political maneuvering. He was well known and respected in much of east Asia before the war, and a natural choice to lead Army efforts against Japan.

Admiral Chester Nimitz – commander of all U.S. Navy forces in the Pacific, and the antithesis of MacArthur. He led a remarkably aggressive push against the initially superior Imperial Japanese Navy. Nimitz ultimately handed command of amphibious operations to MacArthur before the Kyushu invasion.

Clement Atlee – elected Prime Minister of Great Britain in a shocking result in mid-1945, over the long serving wartime leader Winston Churchill. The election cast doubt on English commitment to finish out the war and 'win the peace'.

Major General Charles Willoughby – chief of Intelligence under General MacArthur through the war. Willoughby is often criticized for consistently underestimating Japanese forces and abilities, at great cost to American forces facing them.

Other terms:

Potsdam Conference – After the defeat of Nazi Germany, allied leaders met in the German city of Potsdam to firm up agreements about completion of the war and settlement of territorial occupation duties afterward. The Potsdam Declaration from the same meetings reiterated to Japan that unconditional surrender was required to end the war.

Liberty ship, Victory ship – classes of highly-producible cargo ships which were built by the thousands to support wartime shipping needs. Varieties hauled dry and wet cargo and ordnance of every type. Some went on to commercial service into the 21st century.

USO, United Service Organizations – Founded in 1941, originally under the War Department, the USO is best known for sending entertainers out to remote places to put on shows for troops far from home. It also printed compact books, operated clubs, and a filled a stunning variety of special requests for commanders and servicemen. The USO continues to operate independently, largely on private donations.

NCO, non-com, Non-commissioned officer – any sergeant or corporal, someone who might command other men but who is not a full officer, which is lieutenant and up.

XO, executive officer – second-in-command and/or top administrative officer in a large unit, or on a ship.

CO, commanding officer

BAR, Browning automatic rifle – a light machine gun carried by most American infantry, one or two per squad, with a 20-round detachable magazine of full power rifle ammunition.

MP, military police

OSS, Office of Strategic Services – the intelligence and espionage agency for the United States during World War II.

VE Day, Victory in Europe Day - A celebration over the closure of the first phase of World War Two, officially on May 8, 1945.

Quonset hut - a building with a semi-cylindrical outer shell, usually of corrugated sheet metal.

Seabees, CBs, construction battalions - U.S. Navy engineer units.

Pillbox - common name for any low stone or concrete fortification, typically rectangular with narrow horizontal shooting slits.

CAP, combat air patrol

292

HQ, headquarters

Higgins boats - flat bottomed boats with bow ramps used to unload men and vehicles directly onto a beach, popularized by Higgins Industries of New Orleans.

WAVES, Women Accepted for Volunteer Emergency Service - officially the U.S. Naval Reserve (Women's Reserve).

WAC, Women's Army Corp

Flak - anti-aircraft fire, specifically the type which explodes at altitude spreading shrapnel.

Star shell - one of a variety of light-making devices fired from guns or mortars which stay airborne for some duration.

Weasel - the M29 tracked vehicle, about jeep sized. Variants carried troops and cargo through snow and mud in every theater.

PFC – Private, first class

G-2 – the second group in the traditional general staff system of military organization, the intelligence section.

Additional Reading and Resources

A first stop for more information should be the project web site. It will have the most complete version of this list, more online resources, downloadable color maps, and bits of related historical information.
www.xdayjapan.com

A companion volume is available – *X-Day: Gaming Olympic* is a full color book which illustrates the battle day-by-day in maps and photos with running commentary.
xdayjapan.com/gaming-olympic

Reference materials

Keegan, John, editor; *Atlas of the Second World War*. Ann Arbor, MI: HarperCollins with Borders Press, 1989

Zaloga, Steven J.; *Defense of Japan 1945*. Long Island City, NY: Osprey, 2010

Personal accounts

Green, Bob; *Okinawa Odyssey*. Albany, TX: Bright Sky Press, 2004.

Pyle, Ernie; *Brave Men*. New York, NY: Henry Holt and Company, 1943.

Pyle, Ernie; *Here Is Your War*. New York, NY: Henry Holt and Company, 1943.

Pyle, Ernie; *Ernie's War: The Best of Ernie Pyle's World War II Dispatches*. Ed. David Nicols. New York, NY; Random House, 1986.

Sledge, E. B.; *With the Old Breed*. New York, NY: Random House, 1981.

Tatum, Chuck; *Red Blood, Black Sand: Fighting Alongside John Basilone from Boot Camp to Iwo Jima*. New York, NY: Berkley, 2012.

Tregaskis, Richard; *Guadalcanal Diary*. 1943. New York, NY; Random House

Yahara Hiromichi; *The Battle for Okinawa*, trans. Roger Pineau and Masatoshi Uehara. New York, NY; John Wiley & Sons, 1995.

Other works

Hoffman, Col. Jon T., USMCR; *Chesty: The Story of Lieutenant General Lewis B. Puller, USMC*. New York, NY; Random House, 2001.

Stoler, Mark A.; *George C. Marshall: Soldier-Statesman of the American Century*. New York, NY, Simon & Schuster Macmillan, 1989

Sloan, Bill; *Brotherhood of Heroes: The Marines at Peleliu, 1944 – The Bloodiest Battle of the Pacific War*. New York, NY: Simon & Schuster, 1995.

Sloan, Bill; *The Ultimate Battle: Okinawa 1945 – The Last Epic Struggle of World War II*. New York, NY: Simon & Shuster, 2007.

Eastern philosophy and history

Cleary, Thomas, ed. and trans.; *Training the Samurai Mind: A Bushido Sourcebook*. Boston, MA; Shambhala, 2009.

Sun Tzu; *The Art of War*. Trans. Samuel B. Griffith. London: Oxford University Press, 1963.

Musashi Miyamoto; *The Book of Five Rings*. Trans. William Scott Wilson. Boston, MA: Shambhala, 2012.

Related fiction: Some of our favorite historical fiction explores other endings of WW2, such as if atomic bombs were dropped on cities to force Japan's surrender, or if the bomb simply wasn't available:

Giangreco, D. M.; *Hell to Pay - Operation Downfall and the Invasion of Japan, 1945-1947*. Annapolis, MD: Naval Institute Press, 2009

Frank, Richard B.; *Downfall - The End of the Imperial Japanese Empire*. New York, NY: Penguin, 1999.

Conroy, Robert; *1945 - What if Japan Hadn't Surrendered in World War II?* New York, NY: Ballantine Books, 2007.

Coppel, Alfred; *The Burning Mountain - A Novel of the Invasion of Japan*. New York, NY: Harcourt Brace Jovanovich, 1983. [*This superlative bit of fiction can be faulted only for glossing over the invasion of Kyushu.*]

Maps

Pacific,
http://lukeroberts.deviantart.com/art/Photoshop-Shapes-World-Map-22233322

Japan with Ryukus,
http://d-maps.com/carte.php?num_car=24840

Kyushu,
http://d-maps.com/carte.php?num_car=115469

High quality scans of the original pre-invasion maps prepared by the U.S. Army are available from the University of Texas. In the same collection is a larger scale set for all of Japan, from 1954.
http://www.lib.utexas.edu/maps/ams/kyushu/ [1945, 1:50,000 scale, 20 m elevation lines, VERY detailed]
http://www.lib.utexas.edu/maps/ams/japan/ [1954, 1:250,000 scale, 100 m elevation lines, shaded]

A set of the maps inside this book can be downloaded from http://www.xdayjapan.com.

Brief Historical Context

After the Japanese attack on Pearl Harbor on December 7, 1941, there was a common attitude that it was inevitable that the U.S. would not just fight back but fight to total victory over Japan and permanently extinguish her imperial ambitions. Tempering this attitude, though not near as much as it probably should have, was the reality that another totalitarian threat had swallowed up all of Europe and was pushing deep into old Russia.

Germany only got stronger as it overtook developed countries and their readily accessed labor and resources. From 1933 through 1942 Japan assumed dominion over almost a third of the Earth's surface, but most of that was deep ocean. While many of the island territories taken had rich natural resources, they were raw and it would take time to develop those resources into part of a self-sustaining industrial military machine.

It was agreed among the key "Allies" (The United States, Great Britain, and the Soviet Union) that striking back hard at Japan would have to wait. Among the "Axis" powers (Germany, Italy, and Japan), Germany was the clear and present danger. The very continued existence of the U.K. and of Soviet Russia as an effective fighting force were in doubt if Germany was not checked quickly.

The Japanese knew this and took advantage. Crippling the U.S. fleet at Pearl Harbor and seizing outsized reaches of territory immediately afterward put Japan in a strong strategic position. From there they could pursue their ultimate aim of negotiating with the U.S. to an armistice line in the Pacific. This would leave Japan in place as an undisputed major world power, a position long denied it by the established western powers.

But the Americans did not negotiate. Japan suffered major naval losses during 1942, owing to tactical mistakes, bad luck, and American intelligence successes made public only long after. By the end of 1942 Japan had lost the offensive impetus and was hurriedly rebuilding her navy and especially her naval fighter squadrons.

Elsewhere in 1942, the U.S. and Great Britain traded larger and larger air raids with the Germans. Strategic submarine warfare in the north Atlantic continued and expanded. Germany solidified its hold on Europe, while fighting the largest land battles in history against Soviet Russia. Smaller scale fighting continued across southeast Asia as the Allies tried to get military supplies to Chinese forces lined up against some of the best Japanese divisions, which had been there for a decade.

Even if it was considered inevitable that the U.S. would strike deep into the Japanese empire, it was by no means certain how this would happen. I keep a pull-out poster from an early 1943 newspaper, something we would now call an "infographic," which illustrates Japan's formidable layered chains of fortified islands. The paper pushed for a campaign through mainland Asia instead of "island-hopping."

I think about Tuttle's well-belabored points about logistics and note that eastern China is even farther away than those islands. I leave that option for someone else's alternate history. It was decided that the U.S. military would drive the attack from east to west, building bases on Pacific islands as it went.

It's an age old military problem that a large front or line of positions is difficult to defend if the attacker has good mobility and can concentrate forces on one particular spot at will. Out in the ocean an attacker with a good navy has excellent mobility and can mass firepower and assault forces around any island they wish. The defender has to garrison all the islands. When one of them is attacked, the garrison has to hold out long enough for the defender's navy to get there and meet the attackers. This is the scene that played out repeatedly through 1943 and 1944. Most of the time the Imperial Japanese Navy caught the losing end of the outcome.

American assault forces started as early as possible, even when hamstrung by the emphasis on supplies and troops for Europe. In fact, American Marines landed on Guadalcanal in the Solomons in the fall of 1942, before U.S. Army soldiers joined allied landings in Africa.

With the U.S. still inferior to Japan in naval strength in the area and lacking follow-up troops, the Marines on Guadalcanal fought an epic battle against waves of Japanese reinforcements until the navy was finally able to intercept enemy transports and land reinforcements months later. From there on combat in the Pacific followed a regular pattern.

Naval forces with the Marines took a string of islands across the central Pacific. U.S. Army and Australian divisions did the same further south, including the larger land masses of New Guinea and the Philippines. Both efforts were enormous and accompanied by a buildup of strategic air forces that was able to reach mainland Japan from readily supplied island bases by the fall of 1944. Finally, on April 1, 1945, the two amphibious armies combined on Okinawa in the Ryukus, a few hundred miles south of mainland Japan.

By this time allied forces in Europe had pushed north all the way through Italy. The famous mid-1944 landings at Normandy in France made "D-Day" a brand name. The Soviets and western Allies had pinched the German military into a few shrinking pockets. The war in Europe was officially over in May of 1945. This meant very little to the soldiers and Marines fighting from muddy holes on Okinawa.

Tuttle tried to convey to readers the great scale of the war effort. Most contemporary readers already had direct knowledge of it, as a host of goods were rationed, many prices were controlled, and things like civilian automobiles had simply ceased production since long before the United States was even formally at war.

To help the modern reader, a few comparisons are in order. In 1945 General George Marshall had over eight million men and women in uniform under his direct command – just in the Army. Four million more people filled out the other military services. In 2013 the complete US armed forces came to less than two million people, with multiple wars going and deployments in 150 different countries.

The economists figure 40% of U.S. gross domestic product went directly to the military at the peak of the 1940s war effort. Today prosperous countries are expected to spend 2% of GDP on defense (most spend chronically less).

Popular models of World War II battle tanks or fighter planes were produced in runs of twenty or forty thousand or more. A modern defense company is delighted if a fighter plane sells more than a few hundred copies.

Combat against the Japanese changed through the course of the war. As Tuttle explained, their military tradition is focused historically on offensive action. There may be ample maneuvering and deception, but the focus of it all is pursuit of the final decisive blow that decides a fight, a battle, or a war. Cursory attention was paid in pre-war Japanese military colleges to fixed field fortifications and defensive strategies. They did learn from experience during the war, however.

Early in the war Japanese tactics were anchored on massive human-wave attacks, out in the open. In late 1944 US forces began to encounter extensive layered defensive fortifications, either built up from reinforced concrete or carved into natural rock. The sudden change was an acute shock to American commanders, as exemplified by the brutal fight for the small rocky island of Peleliu, with its unending lines of sharp wavy ridges, which welcomed installation of interconnected and mutually supporting firing positions as if the whole island was purpose designed for it.

It was learned much later just how well coordinated Japanese defenses had been. In particular, one of the senior Japanese officers on Okinawa eventually wrote a book about his experience there. They didn't just have good fixed positions, they maintained communication and control of units right to the end of the toughest battles.

It was also learned that Japanese artillery was well sighted and spotted against advancing Americans, almost without exception. It was not random or desperate. Most famously the top American commander on Okinawa, Major General Buckner, was killed by the first shot of a short barrage when a Japanese gun captain saw a VIP being shown the battle front.

U.S. forces eventually developed tactics (involving lots of explosives, tanks, and flame throwers) for working through such defenses with relatively reasonable losses. It was slow work, and the Japanese presented good reasons to hurry things up at Okinawa. The tactic of flying suicide planes into U.S. navy ships,

300

kamikazes, was not new, but it was scaled up to spectacular effect around Okinawa.

Hundreds of ships were sunk or damaged from the immense supply and fire support fleet as the invasion forces inched along over the island. The dual threats of suicide attacks on the supporting fleet, and the continued pounding of enemy artillery from hidden positions would make it imperative to push through to objectives as quickly as possible. They had to overrun the artillery positions and free the fleet from close support duties near any shore.

Before Okinawa was secure, preparation for the invasion of Japan was well under way. The Army divisions that had taken the Philippines were all still there, refitting and training. The Marine Corps divisions not engaged on Okinawa were doing the same, from bases in the Marianas and the Hawaiian Islands.

The primary home islands of Japan are Hokkaido in the north, Honshu – the largest and most powerful – in the middle, Shikoku and Kyushu to the south of Honshu, with Shikoku east of the larger Kyushu. The invasion of Japan was to be in two parts – southern Kyushu before the end of 1945, and eastern Honshu (around Tokyo) in the spring of 1946. This put the usual winter typhoon season in between.

It was a huge job to shift the logistics chain which had been pointed at the Philippines north many hundred miles to Okinawa and Japan. The major typhoon that hit Okinawa on October 9th, wrecking most facilities and hundreds of ships, delayed the assault on Kyushu from a tentative November 1st to November 15th. Sacrifices were made to sustain a November launch, and it has been argued that the delay should have been longer.

Tuttle's diary chronicles the sixty days of hard fighting after that. As most readers will be aware, even if the rest of this article is news to them, after those sixty days the U.S. Army was bogged down well short of the planned invasion objectives. American bombers then dropped six atomic bombs on Japanese positions, some perilously close to American lines, not knowing for sure just what would happen. The wisdom of that decision, from its immediate costs to the geopolitical ramifications, has been and will be debated vigorously.

One can gather innumerable statistics from the aftermath: hundreds of thousands of soldiers and civilians dead or maimed, two to three million Japanese starved during the winter and following year of costly blockade, half a trillion American dollars spent maintaining the U.S. military across the Pacific until the final cease-fire agreement. Some will question the cost of the entire affair from the start, especially with the extended geopolitical uncertainty and tension it brought. It seemed to some like little was resolved in the Pacific after all.

We bring out this new book at this time because of the impending milestone anniversary of the events it describes and the interest it provokes. Walt Tuttle's voice from that time is a key contemporaneous account from an expert observer. It is a unique point of view that no historian or educated individual should be without in any debate or reflection.

> Shawn D. Mahaney
> Historical Editor
> Stone Lake Press
> Greenville, South Carolina; April, 2015

More Tuttle Columns

Some of Tuttle's regular columns did not rate integration into Kyushu Diary. Portions are reprinted here.

July 18, 1945 : San Diego, California

I went out today with dual purposes. I was to see the Consolidated Aircraft plant, and to arrange my ride out west on one of their new deliveries. Technically it is now a Convair facility, but no one here calls the merged company anything but Consolidated.

It's difficult to describe the enormity of the main aircraft plant in San Diego, partly because there is still some notional level of secrecy maintained about it, being so near the coast where theoretically a sneak attack could still materialize. Mostly the difficulty is that there's nothing to compare it to. The complex is "well over" a million square feet, mostly camouflaged in a way that is conspicuous from the ground. I suppose it looks like farm fields, or maybe a whole new city, or a ski resort, from the air. They say over a third of the people in San Diego work for this facility, and there are a lot more people in San Diego now than just four years ago. I can't think of another good size city that has so much of it tied up in one enterprise.

The plant invites comparison with the effort at Willow Run, Michigan, which is another enormous facility, but one invented from scratch and built up in a largely unpopulated area. In fact, the proud men of Consolidated openly invite the comparison. The automotive men in Michigan set out to put the most modern mass-production methods into creation of complicated airplanes. No one contests that they've done just that, and are kicking out planes at an unprecedented rate. But the traditional aircraft manufacturers have not been sitting around playing with their traditional craftsman's tools, fitting planes together one at a time with shims and grinders.

In this facility there is a moving production line, and there has been since well before the war. A streamlined system of pre-assembly at sub-suppliers has things like wiring harnesses show up pre-checked and ready to install. The whole plane is broken up into sections which multiple men (and women) can get into at once, instead of one or two workers having to crawl into a closed in space. Subassemblies made here are built up on jigs that ensure the parts fit together interchangeably. Almost everything is on movable carts, both for flexibility in production and so that "damage to the plant from military or other causes would create a minimum disruption to production." Consolidated has put out a steady stream of 'white papers' in the trade press touting their advances and accomplishments, its own engineers and managers taking the bylines.

The end result of the work here is several versions of B-24 "Liberator" bombers and PBY "Catalina" seaplanes. I don't imagine either will get the glory of other types, but you readers and the hard working people here in San Diego need to know that these planes have been the real workhorses of this war for our side. (They tell me I have a fair number of foreign readers in Axis territory as well. Greetings to those readers, especially those in the armed forces, who are already well acquainted with the business end of these aircraft.)

The B-24 is not particularly loved by large numbers of people. Certainly it has its fans, such as those who owe their life to its durability. But it's not considered a glamorous or fun-to-fly airplane. The B-17 "Flying Fortress" before it, with a curving fuselage sitting high on a tapered wing, looks like a scaled up fighter plane. Pilots tell me it flies like one, too, responding to inputs with grace. The B-24 looks, and is, more utilitarian. Some say it looks like a boxcar slung under a wing, meaning it as an insult. Others say the same thing as high praise.

The numbers make a simple case in favor of the Liberator – it carries more and farther and faster. With the enormous number produced, well over 15,000 at last count, I don't imagine any other aircraft will add up to the total bomb tonnage dropped by this type. The cutting edge, and much larger, B-29 "Superfortress" has grabbed the headlines lately doing long-range missions across the open Pacific ocean. But types like the B-24 have been there all the way, pushing north from Australia and New Guinea into the

304

Philippines. With Japan now in range from bases on Okinawa, waves of Liberators are sure to be in the fight right on through.

The PBY Catalina has served in every role imaginable, short of dogfighter. Being a seaplane, she was a natural for work in the Pacific, especially early on when friendly airfields were few and far between. We still have special seaplane tender ships that can set up in any harbor or lagoon and support a squadron of sea planes like the Catalina, which can patrol to well over a thousand mile radius. But most new seaplanes have been built as true amphibians, with retractable wheeled landing gear, so they can be serviced on patches of regular old dry land. Until we have mechanics who can walk on water, it's a good solution.

The PBY can hunt submarines, attack surface ships, drop supplies, and perform search-and-rescue operations whenever fliers have to ditch in the ocean. I think they're beautiful to watch turning slow through the air during check-out maneuvers. They must look like an angel from heaven to a pilot stuck on a life raft for days in shark-infested waters.

I'm going to take the first leg of my trip out on a Catalina, one of the very last. She has been ungratefully shown the door in favor of newer larger faster sea planes and dedicated land-based patrol planes. I made the arrangements with the appropriate Navy office, picked up another couple out of town newspapers, and had dinner back at base before starting to pack my things.

December 24, 1945 : X+39 — Onogara-dake, Kyushu

Yesterday I wrote about the trouble we were getting from long range artillery on Sakura-jima. Right on cue Japanese gunners laid out a heavy overnight barrage on the 306th Infantry Regiment. With the 77th Division it had filled in on the right end of the Marine Corps lines, northeast across a small channel from the volcanic mountain. The Army units may have not got the word about trouble from Sakura-jima, because any dumps and big tents in line of sight to the mountain appear to have been key targets. They are cleaning up and moving away from the shore line now.

I made reference back on the 7th to the Pearl Harbor attack of 1941. For me this date, December 24th, Christmas eve, will always remind me more of that horrible fateful day. Because the destruction from the attack didn't end on the 7th. One story of loss will stick with me. On December 8th tapping was heard from deep inside the partially sunk battleship West Virginia, where some number of men were trapped deep below deck. On December 24, 1941, the tapping stopped.

The West Virginia is here with us now, along with four of her sister ships from Pearl Harbor's now infamous 'Battleship Row.' The trouble with sinking ships in a harbor, especially Pearl, is that you can't. It's too shallow. Big ships settle on the bottom, still half above the surface, and a good harbor has every facility one would want to patch up and re-float the ships. In fact the Nevada, the only big ship to get under way that morning, was deliberately grounded after she took damage so she could be recovered and repaired.

The hit at Pearl was a big one for sure, and permanent for thousands of young servicemen, but for most of the big ships ultimately only temporary. Certainly Japanese planners knew this going in. The U.S. Pacific Fleet was mighty thin for the next year, reduced to hit-and-run harassing strikes with the carriers that by luck weren't there in Hawaii. But since then, with scores of new and repaired (and upgraded) big ships joining the fleet, it has leapfrogged the worst nightmares of those admirals in Tokyo.

Much has been said about fast aircraft carriers taking over from the battleships of old as kings of the sea. That may well be true on the ocean, where fleets have engaged in air duels well out of gun range many times across the Pacific. But here on dry land, I can certify that the battleship is very much respected, or feared, depending on which side you're on.

Navy ships sail with bigger guns than any army even attempts to drag along on land. Any place on the Earth within twenty miles of forty foot deep water can be blasted by one ton shells from our newest big ships. Japan is an island nation, and all of her conquests outside of China have been more smaller and smaller islands. All of them are vulnerable to the wrath of naval ordnance over almost all of their surface. Planes could drop bombs

306

of the same size, but low flying planes can be shot down with the smallest of anti-aircraft guns. The only defense against navy guns available to most Japanese garrisons has been to dig and dig and dig, deep down into the rock if they can, and wait to be flushed out by flame throwers once the Army or Marines land under the support of those big old battlewagons.

Here on Kyushu, we found the main beach defenses lined up just exactly beyond the range of most navy guns. At Ariake there were the reverse-slope positions our Navy couldn't get at until sailing into the bay, and that cost us something. But outside of that, the best tactic the Japanese had was to leave old guns in dummy installations near the shore to soak up shell fire.

The ships that came back from the knock-down at Pearl harbor were mostly older slower vessels, but they work just fine for work along the shore. Islands don't move very fast after all. The battleships have been kept very busy. The USS New York just rejoined the fleet after having her guns re-lined. They were worn out from firing so many thousands of big shells at Iwo Jima and Okinawa.

Back to the story of the West Virginia. Re-floating a damaged ship does take some time. She didn't make it into dry-dock for repairs until June 18, 1942. Before that many attempts were made by divers and search teams to enter the lower compartments and rescue survivors or recover bodies. That is also necessarily slow work. Cutting into a closed compartment will flood it, and possibly many more compartments if the hatches aren't all closed. Letting a lot of air out and water in can destabilize the whole ship, sending it over and ruining all chances of rescue or recovery.

I have it on good authority, but off the record, that three young men were recovered from the last compartment opened on the West Virginia. By match light they had marked off the days on a calendar through December 23rd. The Navy has decided never to identify them. They will be officially listed as Killed-In-Action, December 7, 1941.

Scuttlebutt

X-Day: Japan and Kyushu Diary are works of fiction, though based on substantial research into historical facts and documented plans. All characters outside of prominent historical figures and celebrities are fictitious. All actions and statements by the characters are fabricated for purposes of the story. Most ships mentioned in the book are permanent museum ships.

It is explicitly *not* the point of this work to predict the path of history given one change in the timeline. If anything it is to tear up the notion of a "timeline." Events in human affairs are highly volatile and sensitive to subtle influences. The only thing which is inevitable is that surprises will happen. History is a tree, not a vine.

Alternative histories are usually presented with a 'hook,' right up front on the cover. This story is presented from the perspective of individuals who have no access to high level decisions or plans. They are oblivious to the hook. Make what you will of the suppositions that support this alternative history. The contrived result is that the invasion of Kyushu went forward roughly as it was planned by the beginning of August, 1945.

Both sides had much time to adjust between the historical fork of August 6, 1945 and the invasion start. The Japanese could make deeper and different fortifications on Kyushu. The Americans would have had to deal with setbacks from the string of typhoons that hit the southwest Pacific. Assumptions about those actions and responses were made to support the fiction, not to advance any historical theory.

The 'additional reading' section of this book may serve as an actual bibliography. Other resources such as helpful web sites and forums are listed on the project web site at www.xdayjapan.com. Readers are encouraged to join the author and the community there.

When he was ten years old, Shawn D. Mahaney found Guadalcanal Diary in his grade school library. History branched that day.

Made in the USA
Lexington, KY
04 December 2015